RUNNING FROM CUPID

BO GRANT

Published by B. D. Grant, LLC

Copyright © 2024 by B. D. Grant, LLC

Running from Cupid is a fictional work. Characters, places, names, and incidents are used fictitiously or are products of B. D. Grant's imagination. Any resemblances are entirely coincidental.

All rights reserved. No part of this book may be used or reproduced in any manner without written permission except for brief quotations embodied in critical articles and reviews. To make a request of intellectual property contact b_d_grant@yahoo.com.

B. D. Grant, LLC P O Box 1296 Sulphur, LA 70664

Printed by Kindle Direct Publishing

Printed in the United States of America

Cover image by Brittany-see the back of the book for more information

REWARD to readers:

If you are able to get this book in the hands of a director/production company that leads to a movie deal and subsequent film being made, I will show my appreciation by REWARDING YOU the 10% agent fee, not to exceed 10,000 USD to be paid on the day film production starts.

If this interests you and you want to know if anyone has claimed the reward, I will add any claimed rewards to my website. (see last page for website details)

CONTENTS

Chapter 1	1
Chapter 2	15
Chapter 3	19
Chapter 4	27
Chapter 5	31
Chapter 6	35
Chapter 7	44
Chapter 8	52
Chapter 9	55
Chapter 10	60
Chapter 11	65
Chapter 12	71
Chapter 13	76
Chapter 14	82
Chapter 15	86
Chapter 16	95
Chapter 17	100
Chapter 18	106
Chapter 19	108
Chapter 20	119
Chapter 21	122
Chapter 22	132
Chapter 23	136
Chapter 24	145
Chapter 25	148
Chapter 26	156
Chapter 27	160
Chapter 28	164
Chapter 29	169
Chapter 30	174
Chapter 31	178
Chapter 32	180

Chapter 33	186
Chapter 34	190
Chapter 35	194
Chapter 36	207
Chapter 37	211
Chapter 38	218
Chapter 39	222
Chapter 40	235
Chapter 41	239
Chapter 42	247
Chapter 43	253
Chapter 44	262
Chapter 45	268
Chapter 46	277
Chapter 47	287
Chapter 48	292
Chapter 49	298
Chapter 50	300
Chapter 51	306
Chapter 52	313
Chapter 53	317
Chapter 54	324
Chapter 55	334
Chapter 56	342
Chapter 57	346
Chapter 58	354
Chapter 59	362
Chapter 60	366
Chapter 61	376
Chapter 62	380
Chapter 63	386
The End	393
Bonus Chapter	394
Afterword	401

Want more romance by Bo,
check out **BoGrant.com** for exclusive copies, deals, and limited editions not available anywhere else.

More books by Bo that you can read in order
(as listed below) or anyway you like.

Things We Tell Ourselves

Oh My Stars

Bookstores and Boys

The Last Cowboy

Running from Cupid- you got this one!

ONE

The beach should be for sandcastles, summer vacations, and warm kisses. Human kisses, to be specific.

A trip to the beach should never involve waking up to a strange dog bathing your face in slobber.

"You better run," a shrill voice called in the distance. The dog stopped licking long enough to let out a deep bark that echoed painfully through her head.

"Keep it down, will you?"

Whoever's dog this was needed to come and get him. Wiping her mouth off with the back of her hand only helped to smear sand across her face, adding to her overall discomfort. *What happened?* Why was she lying down in the sand? All she could remember was looking at the sunrise blooming over the water.

An older woman ran over to her. "Oh, dear," the woman said in the same shrill voice. She skidded to a halt beside her and then dropped to her knees, out of breath. "Are you—*phew*—okay?"

She opened her mouth to reply, but the dog used that opportunity to attempt to lick her in the mouth.

"No," she spewed at both of them as she pushed him away from her face. "This dog won't leave me alone." As soon as she pulled her arm back, the dog was right in her face again. Something warm ran down her forehead the second she propped herself up on her elbows in an effort to put some space between her and the dog's unwanted affection. "Ugh. Now I am covered in drool." She wiped her forehead with the back of her hand as the woman's eyes widened in horror.

"Oh, that's not drool, honey. That's blood."

"Blood?"

She was right. There was no denying that her hand was smeared with blood. None of this made sense. Why did her head feel so fuzzy, and where did the blood come from? She tried to examine the dog; it looked like a German Shepherd puppy but the graying nose said otherwise. As far as the blood, he was too close to her face for her see anything.

"Where is this...tiny German Shepherd bleeding from?"

"He's a miniature, and he isn't bleeding," the woman said, frowning at the top of her head. "You are."

"*I* am bleeding?"

That did it. The mental fog turned into full-fledged dizziness. She dropped her hand to the sand in an effort to steady herself, but the edges of her vision were already hazy.

"You're okay," the woman told her in a concerningly high pitch. "It's just a cut."

Everything about how she said that, and the way that she appeared to be horrified by the top of her head but at the same time unable to look away, was more than enough to terrify her. She had been injured. That was why she couldn't remember lying down in the sand to watch the sunrise. She couldn't think about it. Her head throbbed at an increasingly alarming rate, and the longer she sat up, the more darkness was creeping in on her vision. She was either going to pass out or throw up.

As if the older woman sensed this, her voice dropped to a more calm, slightly more believable level.

"No need to panic," the woman leaned in closer to her, "The police are on their way, and Milo chased that villain straight into his car. He's long gone now."

Villain? Someone else was involved in this? Her memory of watching the sunset was right there. It was there, her memories, but the pounding in her head kept her from any clear rehashing of events.

"Oh, dear," the woman exclaimed as she stared at her. "Was that *your* car?" They blinked at each other.

Was that my car? She swallowed back the lump forming in her throat. Maybe if she stayed just like she was for long enough, then the nausea and blurry vision would pass.

"Forgive me," the woman interrupted her thoughts. "Where are my manners? I'm Betty."

"I'm..." Her words fell short as she fought to readjust her arms under her without causing her head to hurt worse. All the movement did was make her feel more like she was in a tunnel. Her vision and hearing were going, but she managed to get out, "Who's Milo?"

Betty grinned and hooked her arm around the dog's neck to keep him from jumping back in her face. "You're looking at him." Betty scratched Milo under the chin and got a big thank-you lick in return. It was hard to focus on either of them. "What a good boy," the woman cooed and then looked at her. "I didn't catch your name."

"I..." Darkness consumed her vision. She felt herself falling. Even in this state, she knew that she couldn't tell her the truth. Her words came out as a whisper before hitting the sand, "I don't know."

It was as uncommon in Redrock, South Carolina, to find a woman unconscious on its sandy beaches as it was to have a patient admitted to the hospital whom no one knew.

How did she know she was in Redrock when she couldn't remember her own name? The truth was that she didn't, but everyone from the lady on the beach, the EMTs, the cop, the detective, and the hospital staff asked for her name, and when she couldn't provide it, they asked who she knew in Redrock.

"It's a Jane Doe with amnesia," the nurse explained quietly on the other side of the curtain.

Redrock was a small enough town that the ER rooms were made up of only curtains.

"Got it," an older man's voice said, unabashedly louder than the nurses, "but who is she?"

That question, right there, was how everyone had acted toward her since the ambulance arrived at the beach. She might not know who she was, but everyone looked at her as if they were expecting to recognize her until they actually got a good look at her.

Judging by the man's pristine running shoes that easily cost two hundred bucks, facing the nurse's worn-out Nikes peeking out from under the curtain that stopped short a good foot before reaching the linoleum floor, he must be the doctor or a surgeon. It would take a doctor's salary to be able to afford shoes like that.

Oh, please don't be a surgeon.

Her head throbbed harder at the thought of surgery. Too much had gone right these last few years for her to find herself in some random hole-in-the-wall town needing an operation. That was until she was sprawled out on the cool, sandy beach with a dog licking her face.

A cat meowed somewhere in the distance, momentarily distracting her from the shoes on the other side of the curtain, but the meow undoubtedly came from inside the hospital. *What kind of hospital allows pets?* It had to be her head trauma. She could handle hearing a phantom cat. Hell, she could handle Milo covering her in drool. What she couldn't handle was being in this hospital with everyone walking past her tiny curtain room looking at her, and man, did her head hurt. She needed to get out of here.

"That's just it," the nurse's voice rose, "we don't know *who* she is."

The crisp new running shoes that weren't really made to run as much as show off turned in her direction.

So, maybe she remembered a few things. She had a couple of

pairs of shoes like that years ago to match Humphry's. Her East Coast romance had gotten into running shortly before they started dating, and when you're the kind of wealthy that he was, you run in two-hundred-dollar shoes like they were nothing because at home you have a shoe collection the size of a small shoe stores. Humphrey's had an impressive collection that ranged from the four-figure mark to north of five figures just in shoes, but none of them were as remarkable as the Willem Kooning painting hanging in his study.

A hand pulled back the curtain to her room, and the man stepped forward. Unlike the young, worldly, and always sharply dressed Humphry, with his closet the size of most New Yorkers' apartments, this man was neither young, sophisticated, nor sharply dressed, despite his shoes.

His face fell at the sight of her, just as everyone else's had. Thankfully, it wasn't followed by a look of disgust from her appearance as much as an overall disheartened confusion of yet one more person not recognizing her. The confusion was quickly replaced with an intellectual appraisal of her as he looked her over as he walked up. She could almost see him taking the mental notes. She was in her twenties and in good health, minus her head.

The corners of his mouth dipped into a look of pity. It was one she could almost mirror. *Looks like neither of us is getting the person we assumed was on the other side of the curtain.* She was expecting more of a Humphry's type, and he was expecting someone he knew.

He turned his head to the side just enough to give her a clear enough view of the ponytail at the nape of his neck, which was nothing short of sheer determination since his hairline was thinner than her hospital gown. His white lab coat was completely unbuttoned—not to better make room for his plump midsection, but to showcase the sheer shirt underneath it that was trippy in design, with a kind of nonsensical pattern that twisted and turned so much that it might have a hidden image if she were to look at it long enough, which she could not be paid enough to do. The doctor raised a hand to scratch the back of his neck, causing his coat to open *just* enough that her eyes widened in horror.

There's nothing like seeing your hippie doctor's nipples through his paper-thin shirt the first time meeting him.

"Good morning," he crooned, two seconds after she decided that the safest place for her eyes was on her hands balled up in her lap.

Another meow in the distance made her ears perk up. That was definitely a cat.

"I'm Doctor Eriksen. I'm your doctor for the day."

She relaxed against the bed—not a surgeon, just a doctor. Maybe she still had some luck on her side after all. "Hello," she said gently.

"I hear we got a little bump on our head today."

A *little* bump on the head? All it took was one meek response, and he talked to her like a child—so much for staring at her hands. His condescending tone had her eyes jump up to his, but she checked her temper before it could reach her eyes. She could use that to her advantage.

There was a buzz from the pocket of his lab coat. "Excuse me," he muttered and reached into his pocket to check his phone.

She settled her gaze on the nurse, who was a step behind him. Did she catch how condescending his "little bump" statement came across?

Their eyes met, and despite the nurse stitching her up when she first arrived, she was too out of it and had her head down to notice the nurse's eyes. It was something she regretted now that she saw them. They were the kind of gorgeous bright blue that hypnotized onlookers. The wrinkles at the corners only emphasized their brilliance as if they were arrows to the eyes.

Man, the things she could accomplish with eyes that commanding.

"Sorry about that." The doctor slid his phone back into his pocket.

From the nurse's blue eyes, Kristen looked up at Dr. Eriksen's far less appealing, blood-shot, brown eyes, giving him her best big puppy-dog impression as she stared up through her lashes. She may know far more than she was letting on, but being the timid Jane Doe worked far better for her at the moment.

"Is that what happened?" she asked softly. "I was hit on the head?"

He paused. Clearly, he didn't know, but she didn't let up as she looked up at him expectantly. Someone really should have filled him in on that critical bit of information. If she didn't know, for the most part, what had actually happened to her, then she would not be able to keep this up, but her annoyance with his ignorance fueled her to continue the act. The doctor looked pointedly at the nurse.

"Do we know how it happened?"

Kristen followed suit and looked up at the nurse with hope filling her face that perhaps the nurse would have all of the answers.

The nurse's blue eyes bounced between them before landing on the doctor. "You are more than welcome to ask the detective. He should be here any second."

Where is the detective? Hadn't he met the ambulance on the beach when they were loading her up? The last hour or so was pretty foggy, but she was pretty sure about that. Had he found something on the beach? She gripped her hands tighter in her lap.

"Ah, well," Dr. Eriksen sighed and turned back to her, "if we know the exact cause," his eyes narrowed on the bandages wrapped around the top of her head, "then we need to run cultures to see what kind of antibiotics are needed in case of infection."

He reached out to check under her bandages. She fought not to recoil, thinking him messing with her bandages would worsen her headache, but he barely lifted the edge. He raised his chin and squinted as if he could see something, but it didn't feel like he raised more than the first outer strip, nowhere near the stitches at the top of her head.

Then, just like that, he lowered his hand. Her headache was still at the same level it had been since the nurse gave her two white pills before giving her stitches. She glanced at the badge on the nurse's chest. She was finally close enough to make out her name: Celia.

Dr. Eriksen backed away from the bed. "Ah well," he nodded at Celia, "I'll let you get those cultures started."

Celia took a deep breath. That and the fact that her mouth tightened into a line made her think she was less than enthused at the idea. She also wondered what cultures meant as Celia turned to the drawers-on-wheels.

"Oh, and there's cake in the break room," the doctor added, "they won't let me cut into it until they sing me happy birthday."

"That's right," Celia said, taking something out of the first drawer and moving down to the second. "Happy birthday."

Kristen swallowed hard when she realized that the nurse had just taken out a packaged syringe that was thankfully missing the needle on the end.

"Don't worry," Dr. Eriksen said at the foot of her bed. It wasn't until he added, "We're going to take good care of you," that she realized he was talking to her, not the nurse.

"Oh, uh, thank you." He gave her a nod that was more encouragement to keep talking than an acknowledgment. It took her a second, but she added, "And happy birthday."

He smiled and puffed up his chest as if his birthday were a significant accomplishment and not something that everyone achieved annually. Maybe it was significant, judging by his shaky hands and the fact that he did nothing besides introduce himself. Being a practicing physician at his age was definitely an accomplishment.

"Thank you. Don't take too long," he told Celia on his way out, "there might not be any cake left."

"Ivan's my relief this morning," she said over her shoulder, "so you better make sure they save me a slice."

Dr. Eriksen nodded his way out of the curtained room. "I'll let them know. I'll be in my office if you need me."

"Oh, since you're here first," Celia called after him. "If you haven't heard, the Harrisons are across the hall. Mr. Harrison was asking for you when he came in."

"Ah, well. A doctor's job is never done."

Celia rolled her eyes as he strolled out. "Right," she muttered at the drawers that no doubt held more scary things. They hadn't seemed so worrisome when Celia gathered the stuff for her stitches, but she had been too out of it to care at the time.

"Can we wait until Ivan gets here to do…this?"

The wrinkles at the corners of Celia's blue eyes deepened. "We could. He's a good nurse and all," her voice dropped to a mumble as if she were talking more to herself, "but when the man bothers to call in to let us know he's going to be late, it means that there's no telling how late he's going to be." Celia opened the next drawer, and her voice rose with excitement. "There you are."

Celia withdrew a needle that was surely three times the length necessary for whatever cultures entailed. She turned with a triumphant grin, needle in hand. "So, to answer your question. We *could* wait, but we won't."

Kristen hunkered down in the bed, mentally preparing herself. There was no way she could be a nurse. Even just giving other people shots, there still had to be a chance of accidentally sticking yourself. The thought alone made her cringe even more.

"*Meow.*"

It was loud enough to leave no doubt in her mind that a cat was nearby, and Celia didn't so much as bat an eye. She stared at the nurse, ignoring the syringe, wondering if her head trauma could cause such a clear hallucination. Had getting hit over the head caused her to lose her mind? "Should I be concerned about hallucinations?"

Celia stopped to look pointedly at Kristen. "What kind of hallucinations?"

"A small one, I think. I keep hearing a cat meowing, but it hasn't materialized yet."

Celia giggled and shook her head in amusement.

"Wow, that's rude," Kristen blurted, which caused Celia to giggle harder.

"I'm sorry. I should have warned you. I'm just so used to it." She lowered her voice. "One of our patients acts like a cat. It's not that big of a deal," she added quickly. "She does it for attention."

"Shouldn't she be in a psych ward and not the ER?"

"She would be if we had one, but like I said, she only does it for attention," Celia explained. "The first time she brought herself in, we were getting ready to send her to Charleston to their psych floor, but her husband showed up before the transfer. Once she had a little time with him, she returned to normal. Turns out he planned a work trip on their fifteenth anniversary. He canceled it, and magically, she was cured."

Kristen grinned. "Fascinating." Maybe being a nurse wasn't all torture and sharp objects. "Why is she doing it today?"

Celia shrugged. "We don't know yet, but her husband just got here, so we should know soon. My money is on someone's birthday. The nurse's aide thinks it's one of the kids' college graduations."

A grown woman impersonating a cat to get her way; count her in. "You *have* to let me know when you find out."

"Sure. Now," Celia turned back to the cabinet, "let's get this over with."

Kristen's chest tightened at the reminder of what was coming. The beeping increased from the monitor connected to Kristen's blood pressure cuff, and the thing clipped to the end of her finger.

Celia eyed the monitor. "That's an impressive spike in blood pressure."

"That's an impressive-looking needle," she countered. "You sure you don't have something smaller in there?" She tried to swallow, but her mouth was as dry as the Sahara desert, causing her tongue to stick to the roof of her mouth. She forced her mouth open. "Are you *really* sure we can't hold off on this?"

Celia's blue eyes warmed. "I wish I could; trust me."

Trust. There was a word that was definitely misspelled when it was created. Any word involving one person putting faith in another should be at least ten letters minimum and, more appropriately, have some silent letters thrown in to foreshadow the word's inevitable complications.

Would any sane person trust someone with a sharp object in their hand? Absolutely not.

The weird thing was that Kristen did trust her. It had to be her blue eyes. *Wow,* she thought to herself as she settled back in the bed. *Eyes like that really do work wonders.* But when she ripped open the syringe package, Kristen's entire body recoiled.

"What if I offered to pay you not to do this?"

Celia smirked at her. "That would require money."

Kristen sighed. Celia had helped her change into the hospital gown after her stitches; they both knew she had no purse or cellphone, much less money.

"Do you think you know someone who lives in Redrock?" Celia's question caught her off guard.

"Excuse me?" Kristen asked, too focused on the needle as Celia twisted it onto the end of the syringe.

"The reason you're in Redrock," Celia said, concentrating on her work. "Is it because you know someone here?"

She shrugged. Her heart rate rose again, and the incessant beeping let the whole world know it.

"Or," Celia added slowly and glanced at the monitor, "you could have been driving through, but then..." she took an alcohol swab out from the top drawer without looking along with a rubber tubing, "why would you have stopped next to the beach of all places and so early in the morning unless you *were* meeting someone?"

The beeping slowed, and Celia gave her a puzzled look. She shrugged again.

"Maybe I needed to use the bathroom."

Celia shook her head. "The EMTs said you were on the beach next to the highway on the outskirts of town. There's nothing out there but highway and beachfront."

Gingerly, Celia looped the rubber tubing around Kristen's upper arm. For a moment, she contemplated pulling her arm away like an indignant child and refusing to participate. The tubbing was tied uncomfortably around her arm when a thought came to mind.

If only she hadn't been so out of it when she came in. Being hit in the head had really done a number on her. She should be able to talk her way out of this, but all of her experience getting out of tough situations, not one involved being admitted to the hospital. But, if all her past experiences had taught her anything, it was that she was capable of just about anything. She might have a head injury, but she was clear-headed enough now to think quickly on her feet.

"Surely, I had something on me that could tell us," Kristen said. "If you get my clothes real quick, we could go through them and see."

Celia's eyes narrowed on her. "Didn't you already ask about your clothes?"

Crap. She hoped the nurse wouldn't remember her comment about wanting her pants back once the brain fog settled so she wouldn't be so cold while getting her stitches. All she got out of that was a second, thin blanket to cover her lower body.

"Did I?" she asked, feigning ignorance.

"I'm pretty sure," Celia said, but then she glanced around the tiny curtained-off room. "They would be in a big clear bag if they were here." She shook her head and resumed what she was doing. "I can ask for them once I'm done with this."

Double crap. At the very least, Kristen hoped that the mention of her clothes holding some clue as to who she was would be intriguing enough to prolong what Celia was about to do to her.

"Well," Kristen sighed, "if I could remember, I would tell you."

The beeping from the monitor increased as the rubber tubing became painfully tight around her arm. She shifted uncomfortably in the bed. That's when she noticed a smile playing on Celia's lips.

"What's so funny?" she asked.

Celia's gaze flickered up to the monitor. "If I weren't about to do a blood draw on you, I would say you were lying." Celia glanced at her.

Kristen pinched her brows together in confusion. "Your blood pressure," Celia explained. "Anytime I think my son is up to no good, I hook him to the portable blood pressure monitor I keep at home and ask him questions. If his BP spikes, I know he's lying."

She gaped at Celia. Forget the color of her eyes; this woman was *way* smarter than Kristen had given her credit for. Her shock only made Celia's smirk deepen. "All I had to do a few weeks back was just take it out of the cabinet, and he confessed to sneaking out last weekend with his friends."

"How old is your son?"

"He's in high school."

Kristen hadn't thought Celia was old enough to have a kid that old, but having eyes like that had its consequences. She mirrored Celia's smirk. "So you're getting your money's worth out of that monitor, you say."

For a brief moment, the beeping slowed as she pictured Celia standing over a high schooler, interrogating him like some detective.

"There we go," Celia purred, watching the numbers on the monitor drop.

Kristen followed her gaze to the monitor. The numbers jumped as she realized Celia had not only distracted her but used the blood pressure machine to verify it. The numbers fell as Kristen calmed herself. Celia was growing on her, but she would have to be careful as long as she was hooked up to the blood pressure machine. Celia's gloved pointer finger padded the inside of Kristen's elbow, searching for a vein. When her finger stopped in the middle of her arm and reached for the alcohol swab, any warm feelings she had for the nurse disappeared.

Great. She shut her eyes and leaned her head back against the pillow. *I can do this.*

"There you go," Celia soothed. "Just relax."

Trust, relax; Celia was on a roll today, spitting out all the words that were easier said than done.

"Easy for you to say," she muttered.

Having her eyes closed did help some—too bad shutting her eyes didn't stop the throbbing in her head. The incessant beeping from the blood pressure machine didn't help. The tiny sound of the needle cap popping off caused her to chant louder in her head: *I can do this, I can do this.* She held back a grin despite her nerves as she started chanting *relax* over and over in her head.

"Knock, knock."

She opened her eyes to the curtains pulling farther apart at the foot of her bed.

She blinked hard. Her head trauma must have been playing tricks on her. The man in a white lab coat staring down at her was way too young to be a doctor, but it was the way he was looking at her that transfixed her gaze on his. His right hand clenched at his side.

TWO

It wasn't even nine in the morning, and he already had two missed phone calls and several text messages. Allen knew it was going to be one of those days. That's what a full moon gives you when working at a hospital. It didn't matter which shift you worked; a full moon always brought in the crazies.

Case in point: Mrs. Harrison was one of the two patients listed on the ER's census when he arrived, and the morning shift had only begun.

Allen paused outside of her closed-curtained room.

"Darling, if you would just *tell me* what I forgot, we can go home and spend the rest of the day together," Mr. Harrison pleaded.

She gave a straightforward "*Meow*."

Her husband's voice took on a growl. "I don't care how good our insurance is. I am going to cancel it, and we can go bankrupt from hospital bills if you don't put an end to this madness immediately."

Not one to entertain her husband's empty threats, Mrs. Harrison hissed loud enough that Allen turned on his heels.

They can talk this out on their own. Hopefully, his other patient would be more cooperative. His cell phone dinged in his lab coat pocket. Annoyed, Allen switched it to silent; he should have left it in his office.

He glanced down at the short chart for "Jane Doe," who was thankfully placed on the opposite side of the emergency room, past the nurse's station.

Unidentified patients were rare but usually easy to identify. They typically fell into one of two distinct categories. One percent were unfortunate travelers who ended up in the emergency room, experiencing some major medical event or wreck to where they either couldn't physically speak or were unconscious. Finding their wallet or purse cleared this up. The other ninety-nine percent refused to identify themselves because they were brought in by the police, feigning injury to get out of going straight to jail, and in most, if not all, of those cases, the stubborn individual was already known to police, or someone at the hospital recognized them.

"Morning, Amirah," he greeted the CNA seated at the nurse's station, separating the two halls that make up the emergency room. "You ready for today?"

She spun around in her chair with such force that he froze before she motioned with her one free hand for him to stay put.

"No," she insisted to the desk phone at her ear, "we told officers last time that we would not admit him again."

Allen racked his brain over what patient she could be talking about. There were several patients whom they wished they could ban from the hospital. Take the Harrisons, for example, who used the emergency room for relationship issues, and all it did was waste time and resources for genuine emergency care.

"Hold on a sec." Amirah covered the receiver and looked at Allen. "They're trying to dump that Farris guy on us again."

"Remind me who that is."

"He's the one who was brought in by police a month ago for shouting at vehicles. He freaked out after we admitted him and punched Ivan. Security had to get involved—"

"The schizophrenic," he said. "We transferred him to Charleston. The cops picked him up in Redrock again?"

"Right outside of town," she whispered. "They found him passed out on the side of the road right next to the highway." She nodded at the phone. "It's state police dispatch calling to let us know that they're loading him in the ambulance right now."

"What's his demeanor?"

"Completely out of it. They said that he can barely keep his eyes open."

"Fine, we'll take him, but call Charleston and let them know we'll send him over again today. Hey," he leaned over the counter. "What's the deal with this amnesia patient?"

Amirah's eyes softened. "I don't know. I've been dealing with Mrs. Harrison since she came in, but it sounds pretty sad. Attacked on the beach early this morning and came to with no memory."

He nodded. "That's what I heard too. Any signs of drug use or smell of alcohol?"

"Not that anyone's said." Her hand flew from the receiver. "Yes, I'm still here. I was talking with the doctor. We'll get a room ready—"

"Make sure he's restrained so we don't have to worry about him hitting anyone else."

"Restraints," she echoed into the phone, and he headed off.

He knew from experience that to keep one's sanity on a hectic day meant focusing on one task at a time, and right now, he had a patient with head trauma.

"Knock, knock," he announced, pulling open the curtain.

He opened his mouth to introduce himself but fell short.

All of the times that Allen had accurately envisioned what a patient would look like before seeing them had his words stuck in his throat when he saw her. Whatever he had envisioned, he was wrong.

Jane Doe was fairly attractive, with short, brown curls peeking out from under the bandages, framing her soft face, but it wasn't her appearance. It was her eyes. They were too alert, too aware for someone with amnesia. He expected her to look lost or pissed off, the two most common reactions for people with brain trauma.

Her eyes were full of life.

The same eyes that were studying him, leaving no doubt in his mind: She was lying.

THREE

One look at Dr. Hottie, and she sized him up.

His crisp lab coat was fully buttoned over actual scrubs. Compared to Dr. Eriksen's sheer top, this was what one thought of when picturing a doctor. He was clean-cut and handsome but not intimidatingly so. Maybe not one quite this young, but Jane could see the appeal of visiting a small-town hospital if they had more doctors like him. His scrub pants could use a good press, which was a good sign that he was single; no decent wife or girlfriend would let him leave the house in that state.

The determined look in his gaze gave off the vibe of a young doctor with something to prove. But, if he looked young for his age, then that meant he might be a surgeon.

Great.

He was studying her far too long and not in a good way. He looked…suspicious.

That can't be right.

He did work at a hospital; she could only guess how often doctors were lied to daily. But the way that he didn't even bother to hide it from her was almost like he was rubbing it in her face.

And Kristen thought she had trust issues.

This hospital, man. First, she got a nurse who used medical equipment at home to interrogate family members, then a doctor walking around basically topless, and now Dr. Easy-on-the-eyes with his blatant suspicion. So what if she didn't have amnesia? There was no way he could know that.

And she still didn't know if he was a surgeon or not. There was no way she was going to let Dr. Dreamy operate on her. Her head might hurt, but it was nowhere close to the 'do what you have to do' kind of pain.

"Morning—" he started.

"About time you showed up," Celia grumbled from the side of the bed.

"What are you talking about?" He strolled around the foot of the bed to Celia. "I'm early." He gave Celia an intense once-over. "Aren't you on nights?"

"You're not as early as the birthday boy. And yes, I'm on nights, but Ivan is coming in late. How late, I don't know," she said dryly, "but I did tell him we swapped yesterday and that I had plans with Davie today. So he better be here soon."

He scrutinized Celia for a second. "Who's the birthday boy?"

She paused to cut her eyes up at him. "I am about to take blood to run cultures right now, so who do you think?"

His forehead furrowed. "For a head wound?"

His gaze flickered between Celia and Kristen. Kristen fought to hide the anxiety bubbling up to the surface. She focused on appreciating every second that went by without Celia opening the alcohol swab because as soon as that thing was open, she would be one step away from being stuck with that needle. She didn't even mind Dr. Hot Stuff looking her up and down, trying to put together why Celia was about to take her blood.

His gaze ended at the top of her head. "Was she hit with something rusted?"

"Not that we know of." To Kristen's relief, Celia slid the cap back on the syringe in one practiced swoop. "And it was a pretty clean cut," she told him. "I was the one who stitched her up, but she doesn't know what hit her, and they didn't find anything on site."

He nodded slowly. While they spoke, Kristen scanned him in his wrinkled scrubs in silent appreciation before realizing he was watching her. She swallowed hard and blurted, "Something hard."

His brows pinched together as he stared down at her in silence.

"What was that?" Celia asked and set the alcohol swab down next to the syringe.

Kristen grinned. "He asked what I was hit with. It was something hard."

Celia smiled kindly at her poor attempt at humor while Dr. Grumpy only frowned further. "She's not wrong."

"Good one," he said dryly, stepping closer. "I'm going to take a quick look if you're okay with that."

He cozied up to the side of the bed and leaned toward her. She lifted her chin as he closed in on her. His eyes drifted from the top of her head to meet her gaze. He paused. She hadn't realized until his eyes drifted down to her lips that her mouth was partly open.

Had he asked a question?

"Sure," she managed to get out. He stared into her eyes as he lifted his hands to her temples.

"Not to brag, but"—Celia puffed out her chest beside them, effectively breaking whatever his gaze was doing to her—"it only took me five stitches."

Pfft. *Only five?* Any stitches were too many. A weird noise escaped from her throat. Celia and Dr. Hunkalicious glanced down at her. She waved a hand dismissively. "Don't mind me," she gasped. "Just over here choking on my spit. I'm fine."

And that's when something magical happened, and it had nothing to do with him undressing her "only five" stitches.

He chuckled. It wasn't the chuckle so much as what it did to his face. His smile was *just* deep enough to give her a peek at the dimple on his left cheek. It was gone before she could check the right side.

Of course, men like him have dimples.

"Five stitches isn't a lot," Dr. Dimples said, slowly unwrapping her bandages. "In the grand scheme of things. I gave a patient seven stitches to the back of the head last weekend for getting hit with a whipped cream dispenser, of all things."

Kristen was impressed. "Stitches from a Reddi-wip can?"

"No," Celia said with surprising enthusiasm.

Celia moved closer to them while Dr. Dimples unwrapped the last of the bandages. Kristen couldn't help but notice the hem of Celia's scrub sleeve barely brushed against Dr. Dimples' lab coat in such an innocent way that there was no logical reason jealousy should stir in any sane person, but Kristen felt it.

"The stainless-steel kind," Celia explained. "They use them at the local diner to cream the pies."

Kristen blinked up at Celia, unable to stop the smirk that spread across her face. *Did she really say cream the pies?* Kristen's eyes flickered to Dr. Dimples. There was no way that she was the only one who caught that.

"And from now on," Celia continued, "I will be ordering my pie without whipped cream."

If the doctor had caught what she said, he didn't so much as crack a grin, but the longer he ignored her staring up at him, the more she got the feeling that he definitely caught it. He had a good poker face; she gave him that.

"Keep your head still," he directed when she lowered her gaze.

She did as she was told and realized she had the perfect, close-up view of his upper body and the better part of his lower. It took her a second to realize that his badge was dangling in front of her face. *Dr. Allen Trouth, hospitalist.*

Dr. Dimples was better.

Celia said, "I never asked, but I bet Norah was the one who did it. She's given me that look like she wanted to knock me out more than once."

"What were you doing?" Dr. Dimples asked.

"Asking for a refill."

"Wow," Kristen mouthed, staring at the less attractive picture on his badge.

"You're right," he told Celia, "it was Norah."

"Who's Norah?" she asked, wanting to be a part of the conversation.

"She's a waitress at the diner in town," Celia replied.

Kristen stared at her lap. What does it say about a place where a trip to the local diner could end with more stitches than she had?

"Remind me never to visit Redrock again," she mumbled.

Dr. Dimples sunk into view with a suspicious look plastered on his face again. "How do you know you were visiting if you have amnesia?" he asked, stepping back.

She blinked blankly at him and then chirped, "Oh, I didn't realize you could hear me. You've basically only been talking to her." She cast an accusing glance at him, hoping it would take the conversation off her. "I thought we would just keep acting like I wasn't in the room except for maybe answering the odd question here or there."

She had no real reason to act so petty. She had enjoyed listening to them, but she needed him to stop looking at her like that. And it worked. Dr. Dimples looked at Celia as the nurse gave Kristen a tight, guilty grin.

"Jane," Celia said with a sympathetic tone, "this is Dr. Trouth. He will be your attending doctor for the day."

Two thoughts of how to continue to steer the conversation away from her amnesia came to mind. Ask about what happened to Dr. Eriksen or…

Her face lit up, and she met Celia's gaze, her eyes full of hope. "Jane?" she echoed, with the same small voice she used earlier with Dr. Eriksen.

Celia winced when she realized what she was implying. "Jane Doe, sweetie. That's what we're calling you until we figure out your real name."

"Oh." She visibly deflated and glanced at Dr. Dimples, who was not living up to his nickname, as he glared at her. She looked back at Celia. "Right."

He should have softened at least a little from all of that, but no. He was quickly becoming Dr. Grumpy as his frown turned into a full-fledged grimace. She could see the wheels in his head spinning. His eyes darted between her and the monitor connected to her arm. His lower lip pulled into his mouth, and Kristen watched the wheels in his head turn as his top teeth scratched over his lower lip. He was plotting something. If he were a little less easy on the eyes, then she would not enjoy watching him as much as she did. He finally looked at Celia and pointed at the monitor. "Her blood pressure was elevated when I came in. Does she have a fever?"

Celia shook her head. "Her BP spiked when I took the needle out."

He made a throaty "hmmm" as he eyed the abandoned syringe on the counter before turning back to Kristen. "Do you remember anything that happened to you this morning?"

Her gaze drifted down to her hands. The uptick of beeping from the monitor matched the drumming in her chest. "I...remember looking at the water... I think. Or maybe it was after I came to on the beach from..." She vaguely pointed at the top of her head. Celia nodded along with a pained expression, but not Dr. Grumpy. "Ringing in my ears. I definitely remember that. The throbbing in my head hasn't stopped."

"I can get you something for that," Celia offered.

Dr. Grumpy raised his hand to stop Celia. "Why don't you get those blood samples first." He glanced out the corner of his eyes at Kristen. "After she collects the samples, she can get you something for your headache."

Headache was an understatement as her anxiety from him being onto her turned to panic with the stomach-turning addition of having to worry about more needles. The throbbing turned into pounding in her ears.

Celia gave him a double take. "Really?"

"Yes," he said with an undeniably severe tone. "Really."

"All right." Celia turned back to where the syringe waited quietly to torment its victim.

Kristen winced. "Is it too late to request a different doctor?" She would much rather Eriksen with his sheer top and ponytail than this. Except Dr. Eriksen was the whole reason Celia took that stuff out in the first place.

"It is," Dr. Trouth grinned, clearly enjoying this.

Her blood pressure spiked. He took a step back, giving Celia room as she took out a second alcohol wipe.

"Now," he said, looking her dead in the eye, "are you sure you don't remember what happened today?"

What is with these people and using blood pressure machines as lie detectors?

She gaped at him. "I really don't." Kristen pleaded as Celia wiped the alcohol swab across the inside of her elbow, "This is a joke, right?"

"This is not a joke," Dr. Trouth stated as he slid his hands confidently into the front pockets of his lab coat. "All we need to know is what hit you in the head."

"I told you, I don't remember."

His eyes narrow on hers. "Are you sure?"

She gaped at him. Dr. Growing-less-attractive-by-the-second thought that she was lying, and what made it worse was him threatening her via poor Celia and that god-awful syringe dangerously close to her arm.

Even worse than all that...

He was absolutely correct.

She grimaced across her bed at him and blinked hard at Celia and the needle coming straight for her arm. "Are all of the doctors here terrible?"

BO GRANT

FOUR

Was he being harsh? Probably.

But he knew they were being played when she turned doe-eyed at Celia when she called her "Jane," as if Celia had just magically figured out who she was.

He had to hand it to her, though; her fear of needles was as authentic as it got. A spike in blood pressure like that, and he would usually go into his speech about hypertension prevention, but it was the outcome he was searching for. Her blood pressure had spiked previously when Jane Doe saw the needle come out, but it was nothing compared to the spike he saw now. This was more than a fear of needles driving her blood pressure sky-high.

Celia glanced in Allen's direction. He could tell that she hoped he would come to his senses. They both knew that running cultures on a healthy person was pointless, much like the doctor who prescribed them.

"Are all of the doctors here terrible?"

He had to admit that Jane's comment stung, which was immediately made worse when he noticed her eyes were glistening with tears. He made her cry.

"Stop," he told Celia.

Her lies, his ego at being had by a patient, the truth of what happened to her; none of that mattered. He was not going to sit here and watch one of his patients cry, no matter how sure he was that she was lying. He was a better doctor and, quite frankly, a better person than he was acting right now.

"You sure?" Celia asked with relief; he didn't even have to see that she had already backed away from Jane Doe and recapped the syringe to know how much she agreed with his call.

Allen's job was simple: provide care and do everything he could to ensure his patients lived to see another day. Threatening a patient to get her to talk about her trauma was beyond his job description. He blamed the full moon.

His phone let out one quick vibration in his pants pocket. *Speaking of liars.* It was a quiet reminder that it wasn't just the full moon that had him on edge.

Shutting his eyes for a second, he mentally reset as he took a deep breath. "I'm sure," he exhaled.

As he opened his eyes, the patient stared up at him with her big eyes. She blinked away the tears, but her features were still set in the distress he caused. He opened his mouth... *But to do what, apologize? Say, 'Sorry, you called it; I'm a terrible doctor'?* He couldn't say something like that. It wasn't true.

It may not have been his best moment, but he was a good doctor, great even, compared to doctors like Eriksen. It was nothing short of a miracle that the older hippie was not only still practicing but a doctor altogether with the amount of grass he smoked long before it was medically legal. A twelve-hour shift at the hospital wasn't even enough to clear up Eriksen's bloodshot eyes or the faint smell of pot out of his clothes.

"Thank you," Jane mumbled, pulling him from his thoughts.

"That's not necessary."

All three of them knew that he didn't deserve thanks after how he treated her.

"You want me to...?" Celia nodded at the pile of bandages Allen left on the bed beside Jane Doe.

That's why Celia was his favorite nurse; she was always one step ahead of him.

"That would be great." And to thank her, he added, "You did good with those stitches."

"You don't have to tell me that," she smirked.

Despite Celia moving in close to Jane Doe's bedside to gather up the bandages, Jane's blood pressure monitor remained slow and steady. It's funny what a difference holding a twenty-one gauge up to a patient could make. If people only knew how tiny those needles were compared to the ones used to pierce women's ears. Were Jane Doe's ears pierced? His gaze drifted to her ears before he realized what he was doing and stopped himself. His job had nothing to do with whether or not his attractive patient had pierced ears.

The way Jane Doe stared up at him through her lashes made him self-conscious, as though his thoughts were written on his face.

"All things considered, you're fortunate to have made it out of whatever happened this morning with only stitches and"—he swallowed before forcing out—"a case of amnesia. I have faith that your memory will come back sooner rather than later," he said with a certainty that he hoped she understood. "The stitches will dissolve in a week or two, and we don't want you getting them wet for at least—"

"I went over all that." Celia moved in between them to wrap the bandages around Jane's head. "And I have the care instructions printed out at the nurse's station for her when she's discharged."

Again, that was why Celia was one of their best.

"Good. I'll have Amirah put it in her chart since she'll be here a while."

Celia asked Jane, "Do you remember me going over all that earlier?"

"Keep it dry the first day," she counted off on her fingers. "Clean around it, don't pick at the stitches."

Allen noted how well-manicured her nails were as she ticked off her home-care instructions.

"Don't use alcohol or hydrogen peroxide. Why? Will I be here a while?"

She finally caught on to that. He made sure not to look too pleased. Someone genuinely with amnesia wouldn't mind staying in the hospital while the synapses in their brain worked themselves out, but someone lying about it might.

"That's right," he said with a somber nod as if it were anything close to the bad news he gave hundreds of patients and their families before her. "Since you don't have any next of kin we can contact on your behalf, we have no choice but to keep you here until the amnesia subsides."

"Of course," Jane mumbled, but he could tell by the way she was no longer staring at him but somewhere between them that she was thinking things over.

No doubt she was trying to think of how to miraculously remember who she was without it being apparent that she was lying about it the whole time, and then, of course, she'd have to tell them who left her on the beach.

Someone giving her a laceration big enough to require stitches sobered his thoughts when he considered letting her know how awful the food was at the hospital.

These full moons were no joke.

"Don't worry," he assured her, reminding himself who he was and what he stood for: making people better. "We're going to take good care of you." He felt driven to add, "And we have security to ensure you're safe."

FIVE

She wasn't sure if the security comment was made to comfort or threaten her. A part of her hoped it was a threat.

That would be fun.

She could turn his life upside down if she wanted to. If he only knew. If any of them only knew. In the last twenty-four hours alone, she not only stole from a formal ball in Texas full of wealthy Southerners but did so without so much as turning a head. Well, maybe not exactly, but close enough. She was known for clean escapes. The kind of clean escapes that her male counterparts only dreamt of, and she did it with not just one item stolen from the silent auction but three. She only technically got away with two. She was forced to leave one behind at the last minute.

The sad part was that after all of that, she was reasonably sure that it was the one-of-a-kind Gibson Les Paul guitar, the most expensive item she stole from Texas, was no longer worth what it had been thanks to her no-good back-stabbing partner hitting her over the head with it, but that was beside the point.

She made it out of more jams and tight spots in the last five years, so Trouth's "the hospital has security" comment was utterly laughable. She wasn't stuck in here, and if her enemies wanted to get to her, hospital security wouldn't stop them.

That was the scary part. She wasn't sure *who* her enemies were at this point.

Calvin, her partner from the last job, flipped sides, something that was only made clear when he knocked her unconscious when her back was turned and thus gifted her the "only five stitches" she currently had in her head, but what side did he flip to?

There weren't many options. Plenty of mega-wealthy could afford to dump the truckloads of money on collectible art, vehicles, and precious stones. Still, only a select few of those people were privy to connections to people like her who could procure whatever their hearts desired, even if the current owners had no interest in selling. And man, did they pay for those desires.

In five years, she amassed enough of a fortune that she was getting out of the business after collecting from this job. Her boss wasn't too happy about it, considering she was one of his best, but what happened on the beach was all Calvin—and whomever he was working with now. Her boss was the only person she could trust as much as she could trust another human being. Kristen always got the job done, and she was not going to let this hiccup change that.

And only her boss knew that this one was her last. Maybe if she had let the crew know, then Calvin might have offered to cut her into whatever deal he was working on the side instead of hitting her over the head with enough force that it should have killed her.

The Russians were the worst of the handful of outlaws who played at this level. *God, Calvin. Please don't let it be the Russians.* Old Calvin probably thought he was so smart, waiting until she had done all the hard work these last two years to turn on her at the very end. The last thing she needed was for Calvin to have flipped for the Russians. Out of the handful of outlaws that worked at this level of thievery, they were the most ruthless. The second they got their hands on him, they would not be happy because he didn't have the goods. Not the *real* goods, at least. And once they finished with Calvin, they would be coming for her.

If she could just get her hands on her clothes…

Before Dr. Trouth could leave her room, she spat out a cheery, "I appreciate it." She might as well keep the act up even if he threatened her about security.

His dimple came out. "I'll make sure they get you to a room ready." He had a gleam in his eyes; he was definitely antagonizing her.

That should have been it. Dr. Trouth would be on his annoyingly cute way, and she would talk Celia into finding her clothes for her, and then, when no one was looking, she would slip out. It would be easy. It should have been that easy, but then Dr. Trouth stepped out into the hallway and froze.

Two distinct voices, one male and one female, grew loud enough that her blood pressure monitor's beeping quickened despite trying to keep it together. *Tattletale.*

Judging by how the muscle in Dr. Trouth's jaw tightened as he crossed his arms over his chest, he was equally unhappy to see the pair walking up. He barely moved his lips to grumble through clenched teeth, "I thought I told you to stop coming up here."

The kind, attentive older woman who ran up to her on the beach waltzed right up to Dr. Trouth and stopped smack dab in front of him with only a fraction of the curtain obscuring her from Jane's view.

"Hold still," Celia told her. "I'm almost done wrapping you up."

She straightened her head but strained her eyes, looking out the corner of them to see the woman throw her hands on her hips.

"What did you think I was going to do?" she spat, "not come check up here and see how the poor girl was doing? Did you think I would wait for *you* to tell me, Mr. I-refuse-tell-anyone-what-happens-at-my-job?"

Dr. Trouth raised a hand to his face and pinched the bridge of his nose. "It's called patient confidentiality."

Kristen muttered a thanks as Celia finished and felt around her face. Anywhere she felt her hair sticking out from under the bandages, she tucked it back in.

"It looked better with those pieces out," Celia said, collecting the trash from the cart.

"Oh, I bet," she said sarcastically, but the look Celia gave her caused her to hesitate while stabbing a stubborn lock of hair under the bandages.

Celia was being sincere. *Too bad.* This hair wasn't meant for the world to see. Thankfully, the bandages covered most of it except for the backside. She gave up on the lock of hair to run her hands self-consciously over the back of her head. The motion caused sand, still hiding among the curls, to fall on the pillow behind her. Her hair was a complete disaster.

A throat cleared in the hallway, and she saw Dr. Trouth shifting his gaze from the woman in front of him to the person clearing their throat behind her.

"Allen," the man uttered, quietly out of sight.

The doctor's face softened as he gave the man a nod. "Ed."

"Any changes in our Jane Doe?"

He glanced in Kristen's direction. "Ask her yourself."

The muscle in her jaw flexed. These people were *never* going to give her a moment of peace.

"Wow," Celia chirped from the side of her bed. "You'd think I was trying to take your blood again."

"I'm freezing," she murmured.

"I could get you another blanket."

Kristen took a chance by asking, "Can I put my pants back on?"

"You're not going to let me forget about your clothes, are you?" Kristen didn't say a thing as Celia sighed. "I'll look for them once I put all this up."

SIX

So much for being a great doctor.

At this point, Allen was actively ignoring the blood pressure monitor going off in his patient's room, and the lack of cat noises from the other side of the hallway was probably also a bad sign, but he had no plans of sticking around on the floor. He would pull a page from Eriksen's book and hide in his office for a while. Let Eriksen do his job for once. Man, this full moon was bringing out the *worst* in him.

"How are you doing?" Ed asked, striding into the patient's room with his wallet in his hand flipped open to his detective credentials in case anyone thought to question what he was doing in the emergency room. He wondered what Ed could do to him if Jane Doe told him that she was being threatened by the hospital staff.

"I'm okay." She used an overly soft feminine tone, like silk. Jane Doe's eyes met his as if she knew his thoughts. "They're taking good care of me here."

That was a jab.

"Glad to hear it," Ed said, falling for it hook, line, and sinker. For a detective, one would think he would catch on when being worked over.

If it weren't for those eyes of hers, he might have fallen for it too. They were too sharp then. But the way that she was looking up at Ed with naïve doe eyes was far more convincing. He could almost believe *those* eyes.

"Looks like you're as interested in her as I am."

Allen gritted his teeth. Today was determined to be one of those days.

Case in point, regardless of multiple conversations where Allen had been crystal clear in what was acceptable, his mother was not only showing up at his job unannounced but was also in zero need of medical care, which was unacceptable. It didn't matter what she did this morning; he wasn't in the mood for her antics. At least she didn't bring her dog.

"Excuse me?"

His mother rolled her eyes. "Don't play coy with me. You had that same look in your eyes the first time you brought Gwen to my house."

"What are you talking about?" he spat. "Gwen and I had been dating for months when you met her, and we were in love."

His mother gave him the same annoyed look. "And how did that work out for you?"

"Didn't we agree not to talk about Gwen anymore?"

"You brought her up," she shrugged and missed Allen's grimace deepen. The woman's ability to deflect and deny was award-worthy, and she would continue to deny it if he corrected her since she was the one who brought up his ex.

"So let's go over what you remember from this morning," Ed instructed, with his pen and notepad ready.

"Does she still not remember who she is?" his mother mumbled out of the corner of her mouth.

"So she claims." He could hear it in her voice that she had her own opinion on the woman she saved this morning. "What's your take on her?"

"She's hiding something."

He nodded in agreement. His mother might like to annoy him by showing up at his job after he explicitly asked her not to, but for the most part, they were on the same page.

"I thought so, too."

"No," she said, barely moving her lips, "I mean, she's actually hiding something."

"What do you mean?" he asked, stealing a glance at Jane Doe, who was recounting Milo and his mother coming up to her on the beach.

He and Ed had once shared a laugh over the places they had seen people hide things. Ed found drugs and other contraband hiding in orifices when booking offenders into the jail, and Allen treated patients with things stuck in orifices.

"What I mean," his mother's voice interrupts his thoughts, "she has something hidden in a pocket—"

"Did they not check her pockets at the beach?"

"Are you going to let me finish?" she snapped, loud enough that everyone could hear.

Silence fell over the room beside them. Even Celia glanced over her shoulder at them. Allen gave them an apologetic grin and then took his mother by the arm to steer her away. They made it a few steps before his mother dug her heels in, refusing to go further.

"There was slobber all over my face," Jane was saying, "so I didn't even realize I was bleeding until I touched the top of my head."

"She has a hidden pocket," his mother said, her lips barely moving. "Sewn into the front of her pants."

"She told you this?"

"Yeah," his mother said, rolling her eyes again, "right before she told me her name and who attacked her. Then we had some tea and gossiped until the ambulance got there."

"Just tell me," he encouraged, fighting not to look too frustrated by her unnecessary sarcasm.

"She passed out, so I checked her pockets."

"Of course you did," he sighed.

His mother didn't love snooping per se, but searching an unconscious body in an attempt to figure out who they were was right up her alley.

"Don't act like you wouldn't have done the same," she said indignantly, to which he didn't reply. He could think of worse things he would be willing to do to Jane Doe if she wasn't his patient and didn't possibly have brain damage.

"I would have taken whatever it was out too if the ambulance hadn't gotten there so fast."

"Did you tell the EMTs?" he asked, although he knew the answer.

"You mean those two idiots who spend their days in the diner parking lot and barely kept it together when they saw her head split open? Of course not. What would I have said? 'Oh, by the way, after you stop the bleeding, I found a small pocket hidden in the crotch of her pants'?"

Allen blinked at her. "Her crotch?"

"Yeah. Right next to the front button. It felt like it ran down the side of her zipper. It had something hard about an inch or so long. I could only imagine those two guys bumbling around to be the one to check it out."

Though he wanted to, Allen couldn't dispute that. Their EMTs were decent enough guys, but even he didn't like the idea of either unbuttoning Jane Doe's pants.

"What about Ed? Does he know?"

"No," his mother sighed. "I was going to tell him, but then she came to, and I didn't want her to know that I knew, and then once the ambulance left, all Ed wanted to do was talk about our date."

"You mean that date that you walked out of."

"You make it sound like I walked out on him," she protested. "I only left when *he* didn't show up."

"He sent you a text message telling you that he got caught up with that vandalism at the library."

"He knows that I don't check my text messages. Wait a second," she narrowed her eyes. "Have you two been talking behind my back?"

"He reached out only because *you* weren't answering your phone, and when I asked him what happened, he told me about the whole date thing."

His mother crossed her arms angrily over her chest. "Of course, you would take his side."

Allen let out a loud sigh, happy they were no longer right in front of Jane Doe's room for Ed and Celia to overhear this. "There is no side to take. He ran late at work—no fault of his own. I don't know why you're giving him such a hard time."

His mother uncrossed her arms to slap them at her sides dramatically. "A lecture from you is the last thing I need. I'm going home."

"Mom—" he started.

His mother spun on her heels toward the door. Her hand flew up in the air. "Don't want to hear it," she said. "You can tell Ed whatever you want."

He watched her sashay toward the exit, wondering if he had been wrong about his mother not loving the drama. How she acted undoubtedly seemed that way, and what did she think he would say to Ed? It's not like he would encourage the guy to pursue her when she acted like this over something the man couldn't control. Ed was the only detective in town, so it wasn't like he could pass the work on to someone else. Not that his mother dating wouldn't be a welcomed break for him. Ever since Gwen and he split, it was like his mother was everywhere: his house, his job, even his morning runs weren't safe from her and that dog of hers popping up. That's why he changed his route this morning.

It was then that Allen realized he could have been there when Jane Doe was attacked.

"Everything okay?" Celia pushed the supply cart out of Jane's room.

"Peachy," he said dryly. "Tell Amirah to let the front desk know not to let my mother in from now on."

Celia chuckled. "Unless she needs medical care, right?"

"Sure," he said absentmindedly.

"Will do." She knew his mother well enough to understand.

Celia rolled the cart up against the wall opposite Jane Doe's room. Redrock Memorial had the funds to pay doctors like Eriksen a full salary despite his limited role in anything hospital-related. Still, it didn't have the funds to stock each emergency operatory with its medical supplies. Having one crash cart was one thing, but having to hunt down one medical cart when things got crazy in the emergency room with lives on the line should be against the law.

"Sorry," Celia chimed before walking past Jane's room toward the nurse's station, "she already left."

"It's fine. Thank you, Celia," Ed called after her.

It sounded like Ed was asking for his mother. Allen continued down the hall toward the office wing. Talk about commitment. The man was in the middle of working a case, and he was still trying to smooth things over with her. A meow rang out from the opposite side of the emergency room, and Allen shook his head. The day was just beginning. And now, with every step Allen took away from the ER, soft sobbing grew louder behind him. Allen's shoulders drooped. If Eriksen hadn't locked himself in his office, he could handle the Harrisons.

He would take care of the amnesia patient.

That was why the emergency room floor plan was designed in an "H" shape, as his Chief Physician Ruslan explained. The nurse's station in the small hallway connecting the two halls gave them a central point to conduct all administrative work, and the halls on either side were small enough for one doctor to handle by himself, even at capacity. Not that the ER had even been close to capacity on either side, but that was their excuse for keeping Eriksen on Allen's shift despite Allen being the one doing all of the actual patient care. His morning runs before work prepared him for the running he did at work when things got busy.

Sobbing led Allen to Jane Doe's room. "Hey, Ed," Allen started.

His annoyance with Eriksen bled into his suspicion of his amnesia patient. He was going to tell the detective what his mother told him about something hidden in her pants but stopped short. Ed was standing over Jane Doe, looking on in horror as she wept into her hands. It was a genuine enough cry that Allan got that same uncomfortable would-do-anything-to-make-it-stop lump in his stomach. "Are things coming back to her?"

"Not exact—" Ed started, but Jane stuttered over him.

"I-I...didn't get—" she fought through her tears to get it out, "—to thank her." She burst into full-fledged sobs as soon as the last word escaped her lips.

"Let me get you some tissues," Ed offered, backing away slowly as if any sudden move might upset her further.

"What's going on?" Allen muttered when Ed was close to him.

"Talking about assault is hard on victims," Ed explained sympathetically. "And she wanted to thank your mother for helping her, but she left before she could."

Ed didn't seem to catch it, but the second he mentioned his mother, Jane Doe paused her crying for a fraction of a second. However, Allen saw it. When he looked around Ed, her tear-soaked hands still obscured her face. Perhaps her tear-fest wasn't so genuine if she caught on to Allen being the son of the woman who found her this morning.

She pulled her hands away to wipe her eyes and her red and distressed face—can't fake that.

"I can tell her for you," Allen offered to Jane.

Ed glanced back at Jane Doe, who nodded between wiping her tears.

"I appreciate it," she sniffled.

"Can I have a word with you?" Ed ushered Allen into the hallway with a swing of his arm.

"What's up?" he asked once they were safely out of earshot.

Ed kept his voice low. "I'm not getting much out of her," he admitted, getting uncomfortably close to Allen. "Do you think you could have someone watch her for a little while? I need to comb the crime scene. I wasn't able to earlier with your mother there," he explained as if the mention of Allen's mother was some excuse not to do his job. But, witnessing his mother's mood today, he could see her starting in on poor Ed the second the ambulance pulled off.

"And we don't want some violent husband or boyfriend tracking her down here," Ed continued.

Allen nodded in agreement. He looked around the abandoned hallway to no avail.

"I can ask security to come over to watch her, and I'll have Amirah let admitting know not to let anyone back who isn't a patient in case someone does come looking for her."

"Great, and...uh—" Ed looked Allen over before nodding toward Jane Doe's room. Allen leaned in, confident he was about to question him about her authenticity. "How long does something like that last?"

Allen straightened. *So much for that.* "Depends," he sighed. "It's temporary for most people. It could last minutes, hours, days, but you can run her fingerprints, can't you?"

"I can, but I would need to bring her down to the station, and unless she were already in the system, it would be a waste of time."

"Can't be too sure these days," Allen said, feeling like it was more for himself than Ed.

"Right," Ed said, dragging the word out. "Hey, does your mom like flowers?"

Allen blinked. His question was so far from where Allen was mentally that he could only stare at him. "Flowers?"

Then, Allen understood. Leave it to women like their Jane Doe to pull the wool over an aging detective's eyes. He shouldn't be surprised; Gwen had kept plenty of things from him, and he was in his prime.

Ed lowered his voice even further. "Your mom told me in not so many words that she's still mad about our date."

"I couldn't tell you," Allen said earnestly. "But I better get to it." He took a step back to end the conversation as quickly as possible.

"I got you," Ed nodded. "Once security's here, I'll head out."

Allen nodded along. *To the beach, hopefully, and not to get flowers.*

"Is it Jonesy working today?" Ed asked.

There was yet another small-town reminder that even the sixty-something detective in town knew the twenty-something, once high school football star, Jonesy, well enough to know that he worked security at the hospital. From what Allen had been told, the guy was as big as a building and great at football before he blew out his knee, but he was dumb as rocks.

"Believe so. I'll get them to page him. Shouldn't take him more than two minutes."

Ed gave him a thumbs-up over his shoulder as he walked back into the operatory. "I'll let our Jane Doe know before heading out."

"Good luck," Allen said with no doubt that their Jane Doe was already listening.

SEVEN

After being absent all morning, Lady Luck was finally shining down on Kristen.

The detective was leaving. The mention outside of her room of possibly taking her fingerprints worried her, but there had been no further mention of it since the detective returned to her room.

"If anything comes to you while I'm gone," the detective told her, "have them call me."

"Yes, sir."

He wouldn't be gone for long, but she'd take it. All Kristen needed now were clothes and an exit strategy, fast. It was only a matter of time before the security guard arrived. Kristen listened and silently counted: Five seconds from when the detective took a right out of her room to when the doors slid open at the end of the corridor. She was aware enough of her surroundings when she was rolled in to remember that the ambulance ramp was outside those double doors, but Celia had been out there on the ramp when the ambulance arrived with Kristen. And she was sure that Celia used her badge to open the doors for them. But, the detective wouldn't have a hospital badge, so exiting must not require one.

As if she were summoned by Lady Luck herself, Celia appeared with a large clear bag containing Kristen's clothes.

"Here you go," she set the bag down on the foot of the bed. As Celia pulled the sheet back, it clicked with Kristen what she was doing.

"I can put my pants on myself," she insisted.

Celia's brow rose. "Are you sure? You might get dizzy standing, and I can't have you falling and messing up the great job I did on your stitches."

Kristen felt precious time slipping away from her. "I'm good. Really."

"Okay. I'll shut the curtain, but if you need me, you only have to press the button." She tipped her chin at the button to call the nurse on the arm of the bed. Celia closed the curtain on her way out, leaving a quarter-inch gap.

Kristen stood, testing her stability—no dizziness. She was surprised to find all her clothes and shoes inside the bag. If she worked in a hospital making pennies on the dollar, it would be hard to see a pair of Gucci tennis shoes sitting in a bag and not want to swipe them. The people around here must be clueless when it comes to expensive threads. Kristen took her pants out, and sand hit the floor as the pants unfolded, but it was nothing compared to the appearance of dried blood on her shirt that she used to keep the blood from her eyes while waiting for the ambulance to arrive. Thankfully, she had somehow managed to avoid getting any of it on her white shoes.

She didn't have time to worry about this. With eyes on the gap in the curtain, Kristen pulled off her hospital gown, forgetting about the blood pressure cuff attached to her arm and the thing on the end of her finger. Her stress was apparent by the increasing beeps from the blood pressure monitor.

"You sure you got it?" Celia called.

Kristen dropped the gown and grabbed her pants. "I'm good," she said as the nurse poked her head around the curtain.

"You sure?"

She stepped into one leg of the pants to demonstrate how steady she was on her feet.

"Okay. I won't be far."

Kristen's head pounded as she stepped into the other leg. By the time she pulled the pants over her hips, her monitor was yelling at her. It wasn't her blood pressure so much as her heart rate this time, but without thinking, she walked over to the wall and ripped the top power cord out of the socket, unsure if she had the right one, but sure enough, the beeping stopped. The monitor went dark. No footsteps headed in her direction. Ignoring her head pounding, she dropped to one knee and peered under the curtains. Celia's shoes were nowhere to be seen. The coast was clear.

Kristen pulled on her shirt, careful with the top of her head. She might not make it far wearing a shirt covered in dried blood, but she definitely wouldn't make it out of the hospital wearing one of their gowns. When she paused to look herself over, she realized that it didn't matter if she had on her shirt or the gown; she didn't have a means of transportation. Plenty of cars were in the parking lot, but without her purse, she had no tools to hotwire a car. And that was only the here-and-now issues. She also didn't have a place to go. It's not like she could go to their rendezvous point and get paid because she still didn't know if Calvin had wanted to cut her out of the deal or if he was working for someone else. Once he realized he didn't have the goods, it wouldn't surprise her if he would go to the drop site in hopes of ambushing her.

So, the rendezvous point was out of the question. And hospital security or not, it wouldn't take long for Calvin or whoever he may be working with to hunt her down, so sticking around pretending to have amnesia was also out of the question.

Her apartment would have been the best place. None of the guys in their crew knew about it. It was too bad that she canceled the lease and moved all her things into storage when she took this job, knowing it would take her years to finish. Even worse was that her next set of

IDs and the key to her storage unit with all her belongings were in her purse in the car when Calvin attacked her.

Lady Luck really had abandoned her this morning.

Kristen could feel herself spiraling. She was in a tight spot, with nowhere to go and no means of getting there. With a deep breath, Kristen ran her hand over the hidden pocket in her pants and immediately felt relief. She could get out of this.

All her troubles would be solved if she could somehow let her boss know what happened. He could help her. Why couldn't she have had her cell phone on her when Calvin hit her over the head? One phone call, and she wouldn't be surprised if he had some nearby precinct in his pocket. He would have one of them pick her up and deliver her safe and sound; they could laugh about this by dinner.

She couldn't make a run for it yet—not with how little she had to work with. A phone rang close enough that Kristen froze while pulling the hospital gown over her clothes so that only Celia knew she had changed into her street clothes. It was not only a landline, but it was close by. A woman answered it on the second ring, but it didn't sound like Celia.

Crap. Could she hear Kristen moving around and the fact that her blood pressure monitor was no longer working? Kristen couldn't determine what she was saying until the woman said, "he's giving them trouble on the ramp." Her words echoed down the hall, followed by hurried footsteps.

Double crap.

She dove into the bed as Celia rushed by, thankfully not looking in her direction, with Dr. Trouth close behind.

Shoes, she thought to herself. Whether or not she would run for it, being barefoot left her at a disadvantage. With no security guard in sight, what would stop Calvin from walking in and finishing the job with everyone rushing outside? She envisioned kicking Calvin in the groin. No, she definitely needed her shoes.

She was tying her laces when a woman in scrubs stood before the gap in the curtains, watching the exit. In a panic, Kristen threw the bed sheet over her legs.

"Everything all right?"

The woman opened Kristen's curtain enough to look in on her. "Nothing out of the norm," she assured her.

"The Harrisons are filling out their discharge papers," Dr. Eriksen approached from the opposite end of the hallway, and he stopped beside the woman, smiling happily with himself. "You ready for some cake?"

Any concern the woman may have had for what was going on outside evaporated into a grin as she faced him. "Only every day of my life."

Eriksen chuckled. Before the pair walked off, the woman glanced in Kristen's direction. "You need anything?"

"I'm good," she chirped, banking on the woman leaving with Eriksen to celebrate his birthday at a far enough distance that she could get to that landline, make her call, and be back in her bed before Celia and Trouth made it inside.

As they walked off, Eriksen asked, "Where did everyone go?"

"Trouth and Celia are outside with that new admit. Ivan hasn't made it in yet."

"Two people aren't enough to celebrate a birthday. We'll have to grab HR and billing along the way." Eriksen's voice faded down the hall.

Kristen waited a full two breaths before kicking into gear. She could do this.

It was as if the entire emergency room knew what she was up to and had fallen silent to see if she could pull it off.

A faint meow in the distance was all the reminder she needed to know that as much as it might sound like it, she was not alone in the ER. All she had to do was get to the nurses' station, call her boss to tell him what happened and where to find her, get back in bed—unless keys to a nearby car fell into her hands—and then she would hook back up to the blasted monitor before anyone was the wiser.

However, she would have to watch for that security guard, too. She poked her head out of her room. The nurse's station to her left appeared deserted, with two empty chairs behind the low counter. The ambulance entrance slid open to her right.

It could have been worse, she thought as she dove for the bed a second time. What if she had been on the phone at the nurse's station when they came in? She tossed the sheets over her lower half and adjusted the pillow behind her.

"He's working his right arm free," Celia warned in the chaos of squeaking wheels rolling down the hallway and people talking.

"Told you he's Houdini," a man said.

"I got it," another called.

The gurney came to a halt in front of Kristen's room.

"Get off me," the drunk man on the gurney bellowed at Celia while the EMT on his right pounced on the man's arm as it wiggled free from its strap. The EMT who pushed the back of the gurney hurried to help his counterpart.

The drunk man's clothes put her bloody shirt to shame. His oversized shirt and jeans looked like they would crunch at the touch, and they may have, but she couldn't hear it over the man's incoherent shouts as the EMTs wrestled to secure his arm. The man thrashed around but ultimately lost the battle.

The electric doors slid open down the hall, and Dr. Trouth called, "You got him?"

One of the EMTs turned. "Got him. You good?"

"Nice job," Celia cheered to the EMT who had strapped him down. The two grabbed the gurney railings and pushed forward, leaving the other EMT in their wake.

"I'm good. I found one of my buttons—"

The man on the gurney quickly drowned out Dr. Trouth. "Geeeet off," the man slurred. The other EMT hurried to catch up, and the drunk man's head snapped in Kristen's direction. "Monsterssss."

The way he sneered and slurred his words was pretty creepy, but she shrugged it off. She's been called worse. Not that she ever stuck around long enough to hear any of it. With his wild eyes on her, she realized that her tennis shoes were obvious under the sheets, so she crossed her legs under her.

"You're safe, Mr. Farris," Celia reassured the man.

"Mooonnsstters, get off me," he grumbled, losing the energy in his demands.

"There you go," Celia soothed. "You'll feel better when you wake up."

"And when he gets some Haldol in him," one EMT added.

Dr. Trouth came into view. He was a sight, all rosy-cheeked with his lab coat flapping open in the breeze of his stride. His scrub top was tight enough across his chest that Kristen wished it had been open like that when he was tending to her. He glanced in her direction, and she snapped out of it, giving him a tight grin. He gave her nothing back but a glance at the empty bag on the foot of her bed.

Crap.

If he noticed what it was and the fact that there were no longer any clothes inside, it didn't slow him down. Kristen watched as the closest thing to eye candy strolled out of sight, followed by the disheartening sound of them rolling the man into a nearby room close to the nurse's station.

Double crap.

It was smart on their part to keep him close by, but that made getting to the phone trickier. However, it was still not even close to the most challenging thing she had pulled off.

She once dove off a yacht in the Virgin Islands after the heir of a perfume dynasty proposed with his mother's twenty-carat blue Nile emerald cut ring. Kristen had stolen it back after it was stolen from the original owner years prior. If you ever find yourself in possession of stolen goods, don't post a ton of pictures online showing off said item. For that job, she overcame a very real fear of water and a small fear of heights, jumping off of the yacht and swimming to a boat full of fake paparazzi her boss staged near the yacht. That had been a tough job to pull off. Making a phone call in some hole-in-the-wall hospital without drawing attention to herself would be a breeze.

At the very least, she could pretend that her fake amnesia was lifting. "Can I call my mother?" she silently rehearsed, but then she would have to explain that she knew who she was to call her mom.

If only calling her mother was a real option. Life would be so different.

EIGHT

AMIRAH TRIED TO WARN HIM, but had Allen listened? Nope. And the same patient she tried to avoid admitting nearly punched him in the face because of it. But he couldn't be mad at Mr. Farris; he was having a schizophrenic episode. He didn't know what he was doing, but Allen did.

The first thing he was going to do once he got to his office was email Ruslan about their need for a psych wing, and if not a full wing, then at least one or two rooms that offered a more secure space to put patients like Farris until they could be transferred. They would have a nearly empty emergency room if they had. He did not doubt that one trip to the psych ward would stop Mrs. Harrison's feline antics. Allen could make a case for sending Jane Doe, too.

Though he would miss those eyes of hers.

"Mr. Farris is finally going down," Celia informed him as he walked into the operatory.

"He still needs to be restrained," Allen said, lining the gurney up alongside the hospital bed.

"This is how he was when we picked him up," Jerry, the eldest EMT in Redrock, said.

The other EMT, Isaac, agreed. "When we pulled up here, he popped awake like someone had blown a bullhorn in his ear."

"He's a beast," Jerry nodded. "Until the benzos kicked in."

All four stared at Mr. Farris for a long moment, waiting to see if he would magically regain consciousness.

"No time like the present," Allen said.

The unstrapping was done quickly. They grabbed handfuls of the sheet beneath the man. Counting to three, they hoisted him up and onto the hospital bed in one motion. Everyone froze when a sharp noise escaped Farris. Once he snored, a flurry of hands followed. Allen strapped down Farris's midsection in the five-point restraint. Celia got an arm. Jerry, the other, and Isaac secured both of Farris's ankles.

"Excuse me," Mr. Harrison called from the other hallway. "Is anyone there?"

"We'll be right with you," Celia said.

"I'll see what he needs." As he exited the room, Allen noticed the empty nurse's station. "Where's Amirah?"

"No telling." Celia went from one restraint to the next, checking that two fingers fit under them, ensuring they wouldn't hinder circulation. She met his gaze on her way to Farris's ankles. "It would not surprise me if it was just you and me working the whole floor."

The cold, hard truth of her statement made Allen grin. "No different than any other day."

Jerry looked up. "If you guys aren't happy. We're always hiring."

Allen laughed almost as hard as Celia. Laughing was a welcomed change, considering how today was going, but when his phone vibrated in his pocket, it brought him down from the momentary high. He knew who it was, and he was not going to let her get to him. Farris's snore cut off in the middle of a loud one, and everyone's moment of merriment stopped to confirm that the man wasn't waking up.

"Better put an incline in that," Jerry nodded at the bed.

"I need his med orders," Celia reminded Allen as he approached the nurse's station.

He added that to his list of things to do once he got to his office.

NINE

"You're being awfully quiet." An older man pushed a woman in a wheelchair past Kristen's room.

The woman grumbled, "I have never had to be in a wheelchair to leave here before."

"It's their policy."

"A brand-new policy, apparently," she snapped. "It's ridiculous, is what it is. Just like them thinking they could ship me off to some psych ward in Charleston. Yeah, right."

"They have to have somewhere to send the crazy—"

"Gary, so help me God, if you are calling me crazy—"

"Darling, I would *never*."

Their conversation ended with the sound of the doors at the end of the hallway opening and shutting. There went one ticket out of here. She could jump up, run after them, steal their keys, and take off. But she couldn't do it. As much as Kristen had stolen over the years, she couldn't steal from regular, everyday people. The first time she hot-wired a car, she felt so bad about it that she made the block and parked it a couple of spots from where she had stolen it. She had stolen from Phillip, too, back in Texas. That was a kick to the gut to think about. Her regular-guy Texas fling had been neither a target for a job nor a terrible person. His family may have been well-off, but they didn't have the billions that allowed Kristen to sleep soundly at night post-heist.

"I'm going to put in his med list now," Dr. Trouth said down the hall.

"Don't want to help me get him in a gown?"

"I don't want to get in the way." Kristen could hear the smile in his voice.

She couldn't blame him. If she went to school to become a doctor, the last thing she would want to do was help undress a drunk man. Kristen nestled her head into her pillow and shut her eyes as his steps grew closer. The utter silence in her tiny room was glaringly obvious, but hopefully, only to her. She should have plugged the machine back into the wall before jumping into bed.

Please don't notice that the blood pressure machine is off. Please don't notice that the blood pressure machine is off.

She kept her breathing slow and steady. His footsteps slowed. Just when she thought he was about to walk into the room, his footsteps continued by without a word. Kristen waited a few more breaths until his steps faded into the distance and then opened her eyes. All clear. Luck was on her side.

The phone at the nurse's station rang.

"Amirah," Celia called. It rang a second and third time. "Anyone?" Still, no response.

Kristen leaned forward to listen as Celia marched over.

Please call her away from here.

"This is Celia." The nurse sighed, "Ivan, so help me. You know I have plans today. You better be pulling into the parking lot. Yeah, I'll believe it when I see it." She slammed the phone down.

Something like Velcro ripped nearby.

Celia jogged from the nurse's station. "Hey, don't do that," she warned. "You really are Houdini, aren't you?" A grumble came from the drunk man's curtained-off room, and Celia's voice lowered. "Nope, we are leaving our pants on today, Mr. Farris."

At a curtain pulling shut, Kristen leaped out of bed. This was her chance. As long as that curtain stayed closed with Celia on the other side of it, Kristen could make it to the phone. She'd have to be quiet and keep the call short, but her boss needed to know where to find her and that Calvin was on the run. If anyone saw her, Kristen would act confused and say she was looking for the bathroom.

The coast looked clear when she poked her head out. Staying low, she moved into the hallway partly for stealth, partially because she got up too fast, and standing up straight hurt her head even more.

"How did you get that undone?" Celia said as Kristen got close.

There was a gap in the drunk man's curtains, too, but thanks to good Ole Lady Luck, Celia's back was turned when Kristen passed. By the time Kristen was at the nurse's station, Celia wouldn't be able to see her even if she did turn around.

Kristen maneuvered around the two chairs like landmines in her path to the phone. She gently pushed the first chair out of the way, but the lightweight jacket draped over the back slipped off the second. She caught it mid-air.

"Come on," Celia said impatiently on the other side of the curtain. "Give me your arm."

With the jacket safely back on the chair and out of her way, Kristen made it to the phone. She heard a single beep when she put the phone to her ear—no dial tone. *Come on, Lady Luck. I need you.*

If infiltrating art galleries as an art dealer taught her anything these last two years, all decent businesses required a code to dial out. Apparently, Redrock Memorial emergency room was no different.

"Give. Me. Your. Arm." There were more grunts from the other side of the curtain; Celia was still busy.

If I was the dial-out code, where would I be? She took a guess and dialed nine. Sure enough, that was it. Lady Luck was definitely back.

Kristen dialed the only number she had memorized. *Only for extreme emergencies*, her boss's voice echoed in her head. She held her breath. In the hospital with only the clothes on her back, no clue of if or when Calvin would show up looking for her—this was definitely an emergency, and for her, this was as extreme as it got.

The phone rang, and relief surged through her.

Kristen ducked behind the counter as more noise came from the other room. The phone continued to ring. She wasn't expecting him to answer, but she wasn't exactly sure what she could safely leave on a voicemail. Were calls in hospitals recorded? How vague did she need to be with something like this? It had been years since she memorized the number. She might not have the number right, or the number may not be good. Then, the voicemail picked up. It was total silence and then a *beep*. No personal or automated voice message; she knew she had the right number.

"Hey. I'm in the hospital in Redrock, South Carolina alone. This number is the only thing I can remember. I was hit over the head and left on the beach." If calls were recorded, she couldn't chance mentioning Calvin or that he didn't get away with the goods. "I am okay, but I don't have a ride home."

There was no triumph as she hung up the phone. Sure, she made the call without being caught, but she needed to get back to her room, and then what, sit around and wait for her boss to swoop in and save her?

There was too much unknown as far as how safe she was here. Her eyes were on the jacket on the back of the chair. She made up her mind; she wouldn't wait for her boss. She pulled off the hospital gown, rolled it up, and stuffed it in the trashcan under the counter. A bloody shirt wouldn't keep her from making a clean getaway, and a plan formed as she swiped the jacket off the back of the chair and strolled out from behind the counter, zipping it up. She would hitchhike out of here if she had to.

The second she strolled past the drunk guy's room, all thoughts left her.

It was that sound—like wheezing, but not quite. Kristen peered into the drunk man's room. The sound wasn't coming from the patient but from Celia. The guy had managed to free his arms and wrapped both hands around Celia's neck as she fought to breathe. Tried as Celia might, the man's hands weren't budging from around her throat.

That's not your problem, her boss's voice echoed in her head. *Get out of here while no one can stop you.*

"Let her go!"

TEN

All he needed was ten minutes of peace and quiet reclined back in his office chair—time to decompress and let the morning stress melt away.

Allen got less than five. He had removed one file from the cabinet and sat down when his phone vibrated in his coat pocket. It was a new text, ruining any mental peace he hoped to achieve. Even without looking, he knew it was from someone he did not intend to respond to. He put his phone in his top drawer, where he kept the things he hated, such as the wedding band he would never get to wear.

He set his phone next to the ring when a distant scream shot him out of his chair.

Jane Doe's empty room was no surprise as he cruised past it. She hadn't been connected to her monitors, and the empty clothes bag sat at the foot of her bed when he passed earlier. He was also pretty sure she was pretending to be asleep, but who was he to call her out on it? He felt she would try to leave without filling out discharge papers, which was fine with him. The hospital would eat the costs of her care, and things would go on like normal. It's not like he hadn't told them when he was hired that they needed badge tags on all the doors, so only those permitted would be allowed in and out of floors like the ER and intensive care unit.

The doors that go out to the main hospital floor swung open.

"Better late than never," Ivan called. "Was someone just yelling?"

"Believe so—"

"Code gray," Celia's hoarse voice called out.

Ivan and Allen exchanged a look before running toward her voice. Allen got to Farris's room first and skidded to a halt. Whatever Allen thought he was about to run into was nothing compared to the chaos waiting for him.

I hate full moons.

Jane Doe was on top of Farris's bed, kneeling into the patient's throat in a goddess-like stance, conquering her foe. Her other leg had his right arm pinned against the bed.

Celia snapped him out of it. "Help."

Looking disheveled, Celia used her body weight to keep Farris's left arm near the restraint. Allen hurried over and strapped Farris's left arm with surprising ease, compared to his strength coming out of the ambulance earlier, but that probably had to do with Farris's bloody nose and skin turning light purple under Jane Doe's shin.

Ivan skidded to a halt at the foot of the bed. Like Allen, Ivan stared up in awe at Jane.

"What's going on?" he asked. "Where is everyone?"

"That's a good question," Celia growled.

"Call a code gray over the speaker," Allen said. "That should get our staff back on the floor."

Ivan took off for the nurse's station as Farris's face turned a darker purple.

"He needs to breathe at least a little." Allen tried not to stare up at Jane Doe as she towered over them in a strong stance that was equal parts a turn-on as it was causing his patient to black out.

"ER Code gray, ER Code gray," Ivan's voice chanted through the overhead speakers.

"Let up on him," Celia said.

Jane Doe shifted her weight. With one good oxygen-filled inhale, Farris weakly attempted to free his arms. It took a conscious effort to lower his gaze for Allen to notice that Farris's other arm under Jane's leg was still not strapped down.

"No extra room for his hands and feet." Allen secured Farris's other arm tighter than the recommended two-finger spacing for proper circulation.

"No shit," Celia grumbled, moving down to his ankle next. She wasn't looking too good. Her eyes were red, and her hair was a mess.

"Why don't you go sit down?"

Celia nodded. "I will once everyone gets back on the floor."

Allen cursed under his breath. If everyone had been here like they should have, including Ivan, then Celia wouldn't have been here for this. She brushed her hair out of her face, revealing the red marks around her neck. "Did he choke you?"

His answer was written on Celia's face as she glanced up at Jane Doe with her shin ready to choke Farris out again if he got too rowdy.

"Not for long. Thanks to her."

Jane looked down at them. "Is he good?"

"He's good," Allen said, helping her down.

He was late to the fiasco and utterly wrong about her. The least he could do was be a gentleman and help her off the bed. She faltered, trying not to step on Farris. Allen grabbed her hip, keeping her steady. When their eyes met, he opened his mouth to apologize for earlier, but the heat in her gaze had him transfixed.

"Monsters," Farris crooned, breaking their gaze.

"All good?" Celia asked. Judging by how she looked at them when Allen released Jane, whatever was happening between them was noticeable.

"So," Allen said, clearing his throat. "Which one of you are going to tell me what happened?"

"She'll have to tell you," Jane said, nodding at Celia as she stepped lightly away from him and Farris's bed. "I only came in at the very end."

"It would have been the end," Celia agreed, "if she hadn't flown in here like a bat out of hell and tackled him."

"You tackled him?" he asked, his eyebrows shooting up.

Jane gave him a tight grin, not saying a word.

"It was more of like a wrestling move," Celia explained.

Allen examined Farris's face. "Is that why he has a bloody nose?"

Jane raised her hands defensively. "All I did was get him to let go of her neck."

Celia rubbed a hand over her throat, highlighting how red it was. "I thought he only had his left hand free when I got in here, but his other hand flew up out of nowhere, and before I knew it…" Her words fell short as they glanced in Farris's direction.

Farris was passed out, slack-jawed. His soft snores were deceivingly gentle compared to what he was capable of. Allen checked the medication cart on the other side of the bed. "What did you manage to give him before he strangled you?"

Celia shook her head. "Nothing. I didn't even get the chance to look at your med orders. He must have worn himself out."

Allen checked the man's pulse. Slow but steady. "I haven't put in his med orders yet." Nor had he paged for security in his hurry to get the Harrisons out of here. He was majorly slacking today.

Doors opened and rushed footsteps hurried down the hall before Ivan popped up at the curtains. "Are we all good in here?"

Allen pointed at Farris. "You watch him to make sure he isn't fake sleeping." He couldn't help but glance at Jane Doe, who was trying to be as invisible as possible, staring at the floor. "I'll put in his med orders, and these two," he looked between Jane and Celia, "fill out incident reports."

"You know who this is?" Ivan said, blinking at Farris. "He's the guy who gave us all that trouble a while back."

Allen frowned. "Yes, Ivan. We know. And Celia, you can go

home as soon as you're done." He turned to Jane Doe. "You're coming with me."

ELEVEN

She should have escaped when she could. However, Kristen was in step with Dr. Trouth, who kept looking at her as she pretended not to eye the exit at the end of the hallway out to the ambulance ramp.

"This way." He directed her to the small corridor she hadn't noticed before.

"Where are we going?" she asked, trying not to make it obvious as she glanced back longingly at the double doors leading outside.

"To fill out your incident report."

He led her to the first open door on the right and into a bare walled office with a desk at the center with two chairs from the nineties facing it. A tall, expensive-looking office chair sat behind the desk, but the worn filing cabinet behind it had her attention, with its rust running down the top of it.

"Wow," she said, looking around. Everything but the office chair looked to be at least twenty years old. "Fancy."

"I hear your sarcasm, and you should know that this is my office," he said, walking around her to his desk, "and you should have seen the state of the other office they offered me. You can have a seat."

Kristen eyed the layer of dust on the armrest of both chairs facing the desk. "You know, I could fill the report out in my room."

"But then I would have missed that disgusted look on your face," he said, going to the filing cabinet.

She sat down in the closest chair, holding her breath a second to avoid inhaling the dust she stirred. With how crappy the office was, the chair behind his desk was fancy. It had a tall back, super cushiony like a gamer chair, and looked brand new. He settled for an outdated office, but he did not settle for an outdated chair.

Allen took out a thin folder from the cabinet and then walked to his seat, sitting down with an audible sigh of relief.

Every man had his thing. Humphry's thing was his shoes, and she wondered if her doctor's was his office chair.

"Is an incident report really necessary?" she asked as he withdrew a paper from the folder.

"You will have to fill one out before you leave, and I assumed you wanted to get out of here sooner rather than later, seeing as how you are in your clothes, plus Celia's jacket."

Kristen's cheeks flushed. She wouldn't have taken it if she had known it was hers. That poor woman had been through enough. "Why do you think this is Celia's?"

"I don't think, I know. It's the bleach stains." Allen pointed at the three dots along the edge of the collar Kristen hadn't noticed before. "She came in complaining about her son doing that to a load of laundry last week that included her work jacket."

There was nothing she could say. He caught her. When Kristen unzipped the jacket, Allen grimaced at Kristen's chest. She couldn't blame him. With no other option, she had to use her shirt to keep the blood out of her eyes while they waited for the ambulance once she came to after passing out.

"You know what," Allen said, eyes still locked on her blood-covered shirt, "why don't you keep it on for now?"

For a second, Kristen thought about leaving the jacket unzipped just so he would have to look at it, but ultimately zipped it back up.

Dr. Trouth pushed a piece of paper toward her. "What's this?" she asked. The top of the form read "South Carolina's Women's Empowerment Program."

"Your ticket out of here. If that's what you're after."

Her silence was as close to a confession that he was right on the money as he would get. He needed to get to the point, but he studied her for a long moment before settling his gaze on the paper.

"You fill that out, and it will cover the cost of your medical bills. It's a grant program the state offers." She scanned the paper as he spoke. "It covers medical and recovery costs for battered women. You don't even have to keep the bottom part. We just need your name and social."

At the bottom were various phone numbers for resources like local safe houses and counseling. Having something like that wasn't a bad idea. *A built-in hideout, and surely it had some level of security given the circumstances women would be there; what wasn't to like?* She immediately felt guilty for the thought. It would be a waste of resources, but a safe house was exactly the sort of thing she needed.

"We don't share this with the authorities." Dr. Trouth turned on the computer screen on his desk and began typing. "So don't stress out if you have warrants or anything like that. It doesn't matter."

There it was. He thought she was a criminal. That was a blow to her ego, but the way she jumped on that guy to subdue him, she understood how she might give off the vibe. It was a hard pill to swallow. In all of her years being a criminal, not a single person suspected her of being anything other than what she pretended to be, or at the very least, never came out and said it to her face.

In the polite society of the uber-wealthy, such things were never said out loud, even when you knew it for a fact. Like the guy she dated whose grandfather made his initial millions from insurance fraud in the early nineteen-forties, and by the time authorities found out, he had hidden enough assets before the seizers started so that decades later, his grandchildren were living comfortably without ever having to work a day in their life. That man's eldest grandson,

Edward, had been Kristen's first and easiest mark. He laughed about what his grandfather "accomplished," as he put it when she asked about "the rumors" in private. When she stole over sixty thousand dollars' worth of art from his penthouse a week later, she had laughed too.

But, all was not lost. She could still save this.

"Do you have a pen?" she asked. "And scissors."

His slight smile fell. "What do you need scissors for?" He took a pen from the top drawer of his desk.

"To cut out this bottom part." She pointed at the list of resources and pretended to be preoccupied with filling out the paper, but she could feel his eyes on her. "I want to keep it." Hopefully, that would be an explanation enough.

As she filled out the form, Allen opened the folder on his desk. "Oh," he said solemnly and then shut it. "Right. Uh..." He rummaged through the desk drawer by drawer. "I'll go find some scissors." He typed away for a minute, making Kristen think his way of locating scissors was via email, but then he turned off the screen. "Med orders are done. I'll be right back."

"I'll be here," she said, meaning it as a joke, but Dr. Trouth peered at her.

At first, she thought he would give a look to say, "You better be here," but then she saw it. *Sympathy.* The look he gave her was more like, "You poor thing." It was the last expression she wanted him to give her. She hated sympathy, but it was exactly what she needed to lean into to get out of this.

She diverted her gaze to the paper.

"I'll lock the door behind myself," he said.

"What's the plan? After I fill out this form, I mean," she asked, barely turning her head in his direction.

"You, uh...don't have anyone you can call to come pick you up?"

She hesitated. He was smart; she gave him that. He had been onto her from the beginning. He recognized she was fully clothed and had on Celia's jacket when no one else had. How far was she willing to show him that he was right? Kristen turned fully in her seat to face him. He wasn't letting up, so what was the harm to give in just a little?

"If you mean for me to call the person who did this to me," she pointed at her bandages, "it's not going to happen."

He shook his head briskly. "Of course not. I mean...your mom or dad."

"Dead and no," she said bluntly.

"Siblings?"

She shook her head.

He pinched the bridge of his nose. "But you don't want to stay at the hospital," he said. "Correct?"

There was something in the way he said it. He now knew that she didn't have anyone, and yet, it still sounded like he was willing to let her leave if she wanted. She had never given this much away to someone not in on the con before, but being right on the edge of the cliff with nothing but honesty below, she stuck her toe out just a hair further.

Kristen lowered her gaze to the form, where it asked for the relation of her abuser for statistical purposes. "It'll be the first place he comes looking for me."

"I'll think of something." And with that, he walked out, shutting the door quietly behind himself.

She rose from her seat to check the door, which was locked like he said it would be. For a moment, she envisioned him trapping her in here and calling the detective he was so chummy with to pick her up, but she wasn't trapped. The lock was on the inside. She was safe. All she had to do if she wanted to leave was unlock the door and walk out.

He might not be that great of a doctor, threatening her with a needle, but he was a decent person. Unless, of course, he came back with the detective. But he wouldn't, she told herself. He was a decent person, and decent people helped those in need, and she was definitely in need.

With a moment to herself, she moved around the desk and opened the top drawer. Pens and knick-knacks rolled around. She opened it further and saw a gold band beside a cell phone lying face-down.

Kristen grabbed the ring. Why would it be in his office drawer? He didn't come off as the married-but-only-wore-his-ring-around-his-wife type. Hospital rules, perhaps?

There was a fleeting thought of pocketing the ring, but she set it back in the drawer and grabbed the phone. The screen lit, alerting eight missed text messages. She almost dropped the phone when a ninth came in while holding it. Throwing a side-eye to the closed door for a second, she swiped at the screen. No lock code. *What a life this guy must lead.* Texts filled the screen, all from the same number saved as Do Not Answer. Her eyes widened at the most recent text.

I AM COMING DOWN THERE!

Kristen scrolled up a little to read the previous three texts.

I cannot believe you are going to act like this.

Can you PLEASE text me back?

I can pick it up myself—no big deal—I just need it before next weekend.

Kristen froze as footsteps sounded outside the door.

TWELVE

ALLEN PULLED his keys from the doorknob. Jane sat quietly, filling out her form. As he handed her the scissors, he glanced at the top of the paper. Her handwriting was as terrible as his. He could only make out the first letter of her name. *K.*

"Thank you," she said meekly.

He didn't deserve to be thanked. He hadn't been there when Celia needed him or for Jane Doe, whom he gave such a hard time when he knew she was lying about having amnesia but was the victim of a crime, nonetheless.

So much for his medical ethics oath to help others.

All he could think about while retrieving her scissors was how alone Jane Doe must feel, not having anyone to call. That was if she were telling the truth—he stopped his thoughts there. He decided that he was going to believe her. It was the least he could do after what she did for Celia. Plus, he made a quick phone call at the nurse's station before returning to his office.

"Your ride will be along shortly."

She stopped writing. "My ride?"

"That's right. I got you a ride to the bus station on the other side of town. I figured it was the least I could do." He took out two more folders from his filing cabinet. "Fill these out next." He handed her discharge papers from the first folder, but the incident report folder was empty.

"Okay." She added the discharge papers behind the grant form she was finishing.

"I need to find an incident report for you to fill out, too." He doubled back toward the door. "I'll give the staff a heads-up that you're leaving. Are you thirsty or anything?"

"I'm good, thanks. Here." She cut the bottom section of the form and then handed Allen the scissors.

A patient had amnesia one minute and then was filling out her discharge papers the next after singlehandedly stopping an assault on an employee. He would have so much explaining to do, but he didn't care. Letting her leave could be a huge mistake, but he'll answer to it later if he has to. So many terrible things could have been prevented if someone had just done something; today, Jane Doe did. He'd gladly take whatever chewing out comes his way because of it.

Allen waltzed up to the nurse's station, surprised to find Eriksen standing there. "What happened over here?" Eriksen asked in his chronically chill tone.

The human doctor version of a sloth appeared to only just now be returning to the emergency room floor.

"Did you not hear the code gray?" he asked.

Eriksen's wiry eyebrows rose. "That was for the ER?"

Amirah was seated behind the counter, phone to her ear. She exchanged glances with Allen. "I'm checking on that Charleston transfer," she told him.

"Where are the homecare packets? I need one for stitches."

Amirah pointed him to one of the drawers down the counter from her.

"Is that why Celia was so shaken up?" Eriksen asked as Allen rounded the counter.

Thanks to the craziness of the morning and years of keeping his mouth shut when it came to Eriksen, Allen had enough. He glared pointedly at the older man as he grabbed the drawer Amirah directed him to with his left hand and slung it open. "If *you* had been here doing *your* job, you would know what happened. Hell, if everyone had been where they should have," he cast an accusing glance at Amirah before directing it back at Eriksen, "then Celia wouldn't have been hurt, and we wouldn't have had one of our patients knock out another one to help her."

Amirah's jaw dropped, but she held the phone to her ear.

"Whoa," Eriksen said, palms up in surrender. His gaze was on Allen's right hand. Allen looked down at the scissors he had forgotten he was still holding.

"We were in the break room," Eriksen explained. "Seventy-six candles are a lot to blow out, let me tell you," he chuckled nervously. "I was close to setting off the fire alarm."

Allen rolled his eyes. "Do you hear yourself? You are a grown man off blowing out birthday candles while one of your nurses was attacked *by a patient*."

Eriksen's eyes were still on Allen's right hand. "What are the scissors for?"

Allen slapped them down on the counter. "Those should have been retirement candles you blew out."

Allen marched into his office with a blank incident report and homecare instructions in hand. He hadn't told anyone that Jane Doe was leaving, and he did not feel bad about it. If Eriksen could get away with being a complete waste of a physician, he could discharge a patient without running it by his staff.

Jane stared at him expectantly when he returned.

"What is it?"

"It's nice of you to get me a ride," she told him. "But I don't have any money. Like, zero money," she paused, and Allen stared at her. "For bus tickets."

Allen nodded. Apparently, it wasn't a wad of cash she had

hidden in her pants pocket. "I figured as much." He went around his desk and withdrew his wallet from his back pocket. His empty wallet was a welcomed reminder of why he didn't miss his ex. Emptying out his wallet was the one thing she had been exceptionally well at.

"Looks like you and I are both short on funds." Jane gave him a confused look as he smirked before plopping down in his office chair. He set the papers down on his desk. "But, I have this." He opened the top drawer of his desk. Jane's eyes widened when he withdrew the gold wedding band. She physically recoiled when he offered it to her.

"What are you doing?"

"I'm giving this to you."

Two soft lines formed between her brows. "Because...?"

"Because I want to marry you," he said dryly. "Because there's a pawn shop in town. You take this." He set the ring down in front of her on the desk and leaned back in his chair. "Pawn it, and they'll give you cash—"

"I know how pawn shops work."

"Really? That's hard to believe when you're wearing one of the most expensive knockoff tennis shoes I know of."

"Knockoffs?" she repeated as if the word left a bad taste and glanced down at her shoes. "These aren't knockoffs."

He grinned at the way she seemed to catch herself. "Don't worry. I'm not going to make you pawn them. I needed to get rid of that ring anyway." His mom owned a similar pair of shoes, but he knew hers were knockoffs because he bought them for her. Knowing hers weren't made him curious. "If they aren't knockoffs, how expensive are they?"

She studied her shoes. "I don't know. I didn't buy them."

The way she continued to stare down at them caused Allen to do the same. That was when he saw a drop of dried blood on them. Anger flared up inside of him, but unlike with Eriksen, Allen's anger was with himself. "I'm sorry," he blurted. "Your shoes are none of my business. It's that ring—" he explained, but when he saw her fighting back a grin, he stopped.

"So we're blaming a defenseless ring now?" she asked, the corners of her mouth cracking into a grin.

Allen smiled. "I guess I am."

It felt like she was flirting with him, but he wasn't sure. Her grin disappeared as she resumed filling out the paperwork.

After a moment, he asked, "Who are you?"

There was a pause in the stride of her penmanship. She barely looked up. "What do you mean?"

She was nonchalant, but with the pause in her writing and the looking but not really looking, he could tell that she was throwing up her defenses. Did he want to tell her that she wasn't like other women? Surely, she knew that already. The strong certainty in her eyes was something she had to be aware of. It was certainly something he had never seen in someone so young. What she didn't know was what a turn-on it had been to find her manhandling his other patient like that. Strength in any form was attractive, but there was no way he could tell a patient that, so he said the only thing he could without risking a lawsuit.

"You keep surprising me."

It was as much of the truth as the rest of it. The tension dissipated as Jane set the pen on top of the forms and slid them to him.

"I'm just a regular girl."

"Right," he said, "and I'm just a terrible doctor."

Jane winced. "I'm sorry about that."

"Don't be." Allen leaned forward and nudged the ring closer to her. "I'm serious about—"

"Pawning the ring," she interrupted. "Or did you mean the terrible doctor thing?"

"Both, I guess." He smiled more genuinely before reading her form. "Miss Chanel."

THIRTEEN

"You can call me Kristen." She regretted it the second she said it. It was the same first name she used with Phillip back in Texas, and she had just written it on everything the doctor handed her.

What was this head injury doing to her? She never slipped up like this.

Kristen made it much easier for someone to link her to the items she stole from Phillip and his family. She could have gone with Kristy, Krystal, or anything other than Kristen; it was written all over the papers she slid across the desk. Would he have her committed if she were to snatch it out of his hands and rip them into pieces?

What was she thinking? She had even used the last name Chanel previously, but thankfully, she had never used Kristen and Chanel together. She wasn't thinking. That was her problem. In her rush to fill out the papers to get out of here, Kristen had put herself one step closer to being linked to past jobs.

No, she needed to calm down. It was going to be okay.

He squinted at the paper. "Is that supposed to be Kristen?"

Her chest tightened as he eyed her over the top of the paperwork. She nodded.

"Kristen." He scanned the paper. "I never thought I would say this," he said, setting the papers down, "but I think you might have worse handwriting than I do."

She forced a grin, hiding a cringe at hearing him say her name again. "It is pretty bad, isn't it?"

The messy handwriting was intentional. She only regretted not making it worse.

A soft rumble came from his desk, and Dr. Trouth raised a hand. "Hold that thought." He withdrew his cell phone from the top drawer and grumbled, "Apparently, using a cell phone has gotten easier for the most stubborn person I know since she can miraculously text now."

Stubborn was the last word she would have used to describe someone blowing up his phone with threats in all caps.

"Good news," he said, returning the phone to the drawer, "your ride is here."

"That didn't take long."

He stood and grabbed the other papers from off of his desk. "That's the good thing about small towns," he said, rolling them up and stuffing them into the front pocket of his lab coat. "It takes no time to get from one side of town to the other."

"What about the incident report?" she asked.

"Oh, right. Go ahead and fill that out."

She jotted down the basics of what happened, lessening her role in helping Celia while acknowledging that she was there all the while waiting for her doctor to warn her that his contact, *Do Not Answer*, was her ride out of here, but he didn't say a word. It will be interesting to find out what kind of person warranted that contact name.

He sat quietly, working on his computer, and printed a few things while she finished filling everything out. No more questions about who she was or what happened to her on the beach.

A smirk crept across her face once she headed out of his office ahead of him. She had kept it together pretty well, minus giving herself one of the names she used in Texas.

All in all, it was turning out to be one of the most unforgettable mornings of her life, and that was saying a lot.

"You forgot something."

Kristen turned to see him holding the gold ring. The same ring that she was *that* close to stealing when she was alone in his office. The irony was not lost on her.

"I'm serious about you pawning it," Dr. Trouth said, inching his outstretched hand closer. "You'll be doing me a favor."

It didn't feel like a favor when she reluctantly took it from his palm. It felt more like hush money. For him threatening her earlier or for saving Celia, she wasn't sure. Judging by how heavy it was in her hand, it could be for both. It felt like solid gold. If that was the case, then it should get her enough cash to get where she was going.

"Are you sure?" Kristen slid the ring into the pocket of her pants.

"I am. That thing has been nothing but bad luck ever since I got it."

She froze. "After the morning I've had, any more bad luck, and I might end up decapitated."

Allen shook his head. "I'm being dramatic. If anything, my ex was the bad luck. She was...something else."

Kristen's brows rose. "Yours too?" she asked, leaning hard into the meek, battered woman role. After how she took out that drunk guy, she needed to play up her role as much as possible. She would have to take a break from kneeing people in the face.

A flash of pity crossed the doctor's face. "I think yours was worse."

Kristen nodded. "Agreed." She fell in step beside him down the short hallway. "Let's just hope I can wrap my pretty little head around how to pawn it." She meant it as a joke, but he winced.

"Did it sound that condescending when I said it?"

"Don't worry," Kristen smiled. "You backtracked fast enough that I didn't have time to take it to heart."

"Glad to hear it. Hopefully, this makes up for the rest of it." He took a left as they rounded the end of the hallway onto the emergency room floor, and his face dropped. "So much for emergency vehicles only," he grumbled.

Kristen followed his gaze to the double glass doors leading outside. A car was on the ambulance ramp with both front windows rolled down. To her relief, the person behind the wheel of the black Honda parked smack dab in the middle of the ambulance ramp was a sight for sore eyes.

"You called your mother?" she asked, her jaw happily hung open in disbelief. "I'm surprised she took your call after the big deal you made over her checking on me earlier."

His dimples reappeared as he escorted her to the exit. "Don't let her fool you. She *loves* drama. Her biggest complaint about Redrock is how boring it is. I bet she couldn't get here fast enough. You are the most exciting thing that's happened around here in a while." His smile deepened. "Don't tell her I told you that."

Kristen nodded, feeling unusually complacent on her stroll to the exit. She hadn't achieved anything except pulling one over on her doctor, who was kind enough to discharge her and get her a ride to the bus station. She had forgotten to grab that bottom part of the paper she cut out. Had he not noticed? She could blame it on her head trauma if he did.

Stealing a glance, she wondered if it was worth mentioning. His features looked even better up close. How was that possible?

She spent so many years keeping men at arm's length to avoid this exact kind of close-up examination. She couldn't have the men she was about to steal from notice that the glasses she wore for some of her aliases weren't prescription or that her long blonde hair was a wig. It was impressive how close she could get to someone and their valuables without them realizing that even the color of her eyes was fake.

Being this close, she could see a faint but undeniable scar at the start of his hairline. The way it peeked out from under his hair made her want to reach up and see how much more of it was hidden beneath it. What was it with men with scars? She was so entranced that he caught her staring straight at him when he glanced over at her.

"What?" he asked, neither upset nor uncomfortable to catch her staring, but their closeness, mixed with how he searched her face, made her want to bolt.

Her head snapped ahead as she searched for something, anything, to say. Kristen blurted the first thing that came to mind. "Shouldn't I be in a wheelchair?"

Outside in the car, Betty tossed stuff over from the passenger seat into the back, clearing out room for her up front.

Dr. Trouth raised his arm toward her with concern, looking at her as if she might fall. "Do you feel like you need a wheelchair?"

Kristen forced an uncomfortable grin. "The cat lady was very vocal about the new policy that forced her to be wheeled out—"

"Right," he caught on. "The Harrisons did not like me enforcing that one. Technically, we're supposed to put you in a wheelchair when we discharge you, but we don't enforce it."

"Unless you're acting like a cat."

"Precisely." His dimples reappeared, and she liked being the cause.

After this was said and done, looking for a guy with dimples to date in her new life might be fun once Calvin was a distant thought and she had her money. She could swear that her not-so-terrible doctor looked sad the closer they came to the exit. She patted him on the arm, and her stomach tightened as her touch brought his eyes straight to hers.

"Thank you for your help." His gaze was more intense than she expected, so she added with a coy grin, "Turns out you aren't so terrible of a doctor after all, Dr. Trouth."

The corners of his mouth curled. "You can call me Allen."

Stop looking at the man's mouth. Her eyes flickered to the doors, where Betty was finally emerging from her car.

"No hard feelings?" He offered his hand, and it hung in the air between them.

"Are you talking about threatening me with needles?"

He winced, but Kristen took his hand before he could withdraw it. "No hard feelings…Allen."

Her eyes made their way to his. *What is with this guy and the eye contact?* She pulled her hand away first.

"Hello…?" Betty called from the other side of the glass doors.

Allen pressed the large button, and the doors slid open.

"It looks like we were meant to spend the day together." Betty greeted Kristen.

Kristen smiled. "I can't think of a better person to spend the day with than the one who saved my life."

"Aren't you sweet!" The wind knocked some of Betty's soft, graying bangs into her eyes. She tossed her head in a well-rehearsed motion that sent the hair back to its place swept off to the side. "Are you ready to go?"

"I am."

Allen stood off to the side of the double doors, watching them. Kristen dipped her chin at him. "Thank you."

"My pleasure," he said in a low voice. His dimples reappeared as her breath caught in her throat.

Sweet lord. Did he have any idea how hot that was?

She turned without saying a word. He knew. He had to know.

FOURTEEN

The overwhelming desire to do something like embrace the woman he met a mere couple of hours ago kept him planted right where he was. "You are welcome."

His mother walked around the front of the car. "See you later, Son."

"Oh, and hey," he called. "This is only for ambulances."

She threw her hand up in the air over her head dismissively. "I do what I want."

Allen rolled his eyes. *If that isn't the truth.* Kristen gave him a brief smile and followed his mother to the car. He almost apologized for not finding someone else to drive her, but they would be at the bus station in minutes, and then she'd be out of their lives.

"Wait," he leaped forward as Kristen opened the front passenger door.

"What?" his mother grumbled from the driver's side.

"Not you," he shook his head as he walked up to Kristen. "You," he told her as she smiled encouragingly at him.

"Don't tell me you changed your mind about letting me leave."

"Jacket," he managed to get out as he silently wished he had changed his mind about letting her leave. He pointed his finger at her jacket to clarify. "Celia's…been through enough—"

"Yeah, right," she agreed over his explanation, quickly unzipping and taking off the jacket. "I really wouldn't have grabbed it if I'd known it was hers."

"Thanks," he mumbled, ignoring the fact that she wasn't saying that she shouldn't have taken it all, but he could see the guilt in her eyes as she looked from him down to the jacket and then turned to get into the car. "Be safe," he said, not knowing what else to say.

"I'll do my best."

He walked inside of the double doors and then turned to face them.

Watching her leave almost made him long for the next full moon. Perhaps it would bring another woman with mysterious eyes, but he knew better. Women like that were rare. He welcomed the cool breeze that rushed over him as the doors slid shut in front of him.

"We got a two-car collision headed this way," Amirah announced down the hall. "One unresponsive."

Allen tried not to listen. Something amusing was said, and his mother laughed. Kristen glanced over at him as if having to leave was sad for her, too.

He went to stick his hands into his coat pockets and then slapped the pad next to the doors without looking. "Hold up."

Kristen rolled down the window.

"What now?" his mother asked, leaning over the center console to look at him. He stooped down, ignoring his mother.

"Almost forgot to give you this," he said, taking out the papers rolled up in his coat pocket. "It's your home care instructions. Keep your stitches dry for forty-eight hours—no baths where you submerge your head, that sort of thing. The stitches will dissolve as you heal. They'll come out on their own in a couple of weeks." He pointed at the prescription stapled to the packet. "You have two prescriptions. The antibiotic is the important one. Now this is…" He pointed at the prescriptions for the pain medicine, but as soon as he looked at it, his voice faded as he stared at it. He hadn't even thought about printing out and signing the narcotic for someone who didn't have any form of identification. Without ID, no pharmacy would fill it for her. "Forget this one," he said, stuffing it back in his pocket. "Take the antibiotics no matter what."

"Antibiotics, check."

"As far as medicine for the pain goes," he thought quickly with what she had to work with, "you'll get the best pain relief by alternating Tylenol and ibuprofen. You can get those over the counter—"

"Pick up some ibuprofen, check."

Allen looked around Kristen to his mother. "Do you have any?"

His mother rolled her eyes and reached into the backseat. "What kind of question is that?"

Kristen and Allen glanced into the back of his mother's car. Like usual, it was covered in hats, coats, blankets, empty water bottles, and Milo's seat cover. On the floorboard were shoes, her purse, and more empty water bottles. She grabbed her purse from the floorboard. She reached inside and pulled out a travel bottle of Tylenol. "Here we go." She offered the bottle to Kristen. "The long ones are Tylenol. The small round ones are ibuprofen."

Allen gritted his teeth as she passed Kristen the bottle. "May I?" The last thing he needed was for his mother to give the wrong pill to one of his patients. She handed him the bottle, and Allen opened it to find not just two but three different-sized pills inside.

"Mom, come on." He recognized two of the three and fished out the small white, oblong pill that he didn't. "What is this?"

"Let me see." His mother reached across Kristen to pluck the pill from Allen's fingers and popped it right in her mouth.

"Mom—"

"Fresh mint," she said over him, eyeing the open bottle. "There's more Tic Tacs in there if you want one."

Kristen perked up. "I would love one."

Allen could see from the twinkle in her eyes that she was

enjoying this. He tapped a mint and two Tylenol into her hand. "It's all in there." He handed her the papers.

His mother grabbed a water bottle out of the cup holder. "Here," she offered Kristen. "I haven't opened this one yet."

Allen groaned. "How many times do I have to tell you how bad it is to drink out of plastic bottles you leave sitting in the car?"

"I grabbed this one from the house this morning; thank you very much. Now, I think we're good, so why don't you go be a doctor to someone else?"

Allen grimaced at her before stepping back. "Good luck," he told Kristen, placing his hand on the top of the car. Being in a vehicle with his mother, she would need it.

She gave him a warm grin. "I was wrong."

"Wrong about what?"

"About you being a terrible doctor."

"I could have told you that."

FIFTEEN

"Terrible doctor comment?" Betty asked once the car doors were shut.

Kristen rubbed her palms self-consciously across the tops of her thighs. She was more uncomfortable now with Allen's mom than she was thinking that she was in a car with whoever *Do Not Answer* was in his contacts. *It's okay*, she told herself. If there was one thing she could do well, it was handling the moms. Winning a love interest's mother over was a part of the job. The wealthier they were, the more attached men seemed to be with the women who gave them life. And, in the end, they all ended up liking, if not loving her, before her job was complete.

The key was letting them do most, if not all, of the talking.

"I may or may not have called your son a terrible doctor when we first met."

Betty gave her an unbothered smirk. "Fascinating," she said as she drove the car out of the ambulance ramp. "Those must be the magic words that got him to break you out of the hospital."

She held up the stapled stack of papers Allen gave her. "You didn't break me out. I had to fill out a bunch of paperwork."

Betty smirked. "The man's got an entire staff working for him. For Allen to give you that, he definitely broke you out of there."

"I'm telling you—"

"How are you paying for it?" Betty interrupted. "You didn't happen to find your insurance card, did you?"

Had Allen not told his mother all of this when he called her to come pick Kristen up? She lowered her head and rubbed her palms against the top of her thighs. She needed to play this carefully and appear honest, but not as honest as she had been with Allen. She had patient confidentiality on her side, but she wasn't naïve enough to think that Allen hadn't filled his mother in on at least some of what she told him. The perk of pretending to be a meek, injured woman was that she could simply shut down if the questions got to be too much.

"He got me a form for a funding program for abused women." Kristen glanced up. She might as well be talking about the weather from how Betty looked at her.

"And you could fill it out because the amnesia lifted?"

The woman didn't miss a beat. Allen must not have filled her in at all. The two were definitely related, though, because she gave Kristen the same skeptical look Allen first gave her. She will have to hit her with all the victim vibes she could muster.

"Yes, ma'am," she said meekly.

"That's awfully convenient."

"It was more than I could have hoped for after everything this morning."

Betty's pleasant but suspicious facade broke into a sad frown. "That was pretty awful," she said. "How are you handling it?"

"I'm okay. Thank you, by the way. I didn't get to tell you earlier, but you saved my life." Kristen thought of her mother to get choked up. "It was...really...brave of you."

Betty's frown deepened at the heaviness of Kristen's voice. One hand on the steering wheel, she reached her other arm behind her seat, dug around for a second, and then withdrew an almost empty box of tissues. She handed it to Kristen.

"Don't make me out to be a hero now," she said as Kristen blew her nose. "All I did was take Milo for a walk."

"And save my life."

Betty stole a glance at Kristen, her features hardening. It was the exact opposite reaction to what Kristen had expected.

"I didn't save anyone's life," Betty told her adamantly. "If anything, Milo is the hero." Her features softened. "He's usually a great listener and doesn't get more than a few feet ahead of me, but he knew you needed his help and took off. All I did was chase after him."

And with that, Kristen knew the dog was the way to the woman's heart. "You will have to thank him for me."

Betty smirked. "I know just the bone to give him when I get home."

She could only imagine the level of dog slobber that poor bone would have to endure. "Good." Kristen balled up the slightly-used tissue in her hand.

"What was he yelling at you about?" Betty asked.

"Who?" Kristen asked. Her question caught her off guard, but she knew exactly who she was talking about.

"I want to see what we worked two years to get," Calvin insisted as he pulled onto the shoulder of the highway for their first official stop since fleeing Texas. She had used the backseat to change out of her dress and wig, but she had been wanting to stretch her legs since Georgia.

"It's all in the trunk," Kristen told him.

She exited the passenger side of the car without so much as a second thought of Calvin. Kristen was ready to welcome her new life, starting with sunrise over the water. Her favorite part of mingling with the wealthy was the views. The penthouses overlooking cities and parks were great, but the water views were her favorite. And this right here in Somewhere, South Carolina, would be the last of those views. At least the ones that came from her life of crime.

This sunrise would be as spectacular as the next chapter of her life. She could feel it.

"I wasn't born yesterday," Calvin called through the open passenger door. "You worked two years across three galleries. You can't tell me the junk you stole from that Texas twat last night are the goods."

"Two and a half," Kristen mumbled as she walked to the beach. She hadn't worked *for* any of the galleries either. She used them, and the "Texas twat" had been a decent guy, but Calvin didn't care. He also didn't care when she told him about the strange guy parked across the street from her apartment in Dallas two days in a row, who she was pretty sure had been around the previous gallery she infiltrated in Chicago. And for a guy whose only job was to protect her the last two and a half years, Calvin couldn't be more indifferent.

She met Phillip Decker that night in Dallas after Calvin blew her off about the mystery man following her, and thanks to Phillip, she never returned to her apartment. He had been so truly good to her that she had to hurt him good enough that she wouldn't be tempted to go back once her big job was done.

On her last night with him at his family's fundraiser, after kissing him far too comfortably, she stole from him. It was more from his family, but it was enough to ensure she wouldn't return. And that was how the Les Paul guitar and Benny Goodman clarinet came to sit idly in the trunk. Calvin was right; they weren't the big job, but he didn't need to know that. His only concern should be getting her safely to the drop point in Charleston and getting them paid. Her only concern at this moment was watching the sunrise.

The sun was making her ascent over the horizon.

"I have a right to know," Calvin's voice made her jump, but she didn't turn around.

She hadn't heard him walking up behind her over the sound of her own footsteps and the waves lapping the beach ahead of her.

"Right to know what?" she asked in a daze.

The sun was already doing its magic. She could feel herself being renewed, forgiven even for the past she was officially leaving behind.

"What it is that we stole."

"What does it matter?"

"It doesn't, but you can at least show it to me."

She shook her head. His voice was pulling her out of the sun's trance.

"Come on," he growled. "I know this isn't what the job was."

She should have turned around just then. If she had, Kristen would have seen that he was holding the guitar or the clarinet, but she was too occupied with the view, and his growing anger was rubbing off on her.

"It doesn't matter," she said, far too loud for the serenity she was trying to achieve. "We did our job, and we're getting paid. That's all that matters."

"Hand it over, Sky."

Her hands clenched into fists at her sides. That did it. He used her last name, her *real* last name. It was a no-no in their line of work. And for her, it was a no-no whether they were on a job or not. She never used her real name. Only a few guys who worked with her boss in the early days even knew it. Calvin was one of her boss's originals and one of her least favorites.

"Not happening, Calvin. Now give me ten minutes to enjoy the view."

"I said, give it to me!"

Had she lifted her chin to better allow the sun's rays to warm her face? All she could remember was what Calvin said next before everything went black.

"Have it your way."

"The man who attacked you," Betty responded, driving them out onto the highway.

"I can't remember," Kristen said, blinking the memory away. The throbbing in her head grew. "This morning is still pretty fuzzy."

"But you do know who he was?"

"Yes," she whispered, trying not to let the throbbing encourage a full-blown headache. "I do. I know him—knew him. I can't believe I was so stupid."

"Don't blame yourself. Sometimes people who never had any right to be there in the first place weasel their way into our lives."

"He weaseled his way in for two years too long." The depth of Betty's words washed over Kristen, and she fell silent. *Is that how the trail of men I left in my wake felt about me?* She weaseled her way into their lives, pretending to be whatever version of a woman her research showed they'd be the most attracted to, except for Phillip.

"Attractive older men have always been my thing, too," Betty said.

Kristen squinted at Betty, partly because of her statement and somewhat to help her focus through the banging in her skull. "You saw him on the beach?" It came out like a question, but if Betty knew he was older, there was no question.

"Vaguely. My hearing isn't what it used to be, but I can tell a man's age from a hundred yards away."

Kristen's brow pinched together as the pain radiated through her skull. She also had a sinking suspicion that Betty may know more than she let on.

Had she heard Calvin use my real name?

"I can only speak for myself," Betty continued, "but older men are the most passionate lovers. The things my late husband could do —" Something caught Betty's eye out the windshield. "What a shame," she grumbled with a shake of her head.

Kristen followed Betty's gaze to the water tower in the field to the highway's left, where someone had spray-painted underwear on the side. "Is that pink underwear?"

"Boxer shorts," Betty nodded. "It's become a whole thing since that showed up on the water tower. Even girls are wearing them now.

My neighbor told me that her fifteen-year-old daughter bought a pair."

"Some marketing, huh?" Kristen looked back at the road. "Slow down," Kristen pointed at a small building coming up. "There it is. The pawn shop."

"Why do you need a pawn shop?"

"To pawn this." Kristen withdrew the gold ring from her pocket.

Betty pulled into the parking lot. "You're pawning your ring?"

Clearly, Allen hadn't told his mother much. The way Betty eyed the ring suspiciously as she parked the car made Kristen wonder if it had been for a good reason.

Kristen was unsure if she should tell her the truth, but there was no point in making something up now. "I explained to your son that I didn't have money for bus tickets when he told me you were on the way to drop me off at the bus station, and your son was kind enough to give me this to pawn. He was pretty insistent on it, actually." Betty took the ring from her and looked it over. "He acted like it was a relief to get rid of it."

Betty flipped the ring over in her hand, holding it up so that the sunlight from the front windshield brought the gold to life.

"Interesting," she muttered.

"It took me by complete surprise," Kristen said, worried that Betty might retract her son's offer. "But I wasn't going to ask any questions when I'm alone and don't have anyone else to help."

Slowly, Betty offered the ring back but held onto it when Kristen reached to take it from her. "You sure you don't have *anything* of value?" she asked the second Kristen's eyes met hers.

"I don't."

Betty released the ring. "What about what's in your pants?"

"Excuse me?"

Betty rolled her eyes despite Kristen's obvious offense. "Not *that*. That," she pointed directly at Kristen's crotch, "right there."

Kristen bashfully covered her lap with her hand. "I don't know what you're—"

"I know you have something hidden around your zipper. I felt it after you passed out."

Kristen gave nothing away, but the woman was getting too close to home. Was it too late to shut down and stop talking?

"That's a weird area to feel on an unconscious stranger."

"I was checking your pockets for an ID like the 9-1-1 operator told me to."

Kristen sighed. There was no point in acting dumb; Betty wasn't having it. You always stick with a story until you can't. By the time she reached into the hidden pocket, as she had sewn on all of her jeans and slacks these last two and a half years, she knew what to say.

She could feel Betty holding her breath as she withdrew the key fob.

"VW," Betty read from the back of the fob as Kristen flipped it around in her hand. "Why are you hiding a key to a car?" She reached for it, but Kristen wrapped her fingers around it.

"I would rather you not."

Betty blinked at her. "So you know why you have it?"

Kristen nodded sheepishly and uncurled her hand. She stared down at the fob. Blurry memories of her mother flashed across her mind's eye.

"It sounds ridiculous," Kristen blinked, tears forming quickly, "but I kept a set on me whenever I could. He kicked me out of the car once on the side of the interstate and drove off. I was in the middle of nowhere, and in my head, I thought that if I had an extra set of keys on me that day…"

"He wouldn't have been able to lock you out," Betty finished for her.

Kristen wiped away the tears. "Yeah."

Betty sat back in her seat. Kristen started to return the key fob to its hidden pocket when Betty set her hand on Kristen's arm.

"You don't have to hide that anymore."

Kristen stared at her for a moment and then cried. She didn't need thoughts of her mother. The simple gesture of Betty touching her arm so gently and with such warmth was enough. Maybe it was a little of the head trauma mixed in with an overly emotional morning, but she let it all out right there in Betty's passenger seat. The warmth from her hand spread to Kristen's shoulders as Betty leaned over to comfort her.

"There you go. Let it out. No one is going to hurt you anymore."

SIXTEEN

"How could you?" Betty fussed in Allen's ear.

He silently chastised himself for picking up his office phone. "What are you talking about?"

"How could you give your father's ring to a stranger and tell her to pawn it?"

"You mean the ring I told you I didn't want, and you forced me to take?"

"I mean the wedding band I was kind enough to give you when you got engaged in a misconstrued belief that you would cherish wearing something of your father's."

"You mean the cursed ring?"

"I..." he could hear the gasp as his words sunk in. "What did you say? That ring is *not* cursed."

He shook his head as if she could see him. "That's not what you said when the ambulance showed up."

"What on Earth are you talking about?"

"They told you we couldn't ride in the ambulance with him to the hospital, so you said we'd follow them. That's when they gave you dad's ring and wallet..." Allen paused to wipe a tired hand over his face. "You chewed them out for giving you his cursed ring, and then you handed it to me."

His mother's voice was significantly softer when she replied. "That was so long ago. How do you even remember that?"

"I didn't know I did until you forced Dad's ring on me again when I got engaged."

She sighed. "Son, you need therapy."

"I went to therapy," he tried to get out, but she spoke over him.

"I was cussing those people out because they weren't moving fast enough. He needed to get to the hospital, and there they were, fussing about his belongings as if I cared about any of that. I wasn't being literal."

"The ring is bad luck," Allen stated. If she thinks he needed more therapy, then she was really about to think he needed it. "It killed Dad, and then it killed my engagement. I'm surprised it hasn't killed you or me yet."

"We both know what killed your father, and if we're blaming it for ending your engagement with that nightmare of a woman, then it's a lucky charm if you ask me."

"I'm being facetious."

"Oh, you're definitely being something."

He shouldn't have let it go this far, but sometimes he enjoyed fighting with his mother about his father because it gave them a chance to talk about him without it being all mushy. Allen took a breath. "It's not Dad's ring."

"It certainly looked like his ring."

"Except it's bigger," he said. "And didn't have any nicks and scratches that Dad's had."

"I assumed you had it resized and polished."

"Gwen had her jeweler make one that was similar to his."

"Like I've told you before, never trust a woman with her own jeweler."

"Didn't you use to have a jeweler when Dad was alive?"

"Those were different times. Where is your father's ring, then?"

"In the safe at the house."

"Wow," she said, sounding more at ease. "I'm surprised Gwen didn't try to take that too."

Allen glanced at his desk as if he had X-ray vision to see his phone lying in the top drawer. He could only imagine how many texts Gwen had sent him since he hadn't responded this morning. "She would have if she had known about it, but can we not talk about my ex in front of my patient?"

"Your what?" she asked.

Pretending not to hear him was his mother's new way of rubbing things in his face, like how she made him repeat, "You're right," at least twice before acting like she could finally hear him.

"My patient," he repeated, as loud and clear as he could be without shouting into the phone.

"Your patient, huh? Did you act like calling me to chauffeur her around was a normal thing, or did you tell her that you liked her?"

Allen couldn't sit up in his chair fast enough. "Do you hear what you're saying right now?"

"Don't get your panties in a bunch. She's inside the pawn shop as we speak, and don't worry. I gave her one of my cardigans and a hat to wear."

"What?" Allen checked the time displayed on the office phone. "What have you been doing this whole time?"

"Calm down. We chatted, and if she's smart, which I have the feeling she is, she is trying to get the best price out of them because I told her I would give her whatever they offer for the ring so that if my dear son ever had an engagement that stuck, he would still have the very nice ring that he ignorantly gave to her to pawn."

Allen slumped back. "You didn't," he said, dropping his head back against his office chair.

His mother chuckled. "Not the last part, but I told her I would buy it from her."

"So you mean to tell me you're going to let some stranger see how much cash you carry?"

"You mean to tell me that you were okay giving a gold ring to a stranger so they could get some cash but not okay with me just giving them the cash so I could keep the ring that I thought was my late husband's?"

"All right, whatever, but if she mugs you, don't say I didn't warn you."

"No one is mugging anyone. Ooh," she perked up. "You want to hear what she's hiding in her pants?"

"More than anything," he said dryly.

"Car keys—like a key fob thing. I saw it with my own eyes. She had an awful story to go along with it. He—she's walking out. Gotta go."

"Call me as soon as you drop her off—" *Click.*

He stared at the phone for a second. He had told his mother about Gwen having made a band for him. Perhaps she was as hard of hearing as she pretended to be.

Allen leaned over, elbows on his desk, face in his hands, when Ivan strolled into his office.

"We got three more filling out paperwork out front," Ivan announced, far too cheerily, as he set down a paper in front of Allen.

Slowly, he lifted his head from his hands. "What's this?" he asked before his eyes could focus on a word of it.

"Incident report. They want you to fill one out."

"Done." Allen picked up the identical sheet he had already filled out. "And I need you to drop this off to patient admin for me."

"Will do. It's going to be one of those days," Ivan said, strolling out. "It's a full moon."

"I know, Ivan. I know."

RUNNING FROM CUPID

SEVENTEEN

"It's got to be worth more than that," Kristen insisted to the man behind the counter at the pawn shop. "How much does it weigh?"

Randy turned to look at the digital scale on the counter where the ring was sitting. "Five grams, but like I said, it's not how much you originally paid for it. It's the price of the gold."

She did the math in her head. The last time she checked out the price for gold, it was in the low sixties per gram, putting this ring at over three hundred dollars, and the highest Randy was willing to go was a hundred.

"Randy, work with me here." She leaned over the counter, jutting a cardigan-covered shoulder at him. "We both know the ring is worth three times what you're offering. And I'm not talking about the original cost; we are talking about the gold, so, how about you come up to two hundred—"

Randy shook his head adamantly. "Not gonna happen." He stepped to the side just enough for Kristen to catch sight of herself in a gold-trimmed antique mirror with a three-hundred-dollar price tag.

Betty had scrounged up a baseball cap with a faint musky vanilla scent that made Kristen think of Allen when she carefully slid it on after taking off all of the bandages, except for the one taped to the top of her head. It was a faint smell, but she only thought of it now from smelling the baseball cap. With her hair, the hat with its bulge at the top of her head, and her blotchy, leftover makeup, she could see why Randy wasn't willing to work with her. She looked terrible. She fixed her gaze on Randy and tried to think about her mother.

"I can do a hundred and ten," he said.

She gave him her best, big, puppy-dog eyes. "Is that the best you can do?"

"That's the best offer you're going to get."

Kristen straightened and picked up the ring from the scale. "Agree to disagree, Randy."

Her head was hurting so badly by the time she got back in the car. Kristen shut her eyes as she peeled off the hat, feeling like her eyes might pop out from the pressure if she didn't.

"You okay, hon?" Betty asked.

"Yeah," she sighed with relief. "I think the hat was too much."

"You probably should have loosened the strap some." Betty took the hat and set the strap on its loosest setting. "That should do it." She handed the hat back and dug through her glove box. "I might have a beanie. The weather's not right for it, but I always keep gloves and—"

Kristen stopped listening when her eyes locked onto the handgun sticking handle-side out from under a stack of papers inside the glove box.

"What's wrong?" Betty asked before she spotted it below the gloves and beanie, sitting on the stack of papers. "Oh, don't worry about Sheila." Betty reached as if she was going to grab it.

"Don't!" Kristen jerked and kneed the glove box shut.

Betty slowly sat back in her seat, staring at her. "Did he used to threaten you with a gun?"

Kristen couldn't shake her head fast enough. As much as she wanted to play into her role, she couldn't when it came to guns, even though it would have been a perfect cover story since she had a physical repulsion to them. "No, he never did that. I hate guns."

"A healthy fear of them is good," Betty said matter-of-factly. "It means you respect what they can do."

Kristen wasn't hearing anything she said. All she kept visualizing was that gun inches from her knees. "W-why do you have a gun in your glove box?"

"Well, it's usually in my purse, but my son gets very snippety with me when I carry Sheila inside the hospital, so I put her in the glove box when I went in to see how you were doing."

"You named your gun?"

"Well, you have to so you don't look crazy when you talk to it."

Kristen slowly nodded. First, the crazy cat lady, and now a crazy lady talking to inanimate objects. Was everyone in Redrock mad? It would explain Allen's willingness to give her that ring.

What a day. Now, she was trapped in a car with someone with a gun. Sure, she could get out, but where would she go? That question was starting to *really* get on her nerves.

"One ten," Kristen said.

"What?"

"A hundred and ten," Kristen repeated. She planned on inflating the price significantly since the older woman had already offered to pay whatever the pawnshop offered her, but that went out the window the second her fight-or-flight response kicked in. "That was his final offer, a hundred and ten bucks." She needed to get the money and maybe that bottle of Tylenol and go. The faster, the better.

As if she felt Kristen's anxiousness, Betty reached out and set her hand on Kristen's forearm. When she did that earlier, it was a warm, welcoming feeling. This time, it took everything Kristen had not to rip her arm away from her.

"Breathe," Betty whispered.

Kristen tried not to listen to her soothing tone.

Betty lowered her chin. "Honey, you need to take a deep breath.

You are as pale as a ghost. Do I need to bring you back to the hospital? I thought my son was jumping the gun when he called me to come get you."

Just when she thought she could stop thinking about it, Betty brought up the gun again. God, this lady was obsessed.

"What did the sand feel like? Do you remember?"

Kristen laid her head back against the headrest. "What are you talking about?" Her vision blurred. No—it was darkening. She was about to pass out.

"Tell me what the sand on the beach felt like," Betty said, her tone eerily quiet.

"I-I don't understand."

"Honey, I think you're having a panic attack. Tell me what the beach felt like."

This woman might be crazy, but she was right about the panic attack. She was breathing way too rapidly, and it felt like the inside of the car was closing in on her. Kristen doubled over, her head between her knees.

"Isn't this what you're supposed to do if you're having a panic attack?" Kristen asked.

"Oh, honey, I don't know. The last time I had a panic attack, I threw up."

"You threw up?"

"I did, and it was not pretty."

Kristen groaned. "I don't want to puke."

"I don't want you to either." Betty inched farther from her. "Because let me tell you, it went everywhere, and I don't have anything for you to get sick in." She rummaged around in the back seat. "And you have my favorite hat in your lap. The last time I put it on, I broke Ed's heart." Betty sat back in her seat. "That man has not stopped calling me."

For some strange reason, her rambles settled her nerves. "You mean Ed the detective, Ed?" The darkness around the edges of her vision gradually subsided.

"That's right, and I tell you what, I haven't had this much of a man's attention since I stopped being able to put my feet behind my head."

Kristen's panic turned into shocked giggles, but the pain in her head doubled. She wasn't sure if it was the giggling or her position, so she sat up and held the top of her head to calm down.

"Feet behind your ears—what are you talking about?"

Betty gave her a little wink. "I think you know precisely what I'm talking about."

They broke into a fit of laughter. Betty held her abdomen with the same veracity that Kristen held the top of her head, trying to dampen the impact her laughter had on her stitches.

Betty pointed at Kristen's face. "You're crying."

Kristen wiped the tears on her cheeks and shook her head, still giggling. "I don't know if they're from the laughter or the pain."

Kristen exhaled as the laughter subsided. She lowered her hands to stare dazedly out the front windshield at the pawn shop. "This has been the most bizarre day. First, I got blindsided by someone who should have been my protector, then I had to pull that man off of Celia, and now here I am, freaking out because the person who *did* protect me happens to carry a gun." She chanced a glance at Betty, who had the identical sympathetic look that her son gave her back in his office. This time, it was the look she was going for. "Please don't look at me like that."

"Like what, hon?"

"Like you feel bad for me. I would rather be hit over the head again."

Betty lightly patted Kristen's shoulder. "I was just telling someone else this, but you are due for some therapy."

Kristen stared at her. Add that to her list of firsts. "You were telling someone I need therapy?"

Betty shook her head. "Of course not. I was telling someone that *they* needed therapy. Just about everyone does. I may look like I have it all together now, but therapy helped me through a really dark time in my life."

Searching for something to say, she stole a glance at the glove box and wondered how healed a woman could be when she toted around a deadly weapon. "That's great."

Betty reached into her purse. "Of course, therapy takes time." She dug around and pulled out a wad of cash. "Today is your lucky day. All I have are twenties."

The ring was exchanged for one hundred and twenty dollars.

"Agree to disagree." Kristen smiled. She folded the money in half and stuffed it into her pocket, feeling relieved. Betty's eyes were still on her.

"Are you hungry?"

EIGHTEEN

Ivan stopped Allen in the hallway before he could tell his sixteen-year-old patient that his X-rays showed a broken wrist. "No need to go into five."

"Did his wrist magically fix itself?"

"That would be cool, but Eriksen's in there with them already. As we speak, he's going over everything with the kid and his parents."

"Great," Allen said, surprised by how genuinely he meant it.

Eriksen working rounds on the ER floor meant Allen had enough time to sit in the breakroom for lunch, unlike his typical lunch in his office, where he would review charts, X-rays, and lab results as he wolfed down a sandwich. He was so appreciative that Allen didn't say a word about how it only took chewing Eriksen out to get him to do his job.

"Mr. Bleeker is coming in. His wife called, stating that he isn't making any sense."

Allen was familiar enough with some patients, like Mr. Bleeker, that he didn't even have to see them to diagnose. "It's his blood sugar."

"That's what I said, but she's bringing him in anyway. Amirah is still on the phone with her."

Mr. Bleeker and his unregulated diabetes were nothing compared to his wife, who could talk for hours on end anytime she was given the opportunity.

"Sounds like Eriksen has his next patient of the day." Allen headed for his office. "I'm taking my lunch break."

Zero texts from his mother but four from Gwen. He cleared them from his notifications without reading them and then sent his mother a quick text.

How much did you give her for the ring?

Once he finished the first sandwich, he picked up his phone again.

Please tell me that you dropped her off, and she didn't mug you when she saw how much cash you carry around on you.

He waited a full minute with no response and then sent, **Was your phone in your purse when she mugged you?**

His office phone rang, and he frowned at his cell phone.

"You could have just called me on my cell," he said, expecting his mother.

"My bad," Ivan said. "I wanted you to know I forwarded an email to you from admitting."

"Because…?"

"Because it's about that paperwork you had me turn in to patient administration."

NINETEEN

The diner in Redrock was exactly what Kristen imagined an old-school diner to be, but this one was on the water instead of being surrounded by busy streets.

"What a great location," Kristen said.

"Isn't it?"

The baseball cap felt better now that it was loosened, or maybe it was the Tylenol kicking in. A bell chimed as they entered.

"We need more whipped cream," the waitress called into the kitchen as she backed through the swinging kitchen door. The tray she carried had three milkshakes in big glasses, each topped with an obscene amount of whipped cream, which Kristen had only seen in movies. The second the waitress saw them, her face fell as she frowned pointedly at Betty. "It's you."

Betty smirked. "Great to see you too, Norah."

Kristen looked the waitress over, trying not to make it obvious. That must've been the waitress Celia and Allen spoke of about the whipped cream can incident. *Seven stitches from a whipped cream can from her?* The woman was close to the same age and slightly larger than Betty around the middle. Betty appeared to have a better skincare routine, but nothing gave off a will-beat-you-with-a-whipped-cream-can vibe.

Betty directed Kristen to the nearest stool at the bar that faced the long wall of the diner, which was full of photos from the diner's construction to pictures of patrons over the decades seated in booths and on stools. A few of them had signatures on them.

Kristen eyed the one occupied booth of teenage boys enviously. With the booths lining the exterior wall, they had the best view of the water outside. But Betty had done too much for her not to oblige. Kristen hopped onto the stool without any complaints from her head as Betty sat to her left and dropped her purse onto the one beside her. The medicine was doing its job.

Betty tipped her head toward the waitress as she walked the milkshakes to the booth. "Norah and I are the only single ladies in town of a certain age," she explained. "She acts like we're competing for the single men in town, but I can assure you," she lowered her voice, "I have no competition."

Kristen couldn't help but notice an elderly gentleman staring at them from the other end of the bar. "Is he one of those single men?"

Betty followed her gaze down the bar to the older man grinning at them with bright white teeth. "Oh, heavens no. That man's more of a busybody than I am." Betty waved at him and called down the counter, "Morning, Dwayne. Seen anything worth mentioning lately?"

The man raised his near-empty milkshake glass at her. "Besides the local heathens acting up"—he eyed the booth of boys unapologetically—"nothing."

Kristen stole a glance in the boys' direction. The two whose backs were to them were too busy downing their milkshakes. The one facing them grimaced before grabbing the milkshake straw and vigorously stirring the cup's contents.

He was a cute enough kid, but even from this distance, it was his eyes that she noticed. They were bright blue. She recognized them instantly; those were Celia's eyes.

"How about you?" Dwayne asked.

Betty shrugged. "Same ole, same ole."

"I hear you," Dwayne said. "Who's your friend?"

Norah gave Betty the same curious glance as she walked behind the bar counter with the tray of dirty dishes.

"This lovely young woman is..." Betty looked her over, trying to come up with an answer. "My niece," Betty replied while Kristen blurted, "family friend."

"I claim her as my niece," Betty corrected, smiling at Dwayne. She was fast on her feet; Kristen gave her that. "It's been a long time, but I've known her since she was a little. Her mother and I are good friends."

Kristen tensed at the mention of her mother.

Dwayne raised his glass to Kristen. "Welcome to Redrock."

She forced herself to relax and go along with it. "Thank you."

"I'll be with you in a minute," Norah said from behind the counter as she clanged dirty dishes around in the sink.

Betty pointed at the menu over the bar. "That's everything they have. I recommend the turkey sandwich, chocolate milkshake, and their pies if Norah made them. You made any pies lately?"

"Not for you," Norah called over the sink sprayer.

"That's a yes," Betty said enthusiastically. When Kristen didn't respond, she asked, "Everything okay?"

Kristen was staring down at her hands. "*Were* good friends," she muttered.

"What was that?"

"You *were* good friends with my mother," Kristen said. Over the water and clanging dishes, they were safe from being overheard.

"Oh," Betty said, understanding dawning on her face. "Yes, of course. I don't know how I could have forgotten."

It was trivial, Kristen knew, since they were lying about knowing each other, but she couldn't bring herself to pretend her mother was alive. No matter how nice it would be to pretend.

"I'm ready for my ticket," Dwayne called down the bar.

"Give me a minute, D." Norah wiped her wet hands on her apron. "What can I get for you ladies?"

Betty blinked for a second and pointed at the notepad in Norah's apron. "You're not going to...?"

Norah cocked her head. "Are you trying to tell me how to do my job?"

"Not at all," Betty said. "I'll take tea and a half order of the turkey on wheat, no avocados."

Norah eyed her suspiciously. "No milkshake?"

"Nope, don't need the extra calories."

"Good, because we're almost out of cans of whipped cream." Her gaze moved to Kristen, who tried not to look unnerved at the mention of whipped cream cans. In a town this small, it had to be the diner Allen and Celia were talking about.

"I'll have the same."

"What about the pie?" Betty asked. "You can't go wrong with the pecan or chocolate."

Norah nodded in agreement.

"I'll have the chocolate pie if you have any."

"Good choice," Norah said, heading to the drink station.

"And hold the spit," Betty added.

Norah gave her a wink. "Since you asked."

"I'm going to apologize ahead of time," Betty said once their teas were in front of them, and Norah disappeared to the kitchen. "She didn't write any of that down, so there is no telling what we'll end up with."

"Hopefully, she remembers to hold the spit."

Betty gave her a solemn shake of her head. "I wouldn't count on it." She ignored the loud ding from her purse to tip her chin at the other end of the bar. "Even Dwayne knows it's best to cut his losses."

Kristen peered around her to see Dwayne setting two bills on the bar.

"Tell Norah to keep the change," he told them on his way out.

"Keep fighting the good fight," Betty called before lowering her voice. "You better be happy that I like you because not telling him what happened this morning means I'll be on his shit list once he *does* finds out about it." When Kristen stared at her in confusion, she explained, "He and I swap stories of what's going on around town. That spray paint on the water tower didn't show up until I saw a group of kids having a big bonfire on the beach last weekend." Betty tipped her head toward the boys seated at the booth and raised her voice. "Which would be fine if they would just pick up after themselves, but of course, they don't," she said, satisfied that the teens heard her. "There was a pair of men's underwear in the sand the next morning, and then when I told Dwayne about it"—she leaned in closer to whisper—"he informed me that in the early morning hours, he saw someone buck naked running along the beach."

Kristen giggled, "Are you sure it was kids and not a group of nudists partying on the beach?"

Betty laughed over the distinctive ding from her phone. "There aren't any nudists in Redrock. Trust me, I would know. But you may be right. It might not have been the local high school riffraff, but that's what I put my money on. As far as the naked person, Dwayne could have made that up to feed into me seeing that underwear buried in the sand, but who knows? Dwayne doesn't really come off as the one-upper type."

Kristen couldn't help but ask, "Have you and Dwayne ever dated?"

Betty's eyes widened in such horror as though Kristen had sprouted an extra arm before her. "Me? Date him?"

Kristen worried she had read too much into Betty's entertainment as she glared at her glass of tea in disgust.

"That man doesn't have a single one of his teeth. Any decent woman who takes pride in her hygiene, like me, would never mix with men like that, no matter how informed he was." She shook her head. "And just when I was starting to like you."

"I'm sorry," Kristen chuckled, catching the corner of Betty's mouth curling upwards. "I couldn't tell...about his teeth." Kristen added, "You look great, including your teeth."

Betty smiled wide. "They are great for my age, aren't they? You just wait. You keep your teeth long enough, and you'll be able to spot a pair of dentures from a mile away."

Another ding went off in her purse, but she didn't bat an eye.

"I think your phone is going off," Kristen said, unsure if the woman could hear it.

"Really?" Betty fished out her cell phone. With how far away Betty held it from her face, Kristen could read the texts from the contact: *My sweet boy*.

How much did you give her for the ring?

Please tell me that you dropped her off.

Was your phone in your purse when she mugged you?

"Everything okay?" Kristen asked, acting like she hadn't read the texts as she took a few sips from her tea.

His texts made Kristen anxious. Did that detective show up with news that ruined whatever warmth Betty's *sweet bo*y felt toward her?

"Oh, it's just my son being himself," she said nonchalantly. "He's always worrying about me." Betty slid off her stool, phone in hand. "I'm running to the lady's room."

"I'll be here." Kristen took a quick drink and watched Betty as her anxiety settled in.

Betty was going to the bathroom to call Allen. She forced her shoulders to relax. Checking in with one's family was normal, especially when they were concerned for you. Not that Kristen would know anything about familial concern.

"Not funny," one of the boys in the booth grumbled.

"I'm not kidding. She's gonna be back any minute."

"Wait for me."

Kristen glanced over her shoulder and saw two of the three boys hopping out from the booth. The blue-eyed boy glared at them. "Guys, I can't leave."

"Looks like you're paying then," the taller boy said.

"Thanks for breakfast," another told the remaining boy planted in the booth, surrounded by empty milkshake glasses.

"I've only got ten bucks, guys."

The taller boy snorted. "Then thank your mommy for us."

The kitchen door swung open with a squeak, and the two boys jetted out of the diner.

Kristen straightened in her seat. Norah emerged from the kitchen with a chocolate milkshake without the whipped topping. Oblivious to the boys dashing out to the parking lot, Norah approached Dwayne's empty stool, looking confused by the empty milkshake glass next to the cash he left on the counter.

Tires squealed outside as an old truck flew from the parking lot. Norah eyed the boy alone in the booth and grabbed the cash from the counter. She shoved the money in her waist apron, and Kristen diverted her gaze to her glass of tea as she passed.

A chocolate milkshake slid into her peripheral vision.

"On the house," Norah said, setting the milkshake in front of Kristin and breezing past her. "Welcome to Redrock."

Kristen perked up. "Thank you."

Score! Norah turned into Kristen's favorite person as she peered into the glass. Kristen swirled the large straw around inside of it. It was that perfect milkshake consistency. She took a sip and then another. This town might not be so bad after all.

"I have your ticket right here," Norah said to the boy at the booth. "You ready to take care of that?"

Kristen barely turned her head in their direction. Out of the corner of her eyes, the boy was holding the ticket. Norah hovered over him so he couldn't leave; she was onto his buddies dining and dashing. Kristen had friends like that once upon a time.

"I-I'm waiting for my mom," he said hesitantly. "She's meeting me."

Norah glanced out the diner windows where the two boys were long gone. "She's paying for your friends too?"

He looked at the ticket in his hand and set it face-down on the table. "Yes, ma'am."

Satisfied with his response, Norah turned from the booth. "What do you think of the milkshake?" she asked her.

Kristen smiled. "It's the best I've had."

Norah eyed Betty's purse, sitting abandoned two stools down.

"She ran to the restroom," Kristen said quickly.

Norah gave her a knowing nod. "Fluid pills?"

Kristen remained silent. She wasn't sure if she was asking a question, but all she could think about was what Allen and Betty could be talking about for this long. It must be about Kristen. Betty was probably giving her son an earful about the car key Kristen had sewn into her pants like a psycho.

Had Betty believed her story about Calvin, her supposed nightmare of a boyfriend? What if she hadn't?

Norah was still studying her, so Kristen gave her a tight smile, having lost her train of thought. She gave Kristen a concerned once over. "Your food should be out shortly."

The fluid pills, Kristen realized. It must have been a question. Is something like that a thing that she should know as a niece or a best friend's kid?

The boy in the booth let out a low moan. Kristen glanced over to see him bent over behind his empty milkshake glass with his face in his hands. As he wiped his face slowly, he noticed Kristen watching him and gave her an awkward, dismissive wave.

Kristen turned in her stool to face him. "Hey, you wouldn't happen to be Celia's kid, Dave?"

"It's Davie," the boy answered, sitting up straighter.

"I met your mom this morning. She seems pretty great."

Davie nodded. "You were at the hospital?"

"Yup." Kristen gently lifted the front of her hat. "Stitches."

Davie's eyes widened. "Wow."

"Yeah." She slid off the stool and walked over to him. "Stitches can happen when you hang out with the wrong people."

Davie grimaced as though in pain; she couldn't blame him. She was just some stranger trying to give him unsolicited advice. He glanced from Kristen to the restrooms while a smile worked across his face.

"Dr. Trouth's mom did that to you?"

"No," Kristen laughed. "She's a friend. The good kind, not the kind who would..." she raised a brow at him, "dine and dash."

Davie's face flushed. "You caught that, huh? They don't mean anything by it."

Kristen nodded, knowing all too well. "I had friends who didn't mean anything by it when I was your age. I got arrested for my friends not meaning anything by it when I was your age."

His brows rose. "Was it one of those friends who gave you the stitches?"

She shook her head. "You don't want to know. How much is it?" Kristen tipped her chin at the ticket on the table as she reached into her pocket.

Davie perked up and flipped the ticket over, silently staring up at her with hopeful eyes. Kristen blinked at the total for three sandwiches and milkshakes. The fountain drinks must be included.

"That's cheap."

For a second, she thought about turning on her heels and returning to her stool, but that would be cruel. She took two bills out of her pocket while stuffing the rest of them down to avoid showing him the wad Betty had given her.

"I'm doing this for your mom," she said, setting the money on top of the ticket. "She shouldn't have to pay for your delinquent friends after the day she's had."

Davie brow furrowed. "The day she's had?"

Kristen waved dismissively and then pointed at him. "You need to get better friends."

"You aren't the first person to say that." He hung his head solemnly

"That means you have people who care about you," she said, walking back to her stool. *Like I didn't.*

BO GRANT

TWENTY

"I should tell Ed that he should be looking for a guy driving a Volkswagen, but then I would have to tell him how I know, and then he'll find out I helped his victim flee town." His mother was spinning.

"Forget the car keys," Allen said. He needed her to calm down. If anyone was going to get in trouble for letting her leave, it was him. This was a fine mess he found himself in.

"*Key*," she corrected. "There was only the one." Leave it to his mother to be freaking out and still manage to correct him over the slightest thing. "Honestly, with the texts you sent, I thought you would be more worried about this."

"You don't need to worry about Ed," he insisted. "You need to worry about her."

"I don't know what your deal is. She isn't going to mug me. My purse is at the bar right now with her, and she hasn't run off with it."

"You aren't hearing me. Kristen isn't who she says she is. I'm looking at the email from my people right now. They ran her information, and her social doesn't match up to the name or date of birth she gave us. Kristen Chanel doesn't exist."

For the second time in less than a year, Allen had allowed himself to be played the fool. At least with his ex, Gwen did an okay job hiding her cheating, and then when he found out about it, she cried. Kristen, or whoever she was, had not only written her lies down and handed them to him, but she had the audacity to do it straight-faced while making him feel like some kind of savior.

"Oh yeah?" his mother mumbled like she was barely listening.

"Yes," he said louder, trying to force her to listen. "If she's still lying about her name, what else is she lying about?"

There was nothing but silence on the other end. His words were falling on deaf ears. He squeezed the phone.

"Mom, she could be as dangerous as the guy she was with on the beach."

"I've got a good sense of people," she told him as dismissively as he was being serious, "and all I'm getting from your girl is that she needs help."

"She's not my—" Allen gritted his teeth. She might be listening, but she wasn't *hearing* him. He might as well be talking to a brick wall. "Look at how far your sense of people has gotten us."

It was a dig that clearly struck gold because the silence that followed was deafening.

What was he doing? Hurting Eriksen's feelings was one thing, but his own mother's?

"I'm sorry," Allen choked out.

He was worried that his desire to help now put his mother in danger, and here she was, wanting to help that same someone while he dredged up the past that neither of them could change instead of removing her from the danger.

"I shouldn't have said that."

"You could always make a call."

Allen shook his head. "Just say you are bringing her straight to the bus station."

"That's what I'm doing after lunch."

Allen took a long, patient-filled inhale. "You promise?"

"I will be dropping her off once we leave here, and just so you know, my purse is still sitting there. She's talking to that nurse's kid, you know."

"Who?"

"That kid who's always getting in trouble."

"Davie? Celia's kid?"

"That's the one. ... What in the world?"

Allen tensed. "What is it? Is it your purse?"

"No, no," she said but then fell silent once more.

"Do I need to call the cops?"

"Will you stop it? I can't stick my head out the bathroom door while talking to you and not draw attention to myself."

Allen rolled his eyes. But she could keep sticking her head out of the bathroom door with no problem. Finally, she said something.

"I think she's paying for his meal."

"For Davie's? Why is she doing that?"

"I will find out once you get off the phone with me."

If his mother wasn't the most insufferable woman he knew... "Just tell me. Did you leave Sheila in your purse for her to potentially steal?"

"No," she said proudly. "She is tucked away in my glove box."

Allen frowned. The glove box inside of the car that she would have stolen if she had taken his mother's purse. "Great. As long as you're being safe."

TWENTY-ONE

"And you paid for his friends?" Betty glanced over her shoulder to Davie, who patiently awaited his mom.

"Don't stare," Kristen said, leaning to block her from staring; he didn't need to be gawked at as they talked about him. "His mom had a bad enough day. She shouldn't have an extra bill waiting for her on top of it."

She knew what Betty thought: she was crazy for helping the kid when she only had the money in her pocket, but she needed to do what she did. A teen hanging out with the wrong crowd and a mom getting what she didn't deserve; it all hit too close to home. There was no reason for her to cry right now, so she could not allow herself to think of her mom.

Betty studied her. "Celia had a worse day than you?"

"She could have been killed, so I would say so."

Betty gave her a sympathetic grin. "Honey, you could have been killed this morning."

That hit her like a ton of bricks. She hadn't felt like her life was in danger at the time, but then again, she hadn't seen it coming.

Betty pointed at her milkshake. "Did Celia's kid give you that as thanks?"

The reminder of her milkshake lessened the blow of what she went through this morning. "This is compliments of the house." Kristen stirred the milkshake proudly.

"Norah forgot that she already brought Dwayne his, didn't she?"

"Nothing gets past you, does it?" Kristen smirked. "Want some?"

Betty frowned. "Don't tempt me. I have dating app pictures to look good for."

"Happy I don't have to worry about." She took a drink from the milkshake.

As the cold milkshake made its way to her stomach, Kristen felt awfully close to content. It must be the sugar, or maybe she could tell from how content Betty appeared that she had no reason to worry earlier about her going to the bathroom with her phone.

"That reminds me," Kristen gestured toward the closed kitchen door, "Norah wanted to know if you took fluid pills when I told her you went to the restroom."

"Pfft. What did you tell her?"

"Nothing."

Betty nudged her gently. "Atta, girl."

"Thanks, but I really didn't say anything. She probably thought I was ignoring her." This was her chance to see what Allen's texts were about. "I wasn't, but I kept imagining what could be going on, you know, with Allen texting you so much. Like, maybe...*he* had come looking for me."

Betty couldn't shake her head fast enough. "Heavens, no. My son was texting me... Well, because he doesn't trust you. And not you, per se, but anyone."

"His ex must have really done a number on him."

"Finding out your fiancée is sleeping with one of your coworkers will do that to a man."

Kristen's mouth fell open. "A coworker?"

"Well, an anesthesiologist contracted by the hospital, so basically a coworker. His ex was after the guy with the biggest bank account, and she found it in that chump from Charleston."

"That takes some gall." Kristen knew all too well just how much gall it took to pull one over on someone you were in a relationship with. At least all of her relationships had been with obnoxiously rich men who could afford to lose a girlfriend and whatever item she took with her.

"You don't know the half of it." Betty sighed. "Thankfully, there are enough anesthesiologists in this contractor group that Allen hasn't run into Greg since."

"But still," Kristen said, thinking about Allen and his threats to her with that needle, and she hadn't even so much as seen his ex. "I would be more worried about Allen running into the guy at the grocery store or something."

Betty shook her head. "Oh, no. He lives in Charleston, and Gwen hightailed it to his place as soon as Allen kicked her out."

"Wait, she was *living* with Allen when she cheated on him?"

"I don't know the timeframe for all of it," Betty shrugged. "I think it started after my son bought her the house on the water she just *had* to have," she leaned closer to Kristen, lowering her voice, "before begging him to add a pool. I told him," she said matter-of-factly, "a house on the water doesn't need a pool."

"So this chick cheated on your son because he bought her the house she wanted but wouldn't put in a pool?"

"Oh, no," Betty said. "He got her the pool. Granted, it isn't the big frilly thing that she wanted. I told her flat out, 'Mother Nature gave you all the pool you could ever want,' but who am I to try to talk sense to someone like her? And my son agreed wholeheartedly, but she wouldn't hear it. I mean, why spend all that money when you have the whole ocean—"

"That's crazy."

"That's what I said," Betty sighed. "And I warned him if she was that hard to please, then it wouldn't end with the pool, but when it comes to my son, you can't mess with Cupid."

"Cupid?"

Betty nodded. "That's right. He has a thing about Cupid. It's my fault. His father and I were thrown together at the worst possible time. I was engaged to someone else, and he was..." She shook her head. "Anyways. When I used to tell him how his father and I met, I would laugh about Cupid and how he always knew what he was doing. I think my son took it to heart because flash forward to him meeting Gwen at the hospital when he was covering some shift at the last minute, and here comes that nightmare of woman, and *voila*, he thinks Cupid was behind him meeting Gwen."

"And you believe in Cupid too?" Kristen asked, wondering how deep this belief in make-believe entities went. It did make her feel a little more normal about her affinity for some mystical being behind her luck or lack thereof.

Betty shrugged. "With the Gwen situation, he would have a lot of explaining to do if he is real."

"From the sound of his ex, I don't think Cupid had anything to do with it."

Kristen was a total nonbeliever. Lady Luck, sure. That was fun, but a magical being bringing two people together? She could not get behind that. Not with her track record. And, if Cupid was real, there was no way it would be a guy. No man would put in the effort for something as tricky as true love against all odds. It would have to be a woman behind all of it, and if she were real, Cupid would *hate* her.

"That does explain a lot," Kristen said. "I thought he was nuts giving me his wedding band to pawn. But now, I get it. I wouldn't want to keep it either."

The kitchen door swung open, and Norah backed out with a tray.

"There she is." Betty looked as happy as Kristen was to see the tray containing two turkey sandwiches.

"You think she held the spit?" Kristen whispered.

Betty lowered her voice. "Not a chance."

The fear of food tampering didn't stop Betty from devouring her sandwich, so Kristen didn't let it stop her, and like the milkshake, she had zero complaints.

With one last bite, Betty slid the plate away from her. "They're good, but they aren't my mother's leftover turkey sandwiches the day after Thanksgiving. Her turkey was award-winning."

Kristen's mouth was so full of food that she struggled to reply. "Really?"

Betty nodded, emptying her cup of tea. "She would toast two slices of homemade bread, put the perfect amount of mayo and mustard, and then pack it full of turkey. Cut that sucker in half, and… good Lord, do I miss that woman and her cooking." Betty glanced at Kristen. "I don't have a single one of her recipes either. Not that I could cook any of it as well as she did, but that's life. What about yours? Was she a good cook?"

"I—" Kristen swallowed, "—can't remember. She died when I was little."

Kristen wiped away the layer of condensation on her milkshake glass, ignoring the sad look Betty gave her.

"I'm so sorry, dear."

Kristen focused on her fingertip and the ice-cold glass. "No big deal." She traced another line to distract from the aching in her heart. "It happened a long time ago. I barely remember her at all." In all the times she used her mother's memory to conjure up tears to help manipulate people, this was the first time she found herself pushing them away.

"You know there are things you can do to help you remember her?"

Kristen slid her plate away. "I'm good."

Betty's eyes followed Kristen's hands from the plate to her lap. "I bet your father will be so happy to see you."

Wow. She was bringing up one sore subject after the other. Kristen balled her hands up. "Can we not do this?" She dug her knuckles into the tops of her thighs.

Betty's eyes flickered to her face, her sympathy turning into understanding. "Sure. You ready to go? I'll get lunch," Betty offered. She glanced over her shoulder toward the booths. "Since you already paid for three."

"Thanks," Kristen mumbled.

She waited until Betty was digging in her purse to steal a glance at Davie. Whether he heard Betty's comment or not, Kristen couldn't tell since his nose was buried in his cell phone. But the longer he didn't look up from his phone, the more she was sure he had.

The bus station couldn't come into view fast enough. It took all Kristen had not to jump and run the second the car was parked.

"Thanks for everything, really. It was a pleasure being saved by you this morning."

"The pleasure was all mine," Betty smiled. "And don't worry," she added with a wink, "I have a feeling everything is going to work out just fine for you."

Sure, Kristen thought. Her mind ran through all of the not-so-fine scenarios she had yet to find herself in. Returning to her home base in New York was risky, but at this point, it was her only option. If Calvin had already figured out he had been duped and didn't find her in Redrock, then the city would be his next stop unless he were dumb enough to think she would try to make it to the meetup point in Charleston. It was too much a gamble at this point to go to Charleston. She didn't know who the buyer was or where exactly in Charleston the meet-up point was, because their boss hadn't gotten back with them yet by the time Calvin attacked her on the beach.

Her storage unit was her best bet. Calvin might have the key for it in her bags he took with him the trunk of the car, but he didn't know where or what it went to meaning she would have to break into it. Her stitches would make it hard to wear one of the wigs she kept there, but the storage unit had enough clothes and a stash of cash that should get her through until her boss could meet up with her. She just needed to not run into Calvin and, if her gut was right, the Russians.

"I hope you're right."

"I usually am," Betty assured her as Kristen climbed out of the car.

"Do you want your hat back?" Kristen asked, peering inside the car before she shut the door.

"No, dear. You can have it."

Kristen was unsure if she were telling her it would be too gross to take back; she definitely couldn't blame her. "Thanks."

She had never thanked someone so much in her life and couldn't wait for it to end. There was a pep in her step as she headed into the bus station, but it didn't last. Her head hung in defeat four minutes later when she walked out.

What does a one-way ticket from South Carolina to New York City cost? A hundred and six bucks. The problem was that she only had eighty measly dollars now, and that was if she didn't fill the antibiotics or buy food, and she could forget taking anything for pain other than what Betty had left in her purse.

To hell with it. To hell with Lady Luck and thinking things were going her way. And to hell with being nice. She would have had enough money to get where she needed to go if she hadn't felt obliged to pay for Davie and his stupid friend's lunches. Her boss would have laughed at her being soft.

This wasn't her. She took care of herself. To hell with everyone else.

Kristen would do what it took to get out of there: steal a wallet, purse, and car. She didn't care at this point. She was out of options.

The conundrum building inside of Kristen on whether she needed to scream or cry her frustrations out was interrupted by the unexpected sight of Betty's black Honda parked right where she dropped her off.

"Did you get your ticket?" Betty asked, shutting the trunk of the car.

Kristen's chest swelled with renewed hope. Betty would help her.

"I don't have enough money. Any chance I could give you an IOU in exchange for more money?"

"No can do."

Surely, she didn't hear her right. "I'm sorry. What?"

Betty raised her voice as she walked around the side of the car. "I said, no can do." Kristen would have thought that she had pissed Betty off somehow if she didn't look so content as she came to a stop at the front of her car and then sat down against the hood. "I am retired," Betty explained, folding her arms. "Buying that ring off of you was one thing, but I live on a fixed income. I can't hand money out like candy. But," she said, looking Kristen over. "I do like a good deal. You got anything else I can buy off of you?"

Kristen stared at her in disbelief. What did Betty think she could possibly have on her? All she had on her were the clothes on her back and the key fob that was utterly useless without the car to go with it.

"I don't have anything," Kristen stated, but then a thought came to mind. "I do have a hat," she offered, thinking that maybe this was Betty's way of making it feel less like a handout and more like a purchase of goods like the ring had been. Not that buying back the hat or cardigan she had given Kristen made much sense.

"That's kind of offensive," Betty said dryly. "You're going to sell me back the hat that I gave you for free?"

So, that wasn't it. "Well, if I weren't short of funds, then I would have bought my own hat and clothes to cover the shirt stained *with my own blood*." She fought to keep her temper in check, wondering why in the hell Betty was suddenly acting this way toward her.

"That's right," Betty said, showing no signs of budging. "You're short of funds because you paid for those hoodlums' lunch." She let her words sink in. "How did that work out for you?"

Why was she giving her such a hard time? If it was that big of a deal, she could have snatched those bills right off Davie's booth the second Kristen told her that she had paid for the boys' lunches. It's not like Norah had picked the money up yet. Not to mention the fact that it wasn't like Kristen had forced her to give her the money in the first place. It didn't add up.

"Did I do something to offend you?"

"No, but I saw the way you looked at the phones inside," Betty nodded at the bus station behind Kristen. "Surely, you have someone you can call."

Kristen turned to look through the bus station door. Through the glass door on the wall to the right, Kristen could see three pay phones lined up side by side. She hadn't noticed them when she was in there. If she had looked in their direction, it was only absentmindedly. She had already made the phone call she needed to make, and there was no point leaving a second message just to say, "Hey, it's me again. Just calling to let you know that I'm at the bus station in Redrock but don't have enough money to buy a ticket."

She could imagine what her boss would have said listening to that. *"Then go get the money, for Christ's sake."*

Kristen turned back to her with zero qualms about what she was about to confess. "I don't have anyone I can call."

"Are you sure?" Betty asked, pushing off of the hood of her car.

Kristen was in too much of a bind. If Betty dropped her nice girl act, then so would she. "If I had anyone to call to get me out of this wretched town, then I wouldn't be standing here talking to you right now, would I?"

Betty had saved her on the beach, fed her, and given her a ride to the bus station; what did she do when Kristen snapped at her for not giving her more money?

She *smiled*.

"Atta, girl."

"Excuse me?" Kristen was flabbergasted.

"I know Kristen isn't your real name," Betty said, turning her back to her as she strolled around to the driver's side door. "Allen told me as much when he called me at the diner."

So this was it. All of her lies had caught up with her in the form of being left at a bus station with a head full of stitches and only eighty dollars to her name. *It could be worse*, she thought to herself.

"So let me ask you," Betty said, opening the driver's side door, "do you have a safe place to go if you did have enough money to get to..." she let her words linger, forcing Kristen to speak up.

"Indianapolis," Kristen said, thinking quickly. She needed it to be far enough away to explain the cost of the ticket but nowhere near New York, where she was headed to collect her things and plan her next step until she could meet up with her boss, who was lord knows where. "And yeah. It's safe enough."

Betty continued to stare at her. It was true. New York was safe enough. Even with her storage unit being in the city, all she had to do was keep her head low and stay away from her regular spots. But all it would take was one person to see her, and not knowing if Calvin was acting alone, she would be in danger, and there was no telling how long it would take for her to connect with her boss if he wasn't in the city. Betty was still staring at her when Kristen's shoulders slumped, and she shook her head.

That was what Betty was waiting for, apparently, because she perked up and gave her a knowing nod as if she were already all too aware of Kristen's situation, but then Betty didn't say anything. She just slid into the driver's seat. She was going to leave her—made her admit that she didn't have anywhere safe to go and no one to call, and now she was shutting the car door while Kristen stared in disbelief. How cold-blooded was this lady?

The driver's side window rolled down. "You coming?"

TWENTY-TWO

Over halfway through his twelve-hour shift, a second email came through straight from the top. He had a mandatory board meeting, no doubt thanks to him popping off to Eriksen in front of other staff members, and to top it off, it was scheduled for two days away on his first day off in a week. *Fantastic.*

Allen stared out of his open office door in a daze. He would spend his day off not only at work but getting chewed out for giving Eriksen a piece of his mind.

He picked up his phone to see a text from his mother.

Everything is taken care of.

Finally, some good news. He could take worrying about his mother's well-being off his plate now that she no longer had the mystery woman to deal with. No sooner had he sighed a breath of relief when a notification banner lit up the top of his phone. He clicked on the notification, and his heart dropped as he jumped from his chair. He flew around his desk to shut his door. No one needed to hear this. His mother's phone was ringing before he returned to the desk.

Betty Trouth had not *taken care of anything*.

"Hello, darling."

"Don't do that," he seethed.

"Do what?"

"Play the sweet mother when you damn well know what you've done."

"I don't know what you mean."

"My house. You brought her to *my* house. What is wrong with you?"

"You need to calm down," she insisted. "I am simply killing two birds with one stone."

"Explain." Allen dropped into his chair. All the cushion technology in the world couldn't help him with the stress his mother gave him.

"She needed money," she said. "What I gave her for the ring wasn't enough for the bus ticket—"

"So just give it to her."

"I could, but it doesn't make much sense to shove the poor girl on a bus with more cash if she doesn't have a place to go."

"Get to the point," Allen groaned, aware she was trying to garner his pity.

"Anyway, she needs money and a place to stay. You have the space, and I am going to give her the option to clean your house as a way to earn what she needs plus some—"

This was a joke. It *had* to be a joke. "I don't need anyone to clean my house—"

"You have ants moving into your kitchen like they're your new roommates."

"I don't need a complete stranger in my house, digging around when I'm not home."

"I am not giving her free range of the place. Kristen will only clean while you and I are at the house, and she can stay in and tidy up the pool house while we aren't."

Allen's grip on his phone tightened. "What pool house?"

His mother sighed in his ear. "So I may be using the term pool house loosely, but beggars can't be choosers—"

"If the next words out of your mouth are that you plan to have her stay at my house, so help me—"

"She's not staying at your *house*. She will stay at your *pool house* and only temporarily until she can get her feet under her. You don't have to worry. I will let her in the house to work during the day, make sure she doesn't steal anything, and then lock up when she's done. It'll give her a couple of days to figure out what to do and where to go, and your house really could use it."

Allen *didn't have to worry*. That's a laugh, which he probably would right now if he wasn't so mad. What made it even worse was that she wasn't wrong. His house really did need a good cleaning. He should fight this, leave work right now, force Eriksen to be the doctor he's paid to be, drive home, and bring Kristen, or whoever she is, to the bus station himself. He would buy her the ticket out of town. The second the thought crossed his mind, he knew he wouldn't do any of it.

People lie for a reason. She was lying about who she was, but it was his own mother who witnessed her being attacked on the beach. That had been very real. It was easy to surmise that she was lying because she was scared. Lying to save your life was the most relatable thing on Earth. He couldn't be mad about that. For the life of him, he couldn't stop thinking about what would happen to her once she got where she was going in the state she was in, injured and with no money.

The more he tried to be angry with his mother and her hairbrained idea to keep a total stranger around, the more flashes of Kristen came to mind: her in the hospital bed the first time he laid eyes on her, or when she stood on the hospital bed, knee on Farris's throat.

Both times, his gut was telling him to get closer to her. Because she was pretty? Perhaps. But there was more there than just an attractive face. He could feel it.

Allen rubbed his hand through his hair. She was different, and try as he might, he couldn't deny how badly he wanted to know if she was *his* kind of different. Allen took a deep breath and hoped he wasn't making a mistake.

"And how much am I paying her to do this?"

"That's the great part," his mother said, "since it's my idea, I will pay her to scrub the depression out of your house, and you don't have to thank me."

Allen narrowed his eyes. "Why wouldn't you just give her the money so she can go?"

"Because she doesn't want to feel like a charity case. You should have seen the way she looked when she was walking out of that bus station, knowing that she didn't have enough cash for a ticket," his mother said with a weight of emotion he wasn't expecting. "She was devastated. They had phones in the bus station she could have used to call friends or family, but she didn't, because she doesn't have anyone. She is all alone."

"I get it," Allen said, accepting his fate, whatever it may be. "Has she seen the pool house you expect her to live in?"

"We haven't gotten that far. I was showing her the back of the house when you called."

"Great." Allen grinned at his mother and her antics. "Can't wait to hear what she thinks of it." He almost wished he could be there to see it.

TWENTY-THREE

Kristen should have stolen Betty's car.

Betty's whole idea was pretty straightforward, "I'll give you a free place to stay, and I will pay you to pick up the ground floor."

Kristen couldn't help but glance back at the mess in the backseat. "How much cleaning are we talking about?"

"Don't worry," Betty told her. "I'll let you look the place over first."

She really should have just stolen the woman's car. If she could fill up an entire floorboard and back seat with random items, there was no telling what her house looked like. "Great," Kristen said, while feeling anything but.

They drove out of town the way they came from the hospital. Shortly past the water tower, Betty pulled off the road up to the one house that stuck out from the surrounding classic two-story waterfront properties. It was the only ultra-modern home. Besides being a huge box of a home with floor-to-ceiling windows, it looked brand new.

Living on a fixed income, my ass.

"Nice place," Kristen gaped out the windshield.

Betty stopped short of the closed garage. "It's not really my style, but he got it for a good price."

"He?" Kristen echoed.

"That's right," Betty said, turning off the car and grabbing both her cell phone and a keyring full of keys from the center console before hopping out.

"Whose house is this?" Kristen asked, point blank, as she got out of the car.

"My son's," Betty called. Instead of going to the front of the house, Betty started down the side of the garage to the wooden fence off the back. Who buys a house on the water just to fence in the backyard?

Kristen hurried to catch up with her. Not her son, as in Allen, surely. "How many kids do you have?"

"Just the one."

Fabulous. She *really* should have stolen the woman's car.

Betty unlocked the fence gate and pushed it open. "After you. Oh, did I forget to mention it's Allen's house that I need you to clean?"

Super fabulous. Now, if she did agree to this, she would have to worry about what he was going to say to her about lying on all of those hospital forms.

Just as Betty described, there was a very nice, freshly finished pool in the backyard.

Betty's phone rang. "Speak of the devil," she muttered. "Have a look around." She doubled back out through the fence. "I'll be right back."

At the back of the property, where the yard turned into the beach, the wooden fence transitioned to a metal one, allowing an only slightly obstructed view of the water, but the in-ground pool off the back of the house was what caught her eye. Thanks to the ocean breeze, the top of the clear water shimmered like crystals.

The thought of eavesdropping on Betty's conversation crossed her mind, but a quick scan of the back of the house alerted her to the security camera tucked under the soffit on the back patio. They really were getting good at making cameras blend in. If there weren't a slight reflection on the lens from the sun, she would have missed it. That left her with only one option: to look around.

Eight planters ran down the length of the wooden fence on either side. Each one was filled with the same purple grass-like plant. The symmetry was nice enough, but there was nothing around the pool; no seating, no shade. Even the back patio didn't have so much as a chair to sit in and enjoy the view.

She gazed up at the backside of the house. It was a voyeur's wet dream. The all-glass exterior certainly made her feel like a voyeur, especially when she walked under the back patio and pressed her hands to the glass. She had to see if Allen kept his house as messy as his mother kept her car.

The back patio looked straight into the living room, which could not be more of a sad sight. Apparently, the good-looking doctor didn't have much left after he bought the house and paid for the pool. The living room consisted of one lonely recliner, which looked extra pathetic, with two partially drunk bottles of water on the floor beside it, facing a mid-size flat-screen TV on a wall that could comfortably hold a TV three times the size. She would have thought he was moving in, except that the kitchen off to the left of the living room was anything but bare and twice as depressing to see since she would be cleaning it.

Dirty dishes, utensils, and cups overflowed from the large sink onto the counters. The large kitchen island would look great against the built-in cabinetry behind it that reached the ceiling if it weren't for the big margarita machine surrounded by nearly empty ingredient bottles and cups. Nothing was on the walls except a few empty nails where something once hung. The breakup must be hitting him hard to take down all of the photos. Maybe his ex was one of those take-a-photo-for-everything kind of girl, thus littering their place with selfies and pictures of the two of them, leaving him no choice.

The man wasn't a total slob. The windows needed a light wipe down, and the floors themselves looked clean enough, minus a trail of faint paw prints across the kitchen floor to the front of the house. If he had a dog, the clean floors were even more impressive.

The wall opposite the living room blocked her from seeing the front section of the ground floor. If this was the part of the house visible to the outside world, then she could only guess what the rest looked like. She wondered if the house would smell like him.

Kristen straightened. She didn't need to think about his scent. What she needed was for her boss to show up, tell her that the Calvin situation was handled, and get her paid for her last job so she could move on with her life. She cursed Calvin as she stared through the glass. Playing housemaid was the last thing she should be doing, but until she could get a better handle on her situation, it wasn't the worst idea. Allen and his mother knew she didn't have amnesia, so she could ask to use their phones in a day or two to update her boss.

Stepping back, she caught sight of her reflection. With Celia cleaning her up after the stitches and with the baseball cap on, she didn't look as bad as she felt. Her tired curls looked more like beach waves at this point, sticking out from under the cap. The cardigan covering her shirt helped with her overall appearance.

Give her a pair of rubber cleaning gloves; she might as well be a high-end cleaning service. She was staring out at the pool when she heard Betty's voice.

"You would think that it was my son who was the parent and not the other way around." Betty appeared through the fence.

Kristen turned away from the window. "He called to see what you were up to?"

"He knew," Betty pointed at the security camera Kristen had already noted.

Kristen stared at her. "You didn't tell him what you have planned, did you?"

"Oh, no. I told him. He is positively delighted at the prospect of having help cleaning up the place." Judging by how Betty looked pointedly at the camera as she said that, Kristen knew the opposite was true. "He did make a good point," Betty added, walking past her. "You should see where you'll be staying before you agree to any of this."

Until this point, Betty hadn't given her much of an option. If she wanted the money to leave town, she would have to work for it or find his safe. He might not have much furniture, but all rich people had a safe, usually in the closet of the main bedroom, tucked behind the longest garments or built into the floor.

"Where are you going?" she asked as Betty walked down the back patio, passing the back door into the house.

"To the pool house."

"Pool house?" Kristen blinked. There was the back patio and a pool, but no pool house.

"It's right here," Betty said, walking past the back of the house, where it transitioned to a cement corner with a door that blended in almost seamlessly with the wall if it didn't have the doorknob. Kristen tried to envision what a pool house would look like on the interior when its exterior was so inconspicuous. Betty flipped through her keyring, trying one key and then another. Kristen grew concerned by the third.

"Ever since he changed the locks, I can't keep these keys straight," Betty grumbled. "Allen had an impressive plan on utilizing this space, but that ex of his put a halt to it." Finally, she unlocked the door, swung it open, and flipped on the lights. "Don't mind the boxes."

Kristen stared into the room before entering. It was twice the size of what she expected from the camouflaged corner door. The right side of the room had a kitchen area with a sink, cabinets, and an empty spot for a fridge, which would be nice if the countertop wasn't covered in dust and tools. The wall to her left had the short entertainment center pushed to one side with an old TV to make space for the microwave beside it. In the middle, a couch faced the TV. A random bookshelf was at the far left corner of the room, and a stack of boxes filled the kitchen area. The cabinet on the end of the short kitchen counter appeared partially demoed and covered with clear plastic. Despite that, all in all, it had the makings of a potential...

"Pool house," Betty said. "That's what Gwen was going to use it for after I bought Allen a huge margarita machine he thought was hilarious when he put it on their wedding registry. She hated that thing so much she hid it in here and claimed she would use it once this was a pool house."

Kristen nodded absentmindedly, taking in the room.

This was far from an actual pool house. For starters, it should have at least a window overlooking the pool, if not an entire glass wall like the living room and dining room in the main house. Surely, having zero windows was a housing violation.

A pool house for a property this high-end definitely shouldn't have such a pathetic excuse for a couch as this one did that looked several years older than the home itself. Kristen walked around the entertainment center to find a mini fridge beside it—a *mini* fridge.

No, this was not a pool house. A miniature version of a frat house, maybe, but not a *pool* house. She was honestly surprised that the mini fridge wasn't sitting right next to the couch with an extension cord running to it with the state of things.

"It looks like your son turned it into a..." Kristen searched for the right word, "...man cave."

Betty frowned, strolling over to the plastic-covered wall. "It does, doesn't it? But it was supposed to be a safe room that you could get to from the kitchen. He would do one of those false backs on one of the tall kitchen cabinets. He was going to close in that door," Betty gestured to the door they came in through, "and reinforce the wall here to support one of those fancy safe room doors." She pointed at the missing drywall next to the boxes.

So Allen was the type who loved safe rooms.

Humphrey had been like that. He loved his stupid shoe collection and movies involving panic rooms. He was in the middle of having safe rooms installed in all of his residences when she met him, which spoke to how phenomenal her timing was (*thank you, Lady*

Luck), considering that she came into his life before he could move his Willem Kooning painting into a safe room.

"He must watch a lot of movies," Kristen smiled, imagining Humphry having to make space in his panic room to house his shoe collections since she made off with the painting.

"What do you mean?"

"To want to put in a safe room. The first time I watched *Panic Room*, I wanted to have one too, and I don't have anything worth stealing."

"That must be where he got the idea." Betty looked from the plastic to the boxes. "Better safe than sorry." Her eyes locked onto the open flaps of the box stacked on top of two others and hurried over to it. "Ooh, this was the best part of the whole thing."

Betty effortlessly lifted the box from the top, opened the flap, and peered in. "He must have taken it out already," she sighed, her gaze tracing the room. "He got some security gadgets and computer monitors to set up here so he could see the whole place." Betty scowled. "Gwen better not have taken that too." She threw the empty box to the floor. A wave of air rippled up the plastic with soft crinkles that tickled the ear.

Kristen fought not to smile at the woman's adamant anger toward Allen's ex. What a great mom to rally so hard for her son that she took it out on a cardboard box at the sheer thought of his ex. Most of her target's moms lived in other countries or were so wrapped up in their own lives that they couldn't name their son's exes, much less get physically violent over the mention of them.

"So she buys him all of this stuff, cheats on him, and then takes it all with her to the new guy's house?"

"She didn't buy any of it that I know of, but she cheated, and we don't know what she did with all of it when she left. If she had stayed in Redrock, I would know. I'm sure the anesthesiologist has all of his own stuff, so I bet she sold most of it. Allen says she made him get rid of his stuff to move hers in."

Kristen looked at the partially demoed wall as if she could see through it to the nearly empty living room beyond the kitchen. "Is that why the living room is so empty?"

Betty's brows pinched together. "How do you know that?"

"I could see it through the patio window."

"Oh, I didn't notice." Betty's face relaxed. "He normally keeps the shades closed, but he must have forgotten after I called him this morning," she said and winked. "He was in a rush to see you."

Kristen shook her head as heat rose to her cheeks. "I doubt that," she said, but deep down, she liked the idea of her being the reason a man like Allen would forget his routine. Maybe if Lady Luck or even Cupid were on her side, he might forget to put them down while she was here, and she'd get to see…

"I'm going to have to put those shades on a timer." Betty strolled past Kristen toward the door.

Her comment snapped Kristen right out of the rather delicious visual of Allen minus his lab coat and wrinkled scrubs.

"Oh," Betty said. "I almost forgot to show you your bathroom."

Kristen's stomach tightened. There was no bathroom in here, but there were boxes. In Texas, Phillip had talked about taking her camping before she took off. It would serve her right to end up stuck here with only a camping toilet in the corner, but Betty didn't go to the boxes. Instead, she walked to the bookcase on the left side of the room and pulled one of the books. A latch audibly clicked, and the entire bookcase opened from the wall.

"What. In. The. World?"

"A hidden bathroom," Betty said cheerily. "I think this is what gave him the idea to make this space a hidden safe room."

Kristen wasn't listening. She expected to be impressed since he went through all the trouble of creatively hiding the bathroom, but the door opened to a boring, plain toilet.

What in the trashy *Chronicles of Narnia* was this?

The bookcase being a secret door was cool, but opening to a sad, tiny bathroom canceled it out. The theme of the bathroom must have been standing room only. The proximity of it all was comical. There was no way a smaller shower than the one next to the toilet and across from the sink existed. It looked like she could hold onto the sink while she showered if so inclined.

"The couch folds into a twin-size bed," Betty told her. "You've got everything you need: TV, fridge, toilet, and you're right next to the house you'll be cleaning. What more could you ask for?"

To her credit, Betty managed to say that with a straight face. There was no way Kristen could have acted like a mini fridge and twin-sized bed were the best things ever and not crack a smile. And that was saying something since her job was that of a professional liar.

"How are you with yard work?" Betty asked. "Not like mowing the grass or anything. We have a service that does that, but the plants in the backyard need daily watering, and any weeds that grow in the pots need to be pulled, that sort of thing. I'll pay you extra for that, of course."

That was when Kristen knew Lady Luck had nothing to do with today. This was pure Karma.

TWENTY-FOUR

A GROWN MAN should not talk to his mother this much in one day, especially not when she drove him crazy the way his mother could, but here he was, calling her. For a rare turn of events, she answered on the second ring.

"Are you in a better mood?" she asked.

"Don't try to give me a hard time. Tell me why you're leaving my house without her."

"She has a name," his mother said with an attitude.

"She does," he snapped back. "Too bad we don't know what it is."

"I was going to give her a little time before I asked If you were watching, then you know I left her in the pool house, so you have no reason to have your panties in a bunch."

He did not have time for this, but he knew it wasn't true the second he thought it. He had plenty of time for this. Eriksen was on the ER floor for once, giving him all the time in the world to watch his house through his phone's security app.

"It's not a pool house, and she isn't in it." He hit the speaker button on his phone and swiped over to the app. "She's walking around the backyard."

Kristen walked over to his nearest pot of muhly grass and reached under the plant. What did she think she would find around his potted plants?

"Well, that's impressive," his mother muttered.

He watched Kristen pull her hand back and inspect her dirty fingertips. She must be checking the soil.

"What's impressive?"

"That she's outside getting started on the yard work. I thought she would nap or something while I was out."

"What yard work? You said she was going to clean the house."

"You told me I couldn't leave her alone in your house, so I told her to water those plants you love so much."

"I water my plants every morning—"

"And now she can do that for you too."

"Stop giving her stuff to do at my house without checking with me first, okay?"

Betty paused before answering. "That's fair."

"Where are you going? And it better not to bring Milo back to my house."

"I know how you feel about your baby brother being at your house without you there to watch his every move—"

"Milo is not a *baby*, nor are we brothers. He's a dog."

"Milo will always be *my* baby. I don't care what you say, and if you keep it up, I will go get him as soon as I'm done getting Kristen some groceries since the house is off-limits when we aren't there."

The only thing this conversation had accomplished was raising Allen's blood pressure. "Okay, Mom," he said, defeated. "Be careful and—"

"I know, I know," she interrupted, "call you if anything happens. I will. You don't have to worry about me. You have a good day, sweetheart. I'll see you tonight. I'm going to cook supper for all of us."

His mother didn't cook, but there was so much wrong with what she just said that he didn't have it in him to go into it with her. It was bad enough that he was about to have to sit back and watch Kristen drown his plants.

"See you tonight."

TWENTY-FIVE

If retribution was a date on a calendar, then Karma had today circled and highlighted. Today, Kristen learned that when you wreck people's lives for a living, Karma will stick you with a man's life whose life was wrecked long before you came along and then make you the one to, quite literally, clean up the mess. That was what it felt like, at least.

The dirt surrounding the purple tufts of fluffy grass inside of the pots lining the fence did not feel like they needed to be watered, but, so help her, Kristen was going to water them.

One thing off her list of chores meant one step closer to finishing the job.

She searched for the water hose. A nice house should have a sprinkler system, but who was she to say how her doctor-turned-employer's son spent his money? At the very least, he should fix the drywall in his supposed pool house, but then again, he had a living room with only one chair.

"If I were a water hose, where would I be?" she asked herself.

With the size of the backyard, there should be one on either side of the pool so all of the potted plants could be easily watered, but there was nothing. Back patio, nothing. She walked past the door to the "pool house" and found that the fence didn't meet the back of the house but went down the side several feet. The water hose hung from the metal mount next to the A/C unit a few feet from the fence.

She squatted to open the valve to ensure the hose worked before taking the whole thing off the mount. She turned it on, squeezed the trigger, and a burst of water shot out. An obnoxious amount of hose was looped around the large mount, and the more she unraveled it, the more she felt Karma laughing at her. The last plants on either end looked twice as far away now that she would have to haul a hose to them.

Before she stood, she noticed something on the underside of the mount. It was a magnetic hide-a-key.

What kind of man has no code on his phone and spare keys where anyone could grab them?

"Normal people," she muttered.

Kristen looked up. The only thing under the eave was a spotlight, no camera. She plucked the hide-a-key case out from its home. It was big enough to hold an entire keyring, but it was light and made no noise when she shook it. Jabbing her fingernail under the plastic latch, she popped it open. Nothing, just like she thought. That made her feel better. Unless, of course, someone had already stolen the key. She shook her head at the thought. Allen spent his time saving lives, and as quirky as she came off, his mother was normal enough that Kristen knew she was way safer here than she would have been alone in New York. She was not going to allow paranoid thoughts about a spare key get to her.

The foam insert had the faintest indention. Whatever key it once held didn't hold it for long.

A car pulled into the driveway, and she snapped the case shut before returning it underneath the mount and finished unwinding the hose. That was a quick trip to the grocery store, but if it were Betty, she would find Kristen diligently watering the greenery as instructed. She was watering the second plant by the pool when she heard the gate open.

"That was quick," she greeted without looking up.

"Who are you?" a woman's voice she didn't recognize spat.

Kristen spun to find a woman glaring at her. Her blonde hair was pulled so high in a ponytail that there was no way it was comfortable. With disgust on the woman's face, Kristen thought her stitches had caused it, but then she remembered that she still had the baseball cap on. The look on this lady's face was something else.

The stranger pointed her cell phone at Kristen's chest. "I said, who are you?"

This woman had caught her so off guard that when she opened her mouth to introduce herself, she fell short of remembering what name she was currently going by.

Kristen formed an angry grimace at the woman. "Who are *you*?"

The woman's jaw jutted out. "I'm Gwen," she snapped. "I am Allen's fiancée. Now, who the hell are you?"

Kristen narrowed her eyes on her, looking the woman over. They were close to the same age. Despite wearing yoga pants and a tank top that was too small, she was quite attractive, too, but none of that made Kristen stare at her. The small but pronounced protrusion from her midsection had Kristen's mouth gaping open. This chick was pregnant.

"Were," Kristen corrected.

Gwen glared at her. "Excuse me?"

Kristen walked around the pool, dragging the hose. She pointed the hose nozzle at Gwen's chest. "You *were* his fiancée."

Gwen's eyes jumped to the hose pointed at her. "We only broke up a few months ago," she said, taking a small step back. "For him to move some girl in right after—"

Kristen's eyes locked in on the fat diamond ring on Gwen's left ring finger. "Is that his ring?"

"N-no," Gwen stammered, her right hand moving to cover the ring. "Not that it's any of your business."

"And the baby." Kristen pointed the nozzle at her stomach. "Is that Allen's?"

Both of her hands flew to shield her stomach from the water hose or Kristen's gaze; she wasn't sure. "That is also none of your business," Gwen spat, rounding her shoulders back defiantly. "I don't know who you think you are, but—"

"It's not his baby, is it?"

She could see through the stuck-up woman's facade. But it was worse than snobbery. And, the longer Gwen didn't answer her, the more Kristen knew she was right on the money about the kid not being Allen's.

This chick was on a whole other level. Of all the personality types Kristen pretended to be to get to the goods, it didn't matter how good she was at manipulating people; she could never do what Gwen did. To win a man over, get him to propose, buy her the house she wanted and the in-ground pool, just to end up getting pregnant by another man was low. No, it was lower than low. It was pathological.

What specific mental disorder Gwen had, Kristen was unsure, but she wouldn't be surprised if Gwen were cheating on Allen the whole time, and if he hadn't figured out about the infidelity, then Kristen had no doubt that she would have passed the kid off as Allen's.

What Kristen did to her targets was wrong, but what Gwen did would have broken a lesser man. Maybe it did,

"Let me get this straight," Kristen said. "You not only cheated on Allen, who you were engaged to, but you *got pregnant by the other guy*? And now, what?" Kristen gestured to the ring on Gwen's finger. "And how does your baby daddy feel about you still wearing Allen's ring?"

"Allen's ring wasn't half the carats this one is," Gwen announced proudly. "Greg got me this one." She glanced down at her ring finger.

Kristen could not believe this chick. "You are engaged to the other dude, and you still showed up here because…?"

"I had no choice," Gwen spat. "He won't answer my calls, and I need my margarita machine."

Kristen laughed. "The margarita machine? Is that what this is all about?"

"It was a gift," Gwen said, increasingly annoyed by the second. "I *have* to have it for my party this weekend."

"Oh, you need it for a party." Kristen shook her head. "You are not getting that machine."

Gwen scoffed indignantly. "Excuse me? You have no right—"

It all made sense. The threatening texts from *Do Not Answer*. The house had barely anything in it. Betty told her how Gwen wanted to hide the margarita machine in the pool house that wasn't a pool house.

Her showing up here wasn't about the margarita machine, not really. Gwen wanted to insert herself into Allen's life despite no longer being a part of it, and it was not because she loved him. She was doing this to make him miserable. She probably wore the too-small yoga outfit to show off her stupid baby bump so that it would hurt him that much more. But Allen wasn't here.

She was.

Kristen composed herself. "You heard me," she said. "The sheer audacity for you to show up here like this is unbelievable. You aren't getting anything from him." Kristen closed the space between them. "Not today, not ever, and if you show up here again, I will—"

Crap, what am I going to do? What can I do?

"You have no right to talk to me like this," Gwen cut her off before Kristen could come up with a decent threat. "I'm calling—"

When she raised her cell phone, Kristen plucked it from Gwen's hand.

"You are going to stop harassing Allen starting today." And with that, she chunked Gwen's phone into the pool's deep end.

"What are you doing? That was my phone!"

"You can go get it."

"You are insane."

Kristen couldn't help but laugh. "This is pretty ironic if you think about it."

"What are you talking about?"

"Think about it. You wanted the pool, Allen didn't, and now you don't want to get in it."

"You threw my phone in it!"

Kristen shook her head. "We could talk about this all day, but it won't get you what you want. You're done with Allen if you know what's best with you, and whether you want to admit it or not, Allen is done with you."

Gwen gaped at her. "Are you threatening me?"

Kristen blinked. She wasn't threatening anyone. Until now, she thought she was being pretty civil, considering how Gwen stormed into the backyard. Kristen smirked. "If you need to be threatened, here it is. If you don't respect Allen's wishes and stay away from here," she took a calculated step forward, "I can't promise you won't end up like your phone."

The open-mouth stare Gwen gave her was priceless. "Are you threatening to drown me?"

Kristen shrugged. "Read into that however you like," she said. "Just leave Allen alone."

Gwen spun around to the house. "Did you hear that?" she called out. "This... person is threatening me!"

"What are you doing?" Kristen asked. "No one's here."

"Threatening to drown me!"

Kristen realized she wasn't trying to talk to someone in the house; Gwen was talking to the camera.

Double crap. She was screwed if there was an audio feed, and clearly there was if Gwen talked to it like that. She should have cut her losses, dropped the hose, locked herself in the pool house, and hoped Gwen would leave. But Gwen seemed far from finished.

"She threw my phone in the pool. You need to get over here right now." Allen's ex would not quit. Gwen looked Kristen up and down before turning back to the camera. "Who is this chick anyways?"

There was no being civil with someone like this. Kristen could feel the last of her patience dwindling. Gwen was not just some determined ex-fiancée wanting a margarita machine that she never wanted to begin with; she enjoyed the drama. The way she yelled and threw her arms about at the camera, this is who she was.

The more Gwen yelled, the more Kristen was left with only one option.

"That is enough!"

Gwen turned, mouth open, to most likely yell at Kristen. Kristen squeezed the nozzle, and just like when she played the water gun game "Spray the Clown" at a carnival, Kristen got this clown right in the mouth.

When she stopped, Gwen doubled over to cough up water. Kristen was in her face the second she replaced the water in her lungs with air. "If you ever drive by this house again, I will ruin you." Kristen stepped closer. "You don't call him, text him—"

"How could I do any of that without my ph—"

Kristen spritzed her face again. Gwen groaned and wiped the water from her eyes.

"Don't interrupt me. If you so much as like a picture he posts online, I will find you and rock the very foundation of a life you have made for yourself. No decent human will want you in their lives by the time I get through with you." Kristen lowered the nozzle to Gwen's belly. "And that includes your kid."

It was a lie, or more accurately, an idle threat to keep this psycho away from Allen, but Gwen didn't know that, and it might have been the water in her face, but it looked like Gwen was on the verge of tears.

"Have I made myself crystal clear?" Kristen tightened her grasp on the nozzle.

"You have." Gwen jutted her jaw but wiped her face and ran her hands over her hair as if the water hose could knock down her gravity-defying ponytail.

"And the margarita machine?" Kristen asked.

"He can keep the stupid thing."

"How about your phone?" Kristen pointed at the pool. "I'll give you time to collect it before you leave and never come back."

"And ruin my clothes more than you already have?"

Kristen was thinking more of using the pool skimmer to scoop the phone out, but whatever.

"No thanks," Gwen grumbled. "I'm leaving." As she headed toward the fence, she glanced over at the camera. "I hope you're happy."

"What part of not talking to him do you not understand?"

And with that, Kristen squeezed the nozzle full blast, soaking the back of Gwen's head.

Gwen couldn't get out of the backyard fast enough, and her ponytail, to Kristen's delight, had fallen by the time she let up on the water hose.

"Everything all right?"

Across the yard, on the other side of the metal fence, the older man from the diner was stopped on the beach, staring at Kristen through the metal fence.

She waved. "All good, Dwayne. All good."

TWENTY-SIX

After regretting Kristen—or whomever she was—left alone at his house, his stress was rewarded with her pissing Gwen off to no end. If the security camera on his back patio had two-way audio capabilities, he would have turned it on so that Gwen could hear him laughing as Kristen threw her phone in the pool and dosed her in the face.

He laughed so hard that his eyes watered when it was over.

"What do you want me to do?" his mother asked after he sent her a screenshot of the incident.

"Did you not watch the whole video? Kristen took care of it. Gwen left, and I doubt she'll come back."

"Oh, I saw. She won't be calling you anytime soon, that's for sure." He could hear his mother holding back laughter. "You happy I kept her around now?"

"She is..." Allen thought it through—beautiful, lively, surprising. "...something else. I might have to try spraying you with the water hose to see if it'll keep you from coming over so much."

"Pfft, you love me going to your house."

"You, yes. Milo, not so much."

"I don't know why you act like you don't like your little brother. He's a big sweetheart. You owe him, you know."

"I don't know what you're talking about," Allen said. "He still owes me for pooping on the floor of my brand-new house the day I moved in."

"It was that Mexican food truck that came through town's fault."

"How about my door frame he used as a chew toy a week later? Was that the food truck's fault, too?"

"I'll give you that one," his mother said. "But you did end up getting rid of that door shortly afterward to get that museum-like glass thing to match the rest of the house."

"That was Gwen's idea. Not mine."

His mother sighed. "And I'm not going to tell you I told you so."

"Thanks."

"Speaking of Gwen, I'm going to make a stop by my house and pick up some things for Kristen to thank her for running Gwen off, which you should have done over a year ago."

He had just met Gwen a little over a year ago when she walked into his ER looking for the labor and delivery wing. It had concerned him that she had gotten into the ER without a badge, but by the end of talking to her, he agreed to a date. Only after the failed engagement and split did he find out Gwen was there the day they met to visit her friends and their newborn when a nurse told her about the hot new doctor in the ER. It was funny because Gwen was visiting him during his lunch break when Celia and Amirah told him about the new anesthesiology group out of Charleston joining the hospital. A few days later, Gwen met the man she cheated on him with. He wondered if Gwen had searched for Greg the way she had him.

"You do remember that we still don't know who she really is?"

"I do, but I don't think she's lying about not having anyone."

"They have homes to help women like her get back on their feet. You know that, right? All you have to do is drop her off, and then it won't matter that she's lying about who she is."

"You want to drop her off at some shelter, then you go right ahead," his mother snapped, "until then, I'm going to give her something to do, some food to eat, and clean clothes to wear."

"Including my hat," he said, unwilling to admit that she had called him on his bluff, "that you stole from my house?" He didn't really care about the hat, but even though it was his idea, imagining him or his mother dumping Kristen at some poorly funded women's home was enough to make him *need* to change the subject.

"That's mine now. I wear it when I walk Milo after lunch. Thank you, by the way." She didn't wait for him to say, *you're welcome*—not that he was planning to. "What would you like me to cook for supper?"

"Cook? You don't cook."

"On special occasions, I do."

Allen racked his brain for memories of such an occasion. Nothing came to mind.

"We should celebrate Gwen not getting the margarita machine I bought for you. You seem to be enjoying it a lot, by the way."

"I am," he said.

"And what better way to get to know a new certain someone than over good home-cooked food?"

RUNNING FROM CUPID

TWENTY-SEVEN

THERE WAS a limit in her past pretend lives to how many times Kristen would say thank you on any given day. Going from a teenager raising herself to playing the love interest in the big leagues, she learned quickly how truly unappreciative most mega-wealthy were. When everyone did everything for you, thanking them would be like thanking your lungs every time they filled up with air.

The only caveats were the newly wealthy or, from her time in Texas with Phillip, the occasional southern family who were down-to-earth enough to understand how fortunate they were. Two thank-yous tops. That was what she came up with. Any more, and she risked making the elites suspicious; any less, and she felt guilty for not showing appreciation for the comfortable lifestyle she pretended to be a part of.

Today, there were no limits, apparently.

"Thank you," Kristen told Betty for the thousandth time. She felt like a parrot.

This time, it was for a trash bag full of Betty's hand-me-down clothes she gave her before unlocking Allen's house.

"You are welcome," Betty said as Kristen followed her inside the house. The kitchen looked even worse up close. "Why don't you go ahead and change so I can start working at getting the blood out of those."

"It might be a little too late to save my clothes," Kristen said, taking the cardigan off and handing it over.

Betty didn't bat an eye at the sight of her soiled shirt. "Oh, that's nothing. You should have seen the stuff Allen got on him when that food truck gave half the town food poisoning. It was not pretty."

"I bet," Kristen said, heading for the pool house with the clothes before Betty could go into detail.

"Hang your things outside the door, and I'll get them. Oh, your groceries," she called.

"I'll grab them when I come back." Kristen paused. "You will still be here, right?"

Betty nodded. "I will. No point in driving back and forth when Allen has a perfect washer and dryer upstairs. My housekeeper Penny is probably using mine right now anyways."

Kristen looked at her. So much for living on a fixed income.

"Why pay me to clean Allen's house if you have a housekeeper?"

Betty put a grocery bag of cold stuff in Allen's fridge.

"Penny's booked," she said. "And since she isn't taking on new houses, this killed two birds with one stone."

Kristen nodded, but she had the distinct feeling that this was more than just giving Kristen some cash and getting her son's house picked up.

"Allen clearly isn't equipped to take care of this place in his post-Gwen heartbreak, and you..." Betty unpacked the groceries on the limited available counter space until she ran out of room. "...needed the money." Betty spun to face her, giving up on the groceries. "Can I be honest with you?"

Kristen set the trash bag on the floor. "Please do."

She narrowed her eyes on Kristen as if examining whether or not she truly could be honest with her. "There was a moment when I was sitting in my car outside of the hospital moving some things into the back seat to make room for you, and I glanced up..." She stared expectantly at Kristen as if she should know where this was going. "I saw the two of you talking, and I don't know how you did it," Betty looked away as if she were second-guessing what she was about to tell her.

"Just say it," Kristen insisted, unsure if this would be to her detriment.

Betty looked her dead in the eye. "I haven't seen my son look like that in so long. He was relaxed... Himself." Betty's shoulders sagged as if a weight had been lifted. "After everything his ex put him through, I think you being around Allen could help my son get back to his old self, and," she gave her a tight grin, "I think you could use this too. What better way to see that there are good people out there in the world than by spending time with one? And look at this place," Betty waved her hand around at the disaster of a kitchen. "Someone should put this place in order."

"You think I'm a good person?" Kristen asked. Being "good" beyond being good at her job had been something Kristen had given up on a long time ago.

Betty gave her a thoughtful look. "I do."

"Thank you for saying that," Kristen said, not feeling annoyed at repeating those words this time. She *really* needed to hear it. Even if she knew it wasn't true. She hoisted the trash bag of clothes up over her shoulder. "I think you're a good person too."

Betty smiled. "Must be why we get along so well."

When Betty's words sunk in, Kristen set the trash bag next to the couch.

Is she trying to hook me up with her son?

She carried that thought to the bathroom. There was no way she would change into clean clothes without being clean herself. She could use her short stay in Redrock as a way of making things right to whatever degree that was possible. Her last and somewhat legitimate relationship ended with her on the run with more stolen goods.

This time, she truly would be... good, even if only for a little while.

After a career of taking from others for a living, this was her chance to give back. She would remind Allen that not every woman was a manipulative monster like Gwen, and she would hate herself a little less for the way she abandoned the men in her past. A few ways of how to take Allen's mind off Gwen's betrayal came to mind.

This was going to be fun.

Kristen stepped into the bathroom and realized that showering would be tricky. She needed to keep her stitches dry, but this shower was tiny. She would have to keep her whole head out of the shower to keep it from getting wet. It was sad when she opened the vanity sink cabinet to find one shabby towel folded inside.

"Definitely not a pool house."

After the shower, over the sink, Kristen did her best to clean out the dried blood matted in her hair. It would be so much easier if she could dunk her head one good time, but she fought the urge. She did what she could with her hair and went to the trash bag.

Kristen could see why Betty was so keen on giving this stuff away: a robe, bathing suit coverup, and a heavy coat. When she got down to the t-shirts, she found one that made her laugh out loud.

"Perfect."

TWENTY-EIGHT

Full moons weren't so bad when you focused on the positive.

Stress in the form of the meeting looming over his head was tempered with mental images of Gwen being terrorized by his new housemate. That was how he would think of Kristen: his new, temporary housemate. He kept himself from stressing out about a stranger living at his house by reminding himself that she would be a safe distance away in his so-called pool house.

During his downtime, he took his phone out and watched his ex being sprayed in the face on repeat. He would keep that water hose forever in memory of its part in vanquishing Gwendolyn.

When he made it home, the smell of cleaning supplies and food wafted through the air, making the sight of Milo running up to him almost tolerable.

"You decided to help clean." He greeted the dog with a brief pat on the head that turned into a scratch under the dog's chin, where Milo liked it best.

"He's home," his mother called in an unusually high octave.

Allen found his kitchen half-cleaned, with everything gone from the island he had mercilessly attempted to fill every square inch of with trash since Gwen left. The only remaining thing was his margarita machine that was churning out drinks.

"Here," his mother said. She finished filling up a margarita glass and raised it to him. "We are celebrating." She pushed the drink into his hand.

Allen lifted it to his mouth and looked between his rosy-cheeked mother and Kristen, seated at the far end of the island, eating what was left on her plate. Fresh clothes made a big difference, but that's not what had his attention.

She looked... great. Refreshed, that had to be it. She stared at her plate, but he couldn't see her stitches. She had her hair flipped loosely over them, effectively camouflaging them. His eyes grazed across her chest as he took his first sip.

Choking in surprise, he coughed into the margarita mix. "Nice shirt." He wiped off the margarita he splattered on himself.

Kristen looked at the words printed halfway between the shirt's collar and her chest: "*screaming internally.*"

"I laughed when I saw it, too." She smiled. "Your mom gave it to me."

"I know," Allen said, raising his glass. "I was the one who picked it out."

He tipped it back for a longer drink. It wasn't as good as the drinks he made, but after the day he had, he wasn't going to be picky with his alcohol.

"Don't worry," his mother said. "He gave it to me as a joke."

"As a *gift*," he corrected, "for her to open before I told her where I would work after residency."

Kristen arched a brow at his mother. "You don't like living on the beach?"

"It's not that. It's..." She searched for the words and ultimately decided to take a drink.

"She's used to city life," Allen answered. "Add about fifty-thousand more people, and she would like it a lot more."

"I do like it here," his mother swallowed. "We paid half what we would have paid in Charleston, but he *had* to live and work in the same small town."

"Boring was the word she used the first six months we were here."

His mother nodded. "And it may not have been something I would have picked, but being retired," he kept from rolling his eyes at calling herself retired when she hadn't worked a day in her life, "means I can follow my child around the world if I want, and then when I found out that I was the best-looking woman over fifty—"

"Sixty-five," Allen muttered out of the corner of his mouth.

"Fifty," she repeated, "in the entire town, so like I said, I do like it here now."

"Where are you from originally?" Kristen asked and took the last bite of mashed potatoes from her plate.

The way her mouth made the perfect "O" shape as she slid the fork full of food in her mouth told Allen that he better stop with the margaritas while he was ahead.

"Salt Lake," he said while his mother barked, "Chicago." Allen frowned. His mother's drink was stronger than his.

"She asked where we are from," he said loud and clear at his mother, "not where you want to live."

"Oh, was that what she said? Silly me." She set down the glass and scooped up Milo. "I always wanted to be near the Great Lakes, but my vote for a Chicago or Cleveland hospital was out of the question." Her voice took on an exaggerated baby voice. "If our sweet Milo was the doctor, he would have signed on to one of the big cities I asked for, wouldn't you?" She kissed the dog on the mouth.

"Here we go." Allen rolled his eyes. "Right after he grew opposable thumbs and stopped licking his own butt."

Kristen chuckled. He liked the way her eyes lit up as she laughed.

"Don't listen to your mean big brother," his mother cooed to the dog, "you can lick whatever you want."

"Okay." He tipped his chin at her drink. "That's your last one for the night."

"See," she continued in the dog's ear, "he's just a big meanie."

Allen took another sip of his overly sour drink. "What are we celebrating exactly?"

Kristen cast a curious glance at his mother. "What are we celebrating?" She picked up her empty plate and walked to the stove.

"You, silly," his mother said.

He enjoyed the view of Kristen leaning over to open the stove door to grab seconds a little too much. He forced himself to look at his mother as she kept ahold of Milo and raised her glass.

"To Kristen and threatening to drown Gwen in the pool!"

Allen chuckled and raised his glass with her. "Here, here."

Kristen glanced between them. Her cheeks turned a matching shade of red to his mother's. "You both saw that?"

Allen swallowed. "I got a camera on the back porch," he said with a satisfied smile. "Saw the whole thing."

"It was magnificent," his mother said, saluting Kristen and finishing what was left in her glass.

Kristen smiled sheepishly as she returned to her seat. He still couldn't pinpoint what it was about her eyes that he enjoyed so much, but holding her gaze turned him on.

"You aren't mad?"

He blinked and realized Kristen was talking to him.

"How could he be?" Betty asked, far louder than necessary. "You did what he didn't have the spine to do."

"First, you came for my career choice, and now you're coming for my spine?"

"Not your career choice, my dear boy. Your career *location*, and if you had a spine, you wouldn't have let Gwen take every stitch of furniture except for that hideous recliner I told you to throw out your sophomore year of college."

"That is my favorite chair," he interjected. "I am never getting rid of that thing, and I wanted Gwen to take the rest of it. It was all a bunch of crap she made me buy for this place that I didn't like to begin with."

"I think it was smart," Kristen said in his defense. "Your house is a blank canvas you can make your own."

"Precisely." He looked smugly at his mother.

"Sure," his mother said dryly. "Apparently, we're lying about the furniture too now."

Kristen's brow rose momentarily as Allen laughed, sliding the cup away from Betty. "Okay. It's time for you to call it a night."

His mother gaped at him. "You're kicking me out after I cooked for you?"

Even the dog cast him a judgmental glance.

"You actually cooked," Allen said, following his mother's gaze to the oven. The aluminum tray full of fried chicken was a poor attempt on his mother's part to make it look homemade.

"I sure did. I even made sure there were enough drumsticks to share." His mother looked at Kristen. "Didn't I?"

Allen knew better. His mother never cooked, and the extra drumsticks were because his mother always hogged them all. Sure, she could reheat food other people cooked like a champ, but that was it, and the way Kristen reluctantly nodded in agreement only confirmed that he was being lied to. There was no point in fighting his mother's made-up reality. Allen eyed the oven and rubbed his stomach absentmindedly. He was hungry but wanted to get out of his scrubs more.

"I'm going to change," Allen announced. "Thank you for cooking."

Playing into her delusions was his best bet at a repeat of her supposed "cooking" in the future, and any meal that didn't require him to peel back cellophane and nuke it in the microwave was a win.

TWENTY-NINE

"I'm going to head out," Betty announced as soft thumps of Allen ascending the stairs reached them in the kitchen.

"It's past my bedtime."

Kristen glanced out to the backyard. The sun wasn't even down yet. "You sure?" she asked and rose from her chair.

So much for getting seconds; Kristen wasn't sticking around without Betty there.

"No need to get up," Betty insisted, juggling Milo and her empty glass. "I can see myself out."

She placed her glass in the empty sink that Kristen spent an hour cleaning, along with everything stacked inside. Betty insisted on moving the takeout food into pots and pans to make it look like she had actually cooked. In reality, she was making another stack of dirty dishes that Kristen would have to clean tomorrow. Kristen intentionally did not place a single dish in the sink so she could appreciate her hard work for one evening before tackling the rest of the kitchen tomorrow.

So much for a spotless sink, she thought as the glass peered out almost mockingly at her from the sink.

Memories from her childhood flooded her thoughts. Anytime her father spent time at home, he always left dishes in the sink. It was part of her routine to wait until he packed up to leave for wherever his next job took him for an undetermined amount of time to put everything he left in the sink into the dishwasher.

Equal parts therapeutic and painful, a clean sink meant that she was on her own once again.

Betty turned from the sink, blissfully unaware she had just ruined Kristen's hard work.

"And thanks," Betty said quietly, placing a hand on Kristen's shoulder, "for going along with the food thing." She gently squeezed Kristen's shoulder while Milo stuck his nose out to sniff Kristen. "Not that I think he fell for it," Betty said.

"You got that feeling, too?" Kristen got in a quick pet under Milo's chin; how normal this all felt was weird. This was the sort of life she had imagined for herself once this job was complete, living somewhere with a beautiful view. She could even imagine herself with a pet now that she had warmed up to Milo.

"My son's not an idiot." She turned on her way toward the door. "You two kids have fun." She winked. "Oh, I don't know if you know this, but there's a smidge of dried blood at the back of your stitches. You did a good job covering it up, though. See you in the morning."

Betty left, with Milo staring at her over Betty's shoulder, his tongue hanging from his mouth. Kristen nodded at him.

You two kids have fun and that wink. So much for *it'll be good for each of you to see that there are decent people out there by spending some time with each other*. No, this woman was totally trying to hook her up with her son.

It was a funny thought at first, but then a smirk formed on her lips as she thought about what that would entail. Honestly, Betty was right. Kristen really could use a decent man in her life. She would have preferred it be once she was completely out of her life of crime, but—her smirk deepened—this could be a good sample of what life could be like.

Kristen turned slowly to the island, thinking the logistics over as her eyes fell on her second serving of chicken. What was she going to do? Flirt with Allen over fried chicken?

And her hair. Kristen's hand went right to what Betty was talking about on the backside of her stitches. *Gross.* She definitely wasn't going to flirt with Allen with that in her hair. For all she knew, he had already noticed it. The thought was enough to make her cringe.

She was staring at the reflection of herself in the glass back patio door, trying to see what she could feel at the back of her stitches when she heard Allen's footsteps on the stairs.

Crap. Double crap.

Panic set in with her hair, a plate full of second helpings, and Allen coming down the stairs. She was all for hooking up Allen, but there was no way she would try it like this. Kristen grabbed her plate, took one more bite of chicken, and then chunked the food into the trash. She had the plate in the sink before Allen was off the staircase. When he came into view, wearing loose sweatpants and a t-shirt, Kristen was walking out the back door. She waved at him nonchalantly through the glass, and he waved back. He looked around the kitchen, and his face fell when he realized he was alone.

Kristen quickly looked away, but she carried that sad look on his face all the way to her tiny bathroom mirror.

She moved her hair out of the way and found what Betty mentioned. It wasn't a lot, but even a little dried blood was too much. She lowered her hands to the sides of the sink.

"What are you doing?" she asked herself.

Betty had all but told Kristen flat-out that she should hook up with her son. Slightly disturbing as it was, Kristen wasn't turned off by the idea. The sight of Allen looking worn out at the end of no telling what kind of day he had at the hospital; Kristen could think about ways to wake him up.

She sized herself up in the mirror. She was far from her best, but considering how she must have looked when he first saw her, she wasn't even close to her worst.

After cleaning the dried blood from the back of her stitches, she concluded that she could work with this.

Five minutes later, Kristen emerged from the pool house in the bathrobe Betty bestowed upon her and a vague idea of how she would play this out.

The growing darkness outside cast an illuminating glow on the lights in the house. Allen, chicken leg in one hand and a plate full of chicken and sides in the other, was leaning against the island, eyeing the recliner across the living room as if he hadn't quite decided to sit in it. Kristen smirked. She wasn't sure what was more attractive, his first bite from the chicken leg that he shut his eyes to savor or the loose sweatpants that brought her back to her high school days of guys in basketball shorts and sweatpants. It was a shame she had to cut her schooling short for a life of robbing men in tailored suits.

She tried the back door, not wanting to disturb his fried chicken-induced bliss. In her rush to leave the main house, she hadn't thought to lock the door behind herself. Thanks to Lady Luck, he hadn't locked it behind her.

The thought dawned on her that Lady Luck had nothing to do with this encounter. Cupid was far more likely the culprit. And if Allen felt a certain way toward the mythical winged being, thanks to Gwen, then Kristen was about to turn that feeling on its head.

Cupid, if you're watching, you are going to love this.

RUNNING FROM CUPID

THIRTY

Allen's lingering sense of abandonment from Betty and Kristen abruptly leaving him was replaced with the kind of happiness that only good food can supply. His arteries would pay for the amount of fried chicken he planned on eating, but that was a concern for future him. Something delicious was just what he needed.

If all he had to do were go along with his mother pretending to have cooked the food that he knew came from the diner, then Allen would pretend right along with her if it meant she would "cook" for him again next week. Completely engrossed by his meal, he jumped when the back door opened.

"Didn't mean to scare you," Kristen chuckled as he fumbled to keep ahold of his plate. Thankfully, he stopped himself from chunking it at her when he realized it wasn't a burglar or, worse, his ex.

He played it off as she shut the door behind herself. "You didn't scare me," he said, leaning casually against the island. All the while, his heart pounded in his chest.

She gave him a sultry grin. "It looked like I did." At a flash of

Kristen's leg, he wondered if she had anything on underneath the robe she was wearing.

"You did come dangerously close to being taken out by a piece of chicken." He used the chicken leg to straighten the food teetering on the edge of his plate.

Kristen giggled. "Death by chicken? I could think of worse ways to go."

Allen could relate. "I have seen more than my fair share of those worse ways to go. Fried chicken"—he held up the chicken leg—"would be a cakewalk if we're talking choking or long-term heart disease."

Kristen frowned.

"What? Were you thinking blunt force trauma? Because that would not be pretty."

Kristen shook her head. She lowered her chin as she walked over to him.

"I shouldn't have said that," Allen blurted, realizing that he was discussing blunt-force trauma with someone who had just survived it. "You, uh," her stride turned into more of a sashay, and he swallowed, "caught me off guard, coming in here like that." He fought the urge to look her over but ultimately lost. "And, not that you scared me, but..."

He couldn't stop himself. Allen was babbling like an idiot, and there was only one thing he could do.

Kristen's eyes widened in awe as he shoved the chicken leg in his mouth. He couldn't stop himself. He ripped off a bite twice the size he had any business eating in one bite. His eyes widened to match Kristen's. He couldn't tell if she was horrified at the amount of food he bit off or if she was impressed.

Things got progressively worse when he tried to close his lips and chew, only to find that it was impossible, thanks to the amount of chicken he had just shoved in his mouth. Even worse, the left-over adrenaline rushing through his veins from Kristen scaring him made it seem like it was happening in slow motion, one loud crunch at a time. If there were ever a time to die from eating chicken, Allen silently volunteered himself to be taken in this very moment. His self-deprecating side couldn't help it. He looked at Kristen to witness her disgust first-hand from his display. Only she wasn't horrified or disgusted. The second his eyes met hers, what he could only describe as a miracle happened.

Kristen broke into laughter.

It was contagious. It took him two swallows to get everything down, and then he had to set his plate down to laugh without fear of dropping food. His laughter fueled hers to the point of her having to hold her stomach.

"That—was—impressive," she said, struggling to speak.

Allen wiped his eyes with the back of his hand, still holding onto the chicken leg that was little more than a bone. "I don't know why I did that," he confessed, tossing the chicken leg on his plate on the island. "I don't normally eat like a barbarian."

Kristen shook her head at him. "No, it was great. I was nervous walking in here trying to set the mood, but that really got out of my head."

"Wait, what?" The words fell out of him quicker than he could process what she was saying. "You were setting the mood?"

She giggled. "Not well, apparently."

"No, that's not what…" he paused. What was he doing, talking a beautiful woman out of setting the mood? This was every man's dream.

He fought the urge to wipe his face in disbelief. As shocking as this was, Allen was not going to spread fried chicken grease across his face and add to the ridiculousness of the moment. *Get it together, man.*

Try as he might to pull himself together, too many alarms were going off in his head. *She is your patient. You don't even know her real name. You can't trust her, much less sleep with her. My god, she has great legs.*

"This is unexpected," he said, raising his gaze from her legs. He could see her mentally doubting her decisions as much as he was.

"And if we knew each other better, totally welcomed," he added quickly, his voice hitting an octave he had never heard before. Allen cleared his throat. "It's just that I'm your doctor, and after this morning, I don't know why you would...want to do this—"

Kristen was slowly closing in on him. "Do you mean when you threatened me with your needle?" More of her leg flashed out from under her robe.

Allen fought to keep his eyes above her collarbone. "We're talking about the syringe, right?"

"You know exactly what I mean." Her voice sounded like a purr, causing goosebumps to shiver down his body.

Allen shook his head. "I'm talking about being you being my patient—"

She inched closer, dipping her chin to look through her lashes at him. "I *was* your patient. Just like you *were* my doctor. Past tense."

What her voice and proximity were doing to him, Allen found it hard to focus on the reasons his brain was telling him to slow things down. He knew what was happening. His blood supply was being diverted elsewhere.

"I think we should keep things...professional."

Kristen abruptly stopped in her tracks, feet from him. "Probably for the best."

Allen could almost believe she meant it if it weren't for the heat in her eyes. Then, her gaze flickered to his lower half. Her eyebrows rose, equally arousing as she kept her gaze below his waistline.

"It doesn't look like you want to keep things professional."

THIRTY-ONE

Flirting, and coming onto in general, felt forced with the arrogant trust-fund babies she was used to, but not with Allen. Kristen was thoroughly enjoying herself, and the more he played hard to get, the more she wanted him.

And from the bulge in Allen's sweatpants, he felt the same.

Those sweatpants could win awards with how perfectly outlined he was in them, and he didn't try to conceal it.

"I can't," he said, stepping away from her. It sounded more like he was trying to convince himself than her.

Kristen arched a brow and stepped closer. "Are you sure?"

He took a bigger step back. "I'm positive. Don't get me wrong, you are beautiful, and under normal circumstances, I would be more than happy to," he swallowed whatever he was about to say.

She liked the way his Adam's apple bounced. He genuinely looked anxious by her advances. It wasn't the exchange she hoped for, but it was quite entertaining, especially when she took another step toward him, and Allen immediately stepped back.

"But you should know," he cleared his throat, "that it is normal for you to feel this way."

"I know what I'm feeling is normal," she told him, pausing from slowly following him down the side of the kitchen island. "But I would love to hear what you think I'm feeling."

His mouth hung open a second. "It's simple," he said finally. "After what you went through, you need to feel protected, and you think by being intimate with me, you'll secure me as your protector."

Fascinating.

Here she was, wearing only a robe. A fact that surely he picked up on, and Allen was too hung-up on his belief that she was a domestic violence survivor to act upon the urges he so visibly felt.

"What?" he asked as Kristen shook her head.

"I think you're misdiagnosing me."

"I don't think I am."

"That's fine, but I can tell you I don't need you to protect me."

By how Allen tilted his chin to the side ever so slightly, she could tell he wasn't buying it. He may not know the real story, but she wasn't fooling him. Kristen wasn't fooling herself either.

"Okay," she said slowly, "so I do need protection, but this house is all the protection I need. No one is going to look for me here," she lowered her voice, "which means I can be the person I could never be with him." She watched as Allen's Adam's apple bounced again as he swallowed. "Me coming onto you isn't to get you to do anything for me besides help me feel something again. Do you think you can do that?" Kristen asked and took a cautious step forward.

This time, he didn't move away from her.

Her voice came out like a whisper as her hands reached for his chest. "Help me feel alive again."

THIRTY-TWO

Kristen's hands slid up Allen's chest. He shut his eyes as he fought not to lean in. The question wasn't just whether he could make her feel alive but whether she could make him feel alive again, too. The problem was that he already knew the answer. He hadn't been attracted to anyone like this in a long time, not even with Gwen. He felt electricity between them long before Kristen even touched him.

"I can't," he murmured, trying to collect himself. When he opened his eyes, his hands were on Kristen's forearms, not pushing them off of him but keeping them where they were on his sternum. He was sure they would continue to pull him into a kiss. Kristen gazed up at him, her hands staying happily where they were as her thumbs gently rubbed across his shirt.

"I think you need this too."

Allen could only stare at her. She was right, but he wouldn't admit how right she was. "It's not as simple as that."

"We're adults," Kristen said softly. "We can choose to make it as simple as we want."

She didn't need her hands around his neck; she rose on her toes.

Allen watched as she came in close, shut her eyes, and kissed him. He hesitated, but he found himself kissing her back. It was as intoxicating as he imagined it would be. He released her forearms to wrap his arms around her waist.

"We shouldn't do this," he mumbled against her lips. She tried kissing him, but he kept talking. "I don't even know your real name."

She barely moved her lips from his, "Kristen is my real name."

He turned his head as she tried to kiss him again, giving her his cheek instead. "You don't have to lie to me. I know it's not."

Her head jerked back to stare up at him. "This is the kind of conversation you have with someone before you let them stay at your house. Your mom and I cleared this up—"

"Fucking shades," he growled and dropped his arms from around her, ducking out of her grasp in a flash.

"What's happening?" Kristen called as Allen hurried to his recliner. "Safe words should be one word, not two."

Allen smirked over his shoulder at her as he dug his hand between the cushion and arm of the recliner. "Apple," he said. His fingers reached the side of the remote buried in the chair.

"This is a weird time to offer me food," she said dryly.

Allen couldn't press the button on the remote fast enough. "It's my safe word," he explained as the black-out shades emerged from the top and descended inside the glass wall.

"Oh," Kristen said, watching them descend the length of the windows, "you meant the blinds."

Allen nodded. "I forgot to close them the first couple of nights after I moved in here with Gwen. Mom came over shortly after that and had me look to see if there was a way to make them close automatically, so they'd go down on their own at night. It was her way of letting me know that thanks to me sharing my security camera login with her, she saw us, uh—"

"Enjoying the new place?"

He nodded minutely and stared around the living room. "We enjoyed the place everywhere but on the recliner." Allen paused in shock at his confession. Why were words tumbling out of his mouth like this? Kristen didn't look shocked, though. The corners of her mouth curled up. She looked amused.

"That was a missed opportunity." The way her eyes twinkled drew him in.

Allen closed the space between them.

Kristen stared at the recliner. "Is that the real reason you let Gwen take all the furniture...to make it easier to forget all that...enjoying?"

Allen looked Kristen up and down. "Gwen, who?"

She giggled. "Looks like it worked."

The shades were almost completely shut, meaning his mother wouldn't be able to see anything if she were to check the cameras. The only concern now was what he would do. He knew what he wanted to do, and it was light years away from walking Kristen to the pool house and making sure she locked the door before going to bed himself, so much so that he changed course.

"How is your head?" he asked, turning from her to the kitchen. "When's the last time you had any medicine?"

"I'm fine," she said dismissively. "Betty gave me Tylenol and my antibiotics when we had lunch." Allen opened the cabinet next to the refrigerator. "You keep your medicine in your kitchen?" she asked as he took out a bottle of ibuprofen.

"Doesn't everybody?"

"My dad kept his in the bathroom."

"The bathroom," he repeated, dumping four pills out in his hand. "Did your house only have one?"

Her features froze as he walked over with the pills. "So what if I did?"

Allen shrugged. "Just trying to get to know you," he said, holding his hand out. A frown passed over her features. She seemed as uncomfortable with that thought as with him, learning that she grew up with only one bathroom. Or perhaps it was the pills he offered her, he realized as she frowned at his hand. "Do you not need them? They're for the pain."

"It's not bad," she confessed but took the pills from him and tossed them into her mouth.

"I'll get you something to do—" Kristen swallowed them before he could finish. "Impressive."

Kristen's frown morphed into a devious smirk as she arched a brow at him. "Is it?"

He fought it for a second but ultimately grinned. He hadn't meant it like that, but he couldn't say that her ease of swallowing things hadn't brought other things to mind. "We should—"

Kristen tossed her arms around his neck. "We should," she said over him.

"No, I mean—"

"Tell me," she said, the sleeves of her robe cascading down her upper arms.

She had great forearms. *Forearms? Get it together, man.*

"Why let me stay at your house if you knew I was lying about who I am?" Her grasp around his neck tightened when he tried to back away from her intense gaze.

He didn't have to think about it long. "Because you may have lied about who you were, but my mom could tell you weren't lying about not having anybody." He looked deep into those beautiful eyes of hers. He said softly, "We all need someone."

Kristen's grip loosened. As much as he should want to keep her arms around him, Allen felt panicked about her possibly letting go of him.

"What was I supposed to do," he said quickly, "not give you a place to stay?"

Somehow, that got the response Allen expected from his heartfelt admission; Kristen pulled him closer, pressing him against her and her robe. She rose on her toes.

"That is...exactly what anyone else would have done."

"Are you sure about this?" he managed to get out before she kissed him.

"I've never been surer of anything in my life."

Allen's lips parted to meet hers halfway. If she could be sure about this, then he could, too. He might not know her real name yet, but, as she said, they were adults, and she had been right on the money; he really did need this.

Her lips were as hungry as his. Allen's hands made their way around her waist and down her backside, pushing her closer against him as Kristen's fingers found their way into the hair at the back of his head.

All he wanted was to feel her.

She breathed as he moved his kisses down her chin and neck. His teeth grazed the soft nape of Kristen's neck. Allen's hands made their way around the front, finding the robe's string that kept the thick, fluffy menace of a bathrobe on her.

All he could think about was taking it off her.

Kristen gasped. "Could we," she panted as he tugged on the string, "slow down?"

Shit. "Sorry." He fumbled, dropping the fabric as if it were on fire. Allen went to step back, but Kristen stopped him.

She scooped his cheeks up in her palms, forcing him to look her in the eye. He wouldn't mind it usually, but he felt like an idiot for assuming they were finally on the same page.

"Don't apologize." Her hands slid down to his chest, her gaze following them. "I just...had this whole scenario in my head of how this would go. I really thought I would have to do some heavy cohesion but here you digging it and... it is kind of throwing me off."

Allen raised his brows at her. "Do you want me to not be into it?" He was legitimately confused, garnering a giggle from Kristen.

"I want you to be into it. It's just—" Her hand lifted from his chest.

"Your head," he said, seeing her hand abruptly stop at her ear.

"My head's fine," she told him and tucked hair behind her ear. He couldn't tell if she was being honest or not. Her hand returned to his chest and lightly pushed him back, forcing him to walk backward.

"I think it would be better if you sat down." She walked him to his recliner and then gently shoved him into it. "Have a seat."

"Yes, ma'am," he said, doubt creeping over him. "We don't have to do th—"

"And no more talking," she snapped.

Allen couldn't close his mouth fast enough as Kristen slipped her left knee between his hip and the armrest. *Yeah*, he said to himself, *shut up*. She slid her right knee between his other hip and armrest. Slowly, she lowered down onto his lap, straddling him.

"This is much better."

She read his mind.

THIRTY-THREE

Allen knew Kristen was lying about who she was and gave her a place to stay anyway. No, he gave her a safe place to stay *despite* her deception. Men like him were rare. She thought they only existed in movies and love songs, but here he was. Allen did things because they were the right thing to do.

And for someone who spent her life doing the opposite, being with a guy like Allen was about as much of a turn-on as it got.

All inhibitions melted.

The only thing in their way now were Allen's clothes.

Her hands pulled and ripped until Allen's shirt was over his head. "Touch me," she breathed heavily.

His shirt landed on the floor as her mouth made its way down his neck. He brushed her robe away. One shoulder, then the next. Her robe fell to her waist. The knotted tie was the only thing keeping it on her lower half. In the millisecond between her kisses, Allen lifted her. The greediness with which he took her nipple in his mouth was everything.

She tipped her head back. His fingers and tongue were on her breasts. She wanted to return the favor, but he held her there. Every caress, flick, and pinch heightened the fire burning inside her.

She needed this, but the longer he touched her, the more she needed to feel him inside her. She gazed to see him staring at her. He was doing this intentionally to tease her. Thrusting back, she slid off the chair. It was her turn to tease him.

She went straight for the drawstring on his sweatpants, but it twisted into a knot.

"I got it," Allen offered, swiping the string from her.

He was just as impatient, but the string only tightened the knot even further. Kristen would have informed him of that, but no longer having the drawstrings to worry about, her attention was solely directed at the bulge in his pants. She ran her hand over it, causing Allen to groan.

"To hell with it," Allen grumbled and ripped at the drawstring. It didn't budge. His hand disappeared between the bottom cushion and the armrest, and a second later, a pocketknife emerged.

Kristen sat back on her heels before the recliner and watched him flip open the knife, intrigued as Allen sliced the drawstrings loose. "Do you usually keep a knife in your recliner, or did you drop it down there and never get it out?"

"There's a reason this is my favorite chair," he told her, closing the knife and returning it between the cushions. "It has my knife, lays back without me having to prop up my feet, and you're lying in it."

"Wha—" she started, but Allen stood, scooping her up with surprising ease, and dropped her into the recliner.

"Your turn." With one hand, he pulled the tie at her waist free.

Why couldn't his drawstrings have done that?

"Wait," she muttered as he leaned over and pushed the chair to recline, "You never got your turn."

"This is all my turn," he said breathlessly with a wink.

With Kristen laid back, Allen went right to her soft inner thighs. He kissed one thigh and then the other in silent homage for them parting so that his face could fit between her legs. He held onto her outer thighs, and the work his tongue did on her breasts was nothing compared to what he was doing between her legs. Her back arched.

She had planned to go down on him when she came in here, but this... This was so much better.

Her breath was choppy. "Please," she gasped. She didn't look down as she reached for his hand. "I want to feel you inside of me."

"Your wish is my command."

She smiled at him. "I can give you your turn first."

"I told you," Allen said, sitting up, "this *is* my turn." His hands went to his waistband, and she closed her eyes in happy anticipation.

She waited, but nothing happened besides a whoosh of air. Kristen opened her eyes, expecting to get an eyeful, but his pants were not only still around his waist, but he was standing up with a disconcerting look.

"What?"

He nodded toward the top of her head. "You're bleeding."

RUNNING FROM CUPID

THIRTY-FOUR

"This is what I was coming inside to pretend to need help with," Kristen said to Allen as he sat outside the tub over her head, tending to her stitches.

"Oh, yeah?" When he offered her a towel, she waved it off.

He felt like the luckiest man alive, being allowed to be in the bathroom with her while she got into the bathtub and then a front-row seat, squatting over the tub's faucet while she reclined back.

"It's a little late for modesty," she told him, opting for a washcloth.

He had offered it to her so she could be as modest as she wanted since she didn't have anything on under the robe, but her only concern was keeping the water out of her eyes while he cleaned the top of her head to see why she was bleeding. He basically could see every inch of her. The bad part was that his view was so good that he found it hard to perform his medical duties and hear what she was saying.

It was a good thing she asked for that washcloth. He filled a cup but missed the mark the second his eyes drifted beyond her forehead. Kristen pulled the washcloth up before the water got in her eyes.

"Yeah. I was going to stroll in, talk about how I left my hospital papers in Betty's car, and then ask what the doctor's orders were." She said that last part with a sultry shake of her hips. The washcloth flew up to her eyes again.

"My bad," he said quickly.

Kristen lowered the washcloth, grinning. "I'm starting to understand why nurses give patients their baths."

"It's nurses and nurse's aides," Allen said, looking her in the eye as she gazed up at him. "It can require more than one person when a patient is bedridden. We had one come in last year who needed a special ambulance because of his size. It took six of us and two beds pushed up together to get him in a room. It took the nurses and aides from the entire floor to give him a sponge bath."

Kristen's face contorted as he spoke, and he realized it wasn't water that she blinked out of her eyes.

"Is your head hurting?" he asked.

"I'm fine." She raised the washcloth to her eyes and kept it there.

What had he done? He looked at her stitches, wondering if he had somehow inadvertently hit her head. On the back side of the last stitch, a clump of hair had managed to stick against her scalp in dried blood.

"It's just," she inhaled sharply when Allen tried to tug it free. He stopped expecting Kristen to fuss at him, but all she did was lower the washcloth from her eyes. "This is not how I pictured this going—you're actually cleaning my stitches, not that digging crud out of my hair isn't great and all—"

"Would it be better if I told you about the time I sewed the wrong finger onto a patient?"

Kristen's brows shot up as Allen dipped his right hand in the bath water. "Explain." Thankfully, the movement in her forehead didn't cause any more blood to exude from her stitches.

Allen readied his wet fingers over her matted hair. "Let me start by saying it wasn't my fault. The guy came in missing two fingers and only had one with him. The blood supply of the finger he brought in lined up perfectly with the pointer. By the time his buddies brought in the other one, I already had the first finger sewn up. It wasn't until I looked at the other finger his friends brought that I realized his pointer finger was in the bag, and I had just turned his middle finger into his pointer finger."

She smiled. "What did the guy do?"

"Nothing. I sewed the pointer finger onto where his middle finger went, wrapped it all up, and sent him on his way."

"You didn't," she laughed and winced when Allen pulled the last of her hair away from the suture site.

"Done," he announced. "And you're right, I didn't, but it made for a good distraction." Allen cleaned off his fingers in the bath water. Coming upstairs, Allen feared their activity in the recliner had caused a ripped stitch or two, but it was only some light bleeding besides the troublesome hair. Everything else looked fine.

"Distraction from what?" Kristen asked.

"The hunk of curls matted to the back of your stitches I just pulled out."

"Really?" she looked up at him as her hand lightly padded around the site, now free of knotted hair. Kristen splashed her hand in the water when Allen nodded at her. "Great," she said sarcastically. Allen blinked at her. "No, really," she insisted, "That came out wrong, but I mean it. I'm just mortified that the night turned into *this*."

"Would you like me to distract you by pouring more water into your eyes?"

"Don't you dare," she giggled up at him. "And don't think I don't know you're checking me out every time you do it."

Allen opened his mouth but ultimately just chuckled along with her. There was no point in defending his actions, even if they weren't necessarily intentional on his part. "In all seriousness, though," he said, running his damp fingers gently through her curls, "this is what it's all about."

"What?" she smirked at him. "Checking me out in your bathtub?"

Allen lifted a curl with dried blood on the end of it. *"This,"* he said, using the cup to pour water on the curl until it was clean, "is what life is all about: taking care of each other."

THIRTY-FIVE

Kristen woke in Allen's bed. She stretched, found Allen's pillow empty, and remembered the shower running earlier. With no sounds coming from the bathroom now, she was blissfully alone in the main bedroom. She stared dreamily at his empty side of the bed.

Maybe he was some kind of witch doctor.

He definitely put some kind of a spell on her last night. She had planned to seduce him, but it was Allen who worked his magic on her instead. He tended to her head and said some magical words that only reinforced her witch doctor theory. They ended up curling up in his bed without fulfilling a single one of Kristen's ideas when she sashayed into his kitchen wearing only a robe. The craziest thing had been that she hadn't thought twice about it. How could a night feel so intimate with zero intimacy?

Definitely a witch doctor.

What had Allen said to her when she was in the tub?

Life is about taking care of each other.

No, he wasn't a witch doctor. He was a poet. A doctor *and* a poet?

Allen could almost make her believe that a being like Cupid could be real.

And those sweatpants... Kristen squeezed her eyes shut and rolled over in a huff to forget how great he looked in those sweatpants.

Opening her eyes, she realized she faced a glass wall identical to those downstairs. She should have curled under the sheets and gone back to sleep, but the sunrise peeking out from the edges of the shades made her throw the covers back.

The t-shirt Allen gave her to wear once she was out of the tub fell to mid-thigh as she pulled at the sleeves that rolled up to her shoulders from tossing and turning. If only her stupid head contusion hadn't ruined it, wearing his shirt would signify that something happened last night.

Life is about taking care of each other.

She'd show him; she would "take care" of him in ways he would fantasize about for years after she was gone.

The remote on the nightstand was the same kind he used downstairs to lower the shades.

How much better could the view be from up here?

With one click of a button, she got her answer.

Way better.

Just like Allen, the view was even better than she imagined. The ocean unfolded out as far as the eye could see. Soft waves lapped against the shoreline.

Kristen moved closer to the window to see the hurried footprints of someone running from the back of Allen's property out and down the beach line.

Had last night's antics literally made him run for it?

She giggled. If he knew what was best for him, he would run.

She would have run if it had been her needing to care for him. There was no way Kristen or any of her previous aliases would end a night cleaning out their love interest's gross head injury, no matter how badly he needed it.

In the blink of an eye, her thoughts shifted. Her features hardened in the reflection in the glass.

What if he ran because someone was after him?

Thoughts of Calvin finding them gave way to the Russians.

The trail onto the beach could be from anyone. It played out in her mind: Russians came, hoping they would find Kristen alone, but found Allen instead. They took care of him, something spooked them, and they left out the back before anyone could be the wiser. Maybe they were setting her up as Allen's killer somehow.

That would suck; meet a great guy and then be framed for his murder. *Yeesh.*

"I would have heard something," she said to calm her fears but kept her voice low. If those were Allen's footprints running from the house, she didn't want to lead whoever sent him packing upstairs to her.

Kristen straightened. If she was about to fight someone, she should probably put some pants on. She really needed shoes, but creeping down the stairs in a pair of Allen's would have been the equivalent of clown shoes. Allen's sweatpants left draped on the foot of the bed, and the t-shirt she slept in would have to be enough.

It was easier to be quiet in bare feet anyway.

If anyone were waiting to ambush her downstairs, she would have to run for her life shoeless.

Her thoughts of the Russian thieves' crime ring gave way to thoughts of her mother. Barefoot or not, she was not going to die at the hands of the Russians like her mother had when Kristen was little. Kristen was a lot like her mother, or so her father told her, but unlike Kristen, her mother failed at her first heist job, and she found out the hard way why you never work for the Russians. They may pay more, but if you ever get on their bad side or the job goes sideways, it would cost your life.

Kristen had made it too close to making a clean break from this life for this to be the end.

After a silent pass through the ground floor, she ended up in the living room where the shades were up. The morning sun cast a warm glow inside the house.

As far as she could tell, she was alone.

The recliner's headrest caught her attention. It had been cleaned to show no trace of what her head did to end last night's rendezvous. Kristen had to give credit where credit was due: The Trouth family knew how to clean fabric.

She ran a hand over the headrest and found it was still damp. Something hit the glass behind her.

Ruff!

Kristen nearly jumped out of her skin. Fortunately, it came from outside, not in. When she spun around, there were no Calvin or Russians, only Milo begging to be let in as he pawed at the glass back door.

"Where is your—"

Betty walked into view from the pool house, carrying a much larger purse than yesterday's over her shoulder, keys in one hand, and folded clothes clutched to her chest with the other.

"Hello, dear," Betty waved through the glass, oblivious that Kristen's heart was pounding ninety to nothing in her chest. "Do you mind?" she pointed at the locked doorknob.

Kristen hopped to it. "I assumed it was unlocked," she explained as Betty and Milo trotted into the house, "since Allen went for a run."

Betty chuckled. "You really slept in. He had already gone for his run, came back, cleaned up, and went to work. He called us when he was headed out. It was sweet." She tossed her keys on the kitchen island, offering Kristen the clothes. "He made sure that I knew not to wake you, and don't worry, you don't have to explain a thing to me. Allen already told me about last night, and I think it's great that he let you sleep in the guest room instead of the pool house. I'd feel much safer with others close by, too, if I were you."

The guest room? Kristen stared at the clothes being offered to her. It would have been sweet if Allen had woken her and shared their cover story before leaving for his meeting. Kristen hesitantly accepted them.

"I picked out something more your style," she said, "but the graphic tee was right up Allen's alley."

Kristen bit her tongue. As if she needed a t-shirt to pull a guy in. Apparently, for Allen, all she needed was a robe.

"Do you need help with that?" Kristen asked as Betty struggled to keep her purse on her shoulder. "Is that a computer?" she asked when the thin edge of a laptop became visible.

Betty looked at it as if she were as surprised as Kristen was to see it in her bag. "So it is."

"Betty," Kristen started, but Betty walked past her into the kitchen. She set her purse down on the kitchen island and went to the fridge, acting as if she couldn't hear her. "Betty?" Betty opened the refrigerator—still nothing. "Mrs. Trouth?" she said louder.

Betty spun around with a torn-off piece of chicken skin pinched between her fingers. "Oh!" She tossed the chicken skin on the ground for Milo. "Silly me. Somedays, I just don't feel like a Betty, if you know what I mean."

Kristen nodded along but had no clue what she meant. She really must be deaf. "Did you not know you had a laptop in your purse?"

Betty gave her a peculiar glance. "Of course I did. I..." She looked uncomfortably at her purse on the counter. "I just forgot what the password was so I brought it with me."

"I can try to help you," she offered.

"Oh, no, no, it's fine. All I was going to do was play online, maybe sign up to some more dating sites," she pointed at Kristen, "don't tell my son I said that, but it's fine, really." She waved her hand dismissively. "I was only going to mess with it if you were still asleep, but as it were, you're up. So get dressed, and then we can clean this place up."

She had the distinct feeling that someone had gone through her things as she walked into the pool house bathroom to change into the clothes Betty so thoughtfully picked from the bag of hand-me-downs. It wasn't like she had her own *things* for someone to go through so much as Allen and Betty, but something did not feel right.

Was it the towel? It was in the same corner where she tossed it after drying off yesterday, but it looked like it had been moved around.

She should have stayed in bed. Her thoughts of people coming for her made her paranoid. Kristen made eye contact with herself in the bathroom mirror.

"Get it together, will you?"

She was not going to do this to herself. Look at what happened to her yesterday; it still turned out somewhat okay. Kristen did what she could with her hair before looking herself over. Good Ole' Betty picked out capris with a similar fit to the pants she had on yesterday and a casual blouse. It was not her style, not her *true* style, but it was perfect for the easily forgettable persona she took on. She needed to be as incognito as possible.

Still ruminating on that uneasy feeling, she walked outside to find Betty on the back patio. Milo was sniffing around the side of the house where the water hose was neatly wrapped around its holder.

"What are you searching for?" Kristen called to him.

"Coffee?" Betty asked, raising one of the two mugs she was holding.

"Sure," Kristen said, feeling resolve wash over her as Milo greeted her and Betty handed her a mug.

Who cares if Betty, or even Allen, might have looked through the pool house? She would have done the same thing if she were them, and it's not like they would find anything. Kristen had everything under control. Today was going to be a good day. All she had to do was clean Allen's house. Kristen petted the top of Milo's head and glanced at the water hose.

"I'm going to water plants while it's cool out."

"You don't have to worry about it," Betty insisted, taking a cautious sip from her mug. "Allen took care of it already. Come to find out, he waters the plants every morning so that you can take that off your to-do list."

Kristen gritted her teeth and grinned. "Great."

Everything was fine. Today was going to be a good day.

The kitchen was picked up. The margarita machine was cleaned and stored in the tall cabinet beside the stove that, oddly enough, had one shelf right in the middle of it, ruining any chance of it being utilized for mops or brooms. Allen must have planned to house the margarita machine there because it fit perfectly on the shelf.

Out of necessity, she started in on the floors. Not because they needed it but because cleaning the floors would put some much-needed space between her and Betty, who utilized their closeness while following her around to pepper her with questions.

Not only did the questions not stop as Betty meandered around room to room while Kristen swept, asking about everything from Kristen's favorite foods to whether she liked Allen's house, but it quickly became harder and harder for her to mentally keep track of what her answers were not to contradict herself.

She liked anything not too spicy—a lie created to fit her Kristen Chanel persona. The last one was easy. She loved Allen's house. What wasn't to like, considering she would be homeless without it?

And if the beach had not done it, Allen's dislike for Milo was officially rubbing off on her by the time she made it to the living room. Betty's dog, as it turned out, had an uncanny ability to walk through each and every pile Kristen made. As she swept the kitchen, she scooped anything resembling a pile before Milo could increase his odds of being beaten to death with a broom.

"Where did you grow up?"

"Depends," she muttered.

Kristen could tell where this was headed. Betty wanted to fill in the blanks on her son's housemate, and stalking Kristen while she swept was her way of collecting the intel. Even Milo's ears perked up.

"We moved a lot. I couldn't really tell you why at the time—" she said, preparing for Betty's next line of questioning, "they always had their reasons. But I was a kid, so I was just sad to leave whatever friends I had made. Looking back, I think it had to do with money."

"Isn't most things?" Betty chuckled drily.

Kristen couldn't agree more, but she was too busy mentally treading that fine line of giving just enough of the truth to lessen the lies. It made it easier to remember that way. She had moved a lot, but it was after her mother's death. Before that, all she could remember was being in one home. Her mother had been a stay-at-home mom while her dad traveled for work, and she couldn't remember when that changed, and her mom started working for the people who would ultimately kill her. Anytime she asked her dad about that time in their lives right before her death, he would either get too sad or too mad for her to get much out of him.

"My parents were always looking for better jobs, better pay, but once my mom passed, I know we were evicted at least once. We never lived anywhere with a view like this, I can tell you that." Kristen needed to change the subject; the mental juggle was already wearing on her. "What about you," Kristen asked, "where are you from?"

"Didn't Allen tell you where we're from?"

"He told me you're from the city, but he never said where." Kristen swept up a ball of hair from out of the corner, and no sooner had she had it out in the open than she heard Milo's paws against the floor.

"Milo, come here," Betty called as Kristen used the broom to keep him from the hairball. "I always thought I was made for the city, but small-town life is turning out to be equally exciting," Betty explained without answering Kristen's question.

Milo turned from the broom in his face to trot over to her. She bent down to offer to pick him up, but he walked around the back of her legs instead. Kristen took another long sweep, adding to the pile. Out of the corner of her eyes, Milo came to a suspiciously frozen standstill next to Betty. Milo's eyes were locked on the pile she just made.

"And you can't beat ocean views."

Kristen was nodding, but her sweeping had stopped. *Don't you do it.* She glanced down at the pile. When she looked up, Milo was no longer at Betty's side but charging full speed at her.

"What in the world?" Betty gawked.

Milo was quick, but Kristen was quicker. She grabbed the dustpan and shoved the pile into it so fast that Milo didn't have time to stop. She lifted the dustpan to keep him from slamming into it. Milo skidded past her as Kristen beamed down at him in victory.

"What has gotten into you?" Betty exclaimed. "Get over here."

Kristen added to his defeat by patting him on the butt with her broom as he walked past her.

"So, where are you from?" Kristen repeated, setting the dustpan down triumphantly.

Betty gave her a cross look. "From the city."

"Right."

That exchange taught Kristen two things: Milo was not to be trusted, and if Betty annoyed her with her questions, she could turn them around and get an entertainingly vague response. Maybe it was the woman's age.

And that was how the day went. Kristen cleaned; Milo and Betty harassed in their own unique ways, and when she had enough...

"I'm going to take a nap."

Betty stretched her arms out wide at Kristen's announcement. "I think Milo and I are going to do the same."

Kristen put up the broom and dustpan. *Funny how Gwen didn't take any of the cleaning supplies.*

"Milo and I will lock up here, and when you're ready, just wave at the camera on the patio, and we'll come back over once it sends me the alert."

"Sounds good," Kristen said.

Naps were never her thing, but the worn-out couch in the pool house never looked so good.

When she woke and opened the door outside, the sun was going down. It was quiet out. The last thing she wanted was to wave at the camera and call Betty and Milo over, so she didn't.

She was sitting on the side of the pool, watching the waves in the fading sunlight with her feet in the water happy that she had beaten her fear of water enough to comfortably enjoy this, when the lights under the back patio came on, and she heard Allen's voice behind her.

"You look like a picture."

Kristen shut her eyes and tilted her head back, lavishing in the way his warm, smooth voice made her feel. Today was a good day.

"That is the sweetest thing—" she lifted her feet from the water and turned to him. "What are you wearing?"

His scrubs were two sizes too big, but the bags under his eyes were the most concerning. Today had clearly not been good to him.

"They're the hospital's. Mine are..." he glanced down at the plastic bag in his hand, "in here. I was going to start them in the wash and change before I came to check on you, but then I saw you sitting out here."

"I'm fine," she said, looking him over as she approached him. It was more than the oversized scrubs. "What happened to your scrubs?"

"I, uh, got blood on them." She watched him struggle to swallow. "I lost two patients today." Kristen had her arms around him before he finished his sentence.

It made her realize how lucky she was to have spent her day being tormented by Betty and Milo.

Kristen held him tight. "I'm so sorry."

He held her for only a second and breathed deeply through his nostrils. "It's part of the job," he told her as he let go of her.

Kristen backed up, too, but stayed close. "It's the worst part of the job," she said, not liking seeing him hurt like this.

He shook his head lightly. "It's not the worst part. They both passed pretty quickly, and they didn't feel much. The worst part is when they're in pain, and it takes a long time. Witnessing that is the worst part."

Kristen remained silent as his words settled over them. She didn't know what to say to something like that. Allen gazed around the backyard, seeming to let his words settle over himself as well.

"You cool if it's just us tonight?" he asked after a moment.

"Us?"

"Yeah. Having my mom around after the day I had—"

"That's fine with me." The way Allen said *us*, including her with him, made her feel good, but she kept it to herself, not wanting to grin when the day he had warranted anything but.

They didn't talk much about supper, but when Kristen got up to go to the pool house, Allen stopped her.

"We could...sleep in my bed again tonight. We don't have to do anything," he added quickly, "it's just nice having you there."

And that was how Kristen ended her second night there, holding him just like he had held her the night before.

The next day was much of the same. Allen ran, showered, and then went to work for a meeting. Kristen made sure not to sleep in this time, but he wasn't super talkative. Yesterday must have still been weighing on him the way the day before tried to weigh on her. Kristen pushed it away. She could let herself enjoy this, whatever it was between her and Allen, for at least a few more days before she finished whatever mundane cleaning Betty had in mind and got the cash.

"What do you have for me today?" Kristen asked when Betty and Milo arrived at Allen's departure.

"It dawned on me last night that with the house not full of stuff, it is the perfect time to dust everything."

Kristen held back the sarcasm. "Great."

"And we'll probably hang out in the backyard," Betty volunteered, watching Allen skeptically as he grabbed his things before heading out to the garage. "To give my sinuses a break from the dust," she explained.

"Fine with me," Allen told her, glancing at Kristen. "You have fun."

"Oh, yeah," she said, no longer holding back the sarcasm, "it's going to be a blast." They exchanged grins that Betty watched intently. Kristen expected her to say something about it, but all she did was make sure Kristen had what she needed, made them coffee, and then took her cup outside to throw a ball with Milo.

Note to self: dust before you sweep. Kristen learned that the hard way. By the time she was done, the floor needed to be swept again. She was in the front of the house sweeping when she heard the back door open, and Milo trotted in, out of breath.

"Did you sleep in the spare bedroom last night?" Betty asked as Kristen swept up her pile of dust before Milo could try to run through it, but the dog was worn out from playing outside.

Kristen didn't know exactly how to answer that. She was Allen's mother, and Kristen didn't exactly know what was too much to share with her.

"What?" Betty asked, seeing how Kristen was looking at her.

Kristen shook her head. "It's just—"

Milo let out a low growl that got both women's attention.

They looked at him as he spun around and took off to the back of the house. A door opened, and Milo barked as viciously as he had on the beach at Kristen.

"You can see that it's me," Allen snapped. "Why are you barking? This is *my* house."

Kristen exhaled at the sound of his voice.

"Where's Kristen? Has anyone been by the house in the last hour?" Allen asked his mother in rapid succession.

"Don't you have your alerts turned on for the cameras?" Betty asked.

Kristen rounded the corner behind Betty to see Allen locking the door to the garage.

"I do, but—" When he turned, Allen's eyes locked onto Kristen's. "Thank God."

The way he said it gave her pause. His hair was disheveled, and his collar was wrinkled. He looked like he had been in a fight.

THIRTY-SIX

ALLEN'S MIND was going ninety-to-nothing. Finding Kristen safe and sound at the house was great, but he needed to make sure he wasn't followed.

"No one came by?"

"Um," his mother stared at him as he hurried to the front of the house, "not that we know of. Did something happen at your meeting?"

"The meeting? Oh, uh—" His meeting at work was the furthest thing on his mind. "The meeting went fine. I need to make sure I wasn't followed."

"Followed?" his mother echoed as Allen took off past them. Both women were hot on his trail.

"I'd like to say it was nothing, but I noticed a car behind me this morning, and I'm pretty sure it was following me at a distance when I left the hospital."

"To not make it obvious," his mother mumbled.

Allen went to one side of the front window, happier than ever that he kept the shades down on the front of the house. He barely pulled the edge of the shade and peered out. No cars in either direction. Good.

The shades moved from the other side as his mother also peeked out.

"What kind of vehicle?"

"Dark sedan, four doors."

"Sheila's in my purse on the island," his mother added. "Did you shut the garage door?"

"Of course I did."

"Sheila, as in your gun?" Kristen balked. When his mother gave her a nonchalant nod, Kristen stared at them in dismay. "Wait, are we seriously thinking you're being followed?"

"Sure as sh—"

Allen interjected. "There's something I haven't shared with either of you." He stepped away from the window. "Keep watching the street," he instructed his mother. Allen gently took Kristen's hands in his. "A man came by the hospital asking about you last night."

Her hands tightened in his. "Do they think it was him?"

"The night shift was gone when I got in, but Ivan was told that it was an older guy asking if a woman matching your description was brought in recently."

His mother looked away from the window. "Sounds like your guy."

Allen glanced between them, ignoring the pang of jealousy from the way she said, 'your guy.' He certainly didn't deserve the title of her guy. Allen's brows pinched together.

"An *older* man," he repeated, positive that he must have been misheard.

But his mother nodded. He noticed the way his mother looked at him as she replied, "I heard you." Perhaps she could tell that her comment stung.

"It could have been anyone," Kristen muttered. Her gaze was lost somewhere between him and Betty.

"It could," he agreed, hoping it would calm the worry he could see in her eyes.

Betty scoffed. "Doubtful."

Allen glared in his mother's direction, but she was too busy staring out the window to notice. It's true; the odds that it was anyone besides her attacker were astronomically low, but there was no point in rubbing it in. If she were the one holding Kristen's hand, she wouldn't have said that. Her hands were turning clammy the longer he held them. What he wanted to do was take her in his arms, hold her close, and tell her no one would hurt her ever again. But there was no point in making a promise he couldn't keep if she wouldn't be staying around. So, instead, he rubbed his thumbs over the top of her hands.

"You are safe." When Kristen looked at him, he knew he could lose himself in her eyes. "I won't let anyone hurt you." So much for not making promises he couldn't keep.

"*We*," his mother corrected from the window, "won't let anything happen to you."

Allen could see the resolve washing over Kristen's face before she dropped her hands from his. "I'm fine. It's fine. Even if it is him looking for me, he has no clue where I am. I'm still safe."

"Yes, you are," his mother chirped, "and if he does show up around here, Sheila will drop him like a sack of potatoes." She froze. Something out the window caught her attention. Allen froze, too, expecting the worst. "Just a white van," she said.

Kristen glanced between them. She inched closer to Allen. "The obsession with guns…" she whispered. "Is that normal for people around here or just your mom?"

"We lived in a bad neighborhood when I was a kid," Allen explained, glancing at his mother, who acted like she wasn't listening, but he could tell she was all ears. "We were lucky," he said. "Not everyone else was."

Kristen nodded, looking lost in thought. "Try growing up in Brooklyn," she said out the side of her mouth. Kristen seemed to catch herself. Her eyes came out of the daze as she shifted feet away from Allen, glancing cautiously at his mother, who was still staring out the window. "We weren't there for long, thankfully. I barely remember it." She rubbed her palms down the sides of her hips, looking between them. "Welp, better get back to cleaning."

The house was looking clean enough to him, but he understood. She needed space.

It was a good thing he hadn't told her the bad part.

THIRTY-SEVEN

"What do you mean, he knows she's here?" Betty gasped.

"Keep your voice down," Allen said, then paused.

Kristen kept her sweeping pace steady at the front of the house as if she were still actively cleaning and not listening to their conversation. After Allen motioned for Betty to follow him into the kitchen, she worked close enough to overhear but not be obvious. Milo, unfortunately, kept prancing back and forth to check on her. Each time, she flicked the end of the broom to chase him off. On his last trip to see her, he plopped down in the middle of the wide threshold, alternating his attention from Betty and Allen to Kristen.

"Not like here at the house—here in Redrock. The night shift nurse told Ivan about a man who spoke with one of the aids about the woman found on the beach. He said he was a detective from Texas, so they let him into the ER, and he told them that he thought Kristen might be someone related to a case he was working on."

Kristen shut her eyes. This was what she got for using the same first name from the Texas job. *What an idiot.* She could have at least said a name from a few jobs back. This stupid head injury had thrown her off of her game.

Milo raised his nose toward her as if he could smell the turmoil brewing. She put her finger to her lips for him to stay quiet.

There was no possible way a detective from Texas was onto her that fast, not out here in South Carolina. Unless Calvin tipped them off. No, there was no way. Calvin was dumb, but not *that* dumb. If the cops got to her before he did, he would never get the goods. The Texas detective had to be Calvin. Thinking of the gall it took to strut into a hospital and pretend to be a detective, Kristen was almost impressed.

"He knew her name?" Betty asked.

"I don't know, but he did by the end based on what the nurse's aide told him last night. After you left with her the other day, I told Ivan her name was Kristen. I told him she was a family friend we hadn't seen since she and I were kids, so we hadn't recognized her until she remembered her name—which doesn't matter since it isn't her real name. It also answered why you were the one to pick her up two days ago when she was discharged and why I had accounting bill me for her visit in case word got around about that too."

"You didn't tell me you were paying for her. Does she know?"

Kristen froze. She had no clue. They've already done so much for her. This was too much.

"No, but I—"

"She knows now." Betty's voice rose, "You might as well come in here."

Kristen waited for a beat, continuing to pretend to sweep.

"What are you doing?" Allen asked.

"She's been listening, son. There you are," Betty said as Kristen appeared, doe-eyed with the broom in hand, with Milo jumping from his spot.

"Were you talking to me?"

Betty waved her into the kitchen, where they stood on the other side of the island. "No need to play coy, dear. We can all be honest with each other in this house."

Kristen walked over, not saying a word. She stopped being honest with people in grade school. Growing up around actual juvenile delinquents and con artists will make you that way.

"What all did you hear?" Allen asked, looking relatively unbothered by her eavesdropping.

"Your explanation for why Betty picked me up from the hospital."

Betty dipped her chin at her. "And volunteered to pay for your hospital bills?"

Kristen nodded, looking at Allen. "I'll pay you back."

"With what money?" Betty asked.

Milo sashayed around Betty before dropping his butt to the floor to stare up at Kristen as if he, too, were waiting to hear her response.

Allen waved his hand dismissively. "Doesn't matter. I might not have to pay for it. After I talked to billing about the situation, they said they would still submit it to the program and go from there."

Seeing Milo beside her, Betty bent to scoop him up as if he were a tiny dog and not easily forty pounds. She sighed as Milo happily jumped into her arms. Kristen had to give it to her; Betty lifted him with ease. She nuzzled her nose against his ear. "Might as well tell her everything." Milo's ears perked up as if the instructions were for him.

Allen frowned at his mother. "*You* haven't even heard everything."

"Then what is he waiting for, an invitation?" Betty cooed at Milo.

Allen drew in a long breath before settling his gaze on Kristen. "I didn't want to upset you, but it's worse than I let on. When the man came in, claiming to be a detective, the nurse's aide told him that you had been mugged. But she also mentioned that you were family friends with one of the doctors at the hospital, telling him that once everything was straightened out, the person who knew you took you home. Ivan wasn't sure if she shared my name or my mother's, but the guy knows a local took you home."

Kristen gaped at him. "She just *volunteered* all of that?"

Betty stepped forward. "You have to keep in mind that this is a small town. Unless they have a good reason to be suspicious, the people here take others at face value."

Kristen nodded. It was that generous small-town mentality that had Kristen standing here right now and not in the hospital with the detective in her face. "Did he show her his credentials?"

Allen gave her a somber shake of his head. "The way Ivan explained it, the aide was at the front desk talking to the guy. When the night nurse walked by and heard what she was telling him, she asked what was going on and to see his badge. He told them it was in the car, but when he went outside to get it, he never came back. I spoke with my Chief Physician about it, but he was more concerned about HIPAA laws being broken. Since she hadn't shared more than your first name and no medical information, all we could do was alert security to keep an eye out for him. If he comes back, they'll call the cops."

"So it has to be him," Kristen surmised.

If it had been a detective, he would have returned with his credentials and figured out exactly where and who Kristen was with. As much as she hoped Calvin wouldn't be on her trail again this soon, it was better than some detective from her last job.

"You are safe here," Betty assured her.

"What about the detective working my assault?" Kristen asked, daring to mention the genuine detective whom she wanted nothing to do with. "Does he know Calvin's in town?"

Betty and Allen looked at each other for a long moment. Allen raised his brows at his mom, who stood solid. When their stare turned into seconds, Kristen knew they were having some nonverbal battle. Ultimately, Betty rolled her eyes.

"I told Ed what happened to you and that you didn't want to press charges, but if you changed your mind, I would let him know." She looked pointedly at her son and then back to Kristen. "But, we can tell him about this if you think he *needs* to know."

Kristen couldn't shake her head fast enough. "I don't think so. He had to have only come back to make sure he hadn't"—the words stuck in her throat—"killed me, right?" Tears filled her eyes. Before the first could spill, Allen went to her.

"If he tries anything," he said as he wrapped her in his arms, "I'll kill him."

Murder threats from a man whose life work was to save lives... Kristen could not be more attracted to him right now. She leaned into him.

"It's settled then," Betty said. "I won't mention it to Ed." She set Milo on the ground and slung her purse over her shoulder.

"Where are you going?" Allen asked.

"Didn't I tell you?" She glanced at them from the corner of her eyes, "I have a lunch date."

"Speak of the devil." Kristen smiled, but when Betty and Allen gave her a confused look, Kristen clarified, "The detective?"

Betty chuckled. "Oh, heaven's no. That man will be in the doghouse until he can prove himself worthy of a second chance. I'm going to lunch with—"

Allen cut her off. "We don't need to hear about your dating life."

Betty rolled her eyes at him before heading for the door to the garage. "All I was going to say was with someone from out of town."

Allen shook his head. "Still don't need to hear it."

Kristen enjoyed watching Allen squirm at the mention of his mother's love life. She couldn't just let her leave.

"Wait," Kristen said, catching Betty and Milo before they got to the door leading to the garage. "You said there wasn't much of a selection around here. Is this someone from the dating app?"

Allen glared across the room at his mother. "You better not be on a dating app."

Betty glared right back at him. "So what if I am?" She threw her hand on her hip for good measure.

"In what world would a dating app be a good idea?" The way Allen didn't back down despite the look his mom was giving him was impressive.

"Oh, calm down," Betty grumbled. "Mr. Overprotective. I'm not on any dating apps." Her eyes cut to Kristen, and she winked.

"Mom," Allen gaped.

"I'm kidding." Betty gestured to her figure. "Look at me. Women who look as good as I do don't need an app. Word gets around just fine on its own." Kristen giggled at Allen's face until Betty pulled her attention with a smirk. "If you stick around here long enough, you'll see."

"Okay," Allen said. "You go enjoy your lunch date."

"I'll let you know how it goes." Betty waved as she went on her way with Milo at her feet.

"Please don't," Allen called. He turned to Kristen as the low rumble of the garage opening reached them. "So, what do you want to do today?"

Kristen licked her lips, enjoying Allen staring as she thought of something flirty to say.

The doorbell rang, and the heat forming between them disappeared as they both went into full alert. They shared a look of confusion, knowing it wouldn't be Betty.

Allen scanned the house. "We never use the front door," he said, heading toward it.

RUNNING FROM CUPID

THIRTY-EIGHT

Kristen pulled on his arm when he was halfway to the front door. "Wait," she pled, "what are you doing?"

"Answering the door."

Kristen shook her head in disbelief and glanced at the door. "It could be Calvin."

Thankfully, he had changed the see-through glass panes on the front door to privacy film before moving in. It kept prying eyes from seeing inside as much as it kept them from making out the blurry form standing outside.

"Don't worry, you are going to be fine," he said in the same calm tone he took with patients. "I'll take care of it, but if it is him, you don't need to be standing right here when I open the door." He gestured back toward the kitchen.

Kristen stepped back, looking between him and the front door. "Be careful."

The doorbell rang again as she rounded the corner. Allen rolled his shoulders back. He was going to take care of this. Allen puffed up his chest as he took his cell phone out of his pocket to check the front camera. All he could see was the top of a man's head. If it was the guy who hit Kristen, he was going to make him regret coming back for her.

"What's up?" Davie said the second Allen opened the door. His chest deflated. "You okay?" Davie asked, watching it fall.

"Yeah. I thought you were someone else."

He glanced past the teen to his driveway, where his mother watched them in her car near the road. She must have just backed up and noticed someone at the front door because her front windows were still rolled down, and her hand was out of sight, undoubtedly inside her purse.

"Everything all right?" she called out as Milo jumped into the front seat to hang his head out. He lapped the air with his tongue as if it tasted better than the air inside the car.

"All good," Allen waved.

Davie turned. "Morning, Mrs. Trouth."

Allen's mother's suspicion didn't lessen at the sight of the boy's face, but thankfully, her hand came into view, free of any weapons.

"Get in your seat," she fussed at Milo as she punched the button on her door without so much as waving back at the boy.

"I don't think she likes me," Davie said.

Allen waved at her again before she backed out of the driveway and headed home. "I think you're right."

"Does she know about the advice you gave me?"

"What advice?"

Davie gaped at him. "The 'turn their joke against them' advice. It was the best advice anyone has ever given me."

Allen took a deep breath. "I don't think that's how I said it."

"Doesn't matter," Davie said, offering the poorly folded clothes tucked under his arm. "It worked. Here, I meant to drop these off a couple of days ago, but Mom's having a rough one, so I didn't want to chance her asking questions when she saw me carrying that out." He tipped his chin at the clothes. Allen didn't say it but the boy could have put the clothes in a bag or something. "You heard what happened at the hospital two days ago?" Davie asked.

Allen took the clothes, finding it hard to meet the boy's gaze. "I was there," he said. "Well, not there when it happened, but right after."

Davie's eyes widened. "Did you see that chick who had the guy in a choke hold?"

"It wasn't really a choke hold," he said, on the verge of explaining the difference between a choke hold and what Kristen had done with her knee to the man's throat but thought better of it. "But it did the trick."

"That dude was lucky I wasn't there," Davie said, the tops of his cheeks turning rosy.

"He was lucky that he wasn't in his right mind, or else we all would have wanted a piece of him. How is she doing? I didn't see her at work this morning?"

"All right, I guess." He shrugged. "They gave her today and the weekend off. She was making coffee when I left for school."

Allen dipped his chin at him. "You went to class today?"

"Yup. Only have two classes I have to show up for in the mornings—the rest are online for college credit."

Allen perked up. "College. Celia told me you weren't planning on going."

"I'm not, but the classes aren't that bad, and Mom was excited I signed up for them. You know what I'm excited about?"

From the way he smiled, Allen was almost scared to ask. "What?"

"I have a date with that girl I told you about next weekend."

"The one from the party?"

Davie's smile broadened. "That's right."

"Look at you," Allen said proudly. "You couldn't bring yourself to talk to her the other weekend, and now you've got a date."

"It's just like you said, 'life's too short.'"

Allen nodded. "That it is."

"You should've seen me. I walked right up to her and her friends like it was nothing and asked her out. If I play my cards right, she'll be my girlfriend by next week."

Davie's eyes snapped away from Allen. He craned his neck to look inside. Allen looked over his shoulder to see Kristen leaning against the kitchen threshold, watching them.

"Hi there," Kristen smiled.

"Sorry to bother you guys," Davie called over Allen's shoulder, giving Kristen a double take. "Wait, are you—"

Allen could see Davie putting together who Kristen was. He stepped forward, blocking Davie's view. "Thanks for returning these." Allen waved the clothes as he reached for the door.

"Wait, are you two—"

"Just friends," Allen interjected and lowered his voice. "But if I play my cards right, she might become my girlfriend," he winked at Davie.

A sly smile spread across the boy's face. Allen could hear Kristen walking up behind him. "My man," Davie chuckled. "If you need any advice—"

"I don't. See you later," Allen couldn't shut the door fast enough.

"Did you just call me your girlfriend?"

The sudden closeness of Kristen's voice almost made him jump. "We weren't talking about you," he said far too quickly to sound convincing.

Her brows rose as he turned to face her. "Is that right?"

"It is," he said, cool and collected. "We were talking about the kid having a date next weekend."

"Uh-huh, sure." She moved in closer. "And you were saying something about calling someone your girlfriend...?"

Slowly, Allen shook his head, furrowing his brow at her. "I have no idea what you're talking about."

Kristen chuckled. "Right..." She started back toward the kitchen. "I have to finish sweeping the floors for the second time in two days."

Allen took a moment to enjoy watching her walk away. "Forget the floors," he said. "I have something else in mind."

THIRTY-NINE

Kristen crossed her arms in the passenger seat of Allen's car. "Let me get this straight. You had robot vacuums this whole time, and your mother just sat back and watched me sweep the entire ground floor of your house while I fought to keep Milo out of the piles of dirt not once but *twice*?"

Allen chuckled. When he glanced at her from the driver's seat and saw just how unenthused she was, he cracked up even harder. "Okay, okay." He caught his breath. "To be fair, I don't think she knows about the vacuums."

"Vacuums plural?" Kristen fumed.

"I got them a couple of weeks ago," he said, "and if you were making piles of dirt, then clearly, it wasn't for nothing."

Kristen gritted her teeth. "You definitely need better vacuums, and that is not me volunteering to vacuum either."

"Noted," Allen said. "I'll schedule them to vacuum every day from now on since there's two of us."

Kristen settled back in her seat. He said it as if he were fishing for her to say whether or not she would be sticking around, but she kept quiet. Whether it was Calvin or an actual detective from Texas looking for her, she should not be sticking around for long. Thankfully, she felt like she had a little bit of time with him, or maybe she just *wanted* a little bit more time with him.

When Allen told Kristen he had something else in mind, her thoughts dove head-first into the gutter, thinking he was about to lead her upstairs to the bedroom. Allen meant lunch.

They ordered food from the diner, and when it was time to leave, they both agreed that it couldn't hurt for her to ride with him to pick it up. She wasn't sure of his reasons, but if Calvin were looking for her, the last thing she wanted was for him to find her alone.

When they drove near the water tower, she leaned forward.

"Looking at the graffiti on our water tower?"

"Whoever did it is pretty good. Spray paint is a lot harder to work with than people think."

"Sounds like that's coming from experience."

Kristen met his gaze and shrugged before staring out the window. "Only briefly when I was in my cool kid phase."

"You're still pretty cool," he said.

"Thanks," she said gently. "You aren't too bad yourself."

She watched the water tower fade in the rearview mirror as she reminisced. "So, why did Davie give you those clothes?"

They pulled into the diner parking lot, which was nearly full. Luckily, the car Calvin drove was nowhere in the mix of vehicles.

"He needed...to borrow them the other weekend."

Kristen let that explanation sit for a moment. The first thing that popped into her head was that maybe Allen and Celia had been an item at one point, and Davie ended up with some of Allen's clothes. Celia was older than him by at least ten years, if she had to guess, but who's to say Allen didn't take after his mother and had an affinity for older women? She smiled at the thought of last night. She was close to Allen's age, and he definitively liked her, but what about Davie and the clothes?

"What's wrong?" Allen asked, eyeing her as he searched for a parking spot.

"I'm just wondering if I need to call the cops."

Allen gripped the stirring wheel. "You see him?"

"No," she said. "I'm talking about a local high school kid borrowing clothes from a grown man who doesn't live with him and is not related to him. Sounds like quite the scandal if you ask me."

To her amusement and relief, Allen looked horrified. "It's not like... That's not—" he stumbled over his words. "I barely know the kid."

"That makes it sound even worse," she told him.

"Look," he said, passing several empty parking spots, "I was heading out for my morning jog last Sunday, and I saw this kid staggering down the beach behind my house—"

"Stop it," Kristen said as the pieces fell into place. "Dwayne really saw a streaker on the beach that day, and it was Davie!"

"The kid isn't a streaker." He pulled into a spot between a van and a light-colored sedan with rental plate tags. Thanks to the van, their car would be blocked from the view of anyone driving by.

Out of sight from the road, Kristen thought to herself. *Smart.* Though, the idea that there was a chance of Calvin or the Texas detective knowing what Allen drove made her regret leaving the house. She would have to keep an extra sharp eye out.

"He got drunk at a beach party, passed out on the beach, and those terrible kids he calls friends left him."

"Did they strip him first?" she asked, realizing just how terrible his friends were.

Allen stared out the window shield for a moment. "I'm not sure what happened to his clothes."

Kristen paused thoughtfully. "So, he could be a streaker for all we know."

"It has to be voluntary to be considered streaking."

"Agree to disagree," she said, unbuckling.

He shrugged. "Don't believe me, look it up."

"Sure thing," she said sarcastically, "let me just grab my encyclopedia."

"I have something you can use." Allen smiled and leaned across her to the glove box. Kristen tensed, wondering if Allen was like his mom and had his own Sheila stashed inside. But inside, there was just an old flip phone on top of the car's owner's manual. Allen handed it to her. "Here you go."

Kristen accepted it from him and looked it over. It was brand new, and she peeled the screen protector off the front. It would be a wonder if she could, in fact, look anything up on it.

"I know it's not fancy," he told her, "but I was in a rush, so I grabbed the one with the easiest setup."

"It's a prepaid phone?"

"It looks like one, but it's on my phone plan."

She shouldn't like that the little phone was on Allen's plan. It meant he could see the numbers she called, but she liked that he took time out of his day to add a phone *for her* to his plan. She grinned. "Doesn't sound like a rush job."

"It did take a little time," he admitted. "But I'm not giving it to you to keep. I'll need it back when you...leave." She liked the way he didn't enjoy talking about her leaving. "My accountant and the hospital have been telling me to get a separate work phone since I started this job, so," he eyed the phone, "that phone will be it."

That made sense. Kristen wasn't sure what she liked more: Allen's consideration of getting her a phone under the guise of needing a work phone or his unexpected protectiveness to ensure he wasn't followed home to keep her safe.

"Are you always like this?" she asked.

"Like what?"

She leaned toward him. "Unbelievably great."

"Terrible doctor to unbelievably great." He grinned and leaned in. "I should have given you a phone yesterday."

Her eyes were on his lips. They were the perfect distance for a kiss.

"The phone has nothing to do with it." She closed her eyes and leaned in.

Allen made a slight sound of disgust. "Really?"

Kristen's eyes popped open. Allen wasn't looking at her, nor was he leaning in for the kiss she was positive would happen. He frowned at the diner, where Betty was seated at the window. She waved happily at them.

Allen stared back at her, making no move to return her wave. "Fantastic," he said dryly. "And she's parked right behind us. Did you see her car when we pulled in?"

Kristen gave her a meek wave and then turned in her seat to look out the back windshield. Sure enough, Betty's car was parked in the row behind them; so much for keeping an extra sharp eye out. Betty had to have seen her attempt to kiss her son, but all she did was grin and turn away.

"She did tell you that she was going on a date."

"I know," he said begrudgingly and opened the car door. "Doesn't mean I want to witness it." Kristen opened her door, and he asked, "What are you doing?"

"Coming with you," she said with one leg out the door. "Unless you think it's too dangerous for me to go inside."

She pulled her leg back in the car, giving him a minute to think it over.

"No, you're right." He glanced at Betty, who tried not to make it obvious that she was watching them as she hurried to look away. "If he's in there, we'll call the cops, he'll get arrested, and we won't have to worry about him anymore. But if you stay in the car, not only will I not be able to keep an eye on you, but my mom will think we were trying to spy on her."

"If this is you spying," she said, getting out of the car, "you would be terrible at it."

"That's not fair. We're not trying to spy on her, so you don't know how good or bad I am at it."

As much as she should have been worrying about walking into the diner and running into Calvin, Kristen looked at Allen, enjoying him grappling with his mother's dating. "Have you ever done this before?" she asked. "Interfere with your mom's dating life?"

If her dad would have dated after her mother passed, then that would mean he would have been around. She might have had a traditional childhood if he had.

"I wouldn't say interfere," Allen told her as they walked toward the diner door, "but I put my foot down once when my college professor asked her out on a date."

"You told her not to date him?"

"I did."

"If I could have gotten my dad to date one of my teachers, I would have been all for it." Kristen smiled as Allen opened the door for her. "Your mom would have gotten you an easy A."

Allen gave her a mock, horrified expression at the implications. "I would have rather failed than let her help in *any* way. And I did ace the class." He grinned, but then his expression turned serious. "Let me know if you see him."

Kristen scanned the diner as they walked inside. "I don't see him."

He led Kristen to the two stools at the end of the counter, as far from Betty as they could get. "Good."

Norah exited the kitchen. "They're almost done with your to-go order," she told them as she walked by. She pulled a ticket out from her apron and set it in front of Allen. "I'll be right back for that."

"Talk about service," Kristen murmured.

He smiled. "That's a small town for you."

"Is it right?" she asked, checking the ticket. "She was our waitress yesterday, and I got a milkshake that I didn't order."

Allen's knee grazed her thigh as he pulled his wallet out of his back pocket. Her cheeks flushed. They were in a diner full of people, and all it took was for him to brush against her, and all she could think about was one thing. He seemed to read her mind as his eyes met hers and grinned.

"The kitchen takes the to-go order, but if you want a milkshake to-go, I can add it."

So much for his mind being on the same thing. "No," she shook her head. "It's fine." She settled back in her seat. "Do you know who your mom is meeting?"

Allen shook his head as he set a card on the ticket. "No clue."

"If it's someone you don't know, will you introduce yourself?"

"Nope," Allen said without hesitation.

Kristen smirked. "What if he looks like a total creep?"

He shrugged. "She can take care of herself."

"What if he's in some kind of biker gang that kidnaps women for slave labor?"

"Nah, bikers aren't her type."

"What if he's a serial killer, and you introducing yourself to him is the only thing that stops him from adding your sweet momma to his closet full of heads?"

Allen broke out in laughter. "A closet full of heads?" After a few annoyed looks from the nearby patrons, he settled. "Like I said. She can take care of herself."

Kristen leaned in so only he could hear her. "From murderers?"

She was thoroughly enjoying whatever this was, flirting, joking around, poking fun at a guy whose mother's dating life was a sore spot, but Allen's features darkened. He recovered fast, plastering on an entertained grin, but she had seen it.

"What?"

He blinked at her. "What do you mean?"

She must have crossed the line. "Did I get too dark with it?"

"Nah. It just hit me that she won't be here one day, even if this date is with a normal guy."

"You think she will get tired of you and move away?" Kristen asked, in a poor attempt to make light despite knowing what he meant.

"That would be the day." He smiled, but it didn't reach his eyes.

"Sorry," she said. She placed her hand on his shoulder and squeezed gently. "I shouldn't joke about things like death."

Allen closed his eyes. "That feels so g—"

"You ready for me to take that?" Norah appeared behind them with a handful of dirty dishes. Kristen dropped her hand from Allen's shoulder so he could give Norah the ticket and his card. "Be right back."

"There's no reason to be sorry," Allen said. "Death is a part of life."

"That it is. I was five or six when my mom passed." The words bubbled out of her before she could stop them.

She didn't talk about her mother. Some of her personas spoke about their mothers, but it was always strained or nonexistent relationships with both of her parents to keep the men in her life from asking to meet them. The only time she thought of her actual mom was when she needed to cry. That was as far as it went.

"That had to be hard."

Allen's words brought her back into the moment. When she met his gaze, his eyes were staring right into hers, and the way he looked at her didn't make her uncomfortable or annoyed like sympathetic looks usually did. His eyes were so genuinely warm, like a hug if a glance could hold such a thing.

"It is," she mumbled, meaning to say *was*. Being lost in his eyes made the truth slip.

Allen may grapple with his mom dating, but Kristen, this version of her that felt closer to the real her than any past, made-up identities, has never healed from losing her mother.

Allen broke their gaze to look around them and said quietly, "If you start tearing up, I'm going to tear up. Then everyone around us will wonder how I made you cry."

Kristen blinked a second and then took a sheepish glance around them. The occupants of the booths near them were eating and talking amongst themselves. Only a few people made eye contact with her.

However, the man seated on the other side of Allen glanced away a little too quickly when he caught her gaze.

"See?" Allen said.

Kristen pursed her lips. "I say we both cry just to give them a show."

Allen smiled. "Good idea." His eyes fell to her lips, and she could see his thoughts take a turn as his gaze darkened and the corners of his mouth curled.

"What are you thinking about?"

Color rose to his cheeks as he glanced around them self-consciously.

"Out with it," she insisted.

He dipped his chin at her. "I was thinking we should kiss to give them a show, but you should know that some people at my work mentioned you being my cousin and not a family friend, so there's a good chance the cousin story is what's being spread around town."

Kristen giggled. "That would make us kissing cousins."

"Especially if we kissed right here in front of everybody."

"If it makes you feel any better, your mom told Norah yesterday that she was best friends with my mom, so there is a chance her story is what's making its way around town."

"Only one way to find out," Allen said, his gaze darkening.

Kristen smirked. "To see how shocked everyone is when we kiss?"

"Precisely." Allen leaned in and closed his eyes.

Over his shoulder, a man entered the diner. Betty waved him over. Kristen straightened, nudging Allen's chest.

"I think your mom's date just walked in," she told him as he opened his eyes.

His shoulders drooped as he looked across the diner at the man approaching Betty's booth.

"He's dressed nice," Kristen observed. The man was clean-cut, but for a woman who preferred older men, he looked to be around her age, or maybe he just looked really good for his age. His slacks looked freshly pressed, something she almost pointed out to Allen so he could take notes on how his scrubs should look. "Maybe he's a lawyer," she said instead.

Allen shook his head. "She would never date a lawyer."

"Sure, but she might not know what he does for a living. That's what people find out on the first date."

"That's on blind dates," Allen corrected. "And my mom doesn't go in blind to anything. She knows who he is, where he's from, what he does for a living before a first date. Before my first date with Gwen, she handed me the printed-out copies of the background search she did."

"Like, she searched her social media accounts?"

"Everything: criminal history, public background, online photos, her socials; you name it."

Kristen swallowed. "Impressive."

She looked across the diner, pushing out the thought of what Betty would find if she did a similar search on her. It made her appreciate that she lucked her way into their circle.

"He works in an office." Kristen tried to get a feel for the guy solely based on the back of his head and upper body as he sat across from Betty with his back to them. "He's in okay shape but is definitely a pencil-pusher type. I bet he stays hunched over a computer all day. I'm going to say…an accountant or…software programmer."

Allen grinned, stealing a look at his mother's beau. "I could see a software engineer but not an accountant."

Kristen's forehead wrinkled. "You sure?"

"She's dated an accountant before and told me she would never do it again."

"He's a younger guy," Kristen countered, "and she's told me she likes older men. So maybe there is something about this—accountant—that has your mom willing to step out of her comfort zone."

Allen leaned toward Kristen. "Are you trying to ruin my appetite?"

"Here you guys go," Norah announced with their order packed in a bag and copies of the receipt held together with Allen's card by her pen clip.

Kristen took the bag while Allen handled the rest. On the other end of the diner, Kristen noticed Betty pointing Allen out to her date, who turned in the booth to look.

"Don't look now," Kristen ducked behind Allen, "but your mom is showing you off to her date."

"No, she isn't," he groaned. He glanced in their direction, and sure enough, the man smiled and waved.

"You should introduce yourself," Kristen said, expecting him to refuse.

Allen smirked. "You're right. Here," he handed over the pen and the diner's copy of the receipt. "Fill that out, and I'll meet you at the car." He set his keys on the counter in front of her. It was a moment of proud realization as those keys were laid out in front of Kristen. She could take them and be long gone before anyone noticed. Allen would learn the hard way never to trust a stranger, and Kristen would put some much-needed space between her and the possible detective from Texas, who was likely Calvin, but she didn't. This was her chance to practice living the life she was one payday away from, where good people like the Trouths could trust their valuables around her.

"Be nice," she warned.

For Allen to be this enthusiastic about interrupting the date he didn't want even to hear, he was undoubtedly about to intimidate the man as much as a well-educated son can to a man on a date with his mother, and she wanted to witness it. She could steal his car later.

In Texas, Phillip's sister had been one of those intimidating-the-love interest types when it came to her twin brother, and Kristen had known from their first meeting that she was onto her by the way she always seemed to be looking at her out of the corners of her eyes, whenever she thought Kristen wasn't looking. Had she known that Kristen was about to steal precious collectibles? Obviously not, but somehow, she could tell Kristen had been up to something. But, as

Allen had been onto her in the hospital, Kristen did not doubt that Allen would sniff out any less than honorable characteristics from the man if he and Betty made it past the first date.

It was impressive how something small could make her feel so much bigger. Allen hadn't just given her the receipt to fill out but his card, too. Kristen chalked it up to naivety or maybe a test. He didn't even know her real name. Why give her his card unless this was a test? Giving her his credit card was ludicrous otherwise, but here she was, holding it.

Norah walked by, and Kristen grabbed her attention.

"Is it cool if I keep your pen?" She held up the restaurant's copy of the receipt to show her the more than generous tip they left her.

Norah smiled. "You paid for it." She took the signed copy from Kristen and gestured toward Betty. "Looks like Betty's on a date."

"She is. Do you know him?"

"Never seen him before." Norah squinted across the diner. "He's decent enough on the eyes. Wonder what he's into."

"He likes ocean views, deep, soul-baring gazes," Kristen said dreamily, but she wasn't looking at Betty's date.

Norah snorted. "He looks more like a long walks in The Container Store type of guy."

Allen glanced in her direction, standing at the end of the booth his mother and date occupied, and Kristen held back a smile while studying Betty's date. "You're right, he does."

"You'll have to let me know if they don't work out."

"You're interested in The Container Store guy?"

"What can I say?" Norah shrugged. "Container Store guys are stable, and he's in decent shape. The older you get, the harder it is to find men who take care of themselves." She looked Kristen over with renewed interest. "So, you're family friends with the Trouths?"

"That's right," Kristen began before a thought crossed her mind. She could create her own narrative, starting with Norah. "My mom was friends with Betty when I was growing up. Allen was that cool older guy, you know? He barely noticed me. Not to mention the huge crush I had on him. When I heard he was engaged, I thought I lost my chance." Kristen's shoulders drooped for effect. Norah looked as though she held her breath. "Then, when I found out that they broke up... Call me crazy, but I thought it was now or never, so here I am."

Norah nudged Kristen with her elbow encouragingly. "You get your man."

Kristen grinned proudly, much happier with this version of why she showed up in Redrock. "I plan to."

FORTY

Allen needed to get out of this situation as quickly as possible. He saw Kristen through the window, writing something down in his car.

"It was a pleasure meeting you." Allen was already backing away from the booth.

"The pleasure is all mine." His mother's date smiled at him. It was a mirror image of his mother's smugness. She was loving this. "You are an impressive young man," he told Allen. "Your mother talks about you all the time."

"Funny, she's never mentioned you."

"Be nice to my date," his mother said, trying to sound resolute, but both of them were smirking.

"So?" Kristen asked when Allen joined her in the car. The paper she wrote on was no longer on her lap but tucked into the clear to-go plastic bag. "Are you really not going to tell me how it went?"

"You are not going to believe it," he told her, wondering if she was planning her next move once the house was cleaned.

"What?"

Allen ignored the eyes on them from inside the diner as he started the car. "He's an accountant."

"I told you." Kristen waved at the man seated opposite his mother as they backed out of the parking spot. "What's his name?"

"I can't remember. Once I found out he was an accountant, I stopped listening."

"Lame," Kristen said. "What good are you if I can't send you to get all the details for me?"

"You sent me to introduce myself."

"And that means introduce yourself, pepper him with questions to establish your dominance, slap him around a little if needed, and then report back."

He smirked over at Kristen. "If I had known that was what that meant, then I would have enjoyed it a lot more."

Kristen's brows rose in amusement. "So you would have slapped him around?"

"Only if he wouldn't have answered my question," he played along, "but I definitely would have asked for a full resume so we could go through his work history." Kristen grinned, but he was set on making her laugh. "And if he didn't have that, I would ask for a list of character witnesses—"

"At least," Kristen giggled.

"And," he paused, wondering if he dared and then thought, *why not?* "Last but not least, fingerprints and a blood sample."

Kristen smirked. "Why the blood sample?"

He was impressed that she wasn't interested in the fingerprints, but maybe his mother running a background check on Gwen gave that one away. "To run a full panel, of course." If Kristen had any experience in the medical world, that would have been funny, but she stared blankly at him. "A panel is a fancy word for testing blood for multiple things at once. It alerts us to diseases, allergies, and deficiencies in the body based on components in their blood."

"Fascinating," she mumbled.

"Okay, that one was a flop," he admitted.

"Not at all. I thought it had to do with making sure he didn't transmit anything to your mother."

Allen narrowed his gaze at the road ahead. "Please tell me you don't mean what I think you mean by 'transmit'?"

Kristen leaned on the center console, lowering her voice. "That is exactly what I mean."

Allen gagged dramatically. Kristen giggled deviously. It wasn't how he planned to amuse her, but he would take it.

Kristen turned quickly in her seat toward the back glass.

"Do you see something?" he asked, eyeing the rearview mirror. There was nothing on the horizon in front of or behind them. She sunk back into the passenger seat.

"I thought I saw something, but it must have been my eyes playing tricks on me." All humor had left her features. In its place, she looked…tired.

"Are you okay?"

"I'm fine," she said a little too quickly. The worn-out look on her face didn't go away until she caught him looking at her. "How are you doing now that you know your mom has a thing for guys who are good with numbers?" She smiled mischievously at him.

Allen chuckled. He could recognize a defensive mechanism when he saw one. She was changing the subject because she was not okay. Who would be okay after being attacked by someone they knew?

He narrowed his eyes. "Ask me again at tax season."

She laughed. *Mission accomplished.* Kristen had been lucky that it was his mother on the beach yesterday, and the more he looked into her eyes, the more *he* realized how fortunate he was that it was his mother on the beach yesterday. It had been a hard blow kicking the woman out whom he had thought he would spend the rest of his life with, but with Kristen with him, all of that pain became a distant memory. He could never be playful like this with Gwen, but with Kristen she brought it out of him, and the more she played along, the more he realized that what he had with Gwen wasn't that great.

"I'll get our lunch out," Allen volunteered once they were safely inside the house, and Kristen excused herself to the bathroom. First, he took out the pen and piece of paper. He carefully unfolded it in case he had to return it quickly, but he relaxed when he saw what was written.

It wasn't her plan to leave town. It was a doodle of Allen standing at the end of the booth with his mother and the accountant seated on either side. Drawn over them were two winged babies holding bows and arrows with hearts on the end... Cherubs, it dawned on Allen. His mother's obsession had apparently spread to Kristen unless all women were fascinated with Cupid.

The whole drawing was pretty good, especially for being done in pen. He would need a pencil, one of those big erasers from grade school, and a week to make a drawing half that good. His favorite part was the tiny heart she had drawn on his chest.

"You like it?"

Allen jumped. "Uh, I do." He fumbled as he grabbed the to-go containers.

Kristen smirked at catching him off guard. "You're blushing," she said, taking one of the containers from him.

He handed over the pen and paper next. "Well, you did draw a heart on me."

"It was the least I could do," she admitted unapologetically while unwrapping the plastic utensils. "It's rare to meet a guy with a heart, much less one who shows it."

FORTY-ONE

It was a talent Kristen worked at for years, meeting someone and making them feel as if they were kindred spirits. Her research on the person she was "meeting" helped tremendously. Allen somehow had that same ability and did it without even knowing Kristen's real name.

The ease that being in Allen's presence gave her started wearing off once a silence fell over them as they took lunch back at his place. Kristen began second-guessing not stealing his car. Allen and Betty were great, but was staying here hoping she was safe the smart thing to do?

Allen glanced over at her and she grinned at him as she took a bite. Man, did she like looking at him. As much as she liked Betty, it was Allen that had her coming up with excuses to stay. She liked him, and unlike the targets from all of her jobs, the more she spent time with him, the more she liked him. *What in the world was she doing?*

Kristen was still in her head, when Allen excused himself. A few short minutes later, he reappeared.

"You will never believe what happened upstairs."

"What is it?" she asked, nearly knocking over the bar stool as she jumped out of it.

"You'll see," he said, leading the way to the stairs.

"Do we need to call Ed?" she panicked. The thought of having the detective around was welcome if her fear of being in danger had materialized.

"No. It's nothing like that," he told her. They got upstairs and hooked a left, passing Allen's room. The door he led her to was partially ajar. "I don't know what happened," he explained as he pushed the door open.

Still in fear, Kristen craned her neck to look around Allen into the room instead of walking in.

The spare bedroom with nothing but a bed frame—no mattress, box springs, or other furniture in sight—was covered in a white powdery substance.

"What in the—" Kristen took a cautious step inside, careful to stay within the only clean section of floor at the door. "Did you do this?" she asked, eyeing the abandoned bag of flour on the far corner floor.

Allen stepped into the room beside her. "Why would I do this?"

It didn't take Kristen long to put it together. "Lift your foot," she instructed, pointing at Allen's shoes.

He raised one and then the other. Sure enough, flour coated the bottom of both. "I walked in the room," he shrugged, but they both knew the truth.

"Hey," her eyes narrowed, "you have your shoes on inside."

Allen shrugged. "So?"

"I *just* finished cleaning the floors—"

Allen interjected with a shake of his head. "Correction, my robots finished the floors."

The trail of footprints only led from the middle of the room out. Allen had thrown flour around his spare bedroom as if it were his job to cover the floors and lower parts of the walls in the white substance that Kristen hoped, as his temporary housecleaner, was easy to sweep up.

"Right," Kristen agreed. She walked into the room, no longer caring about not stepping in it. "You came in, saw this mysterious mess, and ran downstairs to tell me," she recounted the made-up scene of events. She didn't have to ask questions; Kristen knew why he did it. She walked across the room to the abandoned bag of flour. "This is going to take at least a day or two to clean up."

"At least," Allen said, trailing her.

Kristen walked across the room to the bag of flour. She leaned down and found it to be over twice the size she expected. "Why do you have a family-sized bag of flour?"

"They were having a two-for-one sale on the ten-pound bags, or so my mother told me when she stuck that in my cabinet."

"It's weird that you call your mom mother."

"Is it?" he asked. "I call her Mom to her face."

Kristen picked up the bag and found it still had a good bit of flour. "I guess not then," she mumbled.

He watched her balance the bag of flour on her hip. "I didn't mean for you to start cleaning up right now. We can finish lunch."

"I'm not," Kristen said, peering into the bag. "So, am I really to believe you didn't do this?"

"Me, do this?" he asked, looking around the room as if being the culprit to this disaster was the wildest thing he'd ever heard. "I would never."

Kristen reached her free hand into the bag of flour. "I'm going to ask you again," she said, narrowing her eyes on him. "Did you make this mess?"

"No," Allen said, finally looking back at her. He eyed her arm in the bag of flour as her fingers grabbed a handful. "What are you doing?"

"Me? I'm not doing anything."

Milo charged into the upstairs bedroom. Kristen managed to grab one more handful of flour as Milo barked wildly at them. Allen moved to stop her, but Milo jumped between them, barking more at him as the aggressor as Kristen chunked another fistful of flour, pelting Allen's face.

"What is going on?" Betty's eyes were saucers as she appeared in the doorway.

"Your son," Kristen gasped, breathless, "thought it would be funny to destroy his spare bedroom."

"I told you," Allen said, reaching for the bag of flour, but Kristen snatched it off the floor. Flour was now covering the floors, most of the walls, half of the ceiling fan, and—Kristen smiled proudly—all over Allen. "It's been like this."

Kristen gawked at him. "You're still not going to take ownership of this?"

Allen shook his head. "I don't know what you're talking about."

Betty stepped cautiously into the room. "What happened?"

"We were eating lunch," Kristen blurted before Allen could misconstrue the truth, "when *your* son, thinking he was being sneaky, snuck an entire bag of flour out of the kitchen and upstairs. The audacity." Her eyes zoned in on a small section at the top of Allen's head that was free of flour. "And then," Kristen said, "when I demanded what he was up to, he told me that there was a room upstairs that I hadn't cleaned yet and proceeded to tell me that *you* won't pay me until this *whole room* was clean." She waved her hand around the room.

Betty looked between them a moment before settling her gaze on Kristen. "He's right. This has to be cleaned before you leave." Milo was belly-up at Kristen's feet, rolling around in the flour, and Betty groaned.

Kristen knelt to rub his belly. "Glad to see you're having fun."

"Let's go home, Milo. Before this gets any more out of hand." Betty backed out of the room as carefully as she could.

"Wait," Kristen said, ignoring how Allen eyed the bag of flour as if he had more plans with it once his mother was gone. "Are neither of you going to acknowledge that this was a clean room before today?" Kristen was guessing because she hadn't actually been inside of this room.

Allen looked at his mother as Betty pursed her lips. She took her time looking Kristen, Allen, and the room over with a look that said she wasn't getting involved.

"Thanks," Allen said quickly, "for honoring my wishes."

Kristen gave them a questionable glance.

"He doesn't want me watching the cameras," Betty explained, watching Milo as he strolled over to her.

"And I appreciate you listening," Allen added.

"Sure," Betty told him dryly as she examined Milo with growing apprehension the closer he got to her, "until something happens, and then you're going to come to me, wanting to know why I didn't know what was going on."

Allen rolled his eyes. "That was when Gwen kept taking my stuff after she moved out."

Milo paused for a second as if he were about to shake, causing Betty to flinch from their proximity. He seemed to think better of it and carried on toward the door.

"You either want me to keep an eye on the place or you—"

"Don't."

"Fine." Betty spun on her heels. "I was going to tell you how my date went, but now I'm just going to go home."

"Wait," Kristen pled, "I, at least, want to hear what you think of the accountant."

Betty looked over her shoulder. "Accountant?"

"You were sitting right there when he told me he was an accountant," Allen told her.

"I never heard him say that, but you know my hearing," she dismissed.

"His name," Kristen whispered.

"I didn't catch his name," Allen grinned.

"Elvie," Betty blurted, then shook her head. "No, that wasn't it. Alvie." She glanced at Allen, who did not look particularly pleased.

They're only talking about the man's name, for heaven's sake. Allen really needs to chill out about his mother's date.

"That's it. Alvie," Betty clarified.

"I like it," Kristen said, hoping her positive attitude would rub off on Mr. I-don't-want-my-mother-dating. "Is it short for Alvin?"

Betty blinked at her. "I think so."

For someone who supposedly does background checks on people, she should know for sure. Kristen pushed that thought away to smile encouragingly at Allen, nudging him to say something nice.

Allen misread it and grimaced at his mother. "What is he, a chipmunk?"

Betty's lips pinched together in frustration. "He is not—" she stopped herself, a move Kristen wished Allen was better at when it came to his mother's attempt at finding love. "It is a perfectly normal name."

"It is," Kristen agreed. "And it is perfectly normal for you to feel jealous," she told Allen.

"Jealous?" Allen shook his head furiously. "I'm not—"

Betty cleared her throat as Kristen silently willed him to get on board with his mother's dating life. If Betty was okay with Kristen quite literally living under the same roof as her son, then he should, at the very least, be okay with her dating. Allen had lucked out with Betty not hitting it off with the detective. But a woman in as good shape as Betty, who lived on the beach and was ready to date, would not be single for long, no matter how much he protested.

Allen exhaled loudly. "You can go out with whoever you want. Hell, join a dating site for all I care—"

"You know what? I think I will." She looked at Milo, whose tail wagged once he had her attention. Light puffs of flour filled the air around him with each tail flick. "Milo, tell everyone bye. We're leaving."

Kristen waved. "See you later."

Allen dipped his chin at the dog. "Get some flour on her, will you?"

Milo blinked and took off after Betty. A second later, they heard the distinct sound of Milo's collar clinking as he shook.

"Milo!" Betty yelped.

"Good boy," Allen called out of the room. "He listened," he beamed at Kristen.

Kristen nodded, walking up to him. "He's a smart dog."

Allen had his guard down. Once she was close enough, Kristen smacked a handful of flour on top of his head.

Allen wrapped her in a bear hug. "That's cheating," he said low in her ear.

"How so?"

"I thought we were done with the flour."

"No, you were done with the flour. The empty spot on your head told me it was missing out, so I had no choice. My head is injured, so I can't be covered head to toe."

He loosened his grip. "My head *told you* it needed flour on it?"

She nodded. "That's right."

"Fine." He raised his arms. "What else needs it?"

She walked around him, taking her time. He was covered in it. "Found a spot," she said. Kristen dipped her pointer finger into the bag and swiped it on the tip of his nose, leaving a bright white dot.

"Thanks," he said, smiling. "I'm happy you're here, genuinely. Thanks for sticking around."

The things this man says. He couldn't have known how close she came to stealing his car.

"For real," Kristen said, looking him straight in the eyes, "why did you come up here and do this?"

He blinked hard. "I don't know." He wiped the flour out from around his eyes, having a hard time meeting her gaze. "You looked like you were stressing out about something. I figured it had to do with you about to be done cleaning my house, so," He shrugged, falling silent.

"You wanted to keep me a little longer?"

He nodded minutely as his eyes met hers.

The last of the flour fell out of the bag as Kristen dropped it. Their lips met each other's halfway. It would have been more; she wanted it to be more, but her stomach chose that moment, locked in his embrace, to let out a loud growl.

"Do we dare to finish eating lunch downstairs like this?" Allen asked.

Kristen kept ahold of him. "There are so many other things I would prefer to do right now than eat lunch." She could see in his gaze that he agreed, but he loosened his grasp instead.

"Your stomach says otherwise."

FORTY-TWO

ALLEN KNEW she was probably mad at him as he walked onto the back patio. After they finally finished lunch, Kristen invited him to help her bathe, but he could tell she wanted more than just help cleaning her stitches. He took a shower in one of the spare room bathrooms instead, offering to meet her downstairs. It's not that he didn't want the same thing—hell, it was all he could think about—but Kristen needed more than a physical connection. He did, too. The physical attraction would be there whether they acted on it, but he had that with Gwen. He wasn't going to use Kristen to repeat the past.

This was going to be something more, or it wasn't going to be anything.

He glanced over his shoulder as he made his way across the backyard. She watched him from inside, through the glass. Allen waved for her to join him.

"What are you up to now?" she asked. She wore fresh clothes and a towel wrapped around her head.

"That doesn't hurt?" he asked, pointing at the towel.

"Some," she admitted, "but it's better than the alternative."

"What's the alternative?"

She took a deep breath and saw that her not answering only made him more curious. "Don't say I didn't warn you." Kristen unwound the towel. From the weight of her wet curls, her hair almost touched her shoulders.

He lifted his chin to examine the top of her head. "You did good cleaning the stitches."

"Flour is way easier to get out than dried blood."

He lowered his chin and looked over the rest of her face and hair. "I don't get it. You look great."

She grimaced and flipped her hair carefully over the top of her stitches to conceal them. "I could almost believe you, but we both know I look like a wet dog." Her gaze moved past him as he was about to disagree. "What's that thing?"

Allen turned, looking down the line of his potted muhly grass. "That is the advanced Nexstar computerized telescope that you watered yesterday." He stepped aside to show it off.

"That wasn't out here yesterday." She approached, eyeing his newest toy.

"It was—it had the cover over it. You probably didn't notice it if you didn't walk all the way down the muhly grass. It was behind the last one."

Kristen blinked. "The grass wasn't muddy."

It took a moment for Allen to realize what she was talking about. "*Muhly*," he clarified. "That's the name of the grass in these pots."

"Oh, I've got you," she said with a shrug. "Learn something new every day."

Allen popped the cover off from the other end of the telescope as she leaned over to peer into the eyepiece. "What do you think?"

"I have to admit, I was wondering why you pointed it at your house in the middle of the day like this, but your roofers did a phenomenal job." She winked.

"It shouldn't be pointed at my roof." Kristen stepped aside so

Allen could look through the telescope. Sure enough, it was pointed at the top of his roof line.

"Don't be modest," Kristen teased, "those shingles look great."

"You can check out my shingles if you want." He made a slight adjustment and ushered Kristen to look. "But this is what I meant to show you."

Her face lit up when she looked through it. "It's even better up close."

Allen gazed past the side of the house to the water tower out in the field, but the sun was too blinding. "Never seen someone so impressed with vandalism."

"I would never condone such a thing." Kristen found the knob on the side to zoom in. "But this is more artistic than typical tagging." She straightened to meet his gaze. "Have a look now."

"Again, this sounds like it's coming from experience." He peeked through the eyepiece.

"I told you, I dabbled in spray paint as an art form—"

"That's right, your cool kid phase."

There was a laugh in her voice. "I thought I was until I got caught and almost ended up in jail."

"Did they not have enough proof to put you behind bars?"

"My dad got me out of it, actually. It was the only parent-ish thing he ever did for me."

Allen peered up from the telescope. "And you don't think he would want to know you're okay?"

Kristen's expression turned somber. "Can we not talk about him?"

He heard her loud and clear. "I think you might need glasses."

Kristen's brows pinched together. "What?"

Allen nodded toward the telescope. "You got this zoomed in so much that all I see is a white line."

"That's what I'm showing you. Whoever did that is a proper artist." She moved in close to him. "That white line you're looking at is one of many highlights." Her hand covered his on the focus wheel.

"And if you zoom out, you'll see the shadowing done to help make it come off the water tower."

He zoomed out. What her momentary touch and gentle voice in his ear did to him.

Good Lord, man, keep it together. He was not keeping it together, but he was thankfully bent over enough that she couldn't tell the effect her voice had on him.

"The placement of the shadows and highlights give it that 3D feel."

Allen zoomed out enough to understand all of what she was talking about. "You have quite an eye." He stepped back, smiling in admiration. "Did you major in art or something?"

She narrowed her eyes on him. "Are you just determined to talk about my past?"

He shrugged, hoping his gentle questioning would encourage her. "Only if you want to."

"I don't," she said, point blank.

So much for that.

He gazed at the water tower as a cloud shielded him from the sun's rays. "Well, you better not let my mother hear you talk about those pink boxers like that. She was not impressed when she saw it."

Kristen returned to the telescope. "Betty told me. I can't remember if she called them delinquents or maybe riffraff—"

"Or vandals, scum, good-for-nothings," he added to the list of names his mother used frequently.

Kristen nodded. "Something along those lines."

"I don't disagree with her, but only a few kids around here deserve those titles."

"Like the ones who painted the boxers?"

He shook his head. "It was just one kid, and besides bad taste in friends, he isn't that bad."

Her brows rose. "You know who spray-painted the tower?"

"I watched most of it happen through my telescope that night."

"And you didn't call the cops on him?"

"You're the first person I've told."

Kristen's eyes widened in excitement. "Don't tell me that it was Celia's kid."

Allen kept a straight face. "My lips are sealed."

Kristen lowered her voice as her eyes twinkled from barely being able to keep in her elation. "It was Davie, wasn't it?"

"I'm not saying a word."

Kristen lightly shook her head in disbelief. "What are the odds?"

"I'm not saying it's him."

"It sure sounds like him," she said, sounding perky with no air of possibly being wrong. "It's a kid with a bad taste in friends, and Davie just so happened to be the kid who left his pink boxers in the sand after the beach party." She evened her gaze at him. "Or did his friends leave the pink underwear as another way to embarrass him?"

"I never said it was a 'him.'"

"You did," she countered with a cocky grin. "You didn't correct me when *I* said 'him.' Does Celia know?"

Allen's shoulders fell. There was no reason to keep up the rouse when she figured it out. "Celia can't find out because I'll be in trouble."

"Explain how that makes sense when all you did was give the kid some clothes to wear so he wasn't prancing around in the nude." Kristen narrowed her eyes as if he admitted to a crime.

He sighed. "It wouldn't make sense if that was all I did. I gave the kid advice. He told me that he knew his friends weren't going to let him live it down, and I told him to turn it around on them."

Kristen blinked. "Wait, *you* are the reason Celia's son spray-painted the water tower?"

Allen glanced around the yard, searching for anyone on the other side of the fence. "Shout it out for the world to hear, why don't you?"

"I'm sorry. This is just all too much. It's your fault that the entire town is tormented by that piece of art." Kristen laughed. "What would your mom say?"

Allen arched his eyebrows at her. "She will never say anything about it because she will never find out." A silent agreement passed between them. "If that's all my mother has to complain about, then I'd say life is pretty great."

"It is." Kristen stepped up to him. "You know what would really make this place great?"

"What's that?" he asked, but Allen knew where this was going by the way Kristen looked at him through her lashes.

"If we were to take this inside." She casually tossed her arms around his neck, but how she gazed up at him longingly had him second-guessing his resolve.

If he went inside with her, all bets were off.

FORTY-THREE

Kristen and Allen might both share the predisposition to give Celia's son unsolicited advice, but today, there was one glaringly obvious difference between them. Still high on their flour escapade, Kristen invited him upstairs to continue the fun, minus the flour, but Allen turned her down. He wasn't harsh about it, but it felt harsh, nonetheless. She wanted him to want her the same, if not more than she wanted him, but then they shared the thoughtful telescope presentation, and she got a better look at the water tower. That was when it happened. She could feel it—this was the prelude to finishing what they started last night.

She watched the way his Adam's apple bounced as he swallowed. "I'm going to go for a walk." He eased out from under her arms to step toward the metal fence lining the property. Allen looked back at her. "You coming?"

A walk. The man chose to go for a walk instead of going inside with her. Had she not made her intentions clear? He held the metal gate open for her to walk ahead of him.

"You do know what I meant when I said we should take things inside, right?"

Allen followed behind her. "I do," he said, locking the gate behind them. "Do you know if you locked the back door when you came out?"

Kristen blinked at him. "I did not."

"It's okay," he said, taking out his phone.

"What are you doing?"

"Locking the back door with my app."

"Impressive," she muttered. "Is that why you didn't want to go inside with me?"

"What do you mean?"

"Do you have an app to take care of that too?"

Allen fought back a grin as he slid his phone back into his pocket. "They unfortunately don't have apps like that."

She stopped. "Don't they?"

"Not one that will take care of it for you."

Kristen stole a glance, expecting him to hold back a laugh, but he appeared perfectly serious about it, as if he may have checked. *Lonely men,* she thought to herself and looked out at the beachline.

"Which way?" she asked.

"Up to you."

Kristen glanced in either direction. The route to her left was shorter, leading to town, while the right drifted off into the horizon. "This way." She recognized the beach on her right to be where Calvin took the stance to officially no longer work with her.

"Good choice," Allen said. "Mom's house is that way," he nodded in the opposite direction of where they were both turning from, "which means we won't have her and Milo running after us."

"Could have surprised me." She crossed her arms over her chest. "I figured you would welcome company with how quickly you wanted to go for a walk instead of going inside." Out of the corner of her eyes, she could see him studying her.

Allen wrapped his arm around her shoulders. "Don't be mad at me," he said, pulling her closer. "I just want this to be more than a one-night stand."

"It would be more than one night," she murmured. When he didn't respond, she glanced at him and saw his gaze narrowed ahead. Kristen followed it to the house under construction two doors down.

Almost all its windows were covered with plastic sheeting similar to the partially done wall of Allen's safe room.

"Do you see that?" Allen asked.

Kristen scanned the back of the house as it came into view. One second-floor window was missing half its plastic sheeting. A man in a suit stepped into view as her eyes locked onto it. She stopped dead in her tracks.

"Calvin."

"What?"

She backed up. "It's Calvin, right there." Kristen pointed up at the second-floor window. He was gone. The window was empty besides the half-fallen plastic. "He was just there. I swear." It came out as a whisper as she found it hard to breathe.

Allen stepped in front of her, shielding her from the window. "Go back to the house. Now." He pulled his phone out.

He didn't have to tell her twice. Kristen's head screamed in pain as she ran. *Calvin is here.* She had been so wrapped up in her doctor-turned-roommate that she nearly missed it. Calvin was here to finish the job. Her heart pounded as she reached the gate, but it was locked.

"I got it." Allen ran up behind her with his phone in hand.

Shouldn't he be calling the cops? Once she was at the back door, she heard it click. She glanced back to see Allen still at the open gate, looking out at the beachline. Finally, he brought his phone to his ear.

"Is he chasing us?" she called.

"There's no one." He shut the gate and locked it as Kristen hurried inside.

She grabbed the cell phone Allen gave her off the kitchen island. This should not be her problem. Her boss should be here. It should be Calvin running for his life, not her. Kristen stared at the phone.

Allen was still outside talking on the phone and watching the beach toward the house. She could call her boss and chew him out via voicemail for him not being here to deal with this nightmare, but it wouldn't solve anything. Kristen would still be here, and Calvin would still be a few doors down.

Every fiber of her being was telling her to run, to steal Allen's car and drive off, but she stayed at the island, not daring to move as if it would somehow bring everything crashing down around her. Slowly, she put her phone inside the island drawer. There were too many variables at play to run for it. At least that's what she told herself, but where would that leave Allen if she left? He had done too much for Kristen to abandon him with someone dangerous nearby. He was innocent in all of this. Betty was, too. Calvin may have hit Kristen over the head, but as much as she lied to others, she wouldn't lie to herself about what Calvin would do to Allen and his mother to figure out where Kristen went.

So, she stayed standing behind the kitchen island. Beyond the threshold was the front door, the garage door straight ahead, and the backdoor was on her right. She stood at the best vantage point to watch all entrances into the house. She needed to stay calm and levelheaded. No matter what, she had to keep her wits about her, for Allen as much as for herself.

"Ed's on the way to the Lintzell's." He locked the backdoor, and when he faced her, Kristen could tell that he was doing the same thing—staying calm and relaxed on the outside while feeling anything but on the inside. "You all right?"

Kristen nodded slightly. "I am. Are you?"

Allen dug for the remote from the recliner. "What exactly did you see?"

"The same thing you did," she said. "The man standing at the window on the second floor."

"I didn't see anyone," he said once the blinds descended. "I only saw where someone tagged the side of the house."

"Tagged?"

Allen gave her a look of concern that she was not particularly fond of. "Spray painted," he sighed. "Someone spray-painted the side of the Lintzell's house."

"Oh, tagged." She was so frazzled that even basic slang was beyond her grasp, and man, did her head hurt from running.

Once the blinds shut fully, Allen turned to her. "Tell me precisely what you saw."

Kristen closed her eyes, taking a moment to center herself. "When we were on the beach, I saw him at the second-floor window where its plastic covering had fallen off. He just stood there, looking down at me."

"What was he wearing?"

"I don't know." The harder she tried to recall him at the window, the harder it was to make out any details. She tried to force what she saw to the surface. "Dark clothes, I think. Maybe a suit?"

That didn't make sense. Why would he be wearing a suit? He was more of a tracksuit sort of guy. After she saw a guy in Texas, who she was sure was watching her back in Chicago, he never even bothered to dress up to shadow her at any of the galleries or events she attended.

"*Best not to make my presence known*," he had told her.

Kristen felt like she was losing it. She opened her eyes, wondering if she sounded as crazy as she felt, but Allen stood before her, looking calm and collected.

"I can't remember."

He asked softly, "Was he holding anything?"

A shiver ran down Kristen's spine as her mind went to the worst-case scenario. "Like...a gun?"

"Like anything."

She shook her head. The memory of him at the window was already fuzzy to recall. "I-I can't remember."

"It's all right," he said, but it wasn't all right. Nothing about this was all right.

"I definitely saw someone at the window." Even as she said it, doubt trickled into her thoughts. Did Calvin have anything in his hands? Did she even see his hands? Had she really seen him at all?

"It's all right. I believe you," Allen said in a rush, and she realized the truth: he was just as freaked as she was. Allen's calm exterior was as much of a façade as her standing frozen behind the island while her insides were doing cartwheels. "We are safe in here," he added, making it feel less safe. "Ed is sending a unit out to the Lintzell's house to see if they can find him. The Lintzells are having it repainted before they put it on the market, so no one should be in it besides painters."

Kristen tried to follow along with her growing self-doubt. "So it could have been a painter."

Allen shook his head. "Not wearing all black."

They looked at each other for a long moment. She was scared, but he still managed to look relatively calm.

"Unless...the painter is in his cool kid phase," Allen said, and when Kristen blinked at him, he clarified, "That was a poor attempt at humor."

Kristen nodded. "I got it." For the life of her, she couldn't force a grin. "What should I do?" As soon as the words left her mouth, she couldn't believe she said them out loud. To herself, sure, but to ask someone else, even if it was Allen, was so not her. She took care of herself, always had, and always would.

"You did what you could do. You told me, then we came back here and called for help." He wrapped his arms around her, pulling her into his chest. "You're safe."

She listened to his words; she shouldn't let him hold her like this. In his arms, she could close her eyes and pretend that he was protecting her. In reality, she was protecting him by sticking around. Seconds turned to minutes. She would get herself arrested or killed, and the longer she let him hold her, the more she was okay with either.

"What am I doing?" Although she meant to mouth the question, it came out as a whisper.

As Allen pulled away, she winced, but when she looked up at him, he wasn't mad or hurt.

"Come on," Allen said. "I'll prove to you that we're safe in here."

Kristen stared after him. The man's house was made of glass. The privacy blinds were great and all, but what was he going to do, demonstrate that the deadbolts worked?

"Come on," he coaxed her toward the stairs.

Out of the corner of her eyes, a figure darkened the front door. Allen, ever her naive protector, stepped in front of her almost instinctively.

"Get upstairs," he said hastily, "go to my room—"

"It's Ed," the detective shouted as Allen's cell phone rang.

He took out his phone to see that Ed was calling him, and they both relaxed. Allen opened the door and ushered him inside.

"Did you get him?"

Kristen stood with her arms crossed over her chest. She must look like a wet poodle with parts of her hair dry enough that her curls were no doubt at full volume while the bottom was damp enough that she could feel locks tickling her shoulders. She didn't like it. She didn't like that Calvin had found her, but she didn't like how the detective looked at her.

He saw her, the *real* her. She was too exposed with no wig or makeup to alter her features, but she didn't like how the detective couldn't look her in the eye the most. She knew what he would say before he even opened his mouth.

"Not yet. My men are still sweeping the place."

She should have left when she had the chance.

"But on my initial sweep, we found signs that someone has been squatting in the house," he added. "It looks like kids, though."

"Kids," Allen echoed.

Kristen's lips pinched together as the men exchanged looks of relief. "How does evidence of someone squatting in a vacant house look like kids? Is there a big population of homeless children in South Carolina?"

"Not children," Ed clarified. "Teenagers. The same ones who got to the water tower, if I had to bet. They spray-painted tornados on the side of the house and in one of the bedrooms. Good job scaring them off. My guys found spray paint cans left behind that we got fingerprints off of—"

"Was it still wet?" Kristen asked.

Ed's brow furrowed. "Excuse me?"

"Was the spray paint on the inside wall still wet?"

"I'm not sure," Ed said, glancing between them. "Want me to ask my guys?"

"Please," Allen said and turned to Kristen.

"The tagging could have been done anytime," Kristen whispered while Ed spoke to one of his officers on the phone. "It still could have been him at the window."

"I'm right there with you." He eased the growing anxiety in her eyes that she had seen someone who wasn't really there.

"It's still damp," Ed announced after thanking the person on the other end of the phone. "So, there you have it. I'm working on getting ahold of the Lintzell family, so once we get a hit on the prints, we can hit them with trespassing and property damage."

"What are the chances of you getting a hit on the prints if it's kids?" Allen asked.

"If it's the group I'm thinking it is, we arrested one of them for shoplifting a few weeks back, so we got his prints in the system." Ed settled his gaze on Kristen. "There is one easy way to take care of it if you still think it was your guy."

Kristen perked up. "What?"

"Press charges," Ed told her without missing a beat, squashing her momentary hope. "I'll be able to give my guys his description, and if he's in Redrock, my guys will find him."

Kristen plastered on a placated grin for Allen and the detective, who were silently encouraging her to press charges. "It's fine. It's not the first time my eyes have played tricks on me," she lied, "but I don't think I'd be able to identify the kid or kids if you found them."

"Shouldn't need you to, but here," Ed handed her a card from the chest pocket of his shirt.

Kristen expected the card to have the detective's contact information, but it was a phone number for an adult survivors' hotline. She had to hand it to him for still trying to help her despite her refusal to press charges or even name her assailant. She wasn't sure she would be so generous if she were in his shoes.

"They offer virtual help," Ed told her, "or in-office appointments here in Redrock if you're going to be sticking around."

"Very considerate of you." Her fingers wrapped around the card.

"You'll keep us updated?" Allen asked as he walked Ed to the door.

"I will, and don't hesitate to use that card," Ed told Kristen.

"Will do," she lied.

As Allen opened the front door for Ed, a dark sedan drove by. Kristen only saw a flash, but it was enough for her to stay back in case Calvin was closing in on her.

Ed paused. "You talk to your mom today?"

Allen let out an exasperated sigh. "Ed, I talk to the woman every day."

"Did she like the flowers?"

Allen glanced at Kristen, who shrugged. It was the first she had heard about it, too. "I'm sure she did," he assured him.

Ed frowned. "I don't know. I had them delivered a couple of hours ago, and I still haven't heard from her."

"I don't know what to tell you. Some women like to play hard to get."

The detective nodded. "Your mother is something else."

Allen grimaced. "Thanks for coming by, Ed," he said, shutting the door behind him.

FORTY-FOUR

"Just say it," Kristen insisted as Allen shut the front door. "You think I'm crazy," she said as he turned to face her. "I think I might be crazy, too."

Allen didn't think she was crazy. If anything, he was worried: worried for Kristen, his mother, and himself. A mystery man hiding out in a vacant house was bad news for all of them. He swiped open his phone screen. "No one thinks you're crazy, especially not me."

"Wow," she muttered. "I almost believe you."

He confidently pointed at Kristen. "All you have to believe is that I will keep you safe." He raised the phone to his ear, forcing himself to look as confident as he sounded.

"Who are you calling?" Kristen asked.

"I'm not calling anyone—" His phone buzzed in his hand on cue. Allen winked as he accepted the call. "What do you know?"

"What do you mean, what do *I* know? I know that man sent me flowers, and if he thinks that's all it takes for me to forgive him for standing me up, he is in for a rude awakening. Don't tell him I called. He needs to squirm a little longer."

His mother was clueless. She thought that the detective was at his house for her. Allen saw her car speed past as Ed left and thought she was headed to check on her house, not trying to dodge the men nice enough to send her flowers.

"He did mention the flowers, but that's not why he was here."

"So he found out about your girl then."

"She's not my—what do you mean, found out?"

Kristen stared at him. "What's she saying?"

"I'm guessing that's her," his mother said in his ear.

Allen raised his pointer finger at Kristen, but when she made no move to give him a moment, he slowly meandered toward the opposite side of the house. "Explain."

"She can't hear me?"

"Nope."

"I got the full report while checking out at the store and secured a date for tonight."

"He's meeting you again, or are we talking about Ed?"

"Not Ed," she spat, "the devilishly attractive man I just met at the store."

"Please tell me you're joking."

Allen saw Kristen's eyes widen as she listened intensely despite not moving from where he left her. She motioned for him to put it on speakerphone, and Allen shook his head. "Come on," she pled. "I want to hear too."

"I have plenty of time to look him up before our date tonight," his mother told him. "He gave me his card and everything."

"You mean tonight, tonight? There's no way this isn't a joke." Allen lowered his voice. "This is a bad time to be playing a joke."

"Like I said, I will look him up, and it isn't any different than you dating Kristen, which is not her real name, by the way."

"You can't compare the two of them when you're the one who trusted her enough to bring her to *my house—*"

Kristen stepped closer. "You know I can tell you're talking about me, right?"

Allen turned his back to her. Leave it to his mother to throw him off when they had a legitimate threat nearby. "Ed was here because Kristen and I went on a walk—"

"See how well my trusting a stranger is working for you—"

"Kristen saw a man at the vacant house two doors down." He paused, but she wasn't caught as off guard as he thought.

"Two houses between your house and mine? That's the Feesmen's vacation home. They have family staying this month."

"No, two doors in the other direction. The Lintzell's house."

"Oh, you mean that adorable house they're fixing up? I hoped to check it out before they put it on the market."

Allen fought to keep his cool. "That's the house," he said, praying that her interest in the house was for design inspiration and not for buying the place. If she moved any closer to him, Charleston would have to make a bed for him in their psych ward. "The family moved out weeks ago, and it looked like the painters finished. Kristen thinks it was her ex." Milo barked in the background. "Is someone at your house?"

"Just my sweet baby boy welcoming me home. Did you see him too?"

"He wasn't in the window when I looked. I called the cops, and we hurried back here." He glanced back at Kristen, who impatiently rocked back and forth on her heels with her arms crossed over her chest as she stared at the blurry front door pane of glass. She pretended not to be listening to every word. He lowered his voice. "She said he was in a suit."

"Fabulous," she said dryly. "Did you make any other calls?"

"Not yet. Ed wasn't far when I called. He showed here pretty quick."

"Should I give you a minute?" Kristen stepped toward the kitchen as if he hadn't just asked for her to do so.

"It's fine," he told her. "My mother's about to come over."

She visibly relaxed. "Good. She can tell me about this new guy you won't let me hear about."

He could see it in Kristen's eyes. She was genuinely looking forward to the distraction that would be his mother's presence. If only she knew how much he needed the distraction, too.

"I'm not coming over," his mother muttered. "I have flowers to put in a new vase, a handsome stranger to look up online, and—"

"No, you should stop by."

He left out the part that they could use her there as a distraction.

"If this is about the report I got, I can forward it to you," his mother said dismissively, making him rethink how badly he could use her ridiculous antics.

"What re—" Allen glanced at Kristen. Her brows rose in a silent question. There was no reason to stress Kristen out more by letting her know about his mother finally getting a report on her. He already knew about her run-in with the cops during her cool kid phase. Allen rolled his eyes for Kristen to see. "Do you really think going on *another* date today is the best use of your time after what Kristen saw on the beach? Think about it. He could be after you too, considering you chased him off and can ID him."

"He was on the beach today?"

"No," Allen grimaced. She was mixing his words up. One more power his mother held over him; she was messing with him, or she was becoming senile. "Kristen saw him in the Lintzell's house. Kristen and I were the ones on the beach."

"That doesn't make much sense. Why not just show up at your house? Put me on speaker phone," she insisted. "Is she still in the room with you?"

"She is," he sighed. "Are you sure?"

"Chop, chop. I don't have all day."

Allen swiped it to the speaker phone. "She can hear you."

"Good job speaking up, dear. Facing your foe is never easy but necessary."

"I wouldn't say that I faced him—"

"Nonsense. That is absolutely what you did, and if he broke into the Lintzell's, they would charge him whether you press charges or not."

"Ed's guys didn't see any signs of him, but I'm sure they'll find his prints," Allen said. "They think it was just the local kids since someone had spray-painted the high school mascot on the house."

"High school mascot?" Kristen mouthed.

"The school mascot is a tornado," he whispered.

"You didn't tell me that," Betty snapped. "They could still use Allen's testimony of seeing him at the house to put him behind bars."

Kristen stared at Allen. Neither corrected her that Kristen was the only one to see him at the house. Not that he wouldn't go on record to say that he had seen this Calvin guy in the Lintzell's house if it meant that the guy would spend some much-deserved time behind bars.

Milo barked loudly. "I know, I know," his mother cooed. "I need to let him out. Allen, I will forward you that thing we talked about."

"I'm not hanging up until you tell me you aren't going on this date."

"Two dates with strangers in one day," Kristen leaned closer to the phone. "I don't know how you do it." She smiled slightly as he grimaced.

"Get yourself a Sheila, and it's easy," his mother said. "I'll tell you all about it tonight if things don't go as well as I hope they will. If they do, I'll see you two in the morning."

The corners of Allen's mouth pulled down even harder. "What do you mean 'as well as you're hoping'?"

They could hear the laughter in Betty's voice. "You know exactly what I mean. Anywho, I'll be by in the morning, no matter what."

"Have fun," Kristen cheered. "Can't wait to hear how it goes."

"I'm serious, I'm not hanging up," Allen warned. "Do you even have his full name?"

"Oh, darling. You know I run background checks. I have his full name, business card, and the license plate number from his Rolls Royce." Allen rolled his eyes. It was the car that impressed her, he would bet, unless this guy were some kind of Casanova. Allen hoped it was just the car. "You're lucky Norah doesn't work evenings," his mother chattered, "or else the whole town would really be talking because I would make him take me to the diner tonight just to rub it in her face."

"You better text me and share your location."

"I am perfectly fine with that."

"And let me know what you find—" She hung up before he could finish.

He stared at the phone like the closed front door after Ed left; as if he didn't have enough to worry about.

"She'll be okay," Kristen reassured him as if she could read his thoughts.

All it took was looking at Kristen, and he felt better. "How can you be so sure?" he asked, closing the space between them.

"Well, she has Sheila for one," she said, "so if anything, we should be more worried about her date's safety than anyone's."

Her grin widened, as did Allen's.

"I don't know if truer words were ever said." Allen offered his hand. "Let me show you what I was trying to show you earlier."

Everything didn't have to be right in the world for him to make it a little bit better for her.

FORTY-FIVE

Try as she might to put herself in a different frame of mind as Allen led her upstairs to his bedroom, all Kristen could think about was the figure at the window two houses down. Had he left once he was spotted, or had he hidden somewhere inside as the cops checked the place, biding his time until he could catch Kristen alone?

She was forced out of her thoughts when she realized Allen was leading her into his closet.

"Please tell me you're bringing me here to watch you change into those sweatpants from last night."

"Better," he said, pulling her inside. The way he shut the door behind them made her start to get nervous.

"What's going on?" she asked. "Are you about to tell me that you think he's in the house? Did you see him on your phone or something?"

Despite her growing panic, Allen remained calm. "Nothing like that. I have to have this door shut so the other one will open."

"The other door?" Kristen looked at the decently sized walk-in closet. Straight ahead were tall, built-in cabinets, while clothes racks were on one side. But there was no other door.

Allen passed her. "This is the only reason I bought this house." He went to the cabinets at the back, opened the second from the bottom door, and reached under its bottom shelf. After a click, the cabinets moved.

"It's like the bookshelf bathroom," she said in amazement as Allen opened the cabinets to reveal it hid another room behind it.

"You are correct." He ushered her into the secret room. "But this one has a reinforced door and walls."

Kristen admired how thick the door was that Allen had opened with ease. "You must be obsessed with the movie *Safe Room*."

"This was here before me, but I don't think it has anything to do with a movie. The original owners were loaded from the sound of it, and I think people with that kind of money know they have a target on their back. My real estate agent kept telling me how they were selling all but one of their U.S. properties and retiring to Singapore, where it was safer."

The irony of him educating her on what wealthy people had in their homes was not lost on her. "Why were you going to turn your pool house into a safe room if you already had this one?" Kristen asked, walking up to a small desk.

This was where all the stuff Betty had looked for in the empty cardboard boxes in the pool house had gone. Three monitors were hooked up on the desk, giving Allen a three-hundred-and-sixty-degree view of the house on small alternating screens. She could see why he wanted the blinds down in the back room because at least one of the cameras under the back patio was pointed right at the back windows.

"I think that's what the original owners intended for that tiny room everyone keeps calling a pool house, but then they decided to sell everything. Think about it," he said, sitting at the desk, "this one's okay, but it's missing key elements."

Kristen blinked at him, playing dumb. "A mini fridge?"

Allen chuckled. "That, and a bathroom." He clicked the screen until all sides of the house came into view across six screens divided across the three monitors.

Kristen swallowed. Even the side of the house where the water hose hung on its mount was visible. "Impressive," she mumbled, wondering if he was about to show her recordings of herself stomping around his property.

"You do not have to worry. If your ex tries to come within a hundred yards, we'll see him coming." An alert popped up on the center screen. Allen sat straighter as Kristen leaned in. A view past the backyard popped up on the monitor as a couple walked the beach line while a toddler ran ahead. "It automatically records movement."

He glanced over at her encouragingly. She nodded, but what he was telling her wasn't helping her anxiety the way he thought it was.

"So you have a recording of us in the living room?"

Seeing the color drain from his face made her feel a little better. *Good. Now, we are both uncomfortable.*

"I did," he admitted.

She raised her brows at him.

"I deleted it before I left for my meeting this morning."

Allen scrolled through the archive, clicked on a video, and then fast-forwarded through Kristen as she ran from the back door and left Allen alone in the kitchen to when she reappeared in nothing but a robe.

"You don't want to watch that part?" she asked quietly in his ear as he continued to fast forward through his mouthful of chicken.

"If I knew you would want to watch too, I would have kept all of it."

She eyed him. He was being cheeky. She liked it.

He stopped fast-forwarding when they laughed over how much chicken he had shoved in his mouth.

Kristen couldn't help it; she giggled at the recording of herself doubled over in laughter. "That really was impressive," she said. There was no audio, but she remembered sharing that with him.

Allen shook his head, holding back a grin. "I was mortified with myself."

Kristen clicked the volume button on the keyboard when the recording version of Allen turned somber.

"You were setting the mood?" Allen's voice came in low through the monitor speakers.

Her giggle came through clearly. *"Not well, apparently."*

The video cut off. Kristen sat up. "That's it?"

"That was the best place to stop. I talked about my ex after that. I swear," he said, sitting back in the chair, "I used to be more charismatic before we broke up."

Kristen's eyes narrowed. "Right… And you are sure that you didn't just move the rest of that recording to a folder you keep elsewhere for…" she winked, "personal use?"

Allen exhaled. "A hundred percent transparency?"

"Please."

He glanced at the video frozen on the two of them, eyeing one another from the view of the camera under the back patio. "Once you fell asleep, I came in here and watched it before I deleted it. I couldn't sleep," he added as a smile crept across her features.

"The only thing you did was watch it?"

He met her sly smile with one of his own. "What do you think?"

"Did you enjoy watching it as much as I imagine you did?"

Allen's lips parted a full second before his lips formed the words, "I enjoyed it, and then I enjoyed it again in the shower after my run just thinking about it."

No other words passed between them. Allen was out of the chair as fast as Kristen could cross the space separating them. Her lips were on his, and her hands were in his hai when she could have sworn he cursed under his breath between gasps for air.

"What is it?" she asked breathlessly when Allen pulled away. His face went from mirroring her lust to anguish. "Seriously. You wouldn't come inside when we were in your backyard, and now you brought me to your room, showed me how safe we are here, flirted with me, and now," her shoulders drooped. "You don't want me."

"That is not it." Allen cradled her cheeks in his hands, forcing her to look him in the eyes. "After...that person I'm not talking about anymore—"

"Gwen?"

"I...really struggled, and as much as I want more recordings to have to delete later, I...need this to be more than that."

There was no way she heard him correctly. She dipped her chin to stare through her lashes. "So you're telling me that you would rather do nothing with me physically," she set her hands on his chest, her fingers tracing his sternum, "than to have some hot, wild, no-strings-attached—" Her hands were about to be at his bellybutton when he grabbed her wrists and thrust her hands behind her back.

He growled in her ear. "That is precisely what I'm saying."

Kristen pressed her body against his as she whispered, "But it doesn't feel like that's what you're saying."

She could feel it. She could feel him giving in. His body conformed, enveloping hers. His mouth was hot against her ear.

"What's your name?"

His question caught her off guard. She was expecting more like, *say my name*, not this.

"What do you mean?"

"I mean, I want to know your name. Your *real* name." He kept a tight hold on her wrists, which she thoroughly enjoyed until now.

"It doesn't matter." She dropped her head.

"It does to me."

Kristen's eyes searched his. "Why? Why do you want to know when this...us...can be so simple."

"It's not simple if I don't know who you are."

Kristen opened her mouth but paused. Was she really about to tell him her real name?

"And don't try to lie to me."

Kristen couldn't help it; she smirked up at him. "I would never."

"I'm serious," he said, though his gaze lightened, and he released her wrists to hold her lower back. "I want to know who you really are."

Kristen lifted her hands and slowly grazed his shoulders. Her vision blur. "What if I told you I don't know who I really am." It was such a true statement; it hurt to say it out loud. Instead of spending her early twenties figuring out who she was, she spent them pretending to be everyone but herself.

Allen's lips were on her cheek. She didn't know she was crying until she realized he was kissing her tears away, moving to kiss the top of her other cheek. He licked his lips as he centered his gaze on hers. "What if I told you that I know?" Kristen blinked at him, not following. "Well, I don't *know* who you really are, but I have it... Your real name and all of that."

"What do you mean?"

Allen shrugged. "Remember how I told you my mother did a background check on Gwen?" Kristen nodded. "She did the same on you." They stared at each other for a long second. Neither made a move. Allen broke the silence quietly. "Want to look at it with me?"

Kristen understood every word he said but didn't feel panic or fear. All she felt was relief.

"I do."

Slowly, Allen released his hold on her and returned to the desk.

"How did she run a background check without my real name?" Kristen asked.

"I think my mother used your fingerprints." He rolled the chair out and offered it to Kristen, but she stood firm, staring at Allen. "Okay, I know she used your fingerprints. She got them off of your margarita glass." Kristen gaped at him as he winced. "Are you mad?"

"No," she replied earnestly, "I thought she was a little crazy, no offense," she added quickly, "but I'm impressed."

"She is crazy," Allen agreed, "but she can also be crazy paranoid when it comes to...outsiders, except for maybe men she meets in the grocery store," he said dryly.

"And men she meets on dating apps."

"She's not on any dating sites," Allen stated. "She only says stuff like that because she knows it bugs me."

Kristen didn't say a word. She wasn't going to be the one to burst that bubble, so she went along with it. "Hence, Sheila."

Allen ginned. "Precisely."

Kristen was playing it off, but her head spun when he mentioned fingerprints. Her initial thought was that Betty's basic online background check would find little, if anything. If she did a face search, there might be an old, outdated profile or two from previous jobs that required her to have social media accounts, but none of them were *her*. The hair, eye color, and face contouring would all be off from this unfiltered version of her. But fingertips. There was a lot that could come up with her fingerprints. Old social media accounts were just the tip of the iceberg.

"So," Kristen said, reluctantly lowering into the chair, "what if it's worse than I think, and I'm on America's Most Wanted?"

Allen gestured to the monitors from over the top of Kristen's head. "They only put killers on those lists, so you would have some idea if you would be on it or not, and if you are," he gave her a mock look of horror, "then I would be more than happy to take you straight to the bus station, buy you a ticket to anywhere you want, and let you be on your way."

"You would buy me a bus ticket just like that?" she teased. "I wouldn't even have to clean up the spare bedroom?"

Allen grimaced at the reminder of the flour-covered room. "Maybe I'd give you an hour or two to get started on that room first."

She liked this about him. Even in the face of potentially having a mass murderer in his safe room with him, he could joke around. Gwen was a fool.

"Here it is." He pulled up his email and opened one with the subject line, **Here's everything I could find on your girl.**

"Betty hired someone?" Kristen asked.

Allen's eyes were locked on the screen. "Not a hire as much as a long-running contract. She only has one person she trusts with this stuff." A hard line formed between his brows.

Here's everything I could find on your girl. I give her three out of five. Watch out for this one.

Kristen's stomach dropped. "What does 'three out of five' mean?" Allen's jaw flexed when Kristen glanced at him.

"It means," he said through clenched teeth, "you could be dangerous." Kristen flinched as Allen spun her chair to face him. He lowered to get eye level with her. "Look, I was joking about your being a killer, but if you are, no matter the reason, then you need to leave, and I mean right now. If you don't, the person who sent this won't be too far behind it, and there will be no lurking in a neighboring house. He will come here and take you. I won't be able to stop him."

Who in the twisted knight in shining armor does this guy think he is?

In light of her potentially being a *murderer*, he was still trying to protect her. His eyes followed her tongue as it traced her upper lip, but she couldn't enjoy it while he thought she was a cold-blooded killer.

"I haven't killed anyone. That I know of," she added, to be safe. "And who exactly did your mother hire to run my prints?"

Allen studied her for a moment. "An old family friend." He hovered the mouse over the attachment. "Last chance to leave without any questions."

Kristen pressed his finger on the mouse, opening the email without a word. She needed to see it.

After years of being someone else, Kristen was under the delusion that one of her aliases would be revealed—one of her earlier ones when she hadn't been as careful not to reveal too much of her identity. But when the email loaded, Kristen's jaw fell.

"Autumn Sky." Allen looked at her. "Is that your name?"

She remained silent, jaw open, scanning the email. All of her years keeping her identity secret, there it was. Her real name was out there for anyone who got ahold of this email. Whoever Betty had a "long-term contract" with had done a better job than all of the investigators, no doubt, hired to find her from her past jobs.

Of course, she thought. You can pretend to be anyone you want, but fingerprints will always tell the truth. She thought she had her cool kid phase arrest to blame for putting her fingerprints in the system but on closer inspection...

Autumn leaned forward and pointed at the line *date entered.* "What does that mean?"

Allen read where she gestured. "Your fingerprints were entered into the system when you were"—he scrolled to the top of the page, where her name and date of birth were listed—"two years old."

"Is that normal?" she asked, though she was certain it wasn't.

Allen shook his head slowly. "I don't know."

She sat back, wondering what it all meant. And how Allen would react. In total, it revealed three things...her name, date of birth, and, thankfully, only a small glimpse into what she did for a living.

FORTY-SIX

THE REPORT WASN'T MUCH, but it gave Allen enough to know who Kristen—or, more accurately, Autumn—was. Her actual name didn't sound like an actual name at all, but he knew without a doubt that the reports his mother got were never wrong, and how Autumn stared in awe assured him that it was accurate.

Autumn Sky was five years and two months younger than him—putting her at twenty-four years old—born in New Jersey, which surprised him since she didn't have a Jersey accent. But, the report's last section would have blown the socks off of a lesser man.

Autumn was wanted in connection with Olivia Chanel, a missing person's report filed under a different name by the woman's fiancé, thanks to fingerprints found at the scene. The missing woman fell off of a yacht outside of the U.S., where a twenty-carat emerald ring insurance claim was attached in the millions. The other was dated one day prior to her showing up in his hospital, where Autumn was wanted for questioning in a case where a Texas family had two instruments valued at over fifteen grand stolen. The only things connecting her to either case were her fingerprints found on the railing of the yacht and the instrument cases. The report also stated that there were no leads in either case besides Autumn's fingerprints being tied to both incidents.

At the end of the report, it listed that her prints were added two years after birth. With no notes of any deaths or injuries related to the crime or missing person's report, Allen could only make one synopsis. "So, three out of five doesn't mean you're dangerous, but that you are—"

"A thief."

"You're admitting it? "Allen asked, standing straighter.

"I guess I am. Now you know who I am, where I'm from, and what I used to do for a living."

He didn't know what to say, and how she sat back in the chair looking him over made him uneasy. Not that she was about to attack him or anything, which had been at the forefront of his mind when he read the three-out-of-five-danger rating, but she had effectively turned this around on him. It was on him to decide how this played out from here. His arms were crossed defensively over his chest, so he uncrossed them. It didn't feel right having his arms at his sides, but he kept them there. He wasn't going to look like he was standing in judgment of anyone. The left side of her mouth curled into a one-sided grin.

"What?"

She gave him an appraising once-over. "You are handling this way better than I thought."

"Uh, well. Considering that I had a legitimate fear that I would find out that you were a serial killer, this is great news. Well, not *great,* but—"

"Better than being a serial killer."

"Precisely."

"So, you don't hate me?"

"I do not." He watched her take a deep breath of relief. "But, I can't say I...trust you around valuables."

"That's fair," she said. "Because I might steal them?"

She said it, not me. "Precisely."

"Because you have so much to steal…" She fought to keep the corners of her mouth from curling up. As they continued nodding, a smile spread across Allen's face, but Autumn busted out laughing.

"I do have stuff worth stealing," he countered. The ridiculousness of how he sounded trying to coerce a self-proclaimed thief into believing that he had objects worthy of stealing did not get past him.

"Right," Autumn chuckled even harder. "You better watch out, or I might take off with your margarita machine."

"See?" He stopped himself from mentioning how he told Gwen it would be a hot item when he added it to their wedding registry. He was serious when he said that he was done talking about her. "Everyone wants that thing. And what about my car? That's definitely worth something."

"I am not going to steal your car," she told him, her laughter fading. "And as much of a killing I would make selling your margarita machine on the black market, you don't have to worry. I'm not going to steal from you. I promise."

Allen nearly opened his mouth to say she couldn't make that promise because, at that moment, he knew she had already stolen something of his.

His heart.

But this wasn't the time to bring it up. All signs of pleasure had left her face. She looked at the report again, her eyes filled with sorrow.

"What happened at the yacht?" he asked.

"What?" She blinked. "Oh, I jumped."

"You jumped?"

Nodding, she sighed.

"And I thought my ex-fiancée was bad."

"We weren't engaged," she said, without looking away from the computer. "Well, I guess we were, but I jumped right after he proposed. I guess he didn't see the boat that picked me up. To be fair, there were a lot of boats out on the water that day."

Allen waited. "Is that it?"

"No," she chuckled dryly and then noticed how he stared at her. "I was after the ring. He proposed, gave me the ring, and that was it. I jumped. There was a smaller boat waiting for me."

"And?"

She shrugged. "And the ring is somewhere in the U.K. if I had to guess."

That wasn't what he was asking. He wanted to know how or if her being a person of interest in those two cases had anything to do with her boyfriend attacking her on the beach. "What about Texas? That just happened."

Sorrow washed over her, sticking to her features more so than before. It was Texas that made her sad. "Yeah," she said softly. "He didn't deserve it."

Allen's brow furrowed. "*He?*" The report said a Texas family, not one man.

"The only 'he' by choice."

"So, your boyfriend—what?—pimped you and this married Texas guy—"

"No, no, no, that's not..." She buried her face in her hands. "You've got it all wrong."

Allen leaned on the desk beside her. "So explain it to me." She lowered her hands to blink up at him tiredly. "Or don't."

With one long, loud inhale and exhale, Autumn rolled the chair back, putting a little distance between them.

"Calvin wasn't my boyfriend. We worked together."

"You never dated?"

"We never so much as flirted." She frowned. "Your mom might like older guys, but I like men a few years older at most."

"And the Texas couple?"

Autumn glanced at the report. "I dated their son."

"And you *actually* dated this guy?"

"Yes, and I genuinely liked him. The others were all assigned to me."

"Others," Allen repeated. "So there are more than just these two?"

"Yes." After a moment, Autumn shook her head in frustration. "But that's not...they're not...it doesn't matter. I'm done with all of it. The Texas couple, it was their son I dated. I never would have hurt him if I wasn't scared that I was being followed—"

"By Calvin."

"No. Calvin was supposed to be my muscle, but he ignored me when I realized someone from our last job followed us to Texas."

She was dumping a whole lot more on him than he expected. Calvin was never her boyfriend. For obvious reasons, it made him feel better. Knowing that it wasn't an ex-boyfriend stalking her made him feel better, but then why would he be stalking her at all?

"Hold up," he interrupted as she mentioned meeting some guy named Phillip. "Was this Calvin guy with you on the beach when my mom found you?" She nodded. "And he attacked you?"

Her brow furrowed. "The last I checked, my stitches were quite real from him, leaving me for dead."

"But why? Why hurt you if the two of you worked together, and why would he come back for you if he left you for dead?"

"Why?" she repeated, taking a moment to contemplate the question. "Because we were both delusional," she sighed. "I thought we were working together when, in reality, he was biding his time for me to get the goods. Calvin thought he had made off with the goods when he left me stranded on the beach and took off with all my stuff."

"He...didn't?" he asked slowly.

"He did not."

Understanding dawned on him. "The USB."

Autumn froze. "What?"

Allen looked her over. "You do know what the key fob is, right?"

"Of course," she scoffed. "It is *my* flash drive. The question is, how do *you* know what it is?"

"Because before watching us last night, I may have also skimmed over your first few hours here."

A scowl passed over her face. It was great that this wasn't the case of an abusive ex like he initially thought, and even better that he currently had so few worldly possessions since, as of a few minutes ago, he found himself saddled up with a self-proclaimed thief. All he had to worry about now, besides his margarita machine disappearing, was Autumn's disloyal coworker, who may be back for the flash drive she hid at his house.

"What did you do with it?" she asked. Her scowl was more worry than anger.

"Not much, but I saw you hide it in my hide-a-key. Though, I would say that if—" he flinched when she lurched forward in the chair. "What are you—?"

"Is it in here?" She made a mad dash to open the drawers. She slammed the top drawer shut when she found it only held some pens and pencils. The second was full.

"That's just old stuff from college," he explained as Autumn rummaged through it. A few USBs of his own spilled out onto the floor. "It's not in there." She plucked out one of the two multi-ended USBs and gave him an accusing glare. "Those are all mine," he explained calmly. "Yours is outside where you left it. I promise."

"We'll see about that." She wrapped her fingers around the USB that looked like hers and slammed the drawer shut, nearly knocking him over when she stood. "How do I get out of here?"

"The keypad—8-8-8-8," he said as he entered it.

"Don't tell me the code," she barked and pushed past him the second the door opened.

She was in more of a rush now than when they returned from their walk on the beach. He caught up to her as she headed out the back door.

"Why didn't you tell me?" she grumbled.

"What would you have liked me to say?" he said. "'Hey, you know that key fob that my mother found because she felt it sewn into your pants?' Yeah, I couldn't get enough of watching us make out, so after I deleted the intimate stuff, I watched all the footage I had of you. I saw you hide it—and I know it isn't a key fob—in the spare key holder Gwen never told me about, which she used to hide a spare key to break into my house and take *my* stuff while I was at work after I was dumb enough to help her fill an entire U-Haul truck full of her belongings when I found out that she slept with our new anesthesiologist."

Halfway through his rant, Autumn glanced over her shoulder when he finally breathed. "See how easy that was," she said with a sly grin. Once she reached the water hose holder, her hand disappeared underneath.

"I moved it," he said when she slapped the empty metal. He reached under and around until he found the edge of the hard plastic. "There's a gap between the house and the... Got it." He plucked it from between the house and the metal water hose holder.

Without a word, she took it from him and hurried back to the house. Allen stuck behind her, trying to figure out what was happening in her head.

Allen tried to assure her it was in there when she stopped in her tracks, unable to open it. "Here," he offered, but she ripped it away when he tried to take it from her.

"I've got it."

He winced at how she dug her nail into the clasp until it finally opened. "Told you," he said as Autumn dumped the contents of the fake key fob into her palm. She pushed past him to the pool house. "What are you doing?"

"Someone found my hiding spot," she hissed. "Now I have to find a new one."

Allen didn't dare mention that he had known about it since the very first day she got here when he rewatched her first few hours at his house, catching her on the side of the house and sticking something under the water hose mount. He had thought that his mother had taken the spare key holder down after finding it after Gwen was able to get into his house and take stuff after moving out.

Allen backed away to give Autumn space when movement in his

peripheral vision made him turn to the beachline. "Evening, Dwayne!"

The older man had his walking cane, which meant he was going for a long evening stroll. Dwayne saluted them with his cane. "I see Norah was right."

Allen smiled and glanced at Autumn, who had a fake smile plastered as she waved back. "What is he talking about, Aut—?" he asked out of the corner of his mouth.

"What was that, Dwayne?" she called out, stopping him.

"Norah," the old man shouted, "she said the two of you were sweet for each other."

"Is that so?" Allen threw his arm around Autumn's shoulders. She tensed, but she didn't jerk away like he expected.

"That was supposed to be a secret," she yelled back, countering Allen's move by slinging her arm hard around his lower back, gripping his side far harder than his grasp on her shoulders.

"Secret's safe with me!" Dwayne yelled loud enough that if the neighbors were home, they were definitely in on the secret if they weren't before. "You two take care of yourselves."

"You, too," they said in unison. Once he looked away, they let go of one another.

"*Kristen*," she said, sticking the key his mother gave her into the pool house door. "You can call me Kristen."

"I can do that," he said. "Allen and Autumn sound too pretentious anyway."

She paused to gape at him, then mumbled something that sounded like cursing, followed by what he could swear was "Cupid," before opening the door.

When he followed her inside, she frowned. "What are you doing?"

"Don't look at me like that," he said, shutting the door behind him. "You think I'm going to leave you alone right after you saw your..." he paused.

"Coworker," she finished for him.

He had been about to say, 'abusive ex.' Her real name was one thing, but it was going to take him a minute to unload his feelings toward the man he managed to hate and be jealous of for being lucky enough to have Autumn's affection, only to hurt her, to him now being merely some dude she worked with. It did not, however, make Allen hate him any less. All he could have done was simply leave her stranded on the beach.

"I'm not a hundred percent sure I saw him," she said, walking over to the tower of cardboard boxes and then glaring at him. Allen stared out the door to give her a sense of privacy.

"Can you look up a picture of him on your phone?" he asked. "Then I can tell you if I saw him."

"You didn't see anyone," she said. "You've said that multiple times. All you saw was the graffiti." Some boxes shifted as she moved around. "Speaking of, shouldn't someone warn Celia that her son is probably about to be arrested for vandalizing your neighbor's house?"

"It wasn't Davie."

The movement of cardboard abruptly halted when Kristen sighed. "You can turn around." Allen did. "Why do you sound so sure that it wasn't Davie?" she asked, opening her palm enough for him to see both jump drives still in it and clanked them together.

"Because it was terrible. Want to see?" He withdrew his cell phone from his pocket as she stared at him quizzically. He pulled up the photo and held back a grin as she moved in closer to see.

"You took a picture of the house?"

"I did, in case I missed something, and to send it to Ed."

"And did you?"

He met her gaze as he handed her the phone. "What?"

"Did you see something you missed?"

He swallowed. "I don't think so."

An internal battle brewed. Should he apologize for seeing what she was hiding on his property? His head told him that he would be a chump if he did. It was his property, after all, but other parts of him wanted to do whatever was necessary to get back in her good graces so that he could touch her when she was in such proximity as she was right now. As it was, he fought not to loop a hand around her waist.

"You're right," she said, drawing him out of his thoughts, "it is horrible. What is it supposed to be?"

"A tornado is what Ed's calling it. The high school mascot."

She held the phone at an angle. "I can see it." She handed it back to him. "But it's definitely not Davie. It looks like a preschooler did that."

"A tall preschooler."

"Like Davie's tall friend who drives that truck." Allen raised his brow. "I only know because his friends were with him before they dined and dashed, leaving him with the bill."

"You paid for him and his friends?"

"How do you know that I paid for his meal?" She pretended to be shocked.

Allen smirked. "I don't think it's a secret that my mother tells me everything."

Her brow arched as she tipped her chin at him. "Surely, you don't tell her everything?"

She was flirting; it was a move in the right direction.

He grinned. "What did you have in mind that you wouldn't want my mother to know about?"

FORTY-SEVEN

Kristen raised her flash drive to his face, keeping his drive in the other hand. "Did you tell Betty about this?"

"She already knew you had it in sewn in your pants—"

"No, I mean about it *being* a flash drive."

There was no real point in her asking; she already knew. He had to have told his mother sometime before, during, or after his morning run. It was the real reason Betty showed up with the laptop in her purse.

"After my run this morning."

"What did the two of you find on the flash drive?"

Allen blinked. "Nothing. I didn't look."

"You didn't?"

He shrugged. "I found it and could tell from the feel that it wasn't an actual key fob."

Kristen kept herself from agreeing. She told her boss the same thing when he handed it to her, explaining that holding would give it away.

"I pressed a couple of buttons, and it opened up to the USB. I might have dropped it"—Kristen's eyes widened—"but it was fine. I moved it to a better spot between the house and the mount, so it was less likely to fall off."

"It's magnetic." It annoyed Kristen that he was acting like he was somehow helping her when he could have broken it for all he knew. "The hide-a-key had been there this whole time and hadn't fallen off, had it?"

"No," he admitted slowly, "but where I put it, it was against metal *and* squeezed against the house, so double protection from the elements and...your coworker."

He was doing it again, saying everything right to make her like him more. Who did he think he was? She didn't need him to protect her. She had it covered. She knew that she wasn't really mad at Allen. She was mad at herself for not hiding the flash drive better.

"So your mom took it upon herself to figure out what I was hiding?"

"She didn't." He shook his head. "Not that she didn't try. She texted me while I was at work, asking if I remembered the password for her laptop, but I didn't get around to my phone until I was rushing to get back here and check on you. She couldn't get into it—"

"Because she couldn't get into her laptop." Kristen laughed, not in humor or anger. This was therapeutic. At first, Allen chuckled with her, but her laughter became more hysterical.

Allen's eyes widened. "You okay?"

Betty hadn't lied to her about needing help getting into her laptop. Sure she may have lied about wanting to sign up to more dating sites, but that wasn't a big deal. Allen hadn't lied either when he told her it was still in the hide-a-key. Sure, they found the key fob and discovered it was a flash drive, but that was it. Her laughter subsided.

"I wouldn't say I'm okay."

Allen looked at her as if he wasn't sure if he should pretend to be entertained or scared.

"I am better than okay. I could have ended up anywhere," she said as she realized how fortunate she had been. "I could have ended up in jail, but instead, I ended up here with you." Kristen took a deep breath. "I just admitted that I could have been arrested, and you know about my past, and *still,* I am not terrified that you will call the cops." She gazed at him, unblinking. "I thought your mom was crazy about the Cupid stuff, but Cupid really does know what she's doing."

"You've been spending too much time around my mother."

Kristen looked up at him in earnest. "How do you do it? I have never felt safe in my life, yet here I am feeling..." she shook her head in disbelief, "safe with you."

"It's easy to feel safe with me because you are," Allen said as he pulled her to him. "When I first saw you in the hospital, I knew..." he paused. "Well, I didn't know it then, but I do now." He wrapped his arms around her shoulders. "You and I are one and the same."

"Is that so?" She peered up at him. "Have you gone to a formal event where you may have allegedly stolen a very expensive guitar and clarinet?"

"No, but I have secrets too. Like one that you may or may not have guessed at." He squeezed her gently. "I love—"

Kristen's mouth met his before he could finish. As much as she wanted to hear him say it, it was more than she could bear. She hated so much about her past jobs: the constant deceit and the schmoozing of rich, ungodly, narcissistic men. If any of them had been half the man Allen was, then she would not have been as successful as she had been. All this time, she planned on a life far away from her past crimes—maybe the Midwest, there weren't any wealthy men looking for her out there—but right now, in his arms, all she could think about was staying here with him.

Even she wasn't dumb enough to think Lady Luck would shine on her twice with a man like Allen.

She slid her flash drive and fake key fob into her front pocket. Allen grinned as he kissed her back. She put his drive into his pocket, giving her hands the freedom they required.

"Is the door—" Allen started as she pulled off his shirt.

Kristen breathlessly glanced to check. "It's locked. We're good."

And Kristen meant it. She was not going to let something like the cut on her head or an unlocked door get in the way this time.

"Sit," she instructed, backing him up to the couch and pushing him down. "Tell me how safe I am." She teased, slowly lifting her shirt.

Allen swallowed. "You've never been safer."

His arousal was as visible through his pants as the intense burning inside her. She tossed her shirt playfully over his face. When he had pulled it off, she unbuttoned her pants.

"Not so fast," he said, leaning forward and grabbing her by the hips. "I want to help you."

He was doing so much more than *helping* her. He kissed her lower abdomen as he slid her pants down her legs. She hated the part of her stomach he was kissing, but with his lips making love to the soft parts, even she couldn't hate it.

"Your turn," she said once she stepped out of her pants. She kicked them to the side, and her toes felt the flash drive inside.

This was for her, not a job or a high-stakes payday. She didn't have to pretend to be someone or something she wasn't. He knew who she was and still wanted her. Allen stood to pull off his pants as she stepped back to watch.

"What?" he asked when a smile crept across her face, his pants falling to the floor.

"No pink boxer shorts?"

He let out a disapproving growl as he saw his gray boxer briefs. "Ah, that would have been perfect."

"No," Kristen stepped forward to press her body against him. "This is perfect." She kissed him, and when his hands went for her bra strap, she shoved him onto the couch. "I undress me," she laid out her terms. "You undress you."

Allen couldn't get his underwear off fast enough. "You look amazing," he sighed, sitting back with only his socks remaining.

She could not agree more.

He relaxed his head against the top of the couch as she removed her bra. Her fingertips traced the waistband of her panties. She stood over him like a goddess and felt every ounce as powerful.

"I don't know what I should do with these," she teased, pretending to pull one side down at a time. "What do you think?"

"I'll take them off with my teeth," he offered, but Kristen shook her finger.

"I told you," she smirked. "*I* undress me."

The muscles in Allen's jaw flexed. "Why don't you come here and have a seat while you think about it."

Kristen took a seat right on his lap. She meant to tease him with her panties on, but after a few seconds of grinding against him, Allen's hand found its way to the inside hem of her underwear. She didn't stop him but ground harder as his fingers made their way underneath. His fingertips touched her, all of her, and then they were inside her. When she thrust against him, his fingers pulled back. She was about to protest until she felt them against her soft, swollen clit.

Her head dropped back, but she would not let history repeat itself. Kristen's hand came down on the other side of his and pulled her panties to the side. His head dropped back in pleasure as she sank on top of him.

FORTY-EIGHT

Bliss.

If Autumn thanked Cupid for their meeting, then he would, too. And, if she wanted him to keep calling her Kristen, he would do it. He would call her anything she wanted after this.

Hell, who was he kidding? It was five minutes, tops. His only vindication for the short time it took him to finish was that Kristen finished first. It made it worth it, the stress, the fear of allowing a stranger with secrets of her own into his life.

Those five minutes were electrifying. Every fiber of his being sizzled. It felt like a fall back to Earth afterward—one that he hoped would involve basking in their feat, holding each other on the couch for a while. It seemed they would when she leaned to give him another long kiss. He tried wrapping his arms around her, but she squirmed out of them with a happy grin and stood.

"How about the couch?" she asked, heading to the bathroom behind the bookshelf.

"What about it?"

"Did you and Gwen ever—"

"We did not." He winced at the reminder of his ex.

Gwen and all her memories did not deserve to be mentioned in Kristen's presence. Not anymore. How five minutes with Kristen could outshine a year-long relationship was beyond him, he thought as he reclined back on the couch. Allen shook his head. He knew what it was, and it wasn't just the entirety of his time knowing Autumn/Kristen but the endorphins flooding his system. Those tiny neurotransmitters that our brains release to keep our bodies moving were why he ran every day since the breakup. Though he preferred this over running any day of the week, his endorphins weren't enough for his mind to ignore what the future held as he rode the high.

"What's going to happen after this?" he asked once the toilet flushed and the sink went off.

She walked around the couch, looking magnificent. "What do you mean?" She picked up her underwear.

"I mean, after this," he said, pulling on his briefs. "Are you going to leave even if they aren't able to catch your ex...coworker?" Mirroring Kristen, he picked up his pants next. He gave her time to think it over as she pulled one leg up and then the other. The longer it took her to answer, the more optimistic he felt.

"Well," she said finally, "with the amount of flour you did or didn't dump in your spare bedroom, it'll take at least a day or two to hold up my end of the bargain I made with your mother."

"If it's money you need, I'll give it to you," he said, sitting back to enjoy the view while he could as she picked up her bra. Kristen arched a brow at him.

"Are you trying to make this a pay-to-play situation?"

"Nah," he sighed. "I could never afford you."

Kristen paused mid-latching her bra strap behind her back. She narrowed her eyes and shook her head disapprovingly. "The things that come out of your mouth."

"What?" Allen leaned forward. "You don't like me telling you how great you are?" He grabbed her hips and tugged her toward him.

"I won't stop you from saying it," she grinned as she obligingly stepped up between his legs. She laid her knees on the couch beside his hip, straddling him. "But it may take me a while to get used to it."

He didn't hide the joy from hearing her say that. "More than a day or two?"

Kristen set her warm hands on his shoulders, looking them over. "I mean, Calvin is still out there somewhere." Her fingers traced the tops of his shoulders so softly that it tickled. "I might need a big, strong man to keep me safe."

She traced down to his biceps. He wrapped his arms around her, trapping her from tickling him further.

"I'll protect you," he growled.

She arched a brow at him. "Are you sure you're strong enough?"

In one swift move, Allen stood. Kristen's legs wrapped around his midsection as he lifted her and turned to lay her on the couch. As he set Kristen on her back, her face contorted in pain.

"What happened?" he asked, releasing her.

Her hands went straight to her head. "I'm fine." He quickly helped her sit up to examine her head. "I think it was just too much of a jostle." She lifted her hands for him to see.

"You aren't bleeding," he said with relief and sat before her. "But that's enough fun for right now. Don't want to overdo it."

"Yeah, no repeat of last night." She smiled coyly as Allen grabbed her shirt from off the floor. "Give me ten, fifteen minutes, and then we can go again. If you have it in you."

"Oh, I have it in me, but as your doctor, I recommend that you keep the physical activity to a minimum—"

"Unless I'm stripping for you in your pool house?" She rolled her eyes at his professional opinion.

He grabbed his shirt but made no move to put it on as Kristen carefully put her shirt on over her head.

"Precisely," he said, tossing his shirt over his shoulder.

She looked from him to the door. "You aren't going to put your shirt on before we go outside? What if your mom happens to be watching your cameras?"

"We don't have to go outside to get to the main house," Allen explained, strolling past the couch toward the small kitchen area. "We can get to it through here."

He peeled the tape, holding the thick plastic drop cloth to the wall, where he planned to convert the space into a large safe room but never finished.

"You don't have to bust through your wall to prove how strong you are," Kristen said behind him.

He glanced slyly over his shoulder at her. "You already know I'm strong, but did you know I'm magic too?"

"Magic?" she frowned.

"That's right." He raised his hand over the drywall, no longer hidden by the plastic hanging loosely on one side. "Abracadabra." He pressed on the halfway point on the left section of drywall. The magnetic latch gave way, and the drywall popped open. "Like I said," Allen stepped back for her to look inside as he opened it, "I'm magic."

"And just when I thought you were about to ask me to add painting the pool house to my to-do list," Kristen mumbled as she peeked inside the small space the drywall opened up into. "Add this to the list of things you've surprised me with."

Allen took the margarita machine off of the single-shelf setup in the cabinet. He wanted to say something about how she kept surprising him, too, but as he turned to place the machine within the pool house, he asked, "Do you like to paint?"

"I used to," she said. When he set the machine next to the boxes, Kristen had already taken down the shelf and handed it to him. "But that is not me volunteering to paint your..." she scanned the pitiful excuse of a room, "pool house."

Allen chuckled, propping the shelf up beside the margarita machine. "It's not a pool house."

"It's really not," Kristen giggled, stepping back to appraise the interior cabinet, now void of obstructions. "I'm pretty sure a windowless pool house is an oxymoron."

"Agreed, and that is because it's a safe room." Allen scrunched his arms into his sides to step into the narrow space and knocked the cabinet door open on the other side.

He stepped out to the other side, walked out into the kitchen, and then offered his hand to help Kristen through. She walked through and then stared at the tall kitchen cabinet that she now knew was the door to what would be a safe room if Allen had finished the project.

"Does every room in your house have a hidden door?"

"Just the master closet and kitchen." He stepped through the kitchen cabinet to shut the drywall door behind them.

"And the pool house."

"It counts as the kitchen." He grabbed the mount inside the door that, from the kitchen, looked like the inside of a typical empty cabinet except that it lacked all of its shelving.

"I'm talking about the secret bathroom in the pool house," Kristen said as he stepped out of the cabinet.

"Oh, right." He hadn't considered the bookshelf door of the bathroom.

"It must be a common trait among the rich."

"What's that?"

"To be paranoid enough to need a safe room, but I get it." She crossed her arms over her chest self-consciously. "When people like me exist, I would want a safe room, too, if I had a ton of money."

"You're right," he sighed lazily as he approached her. She tried to turn from him, but he caught her by the elbow and pulled her into him, hugging her from behind. "I'll have to find a good hiding spot for my margarita machine."

She smirked at him. "You should put it in your safe room," she said as he gently rubbed her upper arms that she kept crossed. "Oh, wait. You told me the code to your safe room."

"I did." Allen froze in mock horror. "That doesn't sound like me."

She barked a laugh. His little joke did its job of getting a laugh from her. "Says the man who doesn't even have a lock on his cellphone."

"Hold up," he teased, "how do you know my cell phone isn't locked?"

Kristen turned, laying her hands flat against his chest. She rose on her toes. Her lips were close enough to his that he felt them part as she whispered, "Wild guess," and gave him a quick peck on the lips.

He released her as she backed out of his arms and into the house as Allen gaped at her. "You dug through my phone?"

Kristen shook her head. "That doesn't sound like me."

"You went through my phone," he repeated. "Hey, where are you going?"

"To clean up the flour."

FORTY-NINE

Having an exaggerated sway in her hips all the way up the stairs was a huge waste of time. Allen didn't even follow her out of the kitchen. When she reached the top of the steps, she gave a sultry turn, expecting to see him waiting at the bottom of the stairs. The sashay and the sultry turn were all for nothing; Allen was nowhere in sight. It looked like she would actually have to clean that room.

She underestimated how hard it was to clean loose flour from a room with only a broom. Sure, it could get the job done, but she had not been literal when she told Allen that it would take her a day or two. At this rate, it might.

After a couple of minutes of using the broom to brush flour off the wall, she was over it. At the same time, the key fob burned a hole in her pocket. It didn't feel right to have it on her person like this. Without having her pants with the hidden pocket, all she could do was put it in a regular pocket, and now anyone could reach in and snag it off of her. It needed to be in a safe place, and she didn't feel comfortable putting it in the pool house when there weren't any cameras that could keep an eye on it.

Allen should not have given her the code of his safe room. Within seconds, she stood in what should be the safest room in his house. She slid open the drawer that held his shoebox full of jump drives and cursed. A key fob would stand out like a sore thumb. The camera's footage flipped through the property on the monitors. Downstairs, Allen had lifted the blinds across the back and stared out with his phone to his ear.

She clicked and held the unlock and panic buttons on the key fob, and it popped open.

Allen was too good for her. He trusted her with his house and the code to his safe room, and when she asked him to call her by a fake name because the made-up name felt more like her than her actual name, he didn't miss a beat.

A thud came from the main bathroom behind her, and Kristen froze. Her mouth opened to call out Allen's name, but her eyes found him still on the ground floor, smiling at his phone. He wasn't in the bathroom behind her, and the only thing separating her from the bathroom was the walk-in closet and the safe room door she left ajar so she could slip out quickly. Maybe she had imagined the sound.

Another louder thud.

She was not alone.

FIFTY

KRISTEN CRIED OUT FROM UPSTAIRS.

"You okay?" he called from the foot of the stairs. When she didn't reply, he took the stairs two at a time.

He found the door to his bedroom ajar. He made a quick round through the room and adjoining bathroom, but no one was inside. Even his safe room was empty. Allen went to the spare bedroom, contemplating mentioning that he caught her via the alerts on his phone that his safe room tagged as the *master closet* had been opened and closed. He chalked it up to Kristen needing to check to make sure the house was still criminal-free—besides herself. For a second, he wished he had listened to his mother when she told him to install a camera in the safe room.

"Looks like you found the upstairs vacuum," he called out as he turned into the spare room, eyeing the clean line leading straight across the room that only the vacuum could make. The blinds were up across the back of the bedroom. He opened his mouth, but the only thing that came out was an audible exhale.

Kristen faced the back of the house in front of the floor-to-ceiling window, framed in the sunlight and ocean backdrop. She looked like an angel.

"I did, and it nearly gave me a heart attack. Why are you looking at me like that?"

"What do you mean?" He broke his gaze on her to ensure he stepped within the one flour-free strip.

"You were staring at me—"

"Because you look phenomenal."

She smirked and shook her head. "There you go again, saying those things."

"What do you mean the vacuum gave you a heart attack?"

He could see her playing back what he had asked. The question was meant as she took it, but he didn't want this to turn into him doting on her if it wasn't what she wanted.

"I was sweeping off the wall," she pointed to his right, where the flour piled against the baseboard, "when I heard someone pounding against the wall in another room." Allen could see where this was headed. "When I walked into your bathroom, no one was there, and I started worrying." She pointed squarely at the small, round vacuum. "But then that thing ran right into my foot. I swear I jumped at least four feet in the air before I realized what it was."

"That was when you screamed?"

"I did not scream."

He dipped his chin at her. "I heard you scream. That's why I came up here."

Her brows shot up. "You heard me scream, and it took you *this* long to get up here? Look," she gazed across the room, "the vacuum's already starting its second trek across the floor."

Kristen was right. Behind him, Allen turned to see the vacuum headed toward him, making a second, somewhat clean line beside the first. "Okay," he said, walking toward her, "so it was more of a yelp."

She pursed her lips, still watching the vacuum. "I may have yelped."

Allen stopped in front of her. "You know, I've never been jealous of a vacuum before." Her brow furrowed in confusion. Allen grinned. "It's supposed to be my job to make your heart skip a beat." She rolled her eyes and turned her back to him to stare back out at the beach. He inched up behind her and slowly wrapped his arms around her. "Since the vacuum should be able to clean half the room," he said into her ear, "why don't you come downstairs and sit with me in the recliner and watch some TV?"

"Half the room?"

"If that," he said. "Those things can hold two cups worth of flour, tops."

She glanced over her shoulder at him. "Two cups? How much did you dump on the floor?"

Allen avoided her gaze. "Not that I would know for sure since, like I told you, there was flour on the floor before I got in here," he tilted his head to the side as if doing the calculations in his head, "I would say the…entire five-pound bag."

Kristen's brows shot up. "Five pounds! How many cups is that?"

"Eighteen, I'm pretty sure."

"Impressive calculation skills," Kristen said. Allen grinned. "You doctors really do know everything."

Being a doctor had nothing to do with it. He became the man of the house out of necessity when his father died. It was also out of necessity that he became the chef, knowing that his mother shouldn't be spending the money on takeout every night once it was only the two of them.

"It's a simple conversation from pounds to cups," he shrugged.

Kristen shook her head. "I'll take your word for it. How long do we have until it's full?"

"If I dump it now, we should be twenty, thirty minutes until one of us needs to check on it again."

"Are we really going to be watching TV?" She eyed him suspiciously.

"Not to take any chance with your stitches," he said slowly, hating the doctor side of himself more than ever at this moment, "I say we just watch some TV."

Sadly, Kristen bobbed her head in agreement. "Okay," she turned for the door, "what do you have to watch?"

Never had the thought crossed his mind that he would be thanking Gwen for her outlandish greediness, wanting everything inside *his* house. As Kristen settled on his lap like they were high school sweethearts who couldn't get enough of each other, he silently thanked Gwen for taking every piece of furniture, minus the recliner they were nestled in.

He spread his legs so she would be comfortable lounging between them and his bare upper body.

"Never would have pegged you for a sports fan," he said, pushing down a hard spot between the cushion and armrest.

"Just the inspirational games."

"Inspirational?"

"You know, like a team on a losing streak who gets a win that turns into a string of wins, and then they make it to the playoffs."

"Like what you see in movies?"

"It's real life, too. I watched a baseball game a while back where this young player was doing horribly; fans booed him nonstop. Then everyone decided to cheer instead of boo him for the next game, and when they gave him a standing ovation when he was on the plate, he knocked it out of the park."

"You mean the Trea Turner story?"

"It's not a story," she said. "It was real life."

So much for her being a sports fan; she doesn't even know the name of the player whose story she enjoyed. "I know the game you're talking about," he said. "The batter's name is Trea. He did a ton of interviews about it afterward."

"Then yeah."

"So you like watching the redemption stories."

"That's what I said, the inspirational stuff."

"So you're an inspirational-against-all-odd sports fan."

She turned her head to smile up at him. "Exactly."

Allen made a mental note to look up a few games to show her. The last thing he wanted was to interrupt her in his arms.

Kristen was scrolling the channels when the doorbell rang. She jumped.

"It's for me," he said, reluctantly lowering the footrest. "I'm expecting a delivery."

"Dinner?" she asked, getting off him so he could answer the front door.

He winked. "Better."

RUNNING FROM CUPID

FIFTY-ONE

"School supplies?" Kristen asked as Allen triumphantly set two oversized plastic bags on the kitchen island. He looked a little disheartened by the way she said it, but she couldn't help it. When he returned with the bags, she was a little disheartened to see that he had put his shirt on, but since he had to answer the door, she couldn't blame him.

"Art supplies," he corrected, removing a sketchpad from the first bag.

"You got someone to deliver art supplies?"

"You did, actually. Norah's sister runs the local craft store and asked how you were doing as soon as she heard it was me," he explained as he continued to unload the supplies. "When I told her I wanted to get you some things since you like to paint and draw, she was keen on getting you the basics which," Allen grimaced inside of the bag as he took out paintbrush after paintbrush, "I had no idea would cost so much."

"How much did you spend?"

Allen enthusiastically shook his head. "You don't want to know."

She could only imagine as she started unloading the second bag.

He spent hundreds, if she had to guess. "Oils and acrylics," she muttered as she took out the twelve-pack of each and a travel-size watercolor palate.

"I didn't know which you preferred, and please don't say spray paint because you *really* don't want to know the price for one of her big canvases." Allen shivered.

Kristen laughed. "Don't worry; I have no interest in reliving that phase of my life."

They finished taking everything out, and Kristen could only grin and shake her head at the stuff across the counter.

"What?" he asked.

Don't cry, don't cry, she silently consoled herself until she could speak without her voice breaking. "This is the most considerate gift anyone has given me."

Of all the honest things she shared with him, this was the truest.

"Better than letting you stay in an oxymoron pool house?"

"A hundred times better."

She could point out that she hadn't spent a single night in his oxymoron pool house, but then she wouldn't want him to think that everything that had happened between them was to keep her out spending the night in there. That was how Kristen would have to look at it when she left. She would compartmentalize everything she felt toward him and tell herself that it was all to give her a place to stay while things died down.

"What's wrong?" Allen asked, seeing the merriment drain from her face.

"I don't know where to start."

He mistook her honest statement about everything swirling around in her head as literal.

"How about starting with the basics?"

He set the pack of pencils and sketchpad in front of her. "You can paint me like one of your French girls." Allen bobbed his eyebrows at her enticingly.

Kristen stared at him. "Are you quoting *Titanic*?"

Allen nodded. "I wasn't sure if you would get the reference since the movie was before your time."

"You aren't *that* much older than me," she countered.

"I know, but…"

"But what?" she pressed.

"Nothing, "Allen shrugged.

Kristen rolled her eyes as she picked up the pack of pencils. "Finish your thought. Let's hear it."

"It was nothing." Allen went to the recliner. "All I was going to say was that…" he seemed to struggle with his words, "I only watched it because my mother made me."

She fought not to laugh, but he was right; hearing it reminded her of yet one more thing she missed out on with her own mother. It was a bit of a shot to the gut, but she survived worse. Being reminded that she had no mother to force her to watch old movies wasn't that big of a deal.

Kristen peeled the plastic covering away from the pencils. "All it took for me to watch it was an extremely boring weekend with nothing to do but watch reruns on TV."

"You've got better options this weekend." He made a show of pulling his shirt off. "You can use *this* physique," he bounced his slightly larger than average pecs at her, "for inspiration."

She watched with enthusiasm until he started to take off his pants. "Hold on there, Mr. Model. Don't forget the blinds are up."

Allen paused to stare disparagingly out the back window before pulling his pants back up.

"Good call," she snickered and glanced at the camera tucked under the back patio.

Her gaze drifted past the patio and over the wooden fence that blocked her view of the neighbor's backyard. Only two houses down sat the house that may or may not have an ex-partner hidden inside of it.

"Want me to close them?" Allen asked, effectively breaking her daze.

"I'm good." She grabbed a sharpened pencil out of its packaging. "I think I'm going to start by doodling. Why don't you sit in your favorite recliner so I may sketch you like one of my French girls."

His face lit up, and he laid back in the recliner. She moved to a stool at the end of the island for a better view, giving her an unobstructed view of the backyard. She opened the sketchbook to the first page but could only stare out at the pool and the lapping ocean water beyond it. The view was beautiful, but staring at the horizon only made her think back to the first sunrise she had witnessed in Redrock before her world was turned upside down.

"You're safe," Allen said from the recliner.

"How do you do that?" she asked, putting pencil to paper.

"How do I do what, this?" He tightened his stomach, ushering a more defined abdomen than most men she knew. She didn't laugh, though she knew that was what Allen hoped for.

"How do you guess what I'm thinking so well sometimes?"

"Sometimes?" he barked indignantly. "We both know I was one hundred percent right." His brows rose, waiting for her to admit he was right, but Kristen kept sketching instead, glancing back and forth from him to her sketchpad. "It's your eyes," he said finally. "They give you away."

The pleasure she experienced sketching in an actual sketchbook, not a napkin or the back of a receipt, was not enough to ignore. "My eyes have never given me away."

"Lie to someone else," Allen stretched out farther on the recliner, throwing off the basic outline of his upper half she started, but she could work with it.

"My eyes didn't give me away when I jumped off that yacht."

"Was it hot outside?"

She stopped sketching to look at him. "On the yacht?" Allen nodded. "Yeah, it was summertime."

Allen picked up the remote. "Were you showing a lot of skin?"

"I may or may not have been in a bathing suit."

Allen smirked. "Then he wasn't looking at your eyes."

Kristen mirrored his expression. "Or you're just full of crap."

Allen's jaw dropped. "Me?"

Kristen threw her hand up at him. "Right there. Don't move."

Allen froze, but his eyes scanned down. "Is this my good side?"

"Don't talk," she instructed. "I'm drawing your face." Allen's face contorted. "What are you doing?"

"I'm giving you the smolder."

"Please don't," she snorted, "you look…"

"Hot?"

"Confused or in pain—I can't tell."

"How about this?" Allen took on a more stoic expression as he stared at the TV.

"Perfect."

She didn't need him to be still to sketch, but she wouldn't get in the flow with him talking about how he could read her solely through her eyes. She'd have to close her eyes when she didn't want him to read her thoughts. Her head still protested from how physical things got in the pool house.

Allen dumped the robot vacuum from upstairs. "I have bad news and good news."

Kristen perked up in the living room recliner. "I would say bad news first, but I already saw you put your shirt back on."

"Having my shirt on is not the bad news, unfortunately. The bad news is that the vacuum is officially dead."

"You sure it wasn't because it was full?"

The vacuum had been sitting idly on the floor the first two times Kristen checked on it, but once she dumped the tray full of flour, it started right back up.

"It is dead, dead. It couldn't even make it to its charger on its own. I had to set it on its charger myself."

"And the good news?"

"Good news," Allen puffed out his chest, "I swept the rest of the flour off the walls, so technically, the room is…"

"Seventy-five percent clean."

"I was going to say closer to fifty, but we can go with seventy-five." He scanned the top of the clean kitchen island. "You put everything up?"

"Everything but my pencil and sketchpad." She raised them from her lap to show him. "I put the rest in the empty cabinet under the island."

Allen noticed the baseball game paused on the television. "Was I right?"

Kristen hit play on the baseball game Allen had paused before he went upstairs. "You were." They watched the batter not only miss the ball but lose his bat, but instead of the crowd booing as they had done every other game, they stood and gave the batter a standing ovation. His next swing, with the crowd cheering him on, he crushed it. "The original clip I saw wasn't in real-time, though. It's kind of sad to see how fast it all happened. The viral video I watched had a bunch of commentary—"

"What in the... Is that Milo?"

By the time Kristen rose from the chair, Allen was at the back door. Milo was on the beach, trotting happily toward the gate on the metal fence.

"Stay here," Allen instructed, unlocking the back door. "Do you have your phone on you?"

"It's in the kitchen cabinet."

He paused to look at her. "Grab it. If I wave at you, call the police."

She rushed to get her phone. "I'll call Betty."

"A step ahead of you," he shouted.

Kristen grabbed her phone and stood at the back door, watching Allen. Milo wagged his tail at the gate. Allen passed the pool when Milo barked happily as Betty appeared from the beach. Kristen headed out the back door.

"I'm happy you put your shirt on now," she muttered to Allen as she hurried up behind him.

He looked as relieved as she felt. "Me too."

"I thought she had a date."

Allen smirked. "Maybe he canceled."

"She looks awfully happy that happened," Kristen noted. Across the yard, at the back gate, Milo waited eagerly for Betty, but she slowed when she laid eyes on Kristen and Allen. She smiled and turned to look behind her.

There was a pause in Kristen's step the second she saw who trailed behind Betty. Allen cursed under his breath, but Kristen couldn't decipher what he said over the cursing in her head.

No fucking way.

FIFTY-TWO

Allen chalked it up to having to put on a fake front as the supportive son who encouraged his mother to find love again back at the diner. He could not for the life of him force his mouth into a smile as his mother, in her infinite ability to piss him off, made introductions to Kristen and himself to the real estate agent standing before them. The worst part was that Kristen looked even more uncomfortable by the encounter than he did. His mother could not pick a worse time to drop in with a guest.

"Back up, Milo," his mother grumbled, using her foot to push Milo away from the man's feet.

"Say that for me again," Kristen said to him.

"Nicola Bray," he repeated with an accent that Allen couldn't place.

Betty stepped over to him and gently elbowed him in the ribs. "You are glaring," she mumbled without moving her lips.

"What brings you to Redrock?" Kristen asked.

"My clients heard about this view," he broadly waved his arm across the beachline, partially turning his back to Allen and his mother, "and I knew that if I didn't find them something out here, they would find an agent who would."

Allen steered his mother a few steps away from them. "How do you expect me to act when you show up here unannounced? When I saw Milo running up to the house without you, where do you think my mind went? And don't get me started on the fact that I know you walked here with someone you just met from your house."

His mother grimaced. "You don't need to worry about my modesty."

"This isn't about you—"

"We stopped by my house strictly for business," she said over him, looping her arm around the real estate agent's.

"What business?" Allen dared to ask. He wanted to see if his mother could think up an excuse with all eyes on her, but Nicola spoke first.

"Real estate," he grinned. "Once your mother and I sat to eat, she mistakenly asked me how I like my job. We ended up on the topic of her house and what she could expect to get with its view because of the market right now. What she didn't tell me was how nice of a property *you* had."

Allen fantasized about ten ways to wipe the grin off of the man's face. "My house isn't for sale," he growled and turned to his mother. "Why did you bring him here?"

"Whoa, whoa," Nicola took a step back, "you misunderstand me—"

"We weren't walking to *your* house," his mother spat. "We were going to look at the Lintzell's house when Milo felt the urge to tell his big brother hi."

Ignoring the comment said to piss him off even more, Allen kept his gaze on his mother. "You cannot be serious about selling your house."

Betty pointedly looked between Kristen and the chump she brought with her. "Will you two excuse me? I need to have a word with my son."

"By all means," Nicola said with the bow of his head.

Kristen nodded. As Betty gripped him by the forearm to pull him, it dawned on Allen how quiet Kristen was. Not only that, but she did not appear to revel in his frustration with his mother like she usually would.

He went obligingly with her, but when they stopped at the metal fence, he made sure to keep Kristen in his eyeline as his mother chewed him out.

"What the hell is wrong with you? I know you may be a little sensitive after the scare at the neighbor's house, but can I not have one adult evening for myself without you losing your shit with me over it?"

"Take as many adult evenings as you want, but *this*," he started to point right at Nicola, but his mother quickly swatted his hand, "is not an adult evening for *yourself* when *myself* is involved." She opened her mouth, but he wasn't done. "And don't come at me with the whole, *but you were outside* bit. You could have waved and carried on down the beach with Mr. Real Estate Agent and had sex on the beach for all I care—"

"That is enough," his mother hissed. "I will have you know..."

Allen stopped listening. When his eyes drifted to Kristen, he lost all interest in the conversation.

The way Kristen kept eyeing the real estate agent piqued his interest. That, and she kept glancing in Allen's direction as if he was missing something. Not in a come-and-save-me way, but more to see if he and Betty were still talking. At first, he pretended he wasn't watching her, but when he stole another glance and caught the harsh manner in which she stared at Nicola, Allen didn't look away.

BO GRANT

FIFTY-THREE

"So," Nicola looked Kristen's face over, "what do you do for a living?"

Kristen could barely keep it together. A part of her wished she would have stayed inside and continued sketching or watching another game. The other part of her knew that this was the natural order of things. It had only been a matter of time before some version of this scenario played out.

"I'm a professional art thief," she said, enjoying the ability to be brutally honest. It had been two years since she had seen him last, but the wrinkles across his face had doubled as if it had been closer to ten. "I also dabble in the occasional jewelry heist."

Nicola smirked, causing the crow's feet etched in the corner of his eyes to deepen. "Is that so?"

"That's right," Kristen said coldly. "I can work my way into a person's life in a matter of hours."

She glanced at Allen; Nicola did the same. Allen had been looking in her direction, but he turned away once her eyes were on him. They didn't have to worry about being overheard. Betty was being too loud as she gave her son an earful.

"Sounds like you're as good at your job as I am."

"Cut the crap. What are you doing here?"

Nicola's corny accent disappeared as he stepped closer to her to quietly say, "Did you think I would leave my most valuable asset stranded alone with no way to get home?"

She narrowed her eyes on him. "You mean, unlike all the other times you've done that to me?"

"Ouch." He pretended to wince. "You called me, remember? Do you have the flash drive on you?"

He didn't waste any time. "I called to let you know that Calvin flipped sides," she said, ignoring his other question. "I can take care of myself. That's why you hired me, remember?"

He narrowed his gaze at her. "Taking care of yourself, huh? Looks like this guy is taking care of you." If there was an insinuation in his comment, she ignored it. "Never pegged you for a tacky glass house kind of girl."

"If anything's tacky, it's that accent."

"Women love this accent." He cut his eyes in Betty's direction. "Took me less than a day to be standing in front of you with none the wiser."

Kristen grimaced at the thought of anyone finding him attractive. Not that her boss wasn't. He had a natural debonair way about him and a terrible accent, but his list of crimes went on for miles past all his charms.

"Where's the drive?" he asked. "We need to get out of here."

"We can't just...run off."

"Yes, we can. It's a short run. My rental is parked at her house. I got a bag of disguises. I'll have us paid by this time tomorrow."

Kristen frowned. "That's the plan? Run off without any explanation? Leave both of them wondering what the hell is going on?" She heard her own words and fought not to wince. "I know," she said, stopping her boss from pointing out that Kristen and her previous aliases had done just that in every one of her heist jobs. However, this wasn't a heist, and Allen was not a job. "We need a better plan."

From how he looked at her, she knew he sensed something was off. "I don't have it on me, and neither of us should be out in the open like this." His smug expression turned to confusion, and Kristen mirrored it. "Did Betty not tell you I'm pretty sure I saw Calvin in the Lintzell's house?"

He smirked. Of all things to make that face at, learning that Calvin was close by should not have been one of them.

"Not possible," he said with a shake of his head. "My guys have been tracking him since he arrived in Charleston. He stayed in crowds so they couldn't grab him, but the last call I got, he was headed north, to New York if I had to guess. They'll have him by nightfall."

"What are they going to do to him?"

He gave her a sinister grin. "It's best if you don't know."

"What are you two talking about?" Betty asked as they strolled over as if she hadn't just been scolding her son, not twenty feet from them.

"She was just telling me about her scare earlier," Nicola explained, his accent returning. His honesty surprised Kristen. "I've had my fair share of scares over the years showing empty houses. I once sold an entire plantation solely on the buyers' beliefs that it was haunted."

"Fascinating," Betty said. "Was it full of ghosts?"

"I didn't see a one, and I spent a week on the property going over it with the buyers. It didn't stop them from turning it into a big tourist attraction, though."

Kristen was impressed. Not only by her boss's ability to tell a good story but also by how hard Betty smiled enduringly at him. Allen's unyielding frown almost made it entertaining, but it didn't stop her boss.

"So," Nicola said, holding his arm out for Betty, "are we ready to go check out the house?"

"Sure am." Betty looped her arm around Nicola's and gave Allen a smug glance.

"Would either of you like to accompany us?"

Allen shook his head as he glared from Nicola to his mother. "If you're going to act like visiting the Lintzell's house isn't the dumbest thing you could do, then you better have Sheila on you."

Nicola glanced between Allen and Betty with his brow raised.

"It's best if you don't ask," Kristen warned as Allen stomped off. "I think we'll stay here."

"Probably for the best," Betty muttered.

Nicola nodded, and off they went. He probably hoped Kristen would tag along to figure out where and when to meet once she had the flash drive, but she needed some distance from him. She had wanted him to swoop in and save the day two days ago. The whole situation in which he popped up today seemingly out of nowhere had thrown her. *Why go through Allen's mother? How did he even know that going through Betty would lead to her?*

"How will you look at a house if no one's there?" Allen called out far too loud for the couple to be only a few feet from them. "Or are you hoping the cops will still be there?"

"Already got the lock box code," Nicola said over his shoulder with a dismissive wave. A grin crept across Kristen's face when he finally caught on to the last part, frowning at Betty. "What cops?"

To his credit, he didn't slow down, nor did he physically pull away when Betty shrugged, Kristen barely catching what she told him. "I told you, the vandals. It wasn't anything serious."

Kristen should have warned him that the house was the same one she may or may not have seen Calvin in, but since he blew off her fears about Calvin being in Redrock, she hadn't said a word. He could figure it out himself.

Kristen smirked, too, imagining him and Calvin bumping into each other inside the house. At least it would be Calvin running for it this time.

Milo tried to wedge himself between their feet, but Betty shooed him away.

Kristen joined Allen by the pool as he shook his head in disapproval.

"Did he say something to you?"

Kristen blinked at him. "What was that?"

"Did he say something that bothered you?"

"No," she swung her arms loosely at her sides, fighting the urge to cross her arms self-consciously over her chest, "it's just, you know, them going to that house worries me for them."

A gleam lit up his eyes. "If I were to call Ed, we wouldn't have to worry about them."

I'm going to miss this, Kristen thought as she giggled at his deviousness. "You wouldn't dare."

Lines formed across Allen's forehead. "Wanna bet?"

"Do you think that's wise to do when your mother was just chewing you out?"

"I hear what you're saying, but I don't hear you saying no."

"Hmm," she thought for a second, "you know what? Call him."

"You sure?" Allen asked, swiping his phone open.

"Better safe than sorry. Call him." Once he had the phone to his ear, she added, "Worst-case scenario, it pisses your mom off enough that he ends up your stepdad."

Allen's jaw dropped, but Kristen could hear the phone ringing in his ear. And, as if on cue, Ed answered the phone before Allen could fully second-guess his actions.

"Hey, man," Allen responded as Kristen cracked up. "I, uh, was calling to see if your guys ever found anything? No... Well," he stared at Kristen, who gave him a thumbs up, "that's good because my mom is headed there now with a real estate agent she either went on a date with or is about to after they look at the Lintzell's place. It's not Sweeney—this guy's from out of town and is checking out some houses for one of his clients. They met at the grocery store. You read my mind. Let me know how it goes." He looked smug as he hung up. "He's talking to my neighbors about what happened, so he'll be there in the blink of an eye."

"What was that?" Kristen exclaimed. "What part of you ending up with a stepdad did you not understand? Are you wanting a stepdad?"

Allen blinked at her. "He's only going over there to double-check that he didn't miss anything. Why are you looking at me like that? You gave me the thumbs up."

"I gave you a thumbs up to get off the phone, not to talk him into going to the Lintzell's when your mom is already mad at you. She's going to kill you if she finds out you were behind Ed showing up while she and Nicola are there." She headed into the house, leaving Allen staring at her. No amount of sketching could lessen today's emotional overload, and it wasn't over yet.

"You're not going to tell her," Allen called after her, "are you?"

RUNNING FROM CUPID

FIFTY-FOUR

"Food's ready," Allen shouted from the kitchen. A few minutes later, when he didn't hear Kristen coming downstairs, he went to look for her.

A toilet flushed as he made it to the top of the stairs. He followed the sound of a faucet running to the main bedroom. Kristen emerged from the bathroom as he entered the room.

"Uh, oh," she said, shutting the door behind her. "Don't tell me you need to use the bathroom too?"

"I was coming to let you know that dinner is ready."

"Oh good," she let out a sigh and grinned. "That saves me the embarrassment of telling you to use a different bathroom then."

"It does," he grinned back, "but it keeps me from experiencing your refreshing honesty."

"What a shame."

"Travesty, really. I hope you enjoyed all the food we've had so far," he said, glancing at the bathroom door behind her before he turned to the hallway, "because all I had to work with were our leftovers. The good news is there's one drumstick left, so if you want it, you better make your plate first."

"You won't hear me complaining," Kristen said, heading for the stairs. "I once lived off of one pizza for eight days."

"Sounds like we had a similar college experience."

Kristen glanced at him. "I was in eighth grade." His head jerked up to look at her as they descended the stairs. "I know, I know, but it wasn't as bad as it sounds."

"It doesn't sound bad at all," he told her. "You were lucky to have a whole pizza. In seventh grade, I spent two months living off of Vienna sausages and crackers. I would have killed for a pizza."

She gave him the same look he had given her before they both smiled. He realized, in their silence, that they were both being honest. Seventh grade had been the saddest year of his life. Had eighth grade been the saddest for her? He should have asked, but he didn't. Other things were weighing on his mind. Like the way he was pretty sure she had been lying about why she was in his bathroom.

"Bon appétit," he announced once they reached the kitchen. "I reheated everything."

The leftovers from her time in his house were buffet-style across the stove and counter.

"Looks great," she said, filling her plate.

Allen set his plate down. "I meant to grab something from upstairs. I'll be right back."

"I'll be here," she said.

Allen hurried to the safe room. Kristen was still downstairs, so he took a beat and looked around. Everything appeared to be how they left it earlier.

The desk drawer—hadn't he shut it all the way earlier? If he had, it wasn't now. Allen pulled it open. All of his stuff appeared to be there still. Not that it would matter if all of his crap were gone. The only reason he kept any of it was because it felt wrong to throw it all out when he graduated. So much money and stress went into medical school that he lugged it all around and kept it in the safe room as if it meant something to him.

He should have a bonfire of all of his old crap. That would be fun.

He shut the drawer, and with two clicks of his mouse, he knew he was good. Kristen could have been checking the cameras, but she hadn't seen his emails to Elvis. Her possible honesty about being in the bathroom made him feel even worse about his secrets. Allen had tried to tell her. No, he hadn't *really* tried because if he *really* wanted her to know, he would have told her. His excuse for an attempted confession failing was his brain winning the war over his heart.

As Allen turned the lights out in the safe room, the motion alert came on the center screen. With it, a view of his driveway popped up of a car pulling into it. The front passenger door swung open as Allen noted the Rolls Royce figurine on the hood.

"Son of a—"

Kristen was walking up from the back of the house as Allen descended the stairs. "I think it's your mom."

Betty's voice rang out through the front door. "It's me." Keys rattled on the other side of the door. Allen paused on the stairs.

"We could act like we aren't here."

Kristen smirked. "And what?" she asked, keeping her voice low. "Hope she can't figure out which key it is?"

It was as good of an idea as any, but his mother's face pressed against the blurred glass. "I see you on the stairs."

Allen deflated. "Let her in, I guess."

The second his mother was through the door, she charged straight for him. "Did you not give me the key to the front door?" she asked, holding up her janitor-sized keyring.

"I gave one to you. I couldn't tell you which one it is."

Kristen went to shut the door but then stopped. "My bad—didn't see you there." She opened the door wider for Nicola. "Is Milo with you too?" She looked behind him.

"We dropped him off at the house," Nicola explained, "and

decided to drive my car. I forget how much a workout walking on the beach can be."

Kristen seemed amused by that. "Done a lot of beach walking, have you?"

Allen frowned at his mother. "Do we just show up to each other's houses now with uninvited guests we don't know?"

"Be nice. We came back as a courtesy," she said, loud enough for the others to hear. "Nicky had the sweetest idea to take pictures so you could see it."

Allen didn't hide his lackluster as Nicola strolled up to his mother's side. "Pictures of what?"

His mother took out her cell phone. "Of the house, silly."

"We're still on that?"

"If I can get it for the price Nicky thinks I can, it's basically a done deal."

Allen grimaced.

"Nicky?" Kristen echoed, joining them.

"It's my new nickname," Nicola grinned proudly as Allen's mother nudged him affectionately.

Allen swallowed a lump of saliva, fighting the urge not to gag in their faces. Kristen appeared equally put off by the exchange.

"You might not want to show him the house," Nicola warned, "he might want to put an offer in, too."

His mother let out an atrocious giggle. If this were how she was going to be around her dates, then it would be the first and last time she brought one around him. "He wouldn't dare."

"No," Allen agreed with zero amusement, "I would not."

"It's hard to see in here," his mother said, flipping through the photos. "Turn on the light, will you?" she asked Kristen, closest to the light switch by the front door.

Nicola eyed the blackout blinds. "If you open some curtains, you'll get that natural light that these homes are known for."

Kristen looked at Allen.

"We can go to the kitchen," he said, reluctantly guiding Nicola and his mother to the back of the house.

"Wait until you see this view, Nicky. You are going to love it."

Allen and Kristen fell in at a distance behind them. He slid his arm over her shoulders to whisper, "Say the word, and I'll kick them out so we can eat in peace."

Kristen shook her head. "It's okay." She looped an arm around his midsection and peered up at him. "I liked watching you and your mom together. It lets me imagine what life would have been like if I hadn't lost mine."

He could see a hint of tears forming in her eyes. *Not tears.* This was not how he wanted their day together to go. No sooner had his lips parted to ask her if she was okay had something caught Kristen's eye ahead of them, and her grip loosened.

Nicola glanced over his shoulder at them as they turned the corner into the kitchen. "Haven't finished moving in, I see."

"It's a long story," his mother said.

Keeping Kristen at his side, Allen mumbled, "Is everything all right?"

"Why wouldn't it be?" she asked, dragging Allen into the living room.

A list of whys popped into his head. "Seeing Calvin earlier, for one," he muttered, not knowing if mentioning Kristen's mother would be wise, given that they were in mixed company. Not to mention how annoyed he was with his mother at the moment.

Before he could decide, Nicola was right in front of them. "We haven't intruded, have we?"

"No," Kristen said as they walked into the kitchen to see the apparent intrusion on their meal. "We were just about to eat, but no big deal."

"We'll be out of your hair," his mother said, her eyes on him before he could utter a word, "once you see how nice they redid the inside of that house."

Allen glanced at Kristen, who gave him an encouraging nod. "All right, show me the house."

The first picture was the back patio with the stickers still on the brand-new barbeque pit built into the mini outdoor kitchen. "You took a picture of cookware you know you won't use?"

"Nicky took that one," his mother said, sliding to the second photograph.

"The floors are in good shape," he muttered to make his mother happy.

"I thought so, too," she beamed.

"That's a nice car out front," Kristen said as Allen pretended to be interested in the Lintzell's house to placate his mother.

"Thanks. It's my first Rolls. Want to take a look at it?" Nicola asked, taking out his keys. "It's nice."

"Sure. We'll be right back."

"Sounds good," his mother said absentmindedly as Allen nodded.

His eyes met Kristen's. He nodded, but she just stared at him, examining him. "Do I have something on my face?" he asked, wiping his hand over his nose and mouth.

Kristen shook her head as Nicola headed to the front door. "You look great," she said meekly. *Were those tears?* She turned around before he could be sure.

Allen looked at his mother the second Kristen and Nicola were out of sight. "Did you notice that?"

His mother's eyes widened at the Lintzell's living room picture. "What is it?" she asked, zooming in on the image.

"Not the house. Kristen. She looks sad, doesn't she?"

"Huh," she glanced up, but they were both out of sight, "she's probably still shaken from seeing someone at the Lintzell's," she shrugged, "or maybe she's feeling guilty for all the lying about who she was." Allen stared at his mother, but she returned to her phone. "Now look at this crown molding. Isn't it something?"

"Wow," Allen said unenthusiastically, "it's great."

"I am telling you, if their house would have been on the market when we moved here, then I wouldn't have even looked at my house. Look at this: their bathroom is even twice the size of mine."

Allen zoomed in on the photo. "There's a bench in the walk-in shower too," he noted, "so when you get old and decrepit—"

"I can take a shower sitting down," she said, finishing his thought. "I was excited about that, too." She looked away from her phone up at him. "How crazy would it be to sell my house and buy this one?"

"No one who knows you would be surprised."

She playfully swat his arm. "You stop it. Why don't you tell Nicky what a nice car he has so we can leave, and the two of you can eat?"

Allen perked up, then glanced at his mother for ending the photo viewing so easily. "You're not coming?"

"No, I'll wait for you in here."

Allen eyed the food on the counter. "You're about to pick over my buffet, aren't you?"

His mother looked at the food as if this was the first time she noticed it. "Of course not. Nicky and I already had supper."

"Right," he said, "you better leave enough for Kristen and me."

Allen strolled out of the front door, made it three feet, stopped, and then casually walked backward inside. "Mom," he shouted, "you're going to want to see this."

"Where did they go?" his mother asked, joining him while holding the last drumstick.

"Good question. You gonna call your guy, or should I call Kristen?"

"I'm sure they just took it for a spin." She took a bite as if this weren't a cause for concern, but he had a bad feeling. They didn't just go for a spin.

"I'll call her then."

Please be in his head. Please be in his head. He dialed his old phone number hoping that his fears of this being more than a joy ride was simply post-traumatic stress from dealing with Gwen for far too long. The ringing went off inside the house right after he put his phone to his ear.

"I think she left her phone," his mother said as Allen went to find the source of the ringing. His chest tightened when he saw it.

Kristen's phone, his old phone, sat in the kitchen cabinet on top of her new sketchpad. So much for calling her. Wouldn't she have taken her phone with her if it was just a spin? He flipped open the sketchpad. His mother meandered her way back into the kitchen; the drumstick was only a bone between his mother's fingers. "Call Nicola," he said, staring down at the second page where Kristen had left her pencil tucked inside the pad.

"I tried," his mother chunked the chicken bone in the trash. "He didn't answer." Out of his peripheral vision, Allen saw her look him over as he scanned the second page of Kristen's sketchbook. "Are we thinking this is more than a joy ride?" she asked.

He finished reading the letter on the second page. "See for yourself." He handed her the sketchbook. "Tell me what you think."

She had to hold it out at a distance.

"*I know I'm the villain in your story*," his mother read from the second page, "*but I need you to know that I did not set out for things to end this way.*" Allen looked away when his mother glanced at him. "*I want you to know that no matter what you may think of me, I am truly sorry for how things ended—*" she flipped the page.

"That's it," he told her as she flipped through the remaining empty pages. Allen wished there had been something, anything else, in the sketchpad explaining what was going on. None of this sat right with him. He knew Kristen wouldn't be here forever, but to just disappear without a word and with some idiot real estate agent?

"So she was writing this to you?"

"That would be something I would ask her if she were here."

His mother flipped back to the letter. "Are we positive that Kristen wrote this?"

"It was brand new. I gave it to her today."

"You got this for her today?"

"I had the sketchpad delivered after lunch." He decided against mentioning the cabinet full of art supplies and the role Norah's sister played in getting everything here, telling himself that it was because of Norah and his mother's not-so-silent competition and not the fact that he spent unnecessary money on yet another woman destined to leave him.

It wouldn't have mattered. His mother wasn't listening anyway.

"It was definitely for you," she grimaced at the book.

His eyes followed hers to the first page. Allen took the sketchpad from her to flip it around.

It was Kristen's drawing of him lying back in the recliner. She had told him that he couldn't see it until it was done, but his entire top half and the recliner beneath him looked finished.

"I knew she would be really good."

"Not *that* good if she took off with *my* date," his mother muttered, raising her phone to her ear. She shut her eyes as her phone rang in her ear. "They're just taking the car for a spin," she repeated quietly.

Allen stared at her in a daze. His mother may hate Gwen now, but there was a short window of time where she was on board with them dating before Gwen started showing her true colors. His mother's attitude changed fast, just like it appeared to be happening in real-time before Allen's eyes. He didn't discourage it when it was Gwen, but he wanted to now. Kristen and Gwen couldn't be more opposite in personality and disposition, but Allen kept his mouth shut because there was a chance that perhaps the two were more alike than he cared to recognize.

The sound of the phone ringing in his mother's ear echoed the slow, pathetic thump in his chest. Had he fallen for another woman destined to break his heart so soon after the last? It had to be a bad joke. *They're just taking the car for a spin,* he tried chanting in his head, but his brain told him otherwise. This wasn't a bad joke. If anything, he was the joke.

"Everyone leaves," he mumbled when his mother hung up the phone.

"Ah, my dear boy." She hugged her phone to her chest. "The right person will never leave." She rubbed her hand over her chest absentmindedly as if trying to soothe indigestion before adding, "Even in death."

Allen understood, but he didn't need to hear this. He shouldn't need to be hearing any of this.

I know I'm the villain in your story...

She hadn't been a villain. Kristen, Autumn, whoever she was, had been a breath of fresh air. Everything between them had been great and only getting better. Allen handed his mother the sketchpad and headed toward the front door.

"Where are you going?" his mother asked.

Allen went through the door and stared out at the empty street.

"Come back... Come back."

"Uhh, sweetheart," his mother called. "You're going to want to see this."

Allen turned reluctantly from the front yard to see his mother looking at her phone. "What is it?"

"It's Nicola's background check."

Allen's brows rose. "What happened to calling him Nicky?"

She held her phone to him. "What do you think I should call him?"

Allen took it from her, scanning the document. "Is this a joke?" he asked, seeing it was one of three pages. None of the background checks his mother had ever gotten were more than one page. Kristen's —or Autumn's, rather—had been the longest they had gotten. Most were nothing more than a paragraph long, but this... This was something completely different. The first thing that jumped off the screen was "wanted by the FBI."

"You think he's the guy who attacked her on the beach?"

"No, but look at his name." Allen started reading the first page. "You need to look at your cameras," she said in his ear, for once being a step ahead of him, "and make sure your girl left willingly."

FIFTY-FIVE

"We both know I should drive."

Her boss was less than enthused to sit shotgun as they left Allen's house. "If you had the flash drive on you earlier, then there would have been no need to drive in the dark."

"We would be driving in the dark with you in the driver's seat anyway since you don't know how to drive over the speed limit."

"That's because you don't break the law—"

"When you're breaking the law," she said in unison with him.

"So don't give me a hard time about my driving," he snapped, "when we would have been long already if you had been prepared."

Kristen gripped the steering wheel tighter in annoyance. Of course, he expected her to read his mind somehow that he would be coming today.

"Right, because that would make *so much* sense when I knew it was only a matter of time before Calvin came back for it once he realized that I had it on me the first time he tried to crack my skull open—"

"Calvin is out of the picture," he insisted. "You have my word. As soon as my guys get him—"

"As soon as your guys *get* him? As in, it hasn't happened yet?" Kristen glanced away from the road to see her boss's mouth tightening into a line. She knew exactly what that meant; he was keeping something from her.

"Spill it," she hissed.

He let out a tired sigh. "While I was at that overpriced house your boyfriend's mom wanted to look at, the guys got back with me. It appears Calvin was able to shake them—"

"They lost him!"

"He won't get far. They're on his trail," he said. "Mark my words, Calvin is as good as dead."

"It sounds like your guys *were* on his trail, and now he's in the wind. Do you have a gun?"

Her boss blinked at her. "Calvin must have really scared you for you to be so concerned about his whereabouts that you're asking me if I'm packing. Which," he tapped on the glove box in front of him, "I am."

Instead of making her feel better, the whole gun in the glove box situation made her instantly on edge and defensive thanks to it reminding her of Betty and what she was running away from. "What part of he tried to fracture my skull do you not understand? I would have to be a complete idiot not to be concerned."

"Speaking of wanting to know where things are," her boss said, "let's see the drive."

She narrowed her eyes at him. "You seem awfully concerned about its whereabouts. Did the flash drive try to fracture your skull?"

"I am being serious, Autumn."

She blinked hard at the road ahead.

The mention of her real name stirred up a lifetime of festering frustrations. So, she did what she always did: She pushed it to the side. She felt bad enough as it was. Allen, with his sweet words and ability to make her laugh, would plague her long enough as it was. The way she left things with Phillip had been uncomfortable enough, and he had just been some nice guy she met when she tried to dodge the person following her.

Allen was different. He wasn't just some nice guy. In fact, he hadn't been all that nice at first, and then the surprising way that they got along afterward... He just understood her. No wonder she had been so honest with him about who she was. Not that she had much choice when his mother's background check unearthed what Kristen managed to keep secret from so many men before him.

Allen was great. But even that wasn't enough to keep her there.

No, that wasn't exactly true. She left in spite of how great he was; staying would have been the truly unkind thing to do. Allen deserved so much more than her and all of her baggage. He deserved someone who could give him lifelong happiness.

She could cry about it later. Right now, she had more pressing matters.

"We don't use real names, Bobby."

That she was reminding him, of all people, about that rule was laughable. He was the one who established it on day one of her being brought into his criminal ring: *no real names*. Sure, at one point or another, they came out when things got heated among the group. Using someone's real name was like a verbal slap in the face, much like how she took the mention of her real name now.

"And if you think throwing my real name around is going to shut me up, you've got another thing coming."

He shook his head. "That's not why I—"

"I have questions you haven't answered, and I'm not handing over the drive until you do."

He exchanged the hard look she gave him with one of amusement, probably because he could see the bulge of the flash drive in her front pocket.

"Let's hear these questions," he said condescendingly.

She started with the question that bounced around in her head since Allen showed her that background check. "Was that emerald ring really stolen?"

"What emerald ring?"

"The only ring that I dove out of a yacht for."

"What kind of question is that? Of course, it was stolen. *You* were the one who stole it."

Kristen gritted her teeth. "I mean *before* I stole it."

It took him a second to reply. "Yeah, that's right. The original owners paid us to get it back when they got word of who had it."

He told her that when he came to her with the job.

"Then how did they have the ring insured if it was stolen to begin with?"

"What do you mean?"

"The people I stole it from," she said, getting annoyed, "had an insurance policy on it."

"How do you know that?"

"I know a lot of things."

His mouth formed a hard line. "If you knew so much, then you would know that you can get anything insured if you know the right insurance agent."

Kristen shot it right back at him. "And if *you* knew so much, you would know that after the engraving system was established for precious stones, the Rare Emerald Exchange Act required proof of ownership of existing stone owners to qualify for insurance, which means that the stone I jumped out of that yacht with wasn't a stolen stone, to begin with. I was lied to from the beginning about that entire job. Why?" She expected to see his wheels turning to devise a reason or way around it. All she saw was him looking at her—really looking at her.

"I didn't lie to you, and it is offensive that you would insinuate one of my buyers was a liar when you know that I vet all of them." She was about to tell him it wasn't the buyer she was calling a liar when he said, "Have I ever told you how I knew that you were going to be so good at this job?"

She shook her head.

"You have always been able to figure things out. The day I was taken to you in lockup, you had already gotten yourself out from behind bars and were talking to a couple of the cops. You were working your way out of serving time." He let out a chuckle. "You were only sixteen—"

"Seventeen," she corrected. The way he stared off into space made Kristen wonder if mentally he was back in that police station all those years ago.

"Only seventeen," he said, "and there you were, some scared kid arrested for the first time, but you weren't behind bars. You were out, telling the cops your life's sob story, and I could see it in your eyes. Hell, I could see it in theirs—they were falling for it. You wouldn't have been able to get them to drop all charges like I could with one phone call, but you would have rallied them to help you get off with a lighter charge. Maybe if I had left you in there, you would have been able to talk your way out of the charges altogether, but that was when I knew you were made for the job." He dabbed at the corner of his eyes.

What was happening? He was getting mushy. The man who evaded police in multiple countries and put together and managed a team of criminals was getting sentimental.

"Why did you come to get me that night?" she asked. "I used my one phone call to call a bail bondsman."

"A bail bondsman I had worked with years prior when I first started in the city. He knew as well as I did that we couldn't have a Sky sitting in prison."

She could laugh at the thought that the name Sky meant anything. "Are you worried about the Russians?"

"Why would I be worried about them?"

"Because that's who Calvin could be working with."

"Calvin isn't working with the Russians. He isn't working with anybody."

"You sound awful sure about that."

"Because I am. After you left me that message, I did some digging and found out that Calvin managed to figure out who my buyer was and contacted them. He negotiated his own deal."

"Doesn't sound like they're awfully vetted if they are turning around to cut you out of the deal."

"It was a business arrangement. That's what this is: a business. They would pay him half what they would pay us, but you don't have to worry. It bit them in the ass. I was going to let it be a surprise, but you're getting a hundred grand more."

"A hundred grand?"

"That's right."

He was saying it as if she should be happy about that, but none of this was adding up, and it wasn't just the numbers.

"What?" he asked dryly. "You've spent so much time around the wealthy that you can't appreciate a hundred grand? You know that's more than most people make in a year?"

"I may not have graduated high school, but I can do basic math. I should be getting half of Calvin's cut."

Laughing was never his thing, but he had to be joking about her only getting a hundred grand more now that Calvin was out of the picture.

"If you don't want the extra hundred grand—"

He was serious.

"Let me get this right," she said. "The original split was half a million for each of us, and now that Calvin is out of the picture, I'm only getting an extra hundred grand?"

He chuckled humorlessly. "I mean, in *addition* to the quarter million you're getting from us splitting Calvin's portion."

Kristen calculated it in her head. It was twice the amount she managed to save over the course of her entire career heisting the most expensive items one can carry out of a place. Eight hundred and fifty thousand dollars.

"Are you okay?"

She had eight hundred and fifty thousand reasons to be okay, but his question made her realize that she was lying when she told him,

"I'm better than okay, minus the stitches in my head. Why are we getting paid so much?"

"What do you mean?"

She wouldn't have worried about it in the past. If rich people wanted to pay her boss ten times the price of whatever the items were technically worth, she didn't blink an eye. The buyer wasn't acquiring it legally, for one, and there was the cost associated with the risk of taking on the job, but this was different. In all of her previous jobs, she knew exactly what she was after. She had pictures of the item and, in some cases, photos of the room within the target's house where she would find it. This two-and-a-half-year job, however, she knew next to nothing about what she was actually collecting.

"Tell me what's on the drive. I want to know what's worth so much money."

"It's not that much money to these people."

"So you're not going to tell me?"

"I know less than you. Is that what you wanted to hear? They gave me the flash drive, and I was told to follow the instructions once it was plugged in. That was that. I gave it to you with the list of places to plug it into. I gave you the key fob to put it in, but you would have to tell me what's on it."

She glanced over at him. The solemn look he gave her would come off as trustworthy to those who didn't know any better.

"It didn't show me anything. All I had to do was click load once it was connected to the laptops."

Bobby shrugged. "There you have it."

"So it was a virus?"

"Could be. Does it matter?"

Her mind had been struggling with something she couldn't articulate. She chalked it up to her leaving the Trouths, but his question, *does it matter*, was her last straw. It did matter. Forget that Calvin gave her stitches because of it. Not knowing the job these last two years was unsettling enough, but it was even sketchier now that she was offered close to a million dollars.

Kristen thought back to each time she watched, her heart pounding as she hooked the flash drive up to the computers and cell phones on that list, using whatever end on the multi-ended flash drive required for the given device. The top art galleries across three states, and she got to every one of them. It was not an easy task in this day and age, when most computers were laptops and, like cell phones, were carried around all day by the gallery owners, but Kristen got the job done just like she always had.

The flash drive didn't give much away, either. It would load for an excruciatingly slow ten seconds, and then a box would pop up with one option: accept. There was no message to tell her what she was accepting or what was on the drive. It continued with some scans before a small upload bar appeared on the bottom right side of the screen with amounts of what it was downloading or uploading or whatever it was up to. It was the only thing it displayed, and it was different amounts on each computer—28, 53, 19; she couldn't remember if the numbers had an MB, GB, or the other abbreviations for data. Would that have told her something if she could remember? No, not her, but maybe someone with experience with computers.

They passed the pawn shop and then the diner. This town was already littered with memories. Kristen slowed when the Redrock bus station came into view. She glanced over at Bobby.

"How much cash do you have on you?"

FIFTY-SIX

"Milo is going to be livid," Betty said as Allen paced the kitchen.

He stopped to gape at her. "Huh?"

"Milo. I didn't think we would be here long, so I didn't feed him. He is going to be furious with me."

Allen sighed loudly. "Come on." He pulled the car keys out of his pocket.

"What are you doing?" she asked, eyeing the keys in his hand as if they were foreign objects.

"I'm going to drive you to your house so you can feed your stupid dog."

"You are not," she snapped, plucking the keys from his hand. "What if they come back? You stay. I'll get Milo."

"Don't *get* Milo. Feed him at your house, and if you want, *you* can come back over, but I don't need to worry about him, too, right now."

"You don't have to worry about him—"

"He pees on my floor. Yes, I do have to worry about him."

"Your brother was just christening your new house," she said on her way to the garage door. "He meant it as a compliment."

"Do not bring that dog back here."

"Love you," she cooed and walked into the garage.

He listened as the garage opened, his car started, and the garage door shut.

Silence. He should welcome it after dealing with his mother and her constant antics, but three deep breaths later, the silence felt like a weight on his chest. Allen walked over to the now room-temperature container of leftover chicken. He grabbed a chicken breast, ignoring the plates and utensils on the counter, and took a loud bite, enjoying the crunchy, fried exterior.

It helped briefly, but then Allen's eyes settled on the empty recliner at the center of his empty living room. Walking over, he picked up the remote on the arm of the chair. The TV screen came to life with the crowd going wild as the closeup of the ball was knocked out of the park. It was like salt was being rubbed into a wound. Allen shut it off and threw the remote down on the chair. He couldn't escape her.

First Gwen and now Kristen; they all left. At least Kristen hadn't gotten pregnant by one of his coworkers. The thought of her getting together with that real estate agent was almost enough to make him lose his appetite. He took another bite and turned angrily from the TV. A piece of chicken fell to the floor, and then another. He ignored the mess he was making and almost welcomed it. It would give Milo something productive to do when he no doubt showed up with his mother. Allen paused at the threshold to the front of the house. If his mother didn't bring Milo back, then he would have to get the robot vacuum from upstairs. He took a slow step forward as his eyes drifted to the staircase. He still had a room covered with flour to worry about. Allen shook his head. Gwen took everything, and Kristen left a mess. Sure, it was a mess that he technically initiated, but a mess nonetheless, and a drawer full of art supplies that he would prefer to dump in the trash than leave it where it was.

What about her hand-drawn picture of me?

He thought about what to do with it as he walked to the front door. It would be hard to throw that one away. The only thing he was sure of was that he was no longer hungry.

His hand jiggled the doorknob, ensuring it was locked when his phone vibrated. Allen used his chicken-free hand to take his phone out of his pocket. A motion alert from the backyard was on the screen of his phone. His mother, he realized when he heard the indistinguishable sound of the back door opening. He shoved his phone back in his pocket. At least Milo would clean up the floor. He really needed to give her his spare garage door opener since, apparently, he wasn't going to have another woman in his life who would need it anytime soon.

"Did you forget something?" he called out as he turned on his heels. "I have an extra garage door opener if you—" His words left him as it dawned on him that his mother left in his car, which had a garage door opener. He skidded to a halt, but it was too late.

Allen's eyes landed on the man wearing all black, down to the ski mask covering his face, walking silently from the back of the house. The man held a gun.

Allen did the only thing he could. With all his might, he hurled the piece of chicken at the man's head.

The man raised his gun to Allen's chest as he ducked with ease. The chicken flew over his head and slid into the kitchen behind him. The intruder glanced over at it.

"Did you just throw a piece of chicken at me?"

"I did," Allen said, having a mental conundrum.

Could a full moon last three days? All of Allen's knowledge from decades of studying, and he wasn't sure. It had to be a full moon. The day might have started great, but losing the girl he was falling for and now staring into the eyes of the man who would kill him definitely had the feel of a full moon.

"It was a reflex," Allen said. He could only imagine the laughs the hitman would get from his buddies later when he retold the story of how this went down. "I normally have better aim than that." Allen shook his head. *What in the hell am I saying?* If this was his subconscious trying to bide his time, he was doing terrible at it. The hitman stepped closer. Allen raised his hands in defense.

"Just do it," he said, closing his eyes. "Get it over with."

He cleared his mind. All his planning for a moment like this just to get caught out in the open with only a piece of chicken to defend himself was a shame. A loud sound made him jump. He waited for the pain that never came. It wasn't a gun going off but a knock at the front door.

"It's me!" Kristen shouted. "Can you let me in? The door's locked."

FIFTY-SEVEN

Kristen juggled the pros and cons of telling Allen and Betty the truth. Not the whole truth, of course, but they helped her once, so if she were honest with them this time, maybe they would help her again. That was if they answered the door. She stepped back, wondering if her thirty-minute absence caused them to go searching for her, but then she saw movement in the blinds.

"I can explain," she called out to the blinds swaying lightly from whoever it was moving away before she could see them. "Please open the door."

The front door unlocked, and it was Allen, his face pale.

"I'm so sorry I left—"

Run, he mouthed silently at her.

"Wha—"

"Let her in," a hushed voice said from inside.

The muscles in Allen's jaw flexed. "She doesn't need to be a part of this."

Kristen didn't think it was possible, but a clicking sound inside the house made Allen tense more.

"I said, let her in."

That voice. Chills ran down her spine. There was no way she heard right. Kristen pushed through the door past Allen. Her heart pounded in her ears.

"You aren't here for her. You're here for me. Let her go, and I can make one phone call. I'll give you all of the account information—"

What is Allen going on about? "He isn't here for you," she told him, looking squarely at Calvin. "He's here for me. Nice facemask."

Calvin's eyes narrowed as he grinned at her. "I thought so, too."

Allen eased his way into Kristen's peripheral vision. "You two know each other?"

"I spent the last two and a half years with him," she said.

"You're Calvin," Allen said, glaring at him.

"You told him my name?"

"Not your real name. He knows that you're my ex, and you hit me over the head," she said, ignoring the look Allen gave her at learning that she lied about Calvin's name. She kept her eyes on her backstabbing ex-partner in crime. "That's it. That's all he knows. We can let him go, and I will give you what you're here for."

"*We?* You and I both know that there is no *we* after I knocked you out—"

"You did more than knock me out." Kristen flipped her hair over, exposing her stitches. "You tried to kill me."

Calvin rolled his eyes. "I knocked you out so you couldn't follow me, but," he held up the gun she had ignored up until this point, "today, I might kill you." Allen stepped toward him, and Calvin pointed his weapon at Allen. "Don't even think about it. You're my insurance policy, but if you act up, I am fine with cashing it in. You," he redirected the gun at Kristen, "hand over the flash drive."

Kristen swallowed hard. "I don't have it."

"Nice try. Where should I shoot him first?" Calvin lowered his gun to Allen's nether regions.

"Don't." She tried to step between them, but Allen pushed her back, keeping himself in the line of fire.

"She stashed it," he told Calvin.

"What are you—"

"I saw her," Allen said over her, not taking his eyes off Calvin. "If it's the key fob you're looking for, I saw her hide it."

"Key fob," Calvin muttered, clearly unaware until this moment that she had been concealing it in the fake key for a Volkswagen. He gave Allen a thoughtful once over and raised the gun. "Look at you, saving your own hide. Smart man. Where did she put it?"

Allen would tell him about the key box stuck to the water hose holder, and if Calvin didn't shoot them right here, he would once he found that there was nothing in the key box. Kristen needed a plan and fast.

"In the living room," Allen told him. Kristen gaped at him, but neither man noticed. *What is he talking about?* "Back here," he pointed toward the kitchen. "I'll show you," Allen hesitated, "unless you want us to wait here."

"Fat chance." Calvin waved his gun for him to lead the way. "Keep your hands where I can see them. You too," he instructed Kristen.

She walked with Allen at her side into the kitchen, wondering where he was going with this. Her nightmare of a heist partner kept his distance behind them. The back door was ajar from where he must have entered.

Calvin is out of the picture, her boss had said. *He's as good as dead.* This was only further proof that she had made the right decision to come back to Allen's house.

"Where's your mother?" Kristen whispered.

"She left before your friend showed up."

"He is not my friend—"

"No talking." In the living room, Calvin barked, "Stop right there."

Allen spun around with his hands up. "I was going to get it for you."

Calvin's eyes darted around at the near-empty living room. "You can tell me where it is."

"The recliner." Allen glanced at Kristen. She still didn't know where this was going but played her part, looking defeated as Calvin smirked. "She stuffed it between the back and bottom cushion."

"What are you doing?" Kristen mouthed. He winked.

"So, are you moving out or moving in?" Calvin asked as he pointed the gun at them with his right hand and stuck his left hand in between the recliner cushions.

"Moving out," Allen said, looking less concerned for his life and more confident the longer Calvin dug between the cushions.

Calvin's hand paused in the cushions, and a second later, he pulled out the pocketknife Kristen had also found in the cushions of Allen's recliner during their first tryst. He tossed the small knife around in his left hand. "Did you think you would do something to me with this?"

Allen's face fell. "I forgot that was in there, I swear."

Kristen was impressed by how believable that sounded.

"Sure you did." Calvin shoved it into his back pocket and continued digging in the recliner. "It better be in here."

Allen tensed when Calvin rounded the cushion against the right arm. At first, she hoped it meant that a mouse trap or something was waiting for him, but the intensity in Allen's eyes as Calvin dug around in that side of the chair made her realize something else was up. She let out an annoyed sigh.

"How do we know you won't hurt us when you get the flash drive?"

Calvin withdrew his hand, and Allen's tense gaze shifted to her. Calvin's eyes were also on her, specifically on her head.

"I get that flash drive," he said, cautiously closing the distance between them, "and I promise to not only leave without hurting another hair on your head, but I also won't kill him." He nodded in Allen's direction. "You have my word."

Kristen gulped down a snarl as if his word meant anything. She would tell him where the flash drive was if she knew that Allen would be safe, but she would be an idiot to believe him. Allen glanced from her to the recliner. *And what is Allen's obsession with the chair?*

"Fine," she muttered, resolve setting in.

Hands still raised, Allen moved toward the chair. "I know it's in the chair."

"Stay where you're at," Calvin warned, but Allen was already there. One arm still in the air, he dug elbow-deep between the right arm and the cushion of the recliner. Calvin's demeanor darkened. "Get away from the chair."

He raised the gun, but Kristen pounced.

It was as though she was at the beach again, but this time, she wasn't staring at the sunrise. This time, she would fight. Calvin was stronger, but she had the element of surprise. She used her body weight to force his hand down before he could point it at Allen. He tried to rip his arm from her grasp, but she wouldn't let that happen. Kristen wrapped her arm around his like a snake, her other hand on his wrist, keeping the gun down.

Calvin let out a grumble. "Get. Off."

Kristen reared her head before snapping it forward. Her forehead made contact with the portion of fabric covering his nose in an audible crack. She immediately saw stars, but she held on to him.

"Kristen," Allen shouted, "get away from him!"

Blood poured from Calvin's nose as he stumbled back. She tripped as her foot tangled in his. She released his hand that held the gun, and she fell to the side in slow motion. When she hit the ground, the stars faded from her sight as Calvin hit the wall behind him with a loud thud. Through her starry vision, she could see Calvin, blood soaking his mask below his nose, glaring at her as he raised his gun.

With a loud bark, Milo flew through the air.

"No!" Kristen shouted as Calvin swung the gun to Milo.

The gun went off with one shot. It was so loud that she wasn't sure if it echoed through the house or just in her head. Everything in the room went still.

Milo cried out.

Kristen propped herself up on her elbows. The stars around her vision wouldn't let up.

Allen ran to her. "Are you okay?"

"Milo," she mumbled and found her voice, "He shot Milo."

Allen shook his head. "Milo's fine." He stepped back, allowing Kristen to see Milo standing across from them, sniffing Calvin on the floor where he lay in a heap. Allen held a gun in his right hand.

"You shot him?"

He gave her a kind grin. "I wish."

"Sheila shot him." Betty appeared out from behind the kitchen island.

"You were hiding behind the island this whole time?"

"Heavens, no," she said as Allen helped Kristen up. "I was feeding Milo when I got the alert on my phone of movement in Allen's backyard. I hoped you and Nicola had returned, but I saw that guy when I clicked on it." She glared at Calvin's body. "I grabbed Sheila and Milo, and we came straight over. You were walking in the front door as I drove up. We ran around the back, almost got caught when you guys walked into the kitchen, and after I finally figured out the key to the pool house—"

"You came through the secret door," Kristen said, seeing the tall kitchen cabinet door open where it led into the pool house.

Betty nodded. "And my sweet boy tried to save the day," she cooed. Milo ran up to her as Betty set her gun on the island to pet him. "Who's my good boy?" Milo's tail wagged.

"How's your head?" Allen asked, examining her stitches.

"The top of my head feels fine."

"Any ringing in your ears?"

"No, but my forehead is going to have a bruise."

"That's an understatement," Allen chuckled. "With how hard you headbutted him, I'm surprised you didn't knock yourself out."

"Good thing Sheila doesn't miss," Betty made smooching noises at Milo, "or else that bad man would have hurt you. Yes, he would have. Elvis is going to be so impressed with us."

Allen abruptly stopped his exam. "Mom," he warned.

"What?" Betty asked, looking up. She glanced between the two of them as she scratched Milo's ears. "There's no getting around her knowing about him now. He's driving in."

Kristen was trying to figure out what was going on, but the way Allen looked like he was about to cover Betty's mouth himself made her wonder if she really wanted to know.

"It's Kristen's ex," he said through gritted teeth. "You could have just called the cops."

"I called the cops, too. Well, I called Ed. Don't look at me like that. Did you really expect me not to call Elvis when I saw a man breaking into your house? And now look," she waved in Calvin's direction. "A man's been shot in *your* house by *me*. If I didn't think having Ed here would help us, I would have only called Elvis."

Kristen shook her head at Allen. "I'm sorry. Am I going crazy, or does she keep saying Elvis?"

"Not that Elvis," Betty and Allen said in unison.

"Police," a voice boomed from the front of the house.

Everyone jumped.

Allen recovered first. "We're back here, Ed."

The detective had his gun drawn as he entered the kitchen from the front of the house. He looked around the room, not lowering his weapon, until he saw Calvin face down dead on the floor. "Everyone okay? What happened?"

"We're all fine," Betty said as Milo ran to check Ed out, "except for Kristen having to fight for her life."

Ed's eyes widened the second they landed on Kristen's face. "I'll call an ambulance."

Allen raised a hand to calm him down. "I think she's okay."

Kristen ran her hands around her face to figure out why he looked so shocked. "What's wrong with my—" her fingers landed on the huge knot forming on her forehead.

"She headbutted him in the fight," Allen said. "She's not showing any signs of a concussion."

"Concussion," Kristen echoed.

"You are okay," Allen said calmly.

"Did you both shoot him?" Ed asked, eyeing the gun in Allen's hand and Sheila on the kitchen island.

"I shot him," Betty said proudly.

"She saved the day," Allen said, lowering Kristen's hands from her forehead. "It would be Kristen and me on the ground if she hadn't shown up."

"What about that?" Ed tipped his chin at the gun in Allen's hand.

"I couldn't get to it in time." Kristen jumped when the magazine of the gun popped out of the end as Allen unloaded it.

"Good thing I always keep Sheila nearby."

When Betty reached for her gun, Ed raised his hand to stop her. "I'll unload it," he offered, stepping in between.

Kristen watched Allen pull back on the top of his gun. A bullet flew out of and onto the floor; Allen picked it up.

"I wasn't going to unload her." Betty frowned.

"It needs to be unloaded before my guys get here. For safety," Ed told her.

Betty crossed her arms over her chest. "You don't trust me with my own gun?"

"Is that who Elvis is?" Kristen asked, "One of the officers?" It was a perfectly logical question, or so she thought, but Allen, Betty, and Ed looked at her like she was crazy.

"She's in shock," Allen said with a polite grin, and he pocketed the bullet and magazine before taking Kristen by the arm. "I'm going to take her upstairs and give her some space from all this."

"Good idea," Betty nodded.

"Leave your gun upstairs, too," Ed called after them.

Kristen started to protest, but Allen was in her ear. "It's okay. We can talk about whatever you want upstairs."

FIFTY-EIGHT

Kristen pulled her arm free from Allen. "Let go of me."

"I'm only making sure you're steady on your feet," he told her as they ascended the stairs.

"I'm fine. You can see that I am fine."

"Are you mad at me?" Allen asked, unsure where her sudden aggression was coming from.

"Yes, I am. You and your mom are obviously keeping something from me, talking about accounts you thought Calvin was after and your mom mentioning some guy named Elvis."

Allen gave her a knowing nod. "I can explain."

"You better."

The way she glared at him as if he was the only one keeping secrets took him aback. "Hold up. If anyone needs to explain themself, it's you. *You* are the one who took off with some real estate agent you just met."

Kristen opened her mouth indignantly as she stomped onto the top step. She snapped it shut a second later. Her face visibly softened when she opened it again. "You are...right. I—"

"What was that?" Allen leaned his ear closer. "I didn't catch it."

She sucked in a breath through her teeth as she followed him into his bedroom. "You are right. Now, do I need to keep repeating it, or can I explain?"

He liked being right but needed to hear why she left him. "Let's hear it. Why did you take off?"

"I didn't feel like I had a choice."

"He kidnapped you?"

"No, I... Look, it's complicated. He isn't a real estate agent. Nicola isn't even his real name. His real name is..." She took a moment to collect herself. Or perhaps she was waiting for him to say she didn't have to tell him. Allen didn't open his mouth. If she wanted him to tell her the truth, he would have to hear the truth from her first. "His real name is Bobby."

Allen was impressed. That was the name on the background check. "And Bobby is?"

Kristen went to his bed as Allen stood, waiting for her response. "He's my boss." She sat at the foot of the bed, gazing at her balled-up hands in her lap, "*Was* my boss."

"Your boss as in...?"

"Stealing stuff, he lined up the jobs, told me who the mark was, what I was after, all of it."

"And he pretended to be a real estate agent because...?"

"Because he knew Calvin turned on me." She met his gaze. "I called him when I was in the hospital—"

"How did you—"

"It doesn't matter. What matters is that I had the flash drive, and he wouldn't let one of his people trying to kill his best thief stop him from finishing the job."

The more he learned about her, the more she made sense. She could be so open, so warm to him at times while keeping him at arm's length. Keeping people you care about at a distance isn't a natural behavior. It's learned through moments of being let down by others. You get to the point where you stop letting people close enough to let you down. He only hoped that she learned it in adulthood and not childhood.

"That can't be the only reason he did all that," Allen said, sitting beside her. "He came here to make sure you were okay."

Kristen grinned at him as if he were some simpleton. "Maybe a normal boss would care how an employee was doing after they were hospitalized by one of their other employees, but I don't have a normal job, and he is far from a normal boss."

"Is that all you are to him, an employee?"

"What else would I be to him?"

Allen didn't want to say it, didn't want her to know what he and his mother saw in the email from Elvis, but as his silence dragged on, her eyes darkened.

"What else would I be to him?" she repeated with an edge that matched her eyes.

Allen wanted to wrap his arm around her and pull her close. Instead, he stayed where he was and asked, "What's Bobby's last name?"

Kristen blinked. With each bat of the eye, he could see her putting it together. "You know?" she asked in a near whisper.

Allen remained silent. Tears filled her eyes, and before he knew it, his eyes were watering too. It had hurt him when he saw that Nicola's true identity was Bobby Sky.

"But how?" Kristen muttered. "The only people who know he's my father are the guys who work with us."

"Your father?" Allen stared at her. His tears disappeared as a smile formed on his face. Bobby Sky was her father.

Kristen's brows rose. "Why are you smiling?"

"I'm relieved," he admitted. "When I saw his last name, I thought you were married to him."

"You thought I married my dad?"

"I didn't know he was your father. I mean, now that I'm saying it out loud, he could have been your uncle or cousin or something, but Mom went on about how you like older men—"

Kristen threw a hand up. "Okay, I get it." She gave him a thoughtful look. "Just so you know, I only like guys a *little* older than me."

"Like five years and two months, a little older than you?" he asked, feeling comfortable enough to slide his arm around her shoulders.

Kristen grinned. "Is that the age gap between us?"

"It is."

"Then you are exactly right." Allen leaned in to kiss her, but Kristen's finger flew to his mouth. "Hold on there, buddy," she said. "It's your turn to explain—"

A single *pop!* followed a shout from downstairs. Allen jumped up.

"Was that a—"

"A gunshot." Allen shoved the magazine into his gun and racked it. "Get in the safe room."

"I'm not getting in the safe room without you," she said, moving with him toward the hallway.

"Do you have one for me?"

Allen barely heard her as he crossed the room. His mother was downstairs. He didn't realize Kristen was behind him until he reached the hallway.

"We're good," his mother called out.

Allen raced down the stairs. "What happened?" His mother appeared through the entryway to the kitchen, carrying Milo under her arm, licking her under her chin.

"Was that Sheila?" Kristen asked behind him.

"It was Ed. I don't know what he calls his gun."

"What was he shooting?"

They charged toward her in unison. "You do not want to go in there," his mother told them. "Apparently, your friend wasn't dead," she told Kristen, "but he is now."

"Ed shot him?" Allen went around his mother, but she grabbed him by the arm.

"Had to," Ed said, appearing in front of him. His gun was in its holster on his hip. "It's best we stay in the front of the house until my team gets here." His eyes landed on Allen. "Did you check his pulse after your mother shot him?"

"I—"

"So much was happening," his mother said.

"He was too busy checking on me," Kristen explained, rubbing the hematoma forming on her forehead.

Allen appreciated them covering for him. "I didn't check for a pulse," he said clearly. "He wasn't moving, Kristen was injured, and you got here right after—"

"I got you," Ed said. Sirens wailed in the distance. "I'm going to need statements from everyone, and if you have security footage of what happened—"

"I can email it to you," Allen volunteered.

"Great. You need to put that up." He nodded at Allen's gun. Allen turned around to secure it upstairs when Ed muttered, "And the dead guy is...?"

Allen looked over his shoulder to see Kristen and his mother exchanging glances. Kristen looked unsure, but his mother was on top of it.

"Her ex," Betty said matter-of-factly. "He waited until he saw me leaving in Allen's car. He must've thought Allen was with me and broke in."

Allen started up the stairs.

"The ski mask, though," Ed said, "you see that in home invasions, not domestics."

"It proves that he was here to kill me," Kristen piped up. "He was going to finish the job he started at the beach when Ms. Trouth stopped him."

"That's right," his mother agreed.

Confident that they had this, Allen hurried up the staircase, stashed his gun in his underwear drawer, and popped into his safe room. He couldn't risk texting if this turned into a full-fledged investigation, but he could email Elvis in code in case he was driving like a bat out of hell to get there.

Everyone unharmed. Threat taken care of by local PD. Incident not related to us.

Ed was already leading two of his guys through the front door to the living room when Allen got downstairs. Kristen and his mother were waiting for him at the foot of the staircase. Kristen's forehead didn't look worse; the hematoma had stopped growing. It would be a nasty bruise, but she was okay. That was all that mattered.

"The story is Kristen's ex showed up to finish the job—" his mother whispered.

"I heard."

"We have to all say the same thing," Kristen said as if this were his first time being interviewed by the police. If only she knew.

His mother spoke quietly. "You let me borrow your car, but I forgot something, so I came back through the back gate like I always do, saw an intruder walking through the kitchen, crept through the open back door, but then hid behind the island when I heard all of you coming back from the front of the house, and then jumped out when I had a good shot."

"So the truth then," Allen said, looking between them.

Kristen nodded. "Except we don't mention the flash drive. He and I dated for two years. You guys just know his first name. I'm sure they'll figure out that his name is an alias, and it will be a surprise to all of us—"

"But all they'll need right now is that he broke in to kill you. We assume out of fear you would testify against him about the assault on the beach and going to jail," Allen said, "and my mother, being who she is, burst through a wall to save us."

His mother smiled proudly. "I sure did."

"That should work," Kristen agreed.

"It *will* work." Forget Kristen's ex-partner showing up—Kristen's return made him feel extra optimistic. Too bad it wasn't rubbing off on her.

"What about the stolen car in the driveway?" she asked, rubbing her palms against the sides of her pants in unease.

"What stolen car?" Allen asked, glancing around to ensure Ed or his guys weren't close enough to hear them.

Kristen eyed Allen's mother with concern as she answered, "The Rolls Royce."

"She knows who Nicola really is," Allen said under his breath.

"Wait," his mother said, staring at Kristen, "you stole Nicky's car?"

"*He* stole the car," Kristen clarified.

Allen rolled his eyes when his mother dared to look shocked. "It can't be that big of a surprise when the man's wanted by the FBI," he grumbled.

"The FBI?" This time, Kristen looked shocked.

"That's right," Betty told her. "I sure know how to pick 'em."

Allen bit his tongue to keep from dropping the real bomb that "Nicola" Bobby Sky was Kristen's father when Ed appeared from the kitchen with one of his guys heading toward the front door.

"My guys are roping off the scene until we can clear the body," Ed said. "I can get you a card for our crime scene cleaner. They're from the town over, but they can usually get to a scene within twenty-four to forty-eight hours."

"I would appreciate it. Should I go ahead and drive us over to the station to give statements or—"

"I need initial statements first, but I used my last forms to interview the Lintzell's neighbors about the graffiti."

"Did any of them see Kristen's ex at the Lintzell's?"

"None of them, but seeing how he's here now, I'll do another walk-through. He had to be hiding out somewhere." Ed glanced around. "I'll go see if one of my men has the forms. After that, I'll have to get recorded interviews in my office."

"You're my hero," his mother said before Ed approached the front door.

"Just doing my job," he smiled at her. He walked out of the front door, leaving it open behind him.

Allen lowered his head, unsure if the other officer was still in the living room with Calvin. "He's your hero?"

"He sure is," his mother smirked at him, "until all this blows over."

FIFTY-NINE

Kristen focused on her throbbing forehead as more and more people arrived at the scene.

"He's here," Allen said, straightening from where they hunched over the hood of Ed's car, writing out their statements.

"Who?" Kristen asked.

Allen and Betty exchanged a look before Betty answered, "Elvis."

First Cupid and now Elvis. What's next, Aphrodite and Einstein?

"There are some things you need to know," Allen said cautiously. "Elvis isn't an accountant—"

Kristen blinked at him in confusion as Betty cut him off.

"You aren't about to tell her—"

"I have to," Allen said. "She needs to know."

"Why don't we wait and see if he thinks it's necessary?"

Kristen followed their gaze to the light-colored sedan with a rental tag on the front license plate. The car looked familiar, and she wondered where she'd seen it before as it pulled in behind the line of cop cars.

"Stop staring," Allen warned, but Kristen's jaw fell when the man in the driver's seat stepped out of the car.

"That's even worse than staring," Betty told her, heeding Allen's advice as she glanced at Kristen before returning to her statement.

"Alvie?" the name fell out of Kristen's mouth. "The accountant you had a lunch date with today?"

"They weren't really on a date," Allen mumbled.

"I could have done better at giving him a fake name," Betty sighed.

Allen glared at her. "You think?"

The man who had been with Betty at the diner strolled over as casually as he had walked into the diner. "I'm getting too old for this."

"Ditto," Betty shot back.

"What do I need to know?" he asked, glancing at the house where an officer stood outside the front door.

"I shot an armed intruder," Betty told him. "Turns out he's Autumn's…" Betty glanced at Kristen, who stuttered.

"E-ex-boyfriend." She couldn't believe Betty used her real name.

"Ex-partner in crime," Allen corrected.

Kristen could feel her eyes bulge out of her head. "What are you—"

"He has to know the truth so that he can do his job," Allen said, leaving Kristen with more questions than answers, but he was already spilling more of her deep, dark secrets to Elvis. "They worked the heists together—"

What was going on? Was he an attorney? He better be and he better represent her when she ended up in jail since Allen was spilling his guts. Hadn't they made an agreement on what to say? What was even more surprising was how well Elvis handled all of this information as if they were discussing the weather, not manslaughter and felonies.

"And he came after you to make sure you wouldn't squeal on him."

"That," Kristen said slowly, wishing there was a rock for her to climb under, "and he wanted what we stole from the last job."

"Did he get it?" Elvis asked.

"No," Allen answered. "She doesn't have it."

Elvis gave her the once over and then looked directly into her eyes. "Is that true?" he asked.

She nodded without a word. He had that same intense peering into one's soul ability that Allen had. He took a step closer to her, but as she started to get nervous, Elvis turned his attention to the papers on the hood of Ed's car.

"Are you giving statements?"

"The detective, Ed, wants us to give recorded statements in his office next," Allen said.

Elvis scooped them up. "No statements of any kind until I get a handle on this."

Betty crossed her arms over her chest, looking smug. "Sounds good to me. Ed's inside."

Elvis's eyes narrowed in on Betty. "Ed, Ed?"

"The detective," Allen said, but Elvis shook his head.

"The same Ed you're mad at for being late to your date?"

Allen looked as shocked as Kristen to hear that the man Betty did *not* have a lunch date with knew about her and Ed.

Allen stared at his mom. "Do you tell him everything?"

"Only the important stuff," she smirked.

"When she isn't sending me pictures of sunrises and Milo," Elvis said, reading the partially written statements.

"You send him pictures of the dog?"

"Like I said," she continued to smirk, "just the important stuff."

"Don't worry," Elvis said, flipping to the next statement, "She sends me pictures of you too."

Kristen stepped forward. "Do you think I could go upstairs? I need to use the restroom."

"Shouldn't be a problem." Elvis glanced at her forehead. "You know you got a pretty big—"

"She knows," Allen told him.

"Come with me," Elvis instructed and headed inside.

"You want me to come with you?" Allen asked.

"I'm fine."

"She is a grown woman," Betty grumbled, "she can go to the ladies room by herself."

When Elvis and Kristen reached the front door, he pulled his wallet out and handed it to the officer. "I need to speak with your Chief. Are they on the scene?"

"Not yet." He gave Elvis's wallet a perplexed look. "Why is the marshal service here?"

Elvis ignored his question, flipping his wallet shut. "How about your lead detective, is he here? Ed, I believe."

The officer stepped back from the door, nodding Elvis inside. "He's in the back of the house, but uh," he stared at Kristen.

"Right," Elvis said, "is there a restroom out of the way she can use?"

"The upstairs restroom," Kristen interjected before the officer could respond. "I'll go straight up to the bathroom and come right back out."

"Sure," the cop said. Kristen ignored the way his eyes lingered on her forehead. "Be quick about it."

"Yes, sir."

SIXTY

"What's with you and following me to the bathroom?" Kristen asked as she stepped out to find him waiting for her.

"I didn't think you would be in the water closet."

Pfft. He felt stupid just saying it, but his realtor had insisted that was the proper term for the small room inside the bathroom that housed the toilet.

Kristen grinned. "Water closet, huh?"

"You think it's a stupid name too?"

"I didn't know they were called that until I was an adult," Kristen said, closing the door to the toilet behind herself. "Why not call it a toilet closet?"

Allen grinned. "That would make more sense."

"Is that why you're up here after I told you I didn't need any help—to discuss water closets?"

"I wanted to make sure you weren't up here getting sick. Vomiting is a sign of a concussion."

"I'm not sick," Kristen told him, crossing her arms over her chest. "Is there another reason you came up here?"

"I wanted to have a moment alone with you," he confessed, stepping up to her to rub his hands on the outside of her upper arms. "You went through a lot today."

"*We* went through a lot today."

"You are right, but I didn't have to deal with my father, who is also my boss, before all that went down. How are you doing?"

"I'm..." she took a second to search for the words, "getting through it."

"And your father? Are you going to tell me why you have his car?" He had so many more questions than that, but Kristen stared at him long enough to wonder if he would get any answers from her.

"I didn't kill him and stuff him in the trunk if that's what you're thinking," she said finally. All the questions froze in his head as Kristen smirked at him. "But I didn't check the trunk, so for all I know, there could be a body in it."

"Is that the kind of man your father is? A bodies in trunks kind of guy?"

"No. None of our crew is particularly violent. Though, if anything like that were needed, he would have one of the other guys take care of it, which is why Calvin having a gun didn't surprise me since his job is—was—to be the muscle if anything went haywire."

"Where is your father then?"

"Probably in another stolen car, if I had to guess, but I dropped him off at the bus station with the cash your mother gave me yesterday."

"Everything all right?" a voice called, too close to be coming from downstairs.

Allen stuck his head out of the bathroom. "She's fine," he said and stepped out when he saw the cop walking up the stairs. The sink turned on behind him. "She's washing her hands."

"Hey," another male voice called from the distance, "you guys know we got a 10-65 in the driveway?"

"What's going on?" Kristen asked behind him.

The cop hurried down the stairs.

"I think they just found out that the Rolls Royce was stolen."

"What do we do?"

Her question was one that he asked himself hundreds if not thousands of times: *what do I do?* He could answer it so easily when a patient coded in his hospital. Here, now, he could see how it was going to unfold. They would piece it all together; Kristen would go to jail for the part she played, and even after all of this, she would still leave him.

Allen faced her and took her hands in his. "You need to run."

"What?" she blinked at him.

He squeezed her hands when she tried to pull away. "Why did you come back?"

"Because," her eyes searched his, "this was my last job. I was out of the game. If I would have left with him, I would have ended up right back in it. If not immediately, then eventually—"

"Why did you come back here?"

"Because I don't trust him…"

"Your father?"

She nodded. "Everything about this last job felt off."

"But why did you come back *to me?* I read your note. I know you were planning to leave."

A line formed between her brows. "What letter?"

"The letter you started in the sketchbook."

Kristen shook her head. "That letter isn't to you."

"I thought we left you outside?" They turned to see Elvis at the top of the stairs.

"You did," Allen told him, trying to wrap his head around what Kristen told him.

"Do either of you know about the stolen car in the driveway?"

"What if we do?" Allen asked before Kristen could confess to it being hers.

Elvis strolled into his bedroom, and Kristen reached for Allen's arm as Elvis casually shut the three inside the bedroom. *It's okay*, he mouthed to her.

"You need to tell me everything."

Kristen stayed quiet, holding Allen's arm. Allen told him everything, starting with the assault on the beach by the dead guy downstairs, ending up at his house, to her boss showing up and pretending to be a real estate agent to take his mother out on a date in a convoluted way of getting Kristen out of there. As he wrapped it up, Elvis settled his gaze on Kristen.

"Is that right? He got the jump drive, and you left him at the bus station?"

"Fake key fob and all," Kristen admitted.

"The local bus station?"

"That is correct."

"And you came back here because…?"

Allen could feel her tense against his arm. She was holding onto him for dear life.

"We have feelings for each other," he answered for her.

Elvis didn't look away from Kristen. "And this Calvin guy breaking in while you were gone—"

"Coincidence," she replied, loosening her grip on Allen's arm. "I feared he'd come for me, but I had no idea he was here when I showed up."

"Would you have come back if you knew Calvin was here?" Elvis asked.

His question hit so hard that Allen found himself looking at Kristen. She glanced back at him before meeting Elvis's gaze.

"I would have come back sooner."

Allen grinned like a lovestruck fool and didn't care. He knew from her eyes that she was telling the truth.

"Are there any bosses or members of your band of thieves we need to be concerned about?"

"I don't think so," she told him, but Allen knew better.

He could see in the way the warmth left her eyes that there was something or someone else she was worried about. He knew he could coax Kristen into admitting whatever it was that she was hiding, and they would be okay, but then Elvis turned for the door.

"I need to make a phone call, and if your mother is still outside, you may want to join her," he told Allen.

"We will in a minute."

Elvis stepped away, leaving the bedroom door open. Allen waited until Elvis's footsteps turned into one of the spare bedrooms to shut the door.

"I know you're lying," he said, turning to Kristen.

"What do you mean?"

"I think there are more people we need to be worried about, but it's unfair for me or any of us to expect you to tell us the whole truth when we're keeping things from you too." He waved his hand at the foot of the bed. "You may want to have a seat."

Kristen didn't move.

"You're in the witness protection program," she stated. Allen froze. She looked almost amused when he met her gaze. "Aren't you." It sounded more like a statement than a question.

"Uh, how do you—"

"Elvis is a US Marshal. He showed the cop his badge at the front door. I put two and two together." She walked past him and sat on the edge of the bed, staring off into space. "It explains why you told Calvin he was here for you, not me. Very heroic of you, by the way, trying to get him to let me go."

"Are you trying to make me feel bad?" he asked, sitting beside her. "We both know you were the real hero."

"Well," she said, smirking at him, "I was just biding you some time to get that gun from your recliner."

"So you knew I had a gun hidden in it?"

"I had no clue," she giggled, "I thought you got your hand stuck in it or something. What would you have done if he'd found the gun?"

"I wasn't thinking that far," he admitted. "I just needed to get to that chair and I knew he would keep us close, so—"

"You sent him to the chair."

"You got it," Allen winked. "Could you imagine if I had gotten my hand stuck?" he chuckled. "Dying with my arm stuck in the recliner that everyone told me to get rid of."

They both laughed a second. Then, a sadness passed over Kristen's face.

"What do you think is wrong with us," she looked him in the eye for a brief second, "to laugh like this about morbid things?"

Allen stared at her thoughtfully. "It's a coping mechanism, laughing at the darker things in life. I laughed the day my father died." Knowing he inched toward his family's deep, dark secrets, he swallowed.

"That's dark."

"It wasn't because he died. Mom and I ended up in a motel after it happened, and I remember sitting on the end of the crappy bed like how we're sitting now, facing the TV, and when I turned it on, a family sitcom was playing. A mom, two kids, and a dad sat together at the dining table. I should've cried, but I didn't."

"You laughed?"

Allen nodded. "Mom walked in and probably thought I had lost my mind or was in shock, but she sat beside me, and we watched the rest of the episode in silence. We're in the witness protection program because of my father. He was an accountant, a good one, or that's what I thought as a kid since I grew up in a huge house in the most expensive neighborhood. I was in private school, and my mother didn't work. In reality, he was the lead accountant for a money laundering ring that had ties with the cartel. Long story short, he started working with the feds, his clients found out, and they got to him before he could testify."

"They killed him?"

Allen hadn't shared any of this with anyone, not even Gwen, but as Kristen's arm looped around his shoulders, he couldn't stop there.

"It's why Mom always packs that gun around with her. Two guys broke into our house in the middle of the day. Mom took off upstairs. I thought she had run off, leaving Dad and me to fend the guys off.

That's where I got this," he wiped his fingertips over the scar on his temple. "The butt of one of the guy's guns knocked me out when I tried to get them off of my father. I came to on the floor. Mom was on the stairs, shooting. She took one down, but the other guy ran off. It was too late, though. They had already shot him. He died in our arms before the ambulance got there.

"It was later in a counseling session together that I learned that those men were about to kill me when she made it downstairs. They had been sent to take out the whole family."

"That makes a lot of sense," Kristen said almost absentmindedly. He thought she meant the men being sent to take them all out, but then he noticed the hint of a smirk on her lips. She looked at him out of the corner of her eyes. "Your mom totally gives off that whole *will shoot you if you mess with my family* vibe."

"She does take the term Mama Bear to a whole other level."

"That's a good one. I could totally see her as a bear. Too bad they don't have opposable thumbs."

"So they could shoot a gun," Allen finished.

"Exactly."

They both chuckled for a second time, laughing over something dark.

Kristen lowered her arm to stand slowly. "Hold on," she pointed at him, "you gave me a hard time for lying about having amnesia when Allen isn't even *your* real name?"

Allen frowned. "That is completely different."

"How so?"

He took a deep breath and stood. If she were going to give him a hard time, he wouldn't take it sitting down. "Amnesia is a major medical event for one—"

"A *major* medical event," she repeated mockingly.

"That's right. True amnesia is a sign that the limbic system has been damaged, which would mean that the very center of your brain wasn't firing properly. The things that make up your...essence, mood, emotions, and ability to learn new things would have all been stunted if not permanently altered."

Kristen threw her hands up at him. "I don't need an anatomy lesson. I want to hear you say that you were lying, too."

"My situation is a little bit different, but okay." Allen straightened and looked Kristen in the eye. "I'm sorry that I lied about my name."

"I didn't mean for you to apologize, but since you did," Kristen stood taller, mimicking him. "I am also sorry for lying about my name. There, now I have something that I should share. Don't make that face," she said, nudging him when he frowned, "it's not anything bad." Allen forced a tight grin. "That's not much better. You know how I told you about my cool kid phase? Well, it was after I got arrested when I was caught tagging in an alley that my dad showed up to bail me out, but instead of being an actual parent and telling me how bad what I did was, he recruited me to join his group of thieves, and…I laughed."

"You laughed?"

"That's right. Looking back, I should have—I don't know—yelled at him or cried for having a terrible dad, but I laughed. Then, I accepted his offer."

He nodded slowly. "You should definitely be in therapy."

"You know, I wouldn't be opposed to going."

Allen smiled, but there was still something on his mind. "So who was that letter for then if it wasn't for me?"

A shadow passed over the brightness in her eyes. "A guy I hurt back in Texas. He didn't deserve me hurting him the way I did. He wasn't one of my marks, and he was a good guy like you."

It was meant as a compliment, he knew, but Kristen saying another guy was like him stung. He didn't want to be like any of the guys in her past. He wanted more than that. He wanted to be her future.

"Did he love you?"

Kristen started to shake her head and stopped. "Wait, are you saying that you love me?"

"Depends," he smirked, "on what you have to say if I do."

She leaned in. "I—"

"Guess no one is concerned about Betty," Elvis interrupted, opening the bedroom door. "She could be down there telling them everything."

Allen glared at him. "We both know that she wouldn't do that, and we," he pointed between Kristen and him, "were having a moment."

"I know. I heard."

"So you were eavesdropping when you were supposed to be making a call?"

"I finished the call, and then I eavesdropped."

"Another eavesdropper," Kristen said lightly. "Welcome to the club."

"My mother can keep secrets when she wants to. I'll bet you twenty bucks that if Ed's outside, she is only talking to him, and it's to butter him up to help all this blow over."

"About that," Elvis said. "I can keep Betty and Allen out of the mess downstairs, but my people agree that we are going to need something from you," he said to Kristen, "if you don't want to face charges, and by charges," he added as Allen opened his mouth to contest, "I mean the heists across the country that are currently open cases."

"I didn't do *all* of the heists across the country. I did a few here or there."

"I believe you," Elvis told her, "but pulling your prints set off alerts that I can't turn off."

The line returned between Kristen's brows. "My prints?"

"For your background check," Allen said. "Mom got your prints off of your margarita glass. That's why they met the next day at the diner. Which," he eyed Elvis, "they could have done at a much less public location."

"I told her the same thing," Elvis shrugged, "but apparently, she wanted to make someone named Norah and that detective jealous."

"I am not surprised," Allen said, expecting to exchange a knowing look with Kristen, but she stared into space. "You okay?" He rubbed her shoulder. "We are going to figure this out."

"I think I already have." She blinked at Elvis. "I can't give you any names because I don't know them, but I can give you this."

She reached into the waistband of her pants and withdrew a flash drive.

SIXTY-ONE

Kristen handed the US Marshal the drive, as shocked as Allen appeared.

"What's this?" he asked, flipping it over.

"A flash drive," Allen answered.

"It's two and a half years of work," she said, "but don't ask me what's on it."

"This is not the time to withhold information."

"I'm not. My boss only told me to plug it into the list of devices the buyer gave him, so I did. It never showed anything on the computers or cell phones I plugged it into—"

"Whose cell phones and computers?"

"Art galleries and the art dealers who ran them," she glanced at Allen but couldn't look him in the eye, "across three states."

"Art," Elvis mumbled.

"If I had to guess, based on how much they were going to pay to get that thing back, it's some kind of money-tracing scheme. It infects everything with a virus, finds out where the money is going, and then redirects money into an offshore account somewhere."

Allen stared at her with the same intensity that Elvis eyed the drive. "How much were they paying you?"

"Eight hundred thousand and some change."

Allen's jaw dropped.

"Trust builder," Elvis nodded at Allen.

"Beg your pardon?"

Elvis pocketed the drive. "Autumn, turning this in is a trust builder."

"He's big on trust," Allen muttered to her.

"Given your track record and our boy's innate ability to pick 'em, I had no reason to trust anything you told me. But now, you have not only started to build my trust but there is a good chance that my people will be willing to add some financial backing for the addition to the family."

All Kristen heard were *might* and *addition to the family*. "What does that mean?"

"It means—"

"It means," Elvis interrupted, "that if you plan on sticking around with the Trouth's, it will be easier for me and my team to tuck you away in the program *if* what you have given me pans out."

"But," Allen added, "you don't have to stay here if you don't want to."

She gawked between the two of them. "If this is your way of asking me if I like Allen enough to stick around, then I would think that the eight hundred and fifty thousand dollars I gave up to return today is proof enough."

Allen grinned as Elvis took out his phone.

"What are you doing?" Kristen asked.

"Taking notes."

"He's going to tell them how much you turned down to be with me."

"Living up to that nickname of yours, aren't you?" Elvis muttered.

Kristen's eyebrow rose. "You have a nickname?"

Allen winced. "The Marshal Service called me Casanova in med school."

Elvis cleared his throat. "Dated a serial killer, this one."

"You *what*?"

"It was one date—I had no idea she was a serial killer," Allen grimaced at Elvis, "and why are you even telling her that when it's your job to keep stuff like that a secret?"

"I was only explaining how you got your nickname."

"Okay, calling him Casanova, I get. But," she gaped at Allen, "you dated an *actual* serial killer?"

"It was one date!"

"I should have warned you that he gets a little sensitive anytime I mention Second Date Cindy," Elvis smirked.

"Being sensitive has nothing to do with it," Allen said.

"Second Date Cindy?"

"She killed them on the second date," Elvis said, heading for the stairs. "She got her name from the first clue they found early on where she signed her name, Cindy, on the restaurant receipt that was the last known location of a dead body that was found a couple of days later. The victim's card had been used though so it took a while before they were able to identify her."

"Turned out her real name was Cynthia," Allen told Kristen as they followed Elvis out of the bedroom. "After she was arrested, they started calling me Casanova."

"Good thing she was arrested before your second date."

"That's why he got the name Casanova," Elvis laughed. "She liked him so much that she ended things before it got to a second date."

"She ghosted me," Allen explained. "Turned out she only went on second dates with guys she didn't like."

Kristen held back a grin. "Explains how she could kill them."

"Wish I could have met that one," Elvis smirked at Allen. "Bet she was more fun than that last one you were with."

Allen stared flatly at him. "Going to bring up all of my exes while you're at it?"

"I met Gwen," Kristen confessed, "and even I would have rather met Second Date Cindy."

"Okay," Allen said as Kristen and Elvis exchanged a grin. "Are you two done?"

Elvis shrugged. "Twenty bucks says your mother is outside talking to that detective."

Allen frowned at the back of the Marshal's head. "Hey, that was my bet."

"No takers then?"

"No," Allen snapped indignantly.

Kristen shrugged. "I'm all out of cash."

The kitchen and living room entryways were taped off with crime scene tape. Allen and Kristen followed Elvis through the front door when a thought came to her mind.

"Man," she said, glancing at Allen as she took his hand in hers, "if Cupid is real, then she sure does have a sense of humor, doesn't she?"

Allen brought her hand to his mouth. "Sure does." He kissed the back of her hand and caught Elvis glancing at them. "Don't ask."

"Inside joke," Kristen winked.

SIXTY-TWO

Three days later
Kristen

"This is the first time I haven't looked forward to coming here," Kristen admitted as Allen pulled into the diner parking lot, where not one but three police cars were stationed around the building.

Allen rubbed her arm supportively. "We don't have to do this if you don't want to."

"It's too late. We're already here."

Allen backed into the farthest parking spot from the front door. "Elvis said they can go off of Mom's ID."

Kristen reclined the passenger seat far enough back that only her eyes were visible over the car's dash. If she was going to be spotted identifying someone for the cops, then she wasn't going to make it easy.

Several scenarios had played out in Kristen's head since she returned to Allen's house and handed over the flash drive from the biggest job she had ever done. Only a couple of them circled what would happen to Bobby once he handed over the fake key fob, and they realized that the flash drive was full of Allen's random medical school notes.

The only thing that would save him if the buyers were prone to physical violence would be that he was the only one who knew where to find her. Once upon a time, she would have believed that her former boss would have protected her. Thus, she never would have swapped drives and put him in such a predicament, but she went with her gut. Finding Calvin at Allen's house only proved how right her gut had been not to trust her father. No, not her father —*Bobby*. Bobby was what she would call him from then on. He was never really a dad to her, constantly abandoning her for the next job, and was just as bad as her boss.

Being able to leave him at the bus station with the fake flash drive and only enough cash for a one-way ticket had been her version of abandoning him. Whether he was aware that it was her cutting ties or not, it wasn't enough to keep him from showing back up to Redrock days later. He at least knew better than to show up at Allen's house, but he messed up when he entered the diner. Betty and Ed, on their first official date since the failed one, were already sitting at a booth.

Note for any potential men interested in dating Betty Trouth: if you mess up on the first date, all you have to do is save her life to win a chance at righting that wrong.

Betty and Ed were enjoying their meal when Bobby walked in and took a seat at the counter. They saw him, but he didn't see them. Kristen imagined Ed's back being to him when Bobby scanned the place. Betty would have used Ed to shield her as Bobby looked around, and he hadn't noticed them because he was still sitting at the counter when the cops arrived.

While Ed called his guys in, Betty texted Allen, Elvis, and Kristen.

Now that Kristen sat in the diner parking lot, waiting to identify her old boss, she had to mentally double down on her resolution that he was not worth protecting.

The screen in Allen's car lit up with an incoming call. "It's Elvis," Allen said. "We'll call him back." He leaned forward, but Kristen beat him, accepting the call.

"We're in the car waiting for them to bring him out," she said quickly.

"That's good news," Elvis said on the other end. "Don't know if what I got for you qualifies as the same."

"What is it?" Allen asked, taking Kristen's hand.

She sunk back in the passenger seat, wondering if this was it. Her paranoia from getting off so easy couldn't take the second of silence from Elvis's end of the call. "I'm going to jail, aren't I?"

The second everything seemed to be working out in her favor, she couldn't help but assume it wouldn't last.

Allen turned out to be the man of her dreams, so it would only make sense for her to be taken from him before they had any real chance to see where this could go. Not that *taken* was the right word. When she left a trail of deceit as vast and wide as she had, it was only a matter of time before it caught up to her.

You can only burn bridges for so long.

Kristen glanced at Allen when Elvis didn't reply. "Have you ever been to the Maldives?" she whispered.

"No. Why?"

"They don't have extradition."

"Sorry about that," Elvis said through the car's speaker, "my supervisor was checking in."

"Kristen is worried that we may need to look into countries with no extradition."

"Well, don't tell him that," Kristen gaped.

"For her father?" Elvis asked.

"No, for—"

"Just say it," Kristen blurted. "Good or bad, just tell us what you got for us."

"We hacked your flash drive, and it's more than a money scheme. It collects accounts, buying history, selling history, addresses."

Kristen's throat tightened. There was no telling what would have happened had Bobby handed it over. Sure, there were plenty of art collectors who were vomit-inducing narcissists who probably deserved to have sketchy, if not downright terrible, people after them. But plenty of decent, ordinary people worked hard enough to invest in artwork they could showcase in their homes. To know that she played a role in making those homes known to criminals would ruin the peace of mind she thought leaving her old life behind would grant her.

"It's an all-or-nothing scheme," she said at the same time Elvis stated, "It has a silent tracking virus to infect the device—"

"Wait, what?"

"It's sophisticated, but whatever computer you hooked it up to, they got everything. I'm guessing that's why they were willing to pay so much to get it back because even my tech team was impressed. From what they told me, it was infecting their computer in the background while they were hacking it. Thankfully, my guys were on a closed server."

The door to the diner opened. Ed stepped out, reading from a small paper in his hand.

"It's him," Kristen said. The second Bobby Sky's face reached the light of day, there was no more second-guessing. All those lives were in danger, not just because of her but because of *him*. "That is Bobby Sky."

"They just walked him out," Allen told Elvis as he rolled his window down and gave the thumbs up to the police car in the parking lot, waiting for Kristen to ID the man she confessed had led the whole operation.

"What do we do now?" Kristen asked. "There's no telling how much personal information was on those computers and cell phones."

"It's not any different than any other data leak, but we will contact everyone you listed, and they will have to notify their buyers and sellers."

Betty walked out behind Ed and Bobby. Kristen frowned as Betty openly admired her father's backside. Kristen had to give it to him; the man still managed to look good, being handcuffed and surrounded by police. He glanced around the parking lot. Kristen sat up.

No more hiding, she decided. She wanted him to see her. She wanted him to know that it was because of her that they would put him behind bars. His eyes landed on Allen's car, and just when she thought he would understand that she was behind his downfall...he grinned at her. Not a sarcastic, self-loathing grin at being caught, but a happy one, as if he was genuinely pleased to see her in the passenger seat, glaring at him.

Kristen sank back.

"They're loading him in a car," Allen narrated.

"Good," Elvis said over the speakers. "I'm about to be there."

Allen looked at the screen in his car displaying *Alvie* as his new contact name for Elvis. "I thought you already left town days ago."

"I'm always close by," Elvis boasted.

"That's not enough," Kristen mumbled.

"I can't hear her if she's talking to me," Elvis said through the car.

"That's not enough," she repeated louder. "These art dealers, it's all about image—they aren't going to reach out to all of their contacts and tell them that they're in danger because someone hacked their files."

"The government deals with cyber threats all the time. Don't worry. The victims will be notified. We'll put out a press release. Right now, we need to focus on this case and hope Bobby Sky flips."

Kristen buckled her seatbelt. "He will never flip."

RUNNING FROM CUPID

SIXTY-THREE

The Next Day
Allen

"What do you mean, he flipped?"

"He means he flipped," Betty said, taking the leash off of Milo as they walked behind Allen into the kitchen.

"That's right," Allen said, but his mother talked over him.

"Your dad admitted to everything you told Elvis—"

Kristen winced. "Please don't call him my dad."

"Bobby," Allen said loud enough that even his mother's feigned deafness could hear, "took full responsibility. He stepped up to the plate to keep you out of jail. He told them who hired him—"

"And who gave him that computer thingy," his mother nodded along excitedly.

"USB," Allen corrected.

"Flash drive," Kristen said at the same time.

Allen nodded and then stared at his mother. "Do you want to tell her?"

"No," Betty shook her head adamantly. "You go ahead."

Allen turned to Kristen. "Basically, he confessed to everything."

She arched her brows. "Everything?"

"Not everything, everything, but everything about this job. They haven't mentioned any past jobs, but Bobby has an attorney now, so I'm sure confessing what happened to the other stuff you've stolen for him will be part of his deal."

"He gets a deal? Do I need to get an attorney?"

When Betty told him how Kristen's father lawyered up the second they slapped cuffs on him, Allen asked the same question. His mother looked at Kristen with the same veracity she had given him.

"Elvis takes you handing the computer thingy over very seriously—"

"Flash drive," Allen and Kristen said in unison.

"Yes, that. But if you need an attorney, we will get you one."

"That's right," Allen agreed, not that his bank account could handle it post-Gwen, but he would figure it out.

A curl came loose as Kristen lightly shook her head. "You don't have to do that."

"But we will," Betty insisted.

Allen's eyes followed Kristen's hand as she tucked the curl behind her ear.

"You're misunderstanding me," she said. "Now that everyone knows who I am, I have accounts I can access." She smiled at Allen, Betty, and Milo. "I appreciate all your support, but I don't need *financial* support."

"Right," his mother said, "as in money from all of your jobs, I am assuming?"

Kristen looked nervous.

"It's all right," Allen told her, knowing where his mother was going with this.

"That's right," his mother said. "You can tell us, but before you tell anyone else, we should talk about moving some of those assets around in case they come for it if all this plays out."

Allen couldn't agree more, but the look Kristen gave them told him that she needed more convincing. "There is a reason my mother never had to work after Dad died."

"I lost my husband. I was not going to lose all of our assets when he had put all of our lives in danger, making that money. I made sure we were cared for outside what the government gave us in the program."

"And that was legal?" Kristen asked.

Betty grinned serenely at her. "What would have been the fun in that?"

Allen rolled his eyes. "Elvis and the Marshal Service are okay with looking the other way as long as it stays under the radar," he glanced sideways at his mother, who ignored him, "but if there are retributions that need to be paid—"

"I'll have to pay it."

"Exactly," his mother agreed as if his 'under the radar' comment hadn't been a jab at how she bought most of her homes with cash. It pissed Elvis off when he found out that they only used the house the program paid for them to live in at their first assigned location temporarily before his mother bought her own under an LLC she paid someone to set up so that it wouldn't be linked back to her and Allen.

It was the last time either of them mentioned new homes to him. His mother winked at Kristen. "We'll just have to take care of any dead bodies ourselves in the future."

"There better not be any dead bodies in the future," Allen said sternly.

His mother shrugged. "Well, I thought I was done shooting people after I shot that man in our house, but here we are." To his mother's credit, she didn't look as sad as she once would have, mentioning the day his father was killed, but then she shocked him by smiling. "I'm keeping a tally now."

Allen frowned. "You better not have it written down somewhere—"

"Don't get snippety with me just because you're jealous that I've taken out two bad guys, and you haven't."

"I'm not jealous—"

Kristen's phone chimed. "I'll be right back. You stay here," she told Allen.

"You can't lie to me," his mother said as they watched Milo follow Kristen out the back door and into the yard. "He *stepped up to the plate?*" his mother mocked his words.

"What would you have said? Her father tried to throw her under the bus for a deal. She already knows her father's terrible. I made him a little less terrible for her."

"That is so sweet."

Allen silently agreed. He couldn't give Kristen a decent father any more than he could bring his own back to life, but he could give her one small lie about her father that made him a tiny bit less horrible of a parent.

"What about the letter?" his mother asked. "I can tell her," she offered, "if you aren't up to it."

Allen let the silence settle back over them as he thought about the hand-written letter Elvis emailed them a scanned copy of. "I want to make sure it's the real deal before she sees it," he said, finally moving to the door.

"It is real," his mother stated, "you know it, I know it, and soon Kristen will too. Here," she said, walking over to her purse on the kitchen island. She took out two papers folded in half. "I printed them out for you. It'll be easier if she reads it herself."

Allen took it obligingly, but he wasn't sure how much easier it would make for her. He slid them in his back pocket.

"You weren't supposed to come outside," Kristen called, hurrying to meet him by the pool.

"I have something—" he mumbled.

"Come on," Kristen insisted, ushering him down the side of the pool. "As soon as I came out here, I knew I would have to show you, but I couldn't wait when he told me it was done."

"Who are we talking about?" Allen asked, wondering who would be texting her on his old phone.

She smirked over her shoulder at him. "You'll see." He trailed behind her, looking around as if he was about to meet whoever was texting her. Besides the two kids on the beach, digging near the waterline while their parents watched a few feet away, it was just the two of them. Milo lifted his leg on the telescope Allen hadn't paid much attention to.

"No, Milo," Kristen jogged to stop him, but it was too late. One leg of Allen's very expensive telescope was soaked in dog piss.

"When did you take this out?" he asked.

Kristen looked from Allen to Milo. "You...you're not...going to yell at him?"

"Who? Milo?" Allen looked at his mother's dog as he pranced up to him proudly. "Nah," he said, scratching Milo's ear. "Ever since I saw him look like he was going to eat Calvin's face off, he's kind of grown on me."

"Good," Kristen said, barely listening as she peered through the telescope. "It's not as easy to see as it will later tonight, but," she backed away, gesturing to the telescope. "Take a look."

Allen hunched over to look through the telescope pointed at the water tower.

"I didn't get to answer you," she said, "when you asked what I would say if you were to tell me that you loved me, so there's my answer."

Written in large letters next to Davie's bright pink boxer shorts were:

I love you —A.

"When did you have time to do that?"

"Your faith in my artistic abilities is honorable, but I didn't do it. I may have contacted the town council and, in exchange for a donation to help repaint the water tower, had a local artist you might know paint it for me."

Allen stepped back from the telescope. "A donation?"

"Nothing exorbitant, just a small donation to get the ball rolling on bringing the water tower back to its original bland, boring state."

He wrapped his arms around Kristen's back as she crossed her arms. "It was Davie that did that, wasn't it?"

She grinned serenely up at him as she leaned into his chest. "I'm not telling you."

He leaned down and gave her a small kiss on the lips. "I've got to know," he said, tightening his grasp around her, "how did you get them to agree to it?"

She pressed her lips together, refusing to say a word, so he kissed her again, taking his time. When he raised his lips from hers, her cheeks were flushed.

"Okay," she said, slowly opening her eyes, "if that is who they hired, it may have been recommended to them by a third party that hiring local youth would empower the next generation and support local talent. They totally went for it when they heard how it could bring the community together."

"Could it now?"

"It could. Not to mention," she said, releasing her arms from her chest, allowing him to hold her closer, "the third party may have explained to the council how much money they could raise by selling short-term ad space on the side of the water tower."

"Good idea," he said low in his throat as Kristen wrapped her arms around him.

"I know, right? They even liked my idea to have a fundraiser where a monthly winner gets a small area to have whatever they want written on it. They could get a picture of it, maybe have it in the local newspaper, then it's painted over, and the small area is used again for the next month's raffle ticket winner."

"You mean the third party who may or may not have gotten Davie his first legitimate art job?"

"Exactly," she said. Kristen tipped her head to the side, thinking it over. "I would call it more his first commission-based project, but close enough."

"Close enough," he chuckled and glanced at the water tower. "So, does this mean I get to start calling you Autumn?"

She winced at the sound of her name.

"The A is for Anonymous. Apparently, there wasn't enough square footage in what I paid to have the whole word written out."

Allen nodded. "So, no Autumn then?"

She stared into his eyes for a long moment. "Allen and Autumn don't sound *that* pretentious."

"Not at all," he smiled. "You know, I once knew a girl with the last name Chanel," he joked about the last name Kristen put on all her hospital forms. "Talk about *pretentious*."

Kristen giggled. "How could she not be with a name like that?" She leaned up to kiss him this time.

The papers were still in his pocket, but this holding her, kissing her took precedence. He couldn't give her the start to the life she deserved, but he could give her this moment. Who was he kidding? He needed this, too. He needed her.

"I love you." He wanted to scream it to the world but settled for saying it between her kisses and his. She smiled up at him.

"I love you too."

~~The End~~
Just the Beginning

BONUS CHAPTER

Betty's Secret Admirer

"It was a body, I am telling you," Dwayne said, not bothering to remind Norah for a second time that he needed a refill. "They were carrying it out of the back of Doctor Trouth's house. I saw it clear as day. They loaded it into the coroner's hearse and everything."

Norah's eyes widened. "The coroner's office has a hearse?"

Dwayne slapped his hand on the counter. "You see? This is why I don't tell you about what I see around town."

"What?"

Norah was as clueless as the day he met her in third grade six decades prior.

"I tell you about seeing a dead body, and you act like hearing the town has a hearse is the surprising part."

Norah threw her hands to her hips. "You know what? You're just mad because you're hungry, and the kitchen is taking their time."

"I'm not—" he slapped the counter again in frustration. It was pointless to have a conversation with her. "Refill my drink, will you?" he asked as she turned her back to him.

"Sure thing," she grumbled, but she didn't turn around to take his glass. "You know, with how much you talk about her, you should ask her out."

"How do you know that I haven't?"

Norah turned to frown at him. "Because I've known you my whole life, Dwayne, and it took Peggy Sue asking you out our senior year for you to get a girlfriend, and that was after you had a crush on her since fourth grade."

"You think you know everything," he grumbled, staring at the glass he wouldn't get a refill of anytime soon. It had actually been the third grade, but he wasn't going to correct her knowledge of his late wife.

"Well, I do know if you don't ask Betty out soon, she's going to be taken with the amount of good-looking men popping up around town."

Dwayne's head shot up. "What are you talking about?"

Norah shrugged. "She was here when this really handsome guy came in and sat at the counter. Before you know it, she and Ed—"

"Ed was here?"

"Yeah, he was having lunch with Betty, but you should've seen how she looked at the guy at the counter. Before I knew it, three police cars were surrounding the place, and then there went Ed and Betty walking the guy out in handcuffs."

"The man at the counter?"

"That's what I said."

Dwayne frowned. She hadn't said that, but this was what it was like talking to Norah these days. It was a miracle the woman was still working.

"Turns out the guy had a bunch of warrants or something."

"You don't know what they were arresting him for?"

Norah shrugged. "I didn't ask. This new fluid pill has me running to the bathroom to pee every ten minutes. By the time I got out, the cops were leaving."

"It sounds like Ed is the only guy I have to worry about if they arrested the other one," he told her, "*if* I was interested in Betty like that."

"I'm not talking about Ed or the guy who got arrested," Norah paused to watch a family walking in who stopped inside the door, looking unsure what to do. "Have a seat wherever you like," she called and then lowered her voice. "I'm talking about the tall guy in a suit who was talking to Betty outside when I got out of the bathroom." Norah took out her pencil and order pad from her apron, eyeing the family as they sat at a booth. "And he and Betty looked awfully chummy." She tapped her pencil on the pad of paper. "Like I said, you better ask her out quick."

"I hear you," Dwayne frowned.

Norah took a step toward the family in the booth. "Hey," she said, glancing back at him, "was it a man or a woman in that body bag?"

Dwayne stared into his empty glass. "The thing about body bags, Norah, is you can't see inside them."

"Yeah, but," Norah's eyes got big, "what if it was Betty being carried out in that body bag?"

"What are you talking about?"

"Think about it. Betty was there when that guy got arrested. What if that was why she was looking at him like that? Maybe *she* was the reason he got arrested. He could have gotten out of jail and went and found Betty and taken her out."

"This happened days ago," Dwayne reiterated.

"I know," she said loudly but quickly lowered her voice, "but people bail out of jail all the time. Maybe he got out and found her at her son's house this morning before your walk."

Dwayne couldn't shake his head fast enough. "You aren't hearing me. I saw them carrying out that body bag days ago."

"Ohhh," Norah said, finally catching on.

Dwayne was officially annoyed, but now he needed to know. "When did you see that guy getting arrested?"

She shrugged. "A couple days ago." But she didn't sound too sure about it.

"Then it couldn't have been her," he said, wanting Norah to reassure him that the timeline didn't work out, but all she did was tap her pencil against the notepad.

"I wonder who it was then," she said absentmindedly and then turned without another word and headed toward the family in the booth.

Dwayne stared after her. He had tolerated Norah his whole life, and at this moment, he wondered why. She was as big of a pain in the butt at ten years old as she was today at sixty-eight. He really should have worked harder at getting Peggy to move once he retired from the Army, but then he never would have met Betty Trouth.

Betty, Betty, Betty. Now, that was a woman. She loved hearing about his daily treks anytime something exciting happened. It's too bad this one involved her son's house.

"Redrock might as well be called Boring-rock," he overheard Betty tell Norah the first time he saw her in the diner. Dwayne could not agree more.

"You must be Betty Trouth," he had said, sliding two stools down. It took her a moment to realize that he was talking to her.

"Sorry. What did you say?"

After that, he made it his mission to make his weekly walks daily from one side of the town to the other. All to ensure that Betty would pay attention to him. Everything he told her made Redrock a little less boring. But, thanks to Betty, his life was no longer boring. It wasn't until he saw that body bag being carried out from Betty's son's house the other day that it dawned on him how devastating it would be if Betty were the one in that bag.

He had been coming to the diner for breakfast every morning, hoping to overhear someone talking about who was in that bag, but no one was talking. It may not have been Betty if the timeline was what Norah said it was, but it could have been her son, and then what would keep her in Redrock?

He put fifteen bucks under his empty glass.

Dwayne would go home, get cleaned up, and go to Betty's house. No matter what had happened at her son's house, he would give her a reason to stick around Redrock. He would not let his life be boring any longer.

RUNNING FROM CUPID

Don't forget to **>>leave a review<<**
on Amazon or Goodreads if you enjoyed it!

I love when a story is nice and wrapped up, don't you?

I do, but what did Betty print out for Allen to give Kristen???

Oh, about that...

You can download the extra jawdropping chapter and see what everyone is talking about by joining Bo's VIPs by going to

https://BookHip.com/XZVTMBR

To find more work by my amazing cover artist, check out @BrittanyKellerArt on instragram.

Milton Keynes UK
Ingram Content Group UK Ltd.
UKHW042103240924
448733UK00007B/524